Goddess of Light

P. C. CAST

BERKLEY SENSATION, NEW YORK

THE BERKLEY PUBLISHING GROUP
Published by the Penguin Group
Penguin Group (USA) Inc.
375 Hudson Street, New York, New York 10014, USA
Penguin Group (Canada), 10 Alcorn Avenue, Toronto, Ontario M4V 3B2, Canada
(a division of Pearson Penguin Canada Inc.)
Penguin Books Ltd., 80 Strand, London WC2R 0RL, England
Penguin Group Ireland, 25 St. Stephen's Green, Dublin 2, Ireland (a division of Penguin Books Ltd.)
Penguin Group (Australia), 250 Camberwell Road, Camberwell, Victoria 3124, Australia
(a division of Pearson Australia Group Pty. Ltd.)
Penguin Books India Pvt. Ltd., 11 Community Centre, Panchsheel Park, New Delhi—110 017, India
Penguin Group (NZ), Cnr. Airborne and Rosedale Roads, Albany, Auckland 1310, New Zealand
(a division of Pearson New Zealand Ltd.)
Penguin Books (South Africa) (Pty.) Ltd., 24 Sturdee Avenue, Rosebank, Johannesburg 2196,
South Africa

Penguin Books Ltd., Registered Offices: 80 Strand, London WC2R 0RL, England

This is a work of fiction. Names, characters, places, and incidents either are the product of the author's imagination or are used fictitiously, and any resemblance to actual persons, living or dead, business establishments, events, or locales is entirely coincidental.

GODDESS OF LIGHT

A Berkley Sensation Book / published by arrangement with the author

PRINTING HISTORY
Berkley Sensation edition / April 2005

ISBN: 0-425-20196-1

BERKLEY® SENSATION
Berkley Sensation Books are published by The Berkley Publishing Group,
a division of Penguin Group (USA) Inc.,
375 Hudson Street, New York, New York 10014.
BERKLEY SENSATION and the "B" design are trademarks belonging to Penguin Group (USA) Inc.

PRINTED IN THE UNITED STATES OF AMERICA

10 9 8 7 6 5 4 3 2 1

continued . . .

GODDESS BY MISTAKE

"A witty retelling of *The Beauty and the Beast* myth with a dash of Celtic lore and a twist of 'You go, girlfriend!'"

—*Bibliora.com*

"A mythic world of humor and verve." —*Publishers Weekly*

"A high-spirited fantasy romp, wickedly funny and filled with action. P. C. Cast turns traditional fantasy elements inside out for a story you won't soon forget. Highly recommended!"

—K. D. Wentworth, author of *Stars Over Stars* and *This Fair Land*

"I hated for it to end." —*Romance Under the Rainbow*

"A funny, sexy heroine . . . the dialogue is well-written, rich with secondary characters and peppered with humorous dialogue. In the battle of good against evil, modern conveniences against ancient culture, and a bit of Beauty and the Beast tossed in, readers will enjoy being transported into this fantasy world."

—*Romance Reviews Today*

"If you like your fantasy novels tongue-in-cheek, you will enjoy *Goddess By Mistake*, the debut novel by an Oklahoma high school teacher with a vivid imagination and a wicked sense of humor." —*The Romance Reader*

"Sassy . . . big points for originality, style, humor and sheer exuberance of storytelling . . . a wild ride and a rollicking good time all around." —*All About Romance*

"A fun read." —Christopher Moore, author of *Bloodsucking Fiends: A Love Story*

With love to the real Pamela,
owner of Ruby Slipper Designs,
who found her Apollo in Keith.
Lucky girl!

Acknowledgments

I am profoundly grateful to my good-humored friend, Pamela Rooks, who let me borrow her name and her business and then let me fictionalize . . . fictionalize . . . fictionalize! I would also like to thank her clients who patiently allowed me to traipse through their lovely homes as I followed their interior designer and asked a zillion questions.

Thank you and a wink to my fabulous webgoddess, Shawn Wilson, who bears an amazing resemblance to Vernelle . . .

And, as always, I am grateful for my Goddess Editor, Christine Zika, and my friend and agent, Meredith Bernstein.

Prologue

—

"I have made my decision, Bacchus. The portal will remain open."

As Zeus spoke, he turned his back on the corpulent god and rested his hands against the smooth top of the marble railing that framed the balcony. He gazed down at the Great Banquet Hall of Olympus. The magnificent room was teeming with young gods and goddesses. Zeus' smile became self-satisfied. The immortals were matchless in their beauty, and when they gathered as they did on this evening, their combined allure was more resplendent than all the stars in the heavens. Then his expression sobered. No matter how perfect their exterior, he had slowly been forced to admit to himself that there was something lacking in the group below him.

They lacked the sublimely mortal touch of humanity.

The Supreme Ruler of the Gods indulged himself briefly in a particularly enticing remembrance. Aegina . . . she had been the most lovely of maidens. Her skin had been seductive mortal cream. He could still feel the imprint of its unique softness as she had pressed herself willingly against his feathered back when he changed himself into a mighty eagle and carried her away to make love to her. No, her body had not had the sheen of perfection that gilded a goddess's complexion, but she had responded to his touch with a naive exuberance that no goddess could ever match.

"Exuberance!" Zeus thumped his palm against the balcony railing, causing thunder to grumble across the sky in response. "That is what our young immortals are missing." He didn't turn to look at Bacchus; instead, his gaze roamed restlessly across the sparkling crowd. Considering, he squinted his dark eyes. What was it that Hera had said . . . *They take for granted the gifts of their immortal power. They need to spend time away from the Ancient World. Somewhere they are not idolized and worshiped.* He had to admit that Hera tended to be right, even though he often had reason to wish his wife's powers of observation were less accurate. He grimaced, wanting to forget the knowing look of her sharp gaze, which always seemed to see into his soul.

"They have languished too long in Olympus. It is past time that they mingle with modern mortals," Zeus said suddenly.

Bacchus tried to keep the irritation from his voice. "But I am the only one of the immortals to ever show an interest in the modern world. Why must you insist that they clutter up my realm?"

Zeus looked over his shoulder at Bacchus. "Demeter and Persephone have recently visited the modern world of mortals, and, as the Goddess of the Harvest told me, Persephone became so attached to a kingdom known as Tulsa that she has made a bargain with a mortal woman so that she may return on a regular basis."

Bacchus drew a deep breath and tried not to squirm under the Thunder God's gaze. "Then why not open the portal in the Kingdom of Tulsa?"

Zeus shook his head, turning back to his contemplation of the crowded hall. His talk with Demeter had convinced him that Tulsa was not a place where young gods and goddesses could come and go without being noticed.

"No, Bacchus. I have given this great consideration. I have searched the modern mortal world. Las Vegas provides the perfect setting with its fanciful mortal re-creation of Caesars Palace and The Forum." Zeus chuckled, remembering the silliness he had glimpsed through the portal.

"But Las Vegas is my realm! You know how much time

I have devoted to making Caesars Palace and The Forum mine. They will be meddling in a part of the world I have chosen as my own."

Zeus' head snapped around, and his eyes blazed. "You presume too much! Have you forgotten that I rule supreme amongst the gods?" Thunder rolled threateningly in the background.

Hastily, Bacchus bowed his head. "Forgive me, Lord."

"Do not forget yourself again, Bacchus. What I have given, I can also take away." He stared hard at the lesser deity before returning to his scrutiny of the crowd. "Look at them. The portal has only been opened to them for a short time, but already I feel a change. Even the nymphs have become excited." He paused, scowling as he remembered how too many of the lovely semideities had chosen to be made stars and flowers and trees because they had become so bored with their lives. "Exuberance . . . that is what Olympus has lacked. And that is what Las Vegas has breathed into us once more."

"But Lord." Bacchus covered his growing anger and pitched his voice to a concerned, paternal tone. "You know what happens when gods and goddesses become too involved in the lives of mortals. Think of Troy. Remember Medea and Jason. Consider what became of Heracles and Achilles. Are you willing to doom the world of modern mortals to chaos and heartache?"

"I do not need to be lectured by such as you, Bacchus." Zeus' voice remained controlled, but his warning was clear. Then, changing moods as easily as a spring storm cleared from the mountains, he smiled. "But I have already considered such things. I have set into place certain . . . *restrictions*"—Zeus drew the word out carefully, his eyes gleaming—"which I intend to announce tonight. My children will simply be gracious visitors, enjoying a much-deserved sojourn in the Kingdom of Las Vegas." He shifted his head so that Bacchus could see his stern, majestic profile. "This discussion is over. My will stands."

Bacchus had no choice but to bow and retreat respectfully from the balcony, but his mind seethed. Once again his needs were to be ignored as Zeus played favorites. He had made

Vegas his own. They worshiped Baccus there. At The Forum he commanded the attention of an audience of mortals every day. They cheered for him. They adored him. And now he was to share his realm with the young, beautiful darlings of Olympus?

"We shall see . . ." he whispered between clenched teeth as Zeus' voice thundered from the balcony, calling the attention of the Banquet Hall to attentive silence.

"Beloved children!" Zeus beamed at the gathering. "It pleases me greatly that you enjoy my latest gift." He stretched his arms, palms open, towards the two pillars that stood in the center of the hall, between which an opaque disk of light quivered and swirled. "This evening I announce more news—I have decided that the portal may be open to our lovely legions of nymphs, as well as the young Olympians!" Excited gasps from the minor female deities and semideities present sounded like sweet music to Zeus. "But remember, my beauties, you are entering a world unused to having gods such as us walk amongst them. You do not go to meddle with mortal affairs but rather to observe and to delight in a unique world. Lest you be tempted to forget that you are only there to visit, I have decided that the portal shall only be opened at limited times."

The glowing faces below him all remained upturned and listening. Zeus searched the crowd until he found Demeter standing regally beside her daughter. He inclined his head to her in respectful acknowledgment before continuing.

"The Goddess of the Harvest has informed me that modern mortals enjoy most of their revelry during a small cluster of days which they call a weekend. So it is during mortal weekends that our portal will be open. You have from dusk on their Friday evening to dawn on their Monday to frolic with the modern mortals."

With a small gesture of one hand, he silenced the enthusiastic whispers that his words evoked.

"And now, I give to you the Kingdom of Las Vegas!" The Thunder God clapped his hands together, and the crowd cheered as the sky roared in response.

Below in the Banquet Hall Artemis laughed and shook

her head fondly at Zeus before turning her attention back to her brother.

"Father is certainly pleased with himself," she said.

Apollo shrugged. "I don't understand the excitement. It is simply the modern world of mortals, not a new Olympus."

Artemis raised one perfect, golden eyebrow at him. "Thus said by the god who spent months spying on a modern mortal in the Kingdom of Tulsa."

"I was simply performing a favor for Demeter," he answered a little too nonchalantly.

Artemis said nothing, but she studied her twin as he flirted halfheartedly with a violet-tressed nymph who had stopped to talk in excited little bursts about visiting the Kingdom of Las Vegas. There was no doubt about it. Apollo had been behaving oddly ever since the Persephone debacle.

Artemis sipped her ruby-red wine, remembering how her brother's surprise at Persephone's sudden rejection and odd infatuation with Hades had turned to outright shock when it had been discovered that the soul that had temporarily inhabited the goddess's body had been that of a mortal woman. Persephone herself had been masquerading as a mortal on modern earth. So it was a mortal woman who had rejected Apollo and fallen in love with the God of the Underworld. Artemis' lovely lips curled into a sneer. Mortals. In her experience they either whined pathetically and needed constant care or were so ridiculously hubris-filled that they self-destructed. All in all, they were only good for mild amusement or dalliance. Not that she would ever want to dally with one, but her brother was of a different mind. Often he had laughed and shared tales with her about his latest seduction of a hopelessly naive young maiden. Artemis took another long drink from her goblet. It was good for a mortal to be gifted by the love of a god. Mortal women should be grateful to be noticed by such a god as her twin brother.

The chattering nymph had drifted away, leaving Apollo to gaze silently at the swirling portal. Perhaps that was it. Apollo needed a diversion. Her brother had spent too much time lounging aimlessly around Olympus, brooding about the silly mortal's rejection. He needed to remember that mortals were weak beings who lived the span of their frantic lives within the blink of an eye. They were easily manipulated—then easily cast aside.

A slow smile spread over her flawless face. What better place for him to be reminded of the insignificance of mortals than in a modern world teeming with the creatures?

"Come, Brother," she said with a cheery smile. "Let us visit the Kingdom of Las Vegas."

CHAPTER 1

God, she adored airports. They reminded her of love and excitement and the promise of new beginnings. Not for the first time Pamela thought that it had probably been her deep and romantic infatuation with airports that had fueled her relationship with Duane. One glimpse of him in his United Airlines pilot's uniform, and all rational thought had leaked out of her body along with her ridiculously girly sigh of pleasure.

What a moron she'd been.

That relationship fiasco was over. Finally. Pamela closed her eyes and ran her fingers through her chic new short haircut. She wished she'd run into Duane somewhere in the Colorado Springs Airport before she boarded the Southwest Airlines jet. She would have loved to have seen his horrified expression as he realized that she had cut off all of that thick, dark hair that used to swing around her waist. The hair that he used to take such pleasure in touching and stroking and . . . Pamela shivered in disgust at the memory. Just thinking about it made her feel suffocated. Getting rid of her long hair had been the final step she had taken to free herself from the shackles of Duane's smothering love. It had been six blissful months since she'd spoken to him. After months and months of refusing his gifts, sending back his flowers, and reminding him that their marriage had made both of them miserable, the end of their relationship had finally sunk in, much to the chagrin of her family, who believed that Duane was perfect for her and

that she was a fool to have left him. She could still hear her
brother, her sister-in-law and her parents. *He's not that
bad. He gives you anything you want. He makes great
money. He adores you.*

He hadn't just adored her. He had wanted to consume
her. Duane Edwards had appeared on the surface to be a
successful, handsome, slightly macho, charismatic man.
But under that surface, where the real Duane lived, lurked
a needy, controlling, passive-aggressive boy/man.

Pamela rolled her shoulders to release the tension
caused by thinking of Duane. On second thought, she was
glad she hadn't run into him at the airport. She hadn't cut
her hair to "show him"! She'd cut it because that's what
she wanted. It fit with the woman she was becoming. She
rested her head against the seat back. Her lips curved up.

She liked the woman she was turning into. *Satisfied,*
Pamela thought. She hadn't been so satisfied with herself
in years. She didn't even care that she was mushed into the
window seat of the Southwest Airlines jet next to a woman
whose bony elbow kept poking her while she struggled to
work the cigarette-scented crossword page of the *New York
Times.*

*Why would anyone obsessively work crossword puz-
zles? Did the woman have nothing better to do with her
mind?* Ms. Bony Elbows cackled and filled in another
blank. Pamela guessed she didn't.

*No! No negative thoughts. Self-fulfilling prophecies are
powerful. Negative thoughts cause negative energy.* Now
she sounded like her mother, God help her. She sighed and
pressed her forehead against the airplane window.

Okay, she'd mentally start over. She wouldn't let the
lady sitting beside her bug her, because that was a pointless waste of time, as was dwelling on negatives in general. Hell, who was she to judge? She glanced down at the
book in her lap. It had been open to the same page for the
entire flight. What had *she* been doing with her mind? Instead of reading Gena Showalter's scrumptious *The Stone
Prince,* she'd been wasting her time thinking about her
horrid ex. She was better than that—she'd worked hard to
make it so.

Purposefully, Pamela shifted her attention to the view outside her window. The desert was a bizarre mixture of harshness and beauty, and she was surprised to realize that she found it attractive—at least from several thousand feet in the air. It was so different from the lush green of her Colorado home, yet strangely compelling. Turning, the plane dipped its wing down, and Pamela's breath caught at her first glimpse of Las Vegas. There, smack in the middle of desert and sand, red dirt and canyons, was a city of glass and light and snaking highways, which she could tell even from the air were choked with rushing cars.

"It's like something out of a dream," she murmured to herself.

"Damn right! Ain't it grand," Ms. Bony Elbows rasped through a throat that had sucked down too many Virginia Slim Menthol extra-longs.

Pamela stifled her irritation. "It is unusual. Of course I knew Vegas had been built in the middle of the desert, but—"

"This your first time in Sin City?" She interrupted.

"Yes."

"Oh, girlie! You are in for the time of your life." She leaned in and lowered her gruff voice. "Remember, what happens in Vegas, stays in Vegas."

"Oh, well, I'm not here for pleasure. I'm here on business."

"A pretty young thing like you can sure find time to mix the two." She waggled her penciled-in brows knowingly.

Pamela felt her jaw setting. She really hated it when people patronized her because she just happened to be attractive. She worked her ass off to be successful. And thirty wasn't young!

"Perhaps I could if I didn't own my own business, and I didn't care if my client recommended my work to others, but I do. So I'm here for professional reasons, not to play."

Her seatmate's surprised look took in Pamela's diamond stud earrings—one carat each—and her well-tailored eggshell Fendi slack suit, the classic color of which was nicely set off by a melon and tangerine silk scarf and shell.

Pamela read the look in her eye, and she wanted to

scream, *No, I did not have some damned man buy me this outfit!*

"Just what is it you do, honey?"

"I own Ruby Slipper, an interior design business."

The woman's crinkled face softened into a smile, and with a start Pamela realized that she must have once been very pretty.

"Ruby Slipper . . . I like that. Sounds real nice. I'll bet you're good at it, too. Just lookin' at you I can tell you got class. But it don't look like Vegas class. What are you doing here?"

"My newest client is an author who is building a vacation home in Vegas. I've been hired to decorate it."

"An author . . ." She fluttered long red fingernails at Pamela. "That's big stuff. Who is it? Maybe I heard of him."

"E. D. Faust. He writes fantasy." Pamela only knew that because she'd looked him up hastily on Amazon during their first phone call. The man had proclaimed himself, "E. D. Faust, best-selling author." She'd had no idea who he was, but when she typed his name into Amazon's search box, her screen had blazed with page after page of titles like *Pillars of the Sword*, *Temple of Warriors*, *Naked Winds*, *Faith of the Damned* . . . and on and on. At that moment he'd instantly had her undivided attention, even though Pamela didn't particularly care for male science-fiction and fantasy authors. She read a little of everything, so she'd tried a few of the giants of the genre, but it seemed they were all too much alike. Swords, magic, spaceships, blood, testosterone . . . blah . . . blah . . . yawn. But she wasn't stupid. Far from it, and one of her primary rules was never, ever say negative things about a client. So she put on a bright smile and nodded in response to her travel partner's blank look like she thought E. D. Faust was Nora Roberts.

"His current release is *Pillars of the Sword*, but he's published more than fifty books, and most of them have appeared on all the major best-seller lists."

"Never heard of him, but then I like a good crossword puzzle more than just about anything." She cackled again.

"Well, anything except a long, tall man in a cowboy hat and a cold beer."

She elbowed Pamela as she laughed, this time on purpose. Pamela was surprised to feel herself smiling back. There was something honest and real about the old woman that made her craggy face and her gruff manner strangely appealing.

"Pamela Gray," she said, holding out her hand.

"Billie Mae Johnson." She returned the handshake with a firm grip and a warm smile. "Pleased to meet ya. If you need a friendly face or a cold beer, come on by the Flamingo. I'm usually working at the bar on the main floor."

"I may just take you up on that."

The stewardess announced that they were landing, and Pamela returned her seat to the full and upright position. Billie Mae shook her head and grumbled at the squares of the crossword puzzle, most of which were still empty.

"Ya have to know that the hoity-toity *New York Times* has gone to hell when they start lettin' divorce lawyers from Texas write their puzzles." She sighed and concentrated on one of the questions before looking askance at Pamela. "Hey, the snooty clue is 'metaphoric emancipation.' The answer has seven letters. All I can think of is Budweiser, but that's nine."

"Is the attorney who wrote the puzzle a man or a woman?"

"Man."

"Try alimony," Pamela said, smiling wickedly.

Billie Mae filled in the letters with a satisfied grunt, then she winked at Pamela as the plane touched down. "You just earned yourself a free beer. Hope you're as good at decoratin' as you are at crosswords."

Pamela approached the uniformed man who was holding a sign that spelled out Pamela Gray, Ruby Slipper, in gold embossed letters. Before she could speak, the man executed an efficient little bow and asked in a clipped British accent, "Miss Gray?"

"Yes, I'm Pamela Gray."

"Very good, madam. I shall take your luggage. Please be so good as to follow me."

She did, and had to hurry to keep up with his brisk pace as he whisked confidently through the crowded airport and out to the waiting limo. Pamela wanted to stand and gawk when he opened the door to a lovely vintage stretch Rolls-Royce, but she slid into the dove colored leather seat gracefully, thanking him before he closed the door.

"Well met, Miss Gray!" a deep voice boomed at her from across the limo.

Pamela jumped. Out of the shadows a man leaned forward, extending a beefy hand. As she automatically grasped it, the crystal chandeliers hanging from both sides of the car blinked on.

"I am, of course, E. D. Faust. But you must call me Eddie."

Recovering her composure, she smiled smoothly and returned his firm grip. Her first impression of E. D. Faust was one of immense size. As soon as he had hired her, she had gone immediately to the nearest bookstore and purchased several of his novels, so she was familiar with his author photo. But the pictures in the back of his books hadn't begun to capture the size of the man. He filled the space across from her, reminding her of Orson Welles or an aging Marlon Brando. And he was dark. His hair, which formed an abrupt widow's peak, was thick and black and tied back in a low ponytail. His long-sleeved silk shirt was black, as were the enormous slacks and the glistening leather boots. Though insulated by layers of fat, the strong lines of his face were still evident, and his age was indeterminate—Pamela knew he must be somewhere between thirty and fifty, but she had no clue exactly where. He watched her watching him, and his brown eyes sparkled with what might have been a mischievous glint, as if he was used to being the center of attention and he enjoyed it.

"It's nice to finally meet you, Eddie. And please, call me Pamela."

"Pamela it is then." Abruptly, he tapped the dragon-head handle of his black cane against the half-lowered panel of glass that divided the passenger area of the limo from the chauffer. "You may carry on, Robert."

"Very good, sir."

The sleek limo pulled away from the curb.

"I trust your journey has not overly fatigued you, Pamela," he said.

"No, it was only a short flight from Colorado Springs."

"Then you would not be opposed to beginning your work immediately?"

"No, I'd be pleased to start right away. Does this mean you've made a decision about the style you'd like for your home?" Pamela asked eagerly. If this exquisite car was an example of Eddie's taste and budget . . . her head spun at the possibilities. A showcase! She would create an exquisite vacation paradise fit for the King of Fantasy Fiction.

"I most certainly have. I know exactly what I desire. I found it here in this magical city. All you need do is to replicate it." Eddie tapped the window again. "Robert, take us to Caesars Palace."

CHAPTER 2

"*Caesars Palace? Isn't that a casino?*"

The folds in Eddie's face crinkled as he smiled. "That is exactly why you are perfect for this job, Pamela. You've never been to Vegas, so you will see everything with fresh eyes, eyes that can truly appreciate and capture the unique ambience I desire for my home. And you are correct. Caesars Palace is a casino as well as a hotel. Actually, except for duplicating some of the elements of the hotel's pool, it's not the Palace on which I want you to focus your attention, but rather the incredible shopping mall that is attached to it. The Forum holds the magic I wish for you to replicate."

"A shopping mall?" Had she heard him correctly? How could he possibly want a vacation home—or any home for that matter—to resemble a shopping mall?

"You shall see, my dear. You shall see." Eddie pointed a thick finger at a silver bucket filled with ice and several bottles. "Would you like to refresh yourself with champagne or Pellegrino?"

"Pellegrino, please." She had a feeling she would need a clear head for what was to come.

A shopping mall vacation home. Now that was an odd request. Not that odd requests from clients were in any way off-putting to Pamela. Since she had established Ruby Slipper three years ago, one of the things that she loved most about having her own design business was that it gave her the freedom to cultivate unique clients and to help those clients turn their individual visions into comfortable, tasteful homes. While Eddie poured Pellegrino into a crystal wineglass she thought about Ruby Slipper's very first client, Samantha Smith-Siddons. Ms. Smith-Siddons, formerly Mrs. Smith-Siddons, had wanted to completely redecorate the 8,000-square-foot home she had kicked Mr. Smith-Siddons out of after walking in on him while he was having sex with his twenty-one-year-old office assistant. Unfortunately for Mr. Smith-Siddons, he had also been wearing women's lingerie, red pumps and a blond wig—a fact that his many patrons (Mr. Smith-Siddons owned the largest chain of funeral parlors in Colorado) would have found deeply disturbing if it had become public in a messy divorce. Mr. Smith-Siddons's unique fondness for women's lingerie had not become public knowledge, and Ms. Smith-Siddons was awarded a sizeable settlement for her tactful silence. When she hired Ruby Slipper she had explained to Pamela that she could not tolerate any color except shades of white because she wanted to begin anew and use the purity of color to banish the stain that had been her marriage. Undaunted by the bizarre restriction, Pamela had focused on textures rather than colors. She had used aged, whitewashed wood floors and shabby chic fixtures, as well as the barest hint of blush and pearl and pewter within shades of snow and champagne and moonlight. The end result had been so spectacular that it had won Ruby Slipper its first full article in *Architectural Digest*.

If she could make Ms. Samantha Smith-Siddons's sterile, almost colorless house into a masterpiece, she could certainly do the same for Eddie's mall fixation.

"I must tell you again, Pamela, how very impressed I was by the exquisite job you did on Judith's boudoir." He chuckled, causing his bulk to vibrate in one gelatinous mass. "Venus rising, indeed. I would have never believed that Judith's rather strange decorating idea would have turned out so lovely. Charles says he doesn't even mind sleeping in a bed that appears to be a giant seashell surrounded by pastels and feminine overtones. Every time Judith steps out of that spectacular bathtub, he can't help but believe he's bedding a goddess."

"It was a challenge, but it came together well." Pamela sipped her bubbly water, thinking that the challenge had been toning down a decorating style that Judith thought of as glamorous old Hollywood, when in actuality it had been bordello-like and tacky. Judith had wanted garish; Pamela had managed to morph it into opulent but tasteful. Charles and Judith Lollman had been so pleased with her work that they had hosted a huge party to showcase their new bedroom suite. Charles Lollman not only produced some of the most successful shows on prime-time TV, but he was a science fiction and fantasy fanatic. One of the many guests he had flown in for the soirée had been the best-selling fantasy author, E. D. Faust. Eddie's phone call had been the first of several referrals that had come from that very successful job.

"A challenge . . ." Eddie lingered on the word like it was a pastry. "Do you like challenges, Pamela?"

Pamela squared her shoulders and returned his steady gaze. Smiling smoothly, she said, "I think challenges make life interesting."

"Ah, the correct answer." His smile suddenly reminded her of Dr. Seuss's Grinch.

"Excuse me, sir." Robert's cultured voice drifted to them. "Shall I take you to the front of the Palace, or do you prefer the VIP entrance to The Forum?"

"The Forum, Robert. And call James. Tell him to meet us in front of the fountain."

"Very well, sir."

Eddie checked his gold Rolex. "Excellent. We should be arriving just in time. I want you to get the full effect."

Pamela wanted to ask him what he meant by "the full effect," but as they turned the corner, Eddie pointed and said, "It looks deceptively simple when approaching it from this angle. But I've booked a suite for you at the Palace through next weekend, to give you plenty of time to absorb the ambience. You will, of course, want to explore the main entrance, as well as the casino and mall, at your leisure."

She blinked at him in surprise. He wanted her to stay a full week just to do research on a shopping mall? She had several other jobs she was in the middle of. Could her assistant handle them alone? Before she could voice any objections, he waved his hand dismissively.

"I understand your time is valuable." He reached into one very deep pocket and pulled out a wad of large bills, counted out several, and handed them to her. "Is five hundred dollars a day an agreeable amount with which to compensate you for the extra time this decorating challenge will require?"

Pamela wanted to shout, *Hell yes!* Instead, her smile was calm and professional as she shoved the money deep within her purse. When she got a minute to herself, the first thing she was going to do was to speed-dial her assistant. Vernelle was going to have a heart attack when she found out that this job was surpassing everything they had imagined. And together she and her assistant had excellent imaginations.

"Thank you, Eddie. That will adequately cover the expense of being away from my studio for a week."

The limo slid to a smooth halt. Robert opened the door and helped her out. Pamela studied the outside of the huge building while Eddie extracted his bulk from the car. The exterior relief of The Forum was simple. It looked like an enormous white marble block with hidden columns forming most of the decoration. *Not bad,* she thought, *even tasteful.* If this was an indication of the interior of the shopping mall, she could expect long, clean lines and understated elegance. Challenge? She wanted to laugh out loud. As Vernelle would say, this job would be as simple as selling feather boas to gay guys.

"The Forum is through here." Eddie led the way through a plain set of white double doors, moving with a surprisingly spry step for such a big man. "I delight in this entrance," he explained to her as they walked down a stark white hallway that looked like it should belong to a large furniture warehouse. "It always makes such an impression. I like to suppose that I'm leaving one world and entering another." His chuckle was deep and infectious. "But mayhap that is because I create worlds for a living. So, you tell me, Pamela." His eyes sparkled as he opened an ordinary-looking fire door for her and gestured magnanimously that she should precede him. "Behold, The Forum!"

Sweet mother of God, was Pamela's first thought. Her second was that she needed to close her mouth. Then she was caught up in a vortex of sight and sound. People crowded what had been built to look like the pretend streets of Rome. Emphasis on the word *pretend.* It was tacky beyond belief. She and Eddie had emerged between stores that emblazoned Versace and Escada in gilded letters meant to imitate ancient Rome. But instead of evoking old-world elegance, it reminded Pamela of a cartoon caricature. It was like someone had taken a crayon to history and architecture.

"Spectacular, isn't it?" Eddie boomed.

"The . . . the ceiling has clouds painted all over it," was all she could manage.

Delighted, he nodded. "It is the exact effect I want for the ceiling in my home. Do you see how they have it lit?" He pointed up. The mock facades that fronted the stores were tall, but they did not reach the domed ceiling. It was obvious that atop the fake roofs were spotlights that shined up, illuminating the pretend clouds. "As you see, right now it appears to be midday, which is what I wish for my home. I want it to be perpetual daylight, so that I may write in an eternal sun."

"Oh, God . . ." The words escaped Pamela's lips before she could think to reclose her mouth.

Eddie's laughter rumbled between them. "You had no idea it would be like this."

"No idea," she agreed numbly.

"Come! The best lies before us." He quickly checked his watch. "We must hurry. There are only five minutes left before the show begins."

"The show?" Pamela forced herself to stop gawking and hurried to catch up with him.

"Yes! It is what I want you to create as the centerpiece of my home. The spectacular fountain."

"You want a fountain inside your home?" Her voice was pitched to be carefully optimistic. She loved water features and believed they were an important part of creating positive chi within a home. Her mind was already whirring . . . she would hire an excellent artist and create . . . she glanced up and tried not to grimace . . . a *tasteful* version of the sky blue and cotton white paint-by-numbers scenery above them. Then she would offset that garishness with a fabulous fountain. Perhaps one imported directly from Italy. Eddie would like that, after all, The Forum was a play on Rome, so it would be natural to want a fountain from . . .

They turned to the left, and Pamela stumbled to a horrified halt.

Opening up in front of them was a monstrosity that spewed bubbling water and naked gods and goddesses. Pamela could feel her head shaking back and forth as if it didn't belong to her. It was atrocious. Huge marble horses lunged from the lighted pool as water frothed around them. Zeus or Poseidon or some other naked god stood atop a platform holding a pointed trident as he stared sternly down at the billowing water. Against one side of the fountain diners sat in little café tables of an obviously popular Italian restaurant. Pamela wondered how they could hear one another over the roar of the erupting water.

"No, no, no, not this fountain," Eddie touched her back, guiding her easily past the wet hulk. "I have no need for an imitation of Trevi. I want something truly unique."

Relieved, Pamela gave him a weak smile.

"I do not like that, either," Eddie said as they hurried by The Disney Store, which hosted a life-sized Pegasus sticking out of the top of it. "A winged horse seems a little too much to me."

Pamela nodded silently. A winged horse was "a little too much," but a domed ceiling painted to look like the sky lit with eternal sunlight wasn't? She set her jaw. She liked a challenge. Really. She was an excellent, experienced interior designer with a keen sense of taste and style. She liked eccentric clients. No, she reminded herself firmly, she didn't just like them, she preferred them. There was no project so weird or tacky or bizarre that she couldn't take it and whip it into something tasteful and refined.

A crowd of people milled in front of them, from the

middle of which a tall man's raised arm caught Pamela's attention.

"Ah, there is James. He has chosen an excellent spot."

Eddie tucked her against him as he plunged into the crowd, propelling them forward like a whale cutting through a school of guppies. When they reached the tall man, Eddie pushed her forward. A little short of breath, she smiled a greeting, but the expression died on her face as she realized where they stood.

It was in front of another massive fountain. This one was shaped like an arabesque window. The center of it was dominated by a gigantic stone man sitting on a throne. Three standing statues ringed the throned figure, but Pamela didn't have a chance to get a clear impression of them because at that instant the eternal sunlight that shined off the domed ceiling faded, and a thick fog began pouring from openings at the base of the throne. Pamela sneezed at the tangy scent of dry ice.

"Bless you!" Eddie said from behind her. Then he leaned down to speak in her ear. "It begins. Watch closely."

Maniacal laughter erupted from the middle of the fountain, and Pamela felt a weird little jolt of shock as she realized that the center statue had become animated. The laughter was issuing from its moving lips. In amazement, Pamela watched as the seated figure swiveled on its dais so that it was facing them.

"It is time! It is time!" The talking statue proclaimed. "I am Bacchus! Come one—Come all! Come to the mall!"

The animated Bacchus lifted his goblet, which suddenly glowed golden. But Pamela spared only a small look at the new special effects. Bacchus' face had captured her attention. She decided he resembled a grotesque reproduction of the Three Stooges' Curly all dressed up in a toga with grape leaves around his bald head and several chins dangling down his neck. More laughter spewed from his mouth as he pretended to drink a toast to the crowd.

"Caesar! Welcome the visitors to our Forum!"

At Bacchus' command, the standing statue that was farthest from them began gesturing with his arms and said something about Bacchus pouring a feast for the crowd.

From where she stood Pamela couldn't quite make out his words. The newly animated arm-flailing statue reminded her of Fred Flintstone.

"Bloody buggering hell," she muttered to herself, using her assistant's favorite oath, "it's like a car wreck."

"On with the party!" Bacchus' statue yelled. "Artemis, speak to your subjects."

The second of the standing statues raised her arm, and Pamela was horrified to notice that her mountainous breasts bobbled in time with her movements.

"From the forest and the hunt only you could entice me to leave—so it is to your Forum that we all must cleave. Shop, drink and be merry—especially if it is Visa that you do carry!" The female voice was tinny sounding, and as she spoke a quiver of arrows and a bow slung over her shoulder glowed an awful neon red.

"Well spoken, my beauty!" Bacchus' head wobbled up and down with a jerky, mechanical movement. "But now it is your brother's turn. Play for the gathering, Apollo!"

The statue directly in front of her began to turn until it was facing the crowd. The harp in Apollo's hands glowed bright green while he stroked it. Music came from a speaker semihidden at Pamela's feet.

"Yes, Bacchus, with my lyre I shall delight and inspire."

"It touches my heart!" Said the fat statue in a canned voice. "Oh, Apollo, what a romantic spell you cast. But enough! It is time to summon the light of day!"

The Apollo statue bowed awkwardly to Bacchus before raising his hand. Abruptly, the domed ceiling came alive with lasers, bouncing in bright colors from cloud to cloud as Bacchus' pleased laughter filled the dry ice air. The slicing lights finally culminated in a burst of brightness that left the fake sky lit as if it was midmorning.

"Now, my friends," Bacchus said as the other statues dimmed and died, and a pink-tinged spotlight illuminated his florid face. "Eat, drink and be merry! And remember— you must return for the special evening show at eight o'clock sharp! Until then, carpe diem!

As his maniacal laughter faded and spontaneous applause broke out, Pamela overheard a woman wearing red sweatpants say to her friend, "Ain't it better than last time we was here?"

"Yep," her friend replied.

"Oh, God . . ." Pamela groaned.

CHAPTER 3

~

"No, you are not to fret. I know exactly what has you looking so concerned." Eddie patted her hand. "Money is not an issue. I will spare no expense to make my vision come to life."

"You may trust his word, ma'am. Eddie will provide you with all the funds that you need."

Pamela blinked woodenly up at the tall man.

"How insufferably rude of me," Eddie said. "Pamela, let me present you to my assistant, James Ridgewood. James, this is our much esteemed interior designer, Pamela Gray."

"A pleasure to meet you, ma'am." James took her hand in a firm, dry grip.

Eddie slapped his palms against his thick thighs. "I can hardly contain my excitement! Now that you have seen the marvelous fountain, tell me, Pamela, what do you think?"

"What do I think?" Pamela stalled by repeating the question. She and Eddie were sitting beside each other on one of the faux marble benches that surrounded the now-silent fountain. Because of the author's girth, the bench that would normally have held three or even four people was full, so James stood beside them. Pamela looked helplessly from Eddie's sparkling eyes up to James, who returned her gaze with the steady, attentive expression of a schoolboy. No help there, she realized. James had bought into the decorating disaster, too.

"Yes! What do you think of fashioning the centerpiece of my home after this fountain?"

Pamela studied Eddie carefully. The big man wasn't pretending. Unfortunately, this wasn't a joke. He really wanted the wretched thing. She cleared her throat and took a deep breath before plunging into her answer.

"It is definitely an unusual idea."

Eddie and James nodded their heads in enthusiastic agreement.

"I do, however, have some initial concerns. First"—she gestured at the enormous water fiasco—"the size. If I remember correctly, you said your home was roughly twelve thousand square feet. That is, of course, a spacious home, but I'm afraid that even an estate of that size cannot accommodate a fountain of such"—she paused, silently editing out words like *monstrous* and *grotesque*—"magnificent dimensions."

Eddie threw his head back and laughed heartily, causing several people to stop and stare at him. "Now I understand your shocked expression, my dear. I do not want the fountain *inside* my home. Rather, I want it to be a focal point in the courtyard. James, show our Pamela what I mean."

Smiling, James lifted a beautiful burgundy leather briefcase and extracted a thick manila folder, which he handed to her. She opened it to find detailed color pictures and floor plans of an exquisite Italian-style villa. It was built in a huge U shape around a lovely marble-tiled center courtyard, which was obviously meant to be the focal point of the home. Pamela felt herself nodding in appreciation of the architectural excellence of the home. Then she blinked and took a closer look at the picture. Across the color rendition of the tasteful courtyard someone had scrawled in changes with a pencil. *Take out trees. Replace with Roman columns, gold perhaps, as in Forum?*

Gold columns? Her eyes drifted to a column near them. Like a bizarre cross between a whorehouse and a funeral parlor, it was covered with tacky faux marble paint. The top of the column was encrusted with gaudy swirls of gold. She was glad she was sitting down, because her knees felt decidedly weak. She looked back at the penciled-in notes.

Instead of tiles, make floor to look like Forum streets. Horrified, Pamela glanced down. The "streets" of The Forum were nothing more than cement that had been textured to look like cheap imitation stone, and then painted muddy brown and varnished. Surely Eddie didn't mean to exchange the fabulous travertine with *cement.*

"Do you understand now? I want to transplant this fountain into the courtyard of my home."

Pamela felt her mouth open and close, fishlike, as she struggled to find something to say.

"Of course I realize that even though my courtyard is large, it is not big enough to hold an exact replica of the fountain. So, what I have decided is that I want a miniature version. Cut out Caesar, Artemis and Apollo." His gaze shifted fondly to the center-most statue. "You must keep Bacchus, though. God of the Vine and Fertility. In my home wine is always welcome, and fertility"—his chuckle rumbled—"well, the rules of chivalry remind me that such risqué subjects are not fit for a lady's ears, so for now I will simply say that I wish to encourage the fertility of creativity and the written word."

Pamela ignored the mischievous glint in the big man's eyes. She certainly didn't want to get into any kind of fertility discussion with him.

"Let me see if I understand you correctly. What you want is the aura of this fountain, something with its basic shape and design, only on a smaller scale."

"Exactly!" Eddie grinned. "And, of course, I will require it to be animated."

This time when Pamela's mouth dropped open, she didn't bother to close it.

"Ex-e-excuse me, uh, M-Mr. Faust?"

Pamela turned to see three zit-faced teenage boys standing behind her. Each of them clutched a hardback copy of *Pillars of the Sword* as they stared rapturously at Eddie.

"It-it is you, isn't it?" the tallest of the three stuttered.

Eddie nodded. "It is I, E. D. Faust."

"Awesome!"

"I told you it was him." The tall boy gave his compatriots a victorious look. "We just bought our copies of *Pil-*

lars. It would be, like, *amazing* if you would please sign them for us!"

Pamela couldn't help smiling at the boys. They were cute in a gawky kind of a way, like young colts. Then she noticed that the pudgy boy standing closest to her was trying to look down her blouse. She frowned at him and re-arranged her jacket. Men: whether they were fifteen or fifty, some things stayed the same.

"It would be my great privilege to affix my signature to these books for you young lads! Come! Tell me your names." Eddie gestured magnanimously.

"Taylor!" The pudgy kid forgot about her cleavage as he beat past his two buddies who were shouting, "Jamie!" and "Adam!"

Eddie's laughter boomed good-naturedly, but as the boys surged forward, Pamela noticed that the author shot his assistant a pointed look.

"Miss Gray," James's voice was hurried as he bent and spoke in her ear. "I'm afraid we don't have much time. Everything you need is in this briefcase," which he handed to her, "including your room key. I have already checked you in, and Robert had your bags delivered to your room."

"It *is* E. D. Faust."

"I thought I recognized that guy from somewhere!"

Pamela looked around in surprise. Several people were pointing at Eddie and shouting.

"It is Eddie's wish that you spend this weekend simply soaking up the ambience of The Forum and Caesars Palace. On Monday morning he will send a car for you, and you will be taken to the home itself. All the details of that are in the briefcase. Until then, think of the next couple days as a pleasant sojourn within the magic of Las Vegas."

"E. D. Faust! Wow!" said a breathless man who rushed up to Eddie, knocked aside the glaring teenagers and pumped his hand vigorously. "I have all your books."

"I applaud your taste in literature, sir!"

Eddie's tone was jovial, but there was no mistaking the pained look he gave James.

"There are more instructions in the briefcase, as well as

contact numbers if you need to reach us before Monday. Now I must tend to him," James finished quickly.

Pamela watched as James maneuvered through the growing crowd to Eddie's side and announced that Mr. Faust must be going, he had an important interview for which he could not be late. Eddie lifted his bulk from the bench, winked at Pamela, and began making his way with well-practiced reluctance to the exit. The crowd followed him, still vying for him to sign a T-shirt or even the back of a hand.

Left behind, Pamela shook her head slowly in amazement. She looked at the crowd as it moved away down the pretend street after the fantasy author, and she felt a little like Alice after she'd fallen down the hole. And the crowd kept growing, mostly teenage boys and men with comb-overs who wore white socks pulled up to their knees. They were mobbing him, and Pamela could see James's tall fig-ure hustling his boss forward while the author's distinctive laughter drifted back to her. Eddie was like a rock star—a dorky rock star, but a rock star nonetheless. It was amaz-ing. She'd had no idea.

Her gaze shifted back to the atrocious fountain that was at the moment, thankfully, silent. She sighed. *One step at a time,* she reminded herself. She'd go to her room, freshen up, check in with Vernelle, then come back down here for dinner and—she thought about what the statue had said— she'd catch the evening show. It couldn't possibly be any worse than what she'd already seen.

"Say again, Pammy, I couldn't have heard you right."

"You heard me right, V. The horrid thing talks. And lights up in honest-to-God neon colors. And he wants one like it in his courtyard." Sitting on the edge of the king-sized bed in her opulent suite, Pamela pulled off one of her stiletto pumps and rubbed the arch of her foot.

"The courtyard in the gorgeous Italian villa-like home?"

"The very same."

"Bloody buggering hell."

"My thoughts exactly," Pamela said.

"It's worse than Venus rising." V snorted. "Silly tripod."

The term made Pamela laugh, as it always did. *Tripod,* Vernelle had explained to her when they had begun working together three years ago, was a lesbian slang word for a man. V was most definitely a lesbian. Not a man-hating, cynical lesbian. Vernelle Wilson liked men. She just didn't like sleeping with them. She had explained it to Pamela like this: "Men bore me. After I've been with one for a little while I think I'd rather blow my brains out than wake up next to him and listen to his inane, manly blather for the rest of my life. Now women . . ." Her hazel eyes had sparkled and her grin had turned her face pixielike. "Women I can listen to forever."

And that was one of Vernelle's many strengths: listening to women. She never rushed a decision from any female client, and she seemed to innately understand exactly what one meant when she wanted "that purpley-blue shade somewhere between the night sky and a pansy."

Although not formally educated in interior design, Vernelle was a professional artist and graphic designer—as Ruby Slipper's amazing Web site and unique logo could attest to. She had an eye for color and texture, as well as being a sharp businesswoman. Hiring V as her assistant had been the first of many savvy decisions Pamela had made when she began her own business. V liked to say that it showed how highly evolved Pamela was that she had chosen her over the bevy of gay guys who had applied for the job.

Pamela stifled her laughter before it became hysterical. "I don't know, V. This may be the job that I can't turn tasteful. I mean, please. He wants Roman Liberace. Totally tacky."

"Hey, it's too early to give up. And remember, it's Friday night, and you're in Vegas."

"Yeah, yeah, yeah. Whatever. More importantly, how is the Katherine Graham project coming? You're obviously still breathing, so she must not have driven you to suicide yet."

"Hey, give me some credit. I like the old broad."

"Sure, *like* as in you *like* going to the dentist," Pamela said.

V laughed. "No, really. She's growing on me. I still hate her zillions of cats, and I have no idea how a woman who chain smokes and drinks brandy like it's water can still be alive and kicking at eighty-seven, but her raunchy sense of humor has become almost charming."

"And her color scheme is . . ."

"I've talked her out of the purples and pinks. We've practically decided on yellow, sage green, and a hint of red. When we get done with the exterior, that gihugic Victorian will look like it's ten years old rather than one hundred and ten."

"Then we'll get to work on the inside."

Together, Pamela and Vernelle sighed.

"So, that's going well. How about the Starnes reupholster job?"

"It's fine, Pamela. And so is the flooring for the Bates formal living room and the window treatments for the Thackerys. Would you please not worry about work? You tied up all the loose ends before you left—and I can take care of the ongoing jobs. If I get stuck on anything new, I'll call you."

"Promise?"

"Absolutely. And hey, here's a thought. How about you take some time for yourself. *You're in Las Vegas,* for God's sake! Hang out, have some fun. Hell, you might as well gamble a little."

"Gamble?"

"Pammy, that is what Vegas is all about," V said.

"I don't think I'd like gambling. It doesn't make sense to me. I'm supposed to give up my money and I don't get food or wine or clothes or a piece of furniture in return? I can't imagine it being fun."

"Pammy, I think you're missing the point."

"Which is?"

"Be a little crazy! Let loose! You might hit the jackpot."

Considering, Pamela cocked her head to the side. "You might have something there, V. Maybe I'm looking at this project all wrong. Instead of thinking tasteful, I should be thinking whimsical."

"Yeah," V said. "The guy's loaded, and even though he sounds a little over the top, you said he seems nice."

"He is," Pamela said.

"Well then, look at it like this: E. D. Faust creates fantasies for a living. He is simply asking that you create one for him to live in. Stop stressing about turning it into an *Architectural Digest* layout. And, Pammy, when I said that you should take some time for yourself, I didn't mean it should have anything to do with work." She paused, and her voice became serious. "How long has it been since you've had a vacation?"

"You and I went—"

"No, I'm not talking about trips to market," V cut her off. "I'm talking about a *vacation*."

Pamela sighed. V knew the answer to that question as well as she did. It had been years. The last vacation she'd taken had been with Duane, and it had been a nightmare. Just the two of them, alone at a chic Mexican resort that catered to couples and their privacy. The resort had provided all the booze Duane could swill and lots of alone time for him to obsess over her. He hadn't let her out of his sight for six days. Just thinking about it made her feel short of breath. Since she'd left him, she really hadn't thought about taking a vacation. When had there been time?

"I didn't mean to bring up bad memories, Pammy," she said softly into the silent phone. "I just want you to think about how long it's been since you've relaxed and really had fun." V paused, took a deep breath, and continued in the same soothing tone. "You haven't even had a date since you left Duane."

"I have, too! I went out with . . . uh . . ." Pamela struggled unsuccessfully to recall the name of the textile representative who had taken her to lunch a few months ago.

"A gay guy doesn't count—especially a gay guy whose name you can't remember," V scoffed.

"What's-his-name wasn't gay."

"If you're calling him what's-his-name, it doesn't matter whether he's gay or not. Who besides him?"

Pamela chewed on her lip.

"That's what I thought. Pammy, you're in Vegas. It's Friday night. You have plenty of money. You are single and very available. No!" she said before Pamela could begin to ague with her. "Don't start. The sticky booger ex-husfreak hasn't bothered you in six months, and you've been officially divorced now for a year and a half. You are definitely not one of the aged or infirm. Hell, you even have all your teeth. If I'm any judge of women, what you are is ripe and ready—and you know I'm an excellent judge of women."

"You think I'm going to leap into some kind of tawdry weekend Vegas affair?"

V didn't need to see Pamela to imagine the stern line she'd pressed her lips into. "Hell no! I'm not that hopeful. Seriously, Pammy, all I'm suggesting is that it's time you loosened up and allowed the opposite sex at least a chance with you. You don't have one damn thing to do until Monday morning, so here's an idea—flirt a little."

"Flirt?"

"Flirt. As in engaging in coy, seductive conversation with a tripod."

"May I call him a tripod?" Pamela giggled.

"Only if you want to join my team."

"It might be easier."

"That's yet another heterosexual myth about homosexual relationships, but we're not talking about my pathetic love life, we're talking about your nonexistent love life. Pammy, it's the right time and the perfect place. You don't have to open your legs—just open your mind. See if you can interact with at least one man in more than a businesslike fashion."

Pamela heard the undercurrent of worry in her friend's voice. Had she really only interacted with men as business associates since her divorce? She didn't even need to finish formulating the question in her mind. She already knew the answer all too well. As she thought about it, Pamela felt a little spark of anger begin to stir within her. Duane would be thrilled to know that he had turned her into an asexual workaholic. It would mean he could still control her.

"Flirt," Pamela said.

"Flirt," V repeated sternly.

"Okay, you're probably right." Pamela forced cheerfulness into her voice. "I have been working too hard. I'm going to think of this weekend as a little escape from the real world, and this job as an adventure into the fantastic."

"And maybe you'll even gamble a little?" V coaxed.

"Maybe . . . a little."

CHAPTER 4

"Modern mortals are odd," Artemis told her brother as she watched a row of dowdy matrons pulling the arms of machines that twinkled and clacked and blared obnoxious things like "Wheel of Fortune." "It is as if the shine and the glitter of the boxes casts a spell on them."

"Slot machines," Apollo corrected her.

Artemis gave him a quizzical look.

"Remember what Bacchus told us? They are called slot machines."

"Slot machines or shining boxes, what difference does it make? Leave it to Bacchus to actually listen to mortals."

A middle-aged woman in an appliquéd sweatshirt and leggings paused to frown at the goddess before she fed her machine more money. Apollo took his sister's elbow and guided her out of earshot of the row of machines.

"You shouldn't let them hear you speak that way. And don't be so hard on Bacchus. You know Zeus commanded him to explain the customs of modern mortals to us so that we could blend more easily with them." Apollo paused as he watched a man in a gaudy white jumpsuit encrusted with rhinestones cause a group of women to squeal in delight as he gyrated his hips and sang something about being "all shook up."

"I, for one, am glad Bacchus understands this world. Much of it is a mystery to me."

"Fine! If it'll make you stop sulking I'll gift the matron to make up for my harshness." With a sarcastic flip of her long, shapely fingers Artemis caused the woman's slot machine to land on a perfect row of cherries. The matron squealed and leapt to her feet as lights flashed and sirens proclaimed her a jackpot winner. Artemis looked on in disgust. "Modern mortals would be much more interesting if they were cute and made noises like puppies, instead of looking and sounding like overfed sows all ready for the slaughter."

"They are not pets. Nor are they animals," Apollo said severely. "And Zeus commanded us not to meddle with the mortals."

"I wasn't meddling. I was gifting. There is a distinct difference. If I was going to meddle I would have made that horrid clothing in which she has covered herself combust." Artemis' self-amused laughter was sweet music, and it caused several men to send her hot, appreciative gazes, which the goddess completely ignored.

Her brother grunted an incoherent response.

"Apollo, what is wrong with you?"

"Nothing is wrong with me," he said, taking her elbow again and steering her past the busy blackjack and roulette tables and towards one of the many little bars that were conveniently scattered throughout the casino. Even though the two immortals were dressed in matching chitons that left much of their sleek bodies bare, they blended well with the colorful mixture of casino employees and Vegas revelers. People noticed their stunning beauty and the unique grace with which they moved. How could they not? But no one thought the appearance of a couple dressed as if they had stepped off the streets of ancient Rome unusual. They were, after all, at Caesars Palace in Sin City. Anything could be expected to happen there.

Apollo reached into a fold in his tunic and extracted the paper that Bacchus had reluctantly distributed amongst the Olympians as he explained that the modern world used it as currency. He caught the waitress's attention, and though it was only his third foray to the Kingdom of Las Vegas, he ordered the drink that the immortals had already become fond of with smooth confidence, "Two vodka martinis, very cold, with extra olives. Shaken, not stirred."

"Who are you, sweetheart?" The waitress gave him a flirtatious flutter of her suspiciously thick eyelashes. "Caesar or James Bond?"

"Neither," he said with a bittersweet smile. "I am Apollo."

"I could almost believe it, handsome." She leered at his well-muscled body and wiggled her way back to the bar.

"Insignificant creatures." Artemis curled her lip after the waitress.

"It's not that they're insignificant. It's just that they have changed."

Artemis shook her head at her brother. "What has happened to you?"

Apollo considered giving his sister his standard "nothing's wrong with me" response, but when he met her eyes he read within them her very real concern. He tried to make his shrug nonchalant. "Perhaps I have changed, too."

Artemis felt a little knot of worry expand and harden. "Changed? What do you mean?"

He didn't answer his sister until the cocktail waitress had deposited their drinks. When he spoke, his deep voice was wistful.

"Have you ever wondered what it is that loves, the body or the soul?"

"What it is that loves? What kind of question is that?" she sputtered.

"The kind of question that was asked of me by a mortal, but which I could not answer. Apparently, you can not answer it either, Sister."

Caught mid-drink, Artemis swallowed carefully while she considered her brother's disturbing words.

"It is that damned confused mortal who inhabited Persephone's body. She has done this to you, hasn't she?" Artemis snapped.

"The mortal wasn't confused at all. She clearly chose Hades over me. As the God of the Underworld chose her over all other women, mortal or immortal."

"Well, I hope the silly mortal is worshiping Hades properly. He may reign over the dead, but he is a god and, no matter how odd his tastes, he deserves abject adoration."

Apollo rubbed his brow as if he had a headache. "It's not like that between them. You should see how they are together, Artemis. There is a contentment about them that is beyond words. Perhaps beyond understanding," then he added as if it was an afterthought, "or at least beyond my understanding."

"You've been watching Hades and Persephone?" Incredulous, she could only stare at her brother.

"It's not Persephone. It's the mortal woman, Carolina. Hades did not desire Persephone. He loved the mortal's soul, not the immortal goddess. And, no, I haven't been watching them. At least not like you're making it sound. I have visited the Underworld as Hades' guest—several times." He finished quickly.

So that was where he had disappeared to lately. She had just assumed he was visiting the Ancient World to oversee his oracle or to stir up something interesting, perhaps a minor war or two. Instead he had been Hades' guest in the Underworld? How strange.

"Hades has always been different from the rest of us. Why are you letting his eccentricities bother you?"

"You don't understand."

His eyes had a sad, introspective cast that continued to trouble Artemis. "Then explain it to me."

"Hades doesn't bother me. The mortal he loves doesn't bother me. I bother me."

"You aren't making sense."

"I realize that. I hardly make sense to myself. All I know is that for the first time in my existence I have glimpsed something that I desire, and I have no idea how to attain it."

Arthemis' first instinct was to scoff and to remind her brother that women were easily had, but something in the tone of his voice stayed her abrupt comment. Instead, she watched him carefully as she sipped her drink. He looked tired, and Apollo never looked tired. Was it possible that he was pining for a mortal woman? She remembered the last mortal who had refused Apollo's love. Her name had been Cassandra, and he hadn't become withdrawn and introspective then, he had become angry—so angry that he had negated the gift of prophecy he had given her. But mortals like Cassandra were the exception. Apollo was a legendary lover. Nymphs swooned when he smiled; even goddesses vied for his attention. Could desire for a mortal have so clouded his memory that he'd forgotten his own powers of seduction?

A commotion drew her attention from Apollo. Not far from them a little group of forest nymphs dressed in diaphanous white robes were talking in excited little bursts, completely unaware that every mortal man within sight was staring hungrily at them.

Apollo followed her gaze and smiled fondly at the bright cluster of nymphs. "It might not have been wise to allow the nymphs access to the modern world."

"Let them have their fun; they're harmless."

"How harmless they are would depend upon whether you are a mortal man caught in the wake of their allure," he said wryly.

As if the handsome god's gaze called to them, several of the nymphs rushed up to Apollo.

"My Lord! Have you heard? Bacchus has asked us to frolic for the mortals!"

"Yes! We are to perform a ritual of invocation."

"You should watch, my Lord!"

"Yes, please come watch us!"

The group giggled and posed alluringly for their favorite golden god before scampering off.

Artemis laughed at their childlike exuberance, but when she glanced at Apollo, she saw that he was staring after the little group, and his brow was furrowed.

"What are they invoking?" Apollo muttered more to himself than to his sister.

Artemis nibbled at her last olive. "Blessings . . . fertility . . . good health . . . you know, the normal things nymphs frolic around invoking. Are you going to eat that last olive?"

Apollo shook his head. His sister stabbed his olive with her toothpick and popped it into her mouth.

"Zeus made it clear that we were not to use our powers to meddle in the modern world."

"By Zeus' beard you have become as dour as dead Tiresias!" Her anger sizzled around them, causing the toothpick that she still held between her fingers to burst into flame. Annoyed, the goddess rolled her eyes and blew away the ash. "Mortal lives are like their little trinkets and playthings: fragile, easily consumed and just as easily replaced."

"You're comparing mortals to a sliver of wood?" he said, still staring in the direction the nymphs had disappeared.

"Why not?" She sighed and shook her head at her obviously distracted brother. "Oh, very well. Let us go make certain the nymphs don't do anything to meddle with your precious mortals." When he hesitated, she pulled him to his feet. "You never know," she whispered in mock concern. "Some unsuspecting mortal might actually blunder into the invocation and ask for our aid. I can hear them now: 'Great Zeus, send a thunderbolt to maim my neighbor's dog who barks all night . . .'"

He shook his head at his beautiful sister as he reluctantly walked with her through the casino. "You should not make light of an invocation ceremony. You know as well as I how much mischief has been caused by mortals binding the gods to aid them."

"Ancient mortals, yes, like Paris or Medea. But this is not the Ancient World. These mortals know nothing of us." Artemis watched in disgust as a balding, rotund man bought a fistful of large cigars from a scantily clad young woman who carried a tray, "All that concerns them now is . . ." She paused as the fat man reached forward to grope up the back of the cigar girl's short skirt when she turned away. With a small movement of her fingers, Artemis caused him to trip and fall face-forward. The goddess smiled smugly as his cigars rolled across the floor and the man cursed loudly. "All that concerns them now is shallow self-gratification," she finished. As they walked past, she stepped purposefully on one of the cigars that had come to rest near them, squashing it nicely into the ornate rug.

"Then they differ little from the gods," Apollo muttered.

Artemis shrugged off the accusatory tone of his comment. "We are gods. Self-gratification is ours by right."

"But what if superior self-gratification is not enough?" he asked, keeping his voice low.

Artemis felt her anger stir. There was obviously something wrong with her brother, but his morose, self-pitying attitude was wearing on her.

"What do you suggest, Brother? What other life could you possibly desire besides ours? Look around you." She gestured at the mortals who scurried past them like brainless ants. "We act superior because we are superior. A mortal's life is a temporary thing. They are like butterflies without the beauty of wings. You say modern mortals are changed? The only real change I see in them is that they no longer recognize us, which tells me that they have lost even the small amount of intelligence they used to have. Look at what they worship now." Artemis paused at the end of the casino and looked out into the shopping area that was The Forum. "Their Gods are Gucci, Prada, Versace, Escada, Visa and MasterCard." She shook her head, annoyed that her brother's silly malaise had gotten so under her skin. "We're wasting time. Are we not supposed to be following the nymphs?"

She nodded at the swirling path of golden glitter that the semideities left behind them. The mortals had, of course, noticed the shimmering trail, and many young females were laughing and dabbing the glitter on their bodies. Artemis frowned again. Their odd-looking clothing was confusing: low-slung, faded things that Bacchus had said they called jeans, and tight, middle-bearing brightly colored tops. Did these fledglings not realize how unattractive it was to display so much chubby skin? Being voluptuous was one thing; drawing attention to the one's body flaws was quite another. The goddess thought they looked like desperate young sausages.

"You may have a point," Apollo said slowly, considering his sister's words as they made their way through the noise and confusion of the busy market. "There is definitely something missing about them. Perhaps it is the absence of gods and goddesses within their lives. But I do not think that modern mortals are all as empty-headed as you believe. Actually, they remind me of myself." He laughed at his sister's shocked expression. "They seem to be searching for something that is just out of reach."

"You are a god. An Olympian immortal. Nothing is out of your reach," she said severely. Then her eyes widened as they made their way past a huge fountain that spewed water around naked nymphs. The central feature of the monstrosity was an enormous, scowling statue of a naked Poseidon, clutching a triton and glaring down at the shoppers. "They are lucky that Poseidon has no interest in visiting their kingdom. This naked rendition of him is definitely lacking"—she glanced at the statue's most intimate parts—"the god's true stature."

Apollo grinned. "That's probably why he's glaring."

Artemis smiled back at him, pleased he was sounding more like himself. Maybe her words were getting through to him at last. "Just the same, it is a good thing that Las Vegas isn't near the ocean. Poseidon can be so touchy."

They passed a large store that boasted the logo Disney as well as a life-sized reproduction of Pegasus flying from it. Artemis peered within. "Apparently modern mortals are obsessed with Hercules, Atlantis, and lions."

"At least they're colorful."

"Hercules wasn't really that handsome," Artemis said, glancing back over her shoulder at the strange shop.

"You never liked him."

"He was balding. I don't find bald men attractive, no matter how many labors they perform."

They turned a corner and saw a large crowd gathered around what appeared to be yet another of the ostentatious fountains, and Artemis wondered what glaring god would be featured atop this one. She and her brother had not ventured into this particular part of The Forum on their other brief visits, and curiosity caught her as they drew closer. The fountain was situated in the middle of a large area ringed with ornately carved columns. The shops that flanked the area were different here than at the other end of The Forum. Here they seemed to be more focused on food and wine than on selling clothing and jewelry. One especially interesting looking café caught her eye. The cheap gold lettering that so liberally proclaimed the names of the shops and boutiques throughout the rest of The Forum was absent at this particular café. Instead ancient-looking carved travertine marble letters were interspersed with living moss and trailing vines. The beautiful travertine spelled out the name of the little wine bar, The Lost Cellar.

Artemis elbowed her brother and lifted her chin in the direction of the café. "Let's go there. I'm in the mood for a bloodred Chianti."

"When are you not in the mood for red wine?" He smiled at her as he took her arm and began steering her along the edge of the crowd.

Suddenly, the lights that illuminated the cloud-filled ceiling dimmed and shifted colors from yellow to mauve and violet. The crowd murmured in anticipation, and Artemis and Apollo halted just outside The Lost Cellar. Though they were both well above average height, it was difficult for them to see over the closely packed people. Artemis made a frustrated sound. Just before she flicked her fingers, her brother whispered, "Be gentle with them." She winked at him and waggled her slender fingers mischievously. The people who had been blocking their view magically lost interest in the show and moved away, and anyone who tried to take their place found that standing in front of the two tall, attractive Olympians caused them to have an uncontrollable urge to pass gas—so violently that they hastily excused themselves and hurried to the nearest restroom facilities.

"Don't worry, Brother," Artemis smiled. "Each of them will find that later tonight they will have incredibly good luck at the . . . what did you call those clanking boxes? Slot . . ." Her voice trailed off as her mind registered the look of shock on Apollo's face. She turned her head and followed his stunned gaze. Her eyes went large and round as the seated statue at the center of the spurting fountain rotated in a slow circle towards them and began to speak.

"COME ONE, COME ALL, COME TO THE MALL!"

"The horrid thing looks like Bacchus," Artemis gasped.

"I think it *is* Bacchus," Apollo said, careful to keep his voice low.

The statue opened its mouth and chortled grotesquely. "Ah, but tonight we have a special show for you! Nymphs, I command you dance for the Vegas revelers, two by two!"

As per his order, pairs of nymphs detached themselves from where they had been standing at the edges of the crowd and, to the delight of the watching mortals, they began a seductive dance around the circumference of the fountain in time to the canned music of bells and pipes and horns. Golden glitter haloed the lovely forest deities as they twirled and leapt and frolicked with superhuman grace.

The Bacchus statue mechanically nodded his head in appreciation. Jell-O-like, his chins wobbled as he continued to speak.

"Nymphs, the magic of your beauty is pure and true. Tell me, Apollo, what thinks you?"

At the sound of the animated statue calling his name, Apollo jerked in surprise and took a half-step forward. Then his body froze as one of the lesser statues rotated and came alive in response.

"I agree they are lovely, fair and bright. Tonight I enhance their beauty with the magic of my immortal light!"

The real Apollo was struck speechless as he stared at the caricature of himself. In the next instant the music intensified as a laser show began and the nymphs stepped up the tempo of their dance to the spontaneous applause of the captivated audience.

"How dare he!" Artemis hissed, but her brother caught her arm as she started forward with fire in her eyes.

"Wait! We can't do anything here before all of these mortals."

"Let me have my bow and but a single arrow, and Bacchus will be eternally sorry for his distasteful little jest," Artemis said.

Apollo shook his head at the statue that was supposed to represent him. "He could have at least made it look more like me."

"It is blasphemous." Artemis' voice was low and dangerous.

"Is my lyre actually glowing green?" Apollo tried unsuccessfully to smother a chuckle. "And please tell me that my head is not that large."

His sister's next words were drowned out by the bellowing Bacchus.

"Lovely Artemis, how fair thou art. It is by your royal command that the invocation shall start!"

It was Artemis' turn to stare, dumfounded, as an unflattering copy of herself came alight. It turned and lifted one thick arm. Artemis gasped as it began to speak, the mechanical female voice sounding nothing like her own.

"It is my intent and tonight I do dare, to send out through the nymphs in the shimmering air, this invocation—this summoning spell. So I cast my power and amidst you tonight it shall dwell."

The nymphs instantly began a hypnotic humming as the canned music faded into vague background noise against their sweet voices.

"He goes too far." Apollo's eyes darkened. No one mocked his sister, not even one of the immortals. But he was surprised to feel Artemis' hand tighten on his as this time it was she who kept him from striding forward.

"Listen to the nymphs." Her voice was thick with tension.

Apollo put aside his anger at Bacchus and listened to the music of the nymphs. The melodic humming had a seductive, familiar tempo, and even before the semideities began to sing the words of the invocation, Apollo felt the hair on his forearms prickle in response to the invisible insurgence of power that poured into the air around them.

"Seekers of the ancient ways, think upon
the coming again of the immortals
and of your distant ancestors
who once honored the old gods
and gave blessing to field and forest, wind and
*   water, earth and air.*
This night we invoke past times—past days."

The nymphs' voices were so beautiful that the listening mortals hardly breathed.

"What are they doing?" Apollo said, feeling a sudden tightening low in his throat. "This is a true invocation ritual. I can feel the power—by Zeus' beard, it is almost visible!"

Helplessly, the two immortals watched as the nymphs continued to spin their magic web.

*"Celebrate the reawakening of the Olympians
and the return of the ancient mysteries,
the quickening of beauty and of fruitfulness.
We proclaim the return of the gods
with spell and chant and song.
Let the aid of the ancients be invoked!"*

"We must stop them!" Apollo began to move forward, but once again his sister's firm grip stayed him.

"How?" she whispered. "How do we do that without causing a horrendous scene?"

Apollo's jaw tightened. "But we cannot allow them to complete the invocation. Think of the consequences of a modern moral binding the aid of a god!"

"You are the one who should think, Brother. The invocation is harmless."

"How can you say that? The power feels magnified tenfold! The long absence of magic in this world must be acting to intensify the ritual. This binding will be unbreakable," he said through clenched teeth.

"This binding will never happen," Artemis insisted. "Who here knows how to complete the ritual?"

The sensuous song of the nymphs continued to fill the air.

*"Soft and whispering winds from afar,
greetings be unto thee . . ."*

"Wine from the ancient land must be poured in libation," Artemis reminded him. "Then blood must be mixed with the wine." The goddess's lips quirked smugly. "How many eons have passed since these mortals made blood sacrifice and libation? And that doesn't even fully bind the ritual."

> *"In the names of*
> *Bacchus and*
> *Apollo and*
> *Artemis,*
> *blow the power of the Gods clear and fresh and*
> *free . . ."*

"A true desire of the heart must be spoken aloud as the invocation concludes," he finished for her, and his shoulders began to relax. "You're wiser than I, Sister. No modern mortal could possibly know how to complete the ritual."

Apollo smiled at Artemis and turned his attention back to the luscious nymphs. Now that his fears for the mortals surrounding them were alleviated, he allowed himself to enjoy the eternal grace of the ancient ritual. It was a rite so powerful that he could not remember the last time the nymphs had preformed it in the Old World. *They possess such ethereal beauty,* he thought as he allowed the spell to touch him and wrap around his spirit. Their invocation was pure and heartfelt. As usual, the nymphs desired only to please mankind, and Apollo felt the immortal essence within him respond to their plea. At that moment he wanted to stride amongst the dancing nymphs and allow the mortals a glimpse of his true power. He wanted to reveal to them the glory of a living, breathing god, and then grant those of them who were most deserving the desires of their hearts, even though he knew it was an impossible fantasy. Zeus had forbidden their meddling with humans, and he had to admit that for once he agreed with his father. Modern mortals were best off without the interference of ancient, forgotten gods. But as the nymphs' ritual washed magically around him, the thought that these mortals no longer looked to Olympus made him strangely sad. Apollo felt flushed with equal parts of power and disappointment as the ritual came to its climax.

"Immortal aid is bound
with a spoken desire, and by a heart's sound.
Cast doubt aside; give voice to your soul,
for tonight the truth of love is our goal.
May heartfelt wishes come to thee
as it is spoken—so shall it be!"

As the closing words of the invocation were spoken, Apollo and Artemis suddenly felt an inexplicable pull, as if their minds had been tethered and whoever held the reins had just given them a tug. Their golden heads turned as one to stare at a small, round table that sat in the area built to look like an old-world Italian patio in front of the entrance of the little wine bar. Brother and sister watched in horror as a petite mortal who was sitting alone knocked over her long-stemmed glass, causing the delicate crystal to shatter and slosh red wine. The power lingering in the air caught the spilling wine, magically distributing it around her in a perfect scarlet circle. The mortal hastily tried to mop up the growing pool of wine with her linen napkin. Then she made a small sound of dismay as her finger caught on one of the glass shards, cutting a neat slice through her soft skin.

"No!" Artemis gasped as the mortal's blood mixed with the Italian wine.

"She can't—" Apollo began, but his horrified words were cut off as the woman opened her mouth and uttered the words that would forever alter their lives.

CHAPTER 5

Pamela was definitely feeling the wine. She hiccuped softly, and almost giggled at herself.

"But, hey, I'm in Sin City. Why not?" She said her giddy thought aloud.

"You sure are, sweetheart!" The man sitting at the table closest to her called. Then he gave her a wolfish smile.

Pamela looked from the blinding whiteness of his teeth, to the strategically colored darkness of his hair and down to the glint of the heavy gold chain that nestled in the thatch of thick black hair that forested the area just under his neck. He winked at her. His two buddies leered appreciatively. Pamela grimaced and rearranged herself so that her back was to them. She opened the slick lilac-colored cover of the Special Annual Edition of *California Home & Design* that she had just bought at a mall kiosk, and buried her nose in an article on EuroStone and their hard-to-find granites, marbles, quartzites and French limestones.

Please. She wasn't *that* tipsy. Actually, she didn't think she'd ever been *that* tipsy.

When the waiter appeared with a glass of cheap Chardonnay sent from "Her gentleman friend at the next table," she wasn't really surprised. Her sigh was long-suffering.

"Thank you, but please send it back," she said, all of a sudden feeling much more sober. "I don't accept drinks from men I don't know."

The waiter actually looked surprised, which Pamela

found annoying. Sure, she'd been out of the dating scene
for . . . her mind skittered past the actual number of years,
thereby refusing to acknowledge how much of her life she
had wasted on Duane. Had dating really changed that
much? God, she felt old.

"Then what may I bring you, ma'am?" the waiter asked.

He'd called her ma'am. There was no doubt about it.
She must look as old as she felt. Her eyes drifted back to the
long, slender menu that was filled with an excellent assort-
ment of wines on one side, and appetizers on the other.
Though she'd eaten a huge salad and drank half a bottle of
wine at the Italian restaurant situated next to the other fountain, the long, depressing trek around the shopping mall and
the casino had left her feeling like she needed something to
munch on, as well as another drink. Definitely another
drink. Her eyes lit on the appetizer that was a selection of
olives, cheeses and fresh bread. *Why not?* she thought. She
was old. She might as well be fat and happy.

"Please bring me the olive and cheese appetizer tray
and a bottle of . . ." She studied the Italian reds listed under
Chianti Classico with three glass ratings, and her eyes lit
up as she recognized the '97 Castello di Fonterutoli Riserva. She'd stumbled on a fantastic Italian wine article in
the last issue of *Wine Spectator's Magazine*, and she was
sure that she remembered the name. "A bottle of the '97
Castello di Fonterutoli Riserva Chianti Classico."

"Excellent choice, ma'am. From Tuscany. The wine
maker boasts that in ancient times the gods themselves
strode through their vineyards."

"That figures," she muttered under her breath after he'd
turned to go. "I'm trapped in a trailer park version of ancient Rome, and now I'm going to go from tipsy to thoroughly toasty on wine from a deluded wine maker."

Pamela sighed again. She'd had such good intentions at
the beginning of the evening. After V's pep talk she'd
taken a long shower and towel dried her short hair into a
mussed, sexy tousle. Dressing for success, she'd chosen to
wear the little black dress she'd practically stolen at the
Denver Saks end of season sale. She loved the way it
ended in a soft, feminine ruffle a few inches above her

knees. And then she'd completed the ensemble with delicate onyx chandelier earrings and a glittery purse that was as ridiculously small as it had been expensive. She'd finished with the pièce de résistance—a to-die-for pair of Jimmy Choo black silk slides with mod butterflies and hearts embroidered on them in bright, retro colors.

She'd checked her reflection in the gilded floor-to-ceiling mirror before she'd left her suite. She looked good. Very good. The black dress hugged her petite body, and the slides leant her five-foot-one-inch frame three and a half much-needed inches, making her calves look long and lean.

Yes, she had been ready to flirt.

Until she'd paused at the entrance to the casino to ask a nice-looking man in the casino's distinctive Romanesque uniform where she paid the cover charge. He'd laughed so hard that he'd snotted on himself.

"Lady, you're missing the point," he'd said between chortles. "Casinos *want* people to come in. The more people, the more money they spend."

He'd walked away laughing and shaking his head. Her evening hadn't gotten any better. Her dinner had been fine, but the scenery had continued to weigh on her. She'd told V that she was going to change the way she looked at this job—to shift from tasteful to fanciful. But the more she saw of The Forum, the more desperate she felt. It was just all so incredibly tasteless, inelegant, cheap and gaudy.

No, she corrected herself, scratch the cheap. Her eyes drifted back to the enormous fountain that held the grotesquely animated images of Bacchus, Caesar, Apollo and Artemis. That had definitely cost serious money, as would the ridiculous reproduction Eddie wanted in his home.

The waiter reappeared with her olive tray and a crystal carafe of wine the color of blood. She inhaled the rich Chianti aroma, which automatically brought to mind Marilyn's Pizza House, her favorite pizza place in the world, which was conveniently located just down the street from her design studio. Marilyn's always had a great selection of Italian reds, as well large-screen TVs that endlessly played Marilyn Monroe movies. This Chianti was definitely worthy of Marilyn. She savored the soft, lingering taste of the excellent wine with slow sips and chose a dark kalamata olive. She took a bite of thickly sliced buffalo mozzarella. It was all delicious.

Life in The Forum, she decided with a full mouth, did have some positives. The food was excellent and the selection of wines, superb, even at a small café such as this one. And, she begrudgingly admitted to herself as the Chianti spread its red magic through her body, although the exteriors of the shops were gaudy and their design horrid, the interiors were couture heaven.

Sure, her foray into flirting hadn't gone so well. But that really hadn't been her fault. The only prospect she'd had so far had been wearing a gold chain. He couldn't count. It's true that she'd been scared away from the casino by the cover charge debacle, so her gambling had been, thus far, nonexistent. But the weekend was just beginning, and she shouldn't think of it as a complete loss, at least not yet. Maybe she would just turn it into a shop-a-thon. Or at the very least a shoe-a-thon.

The thought of buying more shoes temporarily brightened her mood, until she imagined what V would say about her being stuck in a rut and falling back on old habits instead of embracing new experiences. Pamela chewed an olive as the waiter paused at her table to refresh her glass of wine. V might be right. Maybe she wasn't trying hard enough.

Resolutely Pamela closed the magazine and refocused on her surroundings. The crowd around the fountain had definitely thickened. A young woman who had impossibly beautiful blond hair caught her attention. She was talking to another girl whose hair was equally lovely, flowing in a thick, silver-colored wave down to her waist. Both girls were wearing costumes that Pamela supposed were meant to look as if they had stepped from the streets of ancient Rome. Sheer, cloud-colored fabric floated in seductive drapes around their lithe young bodies. One instant they appeared to be fully covered and modestly clad, then one of them would laugh and turn gracefully—almost as if she was a dancer—and a cunningly concealed fold in her robe would open to expose a glimpse of creamy skin. Also it seemed that the girls were covered in some kind of golden glitter, because as they moved through the tourists and towards the fountain, they left a sparkling trail in their wake. Pamela pulled her eyes from the duo and looked at the rest of the crowd. None of the men seemed to be able to keep their eyes from the seductively costumed women.

It was, she decided, an excellent publicity ploy. At least from the male perspective. And wasn't that just typical? She cast her eyes through the growing group of people who were congregating around the fountain. Just as she thought, most of them were female. Yet the duos of scantily clad young *women* kept increasing. And did one handsome young lad equally as revealingly dressed join them? Of course not.

"I'll bet women didn't really dress like that in ancient Rome," Pamela grumbled to herself. "They'd catch their death."

"COME ONE, COME ALL, COME TO THE MALL!"

Unexpectedly, the center statue's canned voice boomed over loudspeakers, catching Pamela unaware. She glanced at her watch, surprised that it was already eight o'clock.

"Ah, but tonight we have a special show for you! Nymphs, I command you dance for the Las Vegas revelers, two by two!"

Well, that made more sense. The actresses were meant to be portraying nymphs. As the similarly attired young women stepped from the crowd and began to dance around the fountain, Pamela had to acknowledge that they were very attractive. She watched the show as she sipped more wine, thinking that she had never seen so many expensive hair extensions. The "nymphs" twirled and laughed and leapt in a graceful circle, flinging their thick manes as if they had been born with them.

The awful statues of Apollo and Artemis came alive, one right after another. It seemed the evening show focused on the dancing nymphs, who were admittedly more entertaining than the animated statues who spoke in bad rhymes. Pamela even realized that her foot was tapping in time to the pulsing rhythm of their dance. It really wasn't a bad show, she thought as she refilled her glass again.

> *"Seekers of the ancient ways, think upon*
> *the coming again of the immortals*
> *and of your distant ancestors*
> *who once honored the old gods*
> *and gave blessing to field and forest, wind and*
>   *water, earth and air.*
> *This night we invoke past times — past days."*

When the dancing girls began to sing, she was pleasantly surprised. Their lyrics were far better than the nonsense that the mechanized statues spouted. And their voices! They were incredible. Entranced, Pamela listened as the song brought alive a time long dead when people actually believed gods and goddesses walked amongst them and granted their wishes. Despite her cynical opinion of her surroundings, she felt herself caught up in the performance, so much so that she wanted to slide off her stool and join them in their hypnotic dance.

That, she thought with a tipsy giggle which quickly turned into a snort, was utterly ridiculous. Especially in her three-and-a-half-inch Jimmy Choo slides. But for some reason her unusual desire to frolic with the pretend nymphs didn't shock her. She eyed the half-empty carafe; it must be the wine.

She blinked as the tempo of the dance increased, and the glitter that surrounded the nymphets seemed to blur her vision, so much so that when she reached for her glass of wine, she misjudged the distance and bobbled it. In slow motion, she watched as the crystal stem fell over, shattering on the marble tabletop and spraying red droplets in a crimson arc over the floor around her. Guiltily she snatched up her linen napkin and tried to soak up the quickly spreading stain. Thank God the glass had fallen away from her; she would have hated for her chic dress to have been covered in Chianti. Jeesh, what a mess she'd made. She was just thinking that she'd have to leave the waiter an extra big tip when she wiped at the table a little too enthusiastically and a sliver of glass sliced across the pad of her index finger.

"Ouch!" She shook her hand as if the sharp pain

burned. "Oh, bloody buggering hell." She couldn't believe the amount of blood that was running from one little cut. It even made her stomach feel a little queasy as it mixed with the pooling Chianti.

She pressed the already soaked napkin to her finger, but even the sting of the fresh cut didn't distract her from the conclusion of the nymphs' fabulous show. They were so graceful, and their silky voices seemed to call alive poignant emotions that she usually repressed . . . desire stirred within her . . . desire for something she couldn't— or wouldn't—quite name . . .

> "Immortal aid is bound
> with a spoken desire, and by a heart's sound.
> Cast doubt aside; give voice to your soul,
> for tonight the truth of love is our goal.
> May heartfelt wishes come to thee
> as it is spoken—so shall it be!"

Heartfelt wishes. Well, she wished that she hadn't spilled her wine or cut her finger. But the instant her mind formulated the thought she felt the wrongness of it. Wishing something so trivial after the beautiful dance seemed almost blasphemous. As she unclasped her purse and dug for a tissue to wrap around her finger, she was suddenly filled with sadness that her heart's desire had been nothing more than to undo an insignificant accident. Surely she had more heart than that left in her. Surely Duane hadn't destroyed it all.

> Cast doubt aside; give voice to your soul.

The echo of the words beat through her body in time with the pulse she could feel in her finger. Duane couldn't have ruined romance for her; she wouldn't let him.

> May heartfelt wishes come to thee
> as it is spoken—so shall it be!

Impulsively, she raised her chin and stared at the group of nymphs who were smiling and sinking into graceful prima ballerina curtsies as the crowd broke out in applause. Then Pamela blurted the thought that had been haunting her mind since her conversation with V.

"My heartfelt wish is that my stupid ex-husband hasn't sucked all the romance out of me, but the truth is that I'm afraid he has. So if you want to help me out . . ." She paused, trying to remember the goddess's name (asking the female deity to bring romance back into her life seemed to make the most sense) and then feeling a little foolish, even though the crowd's cheers drowned out her words, she continued, "Uh, Artemis, you could bring romance into my life." Then, remembering the disgusting, gold-chained gigolo, she added, "Oh, and Artemis, I'm tired of men who think they're gods. If you want to grant my wish, bring me a man who is really godlike for a change."

CHAPTER 6

"How could this have happened?" Artemis exclaimed after pulling her still-staring brother into a relatively quiet corner. "The mortal completed the invocation!"

Apollo nodded his head numbly. "She even used your name."

Artemis wanted to strangle him. "You think I don't know that! I feel it." She narrowed her eyes and glared around them. "Where is that rotund fool Bacchus? This was his doing. His stupidity caused this; he should be involved in cleaning up the mess."

"Cleaning it up?" Apollo pulled his gaze away from the mortal woman who had just unknowingly bound an ancient goddess to fulfill her heart's desire. "Don't you mean granting it?"

The goddess opened her mouth for a hot retort—and then closed it just as quickly. Her brother was right. There was no getting around it. The bond had been forged and then neatly soldered into place. She could feel the weight of it like an iron shackle.

"All right. It has happened. There is nothing to do but fulfill the mortal's whim and be done with it."

Apollo said nothing, but his eyes moved from his sister's angry face back to the mortal woman. He couldn't stop staring at her. She had wrapped a flimsy piece of something around her wounded finger, and she was still trying—unsuccessfully—to wipe up the spilled wine. *She'll probably cut herself again,* he thought, and he had a sudden urge to rush over to the table and caution her. He actually breathed a sigh of relief when a servant arrived with a cloth and made short work of the mess. Apollo watched as the woman smiled sheepishly. He couldn't be certain, but he thought that her cheeks were flushed. They were nice cheeks, he decided. High and well-formed. They complemented her heart-shaped face. He felt himself smile. That hair! He should have loathed the fact that a woman would cut her hair so short, but on her he found the shorn locks strangely attractive. It gave her a fey look and made her appear delightfully rumpled and mussed, as if she had just tumbled from her lover's bed.

Artemis followed her brother's rapt gaze. The goddess's sharp eyes evaluated the mortal woman. She appeared completely unaware of what she had done. She was petite and dressed in a surprisingly pleasing fashion, despite her outrageously cropped hair. Her age was indeterminate. All Artemis could discern was that she was older than a youth and younger than a middle-aged matron. She seemed attractive, and the very nature of her spoken desire proved that she was not currently pledged to any man. Artemis felt a small sense of relief. At least the mortal hadn't asked for her to begin a war, or worse, to bring about world peace. All she desired was a god to romance her. She looked at her handsome brother, whose expression obviously showed that he was, indeed, interested in the woman. Artemis' relief expanded. This couldn't be that difficult.

"I believe I'm overreacting. The mortal simply wants to be seduced by a god."

"She didn't say she wanted to be seduced. She asked for romance to return to her life," Apollo corrected her. His lips were tilted up in a slight smile as his eyes remained on the mortal.

"In the form of a man who is godlike. You, my dear Brother, *are* a god. So, what are you waiting for?" She shook her head at Apollo. Had he suddenly become dense? "I certainly am not what she desires, but she has bound me to fulfill her wish. You are my brother. The god closest to me in all of Olympus. That makes you the perfect god to rid me of this ridiculous problem."

"Yes, it certainly does." His smile widened.

"Of course it does," she agreed with him, noting his smug smile. Wasn't this really what he desired, too? Wasn't it just a few moments ago that he had been waxing poetic about Hades and his mortal lover? Now he had a chance to experience the love of a modern mortal—one who wasn't already enamored with another god. For an instant she wondered if this mistake might actually be more than a coincidence. She glanced surreptitiously around them. Could Zeus be plotting something? No, she rejected the thought. It had been her idea alone to bring her brother to the Kingdom of Las Vegas to cheer him up. Apparently, the impulse had been a good one. The old-fashioned seduction of a mortal woman ought to do wonders for his morose mood. Feeling rather pleased with herself, she rested a hand on his shoulder. "Go to her. Romance her. Take her to bed. Fulfill her every erotic desire. Just be quick about it. It would probably be best if Zeus doesn't hear about this. You and I can deal with Bacchus ourselves." Then she added quickly, "You probably shouldn't reveal yourself to her. It wouldn't do to have a mortal woman telling others how she managed to bind the aid of a goddess and invoke golden Apollo to her bed."

He frowned at his sister. "Of course I won't tell her."

"Excellent," she said, rubbing her hands together as if she had just completed a job well done.

"Where will you be?"

"Well, I certainly won't be with you!" She grinned and gave his shoulder a playful punch. "I'm going to have one more of those lovely martini drinks, and then I'm returning to Olympus. I'll meet you there tomorrow after the invocation has been fulfilled. You can give me a full report, and then we'll decide what to do about Bacchus." She gave him a little push forward and watched him walk towards the mortal who had unwittingly bound the aid of a goddess. She patted her hair, which was, of course, already perfectly arranged. Apollo should be back to normal by morning.

*   *   *

"*. . . If you want to grant my wish, bring me a man who is* really godlike for a change."

As she finished speaking, the hair on Pamela's forearms tingled like a jolt of electricity had zapped its way through her body. *Wow!* She smiled an apology to the waiter, who quickly cleaned up the mess she'd made. She usually had a pretty good tolerance for wine, but her head was definitely feeling woozy. Good thing she wasn't driving.

"I'll bring you another glass, ma'am," the waiter said. Then he glanced at the tissue wrapped around her finger. "And how about a Band-Aid, too?"

"Thank you, that would be nice," she said, ignoring how flushed she felt. He'd already turned away when she thought that she should probably have told him she'd just cork the bottle and take it to her room. That would be the sensible thing to do. She fiddled with the tissue. She didn't feel like being sensible. Actually, besides being a little flushed and tipsy, she felt invigorated. It had been empowering to admit her desire aloud. Okay, the wine may have had something to do with it, but she liked to think that that wasn't all there was to it. She had finally acknowledged something that had been unconsciously eating away at her for months, maybe even years—that Duane had somehow invisibly branded her as Nonromance Material. And now that she had given voice to her fear, it didn't seem so monstrous. It was like taking a midnight trip to check the closet for the boogie man—the walk was scary, but after the door was open, the return wasn't so bad. So she'd just start her return. As V would say, she needed to get out there more. Make herself available. Stop thinking of men only as business acquaintances. Well, she couldn't do that by corking the bottle and scuttling back to her room.

"I hope it does not pain you too badly."

Pamela looked up from her finger . . . and up and up . . . into eyes so blue that they couldn't possibly be real. And just how tall was he? Her brother was six two, and this guy had to be at least a couple of inches taller than that. Then her gaze widened to include his face, and all thoughts of blue eyes and her brother disappeared. What a scrumptious man! The lines of his face were firm, his chin square and strong. His hair was the gold of summer sun, thick and curly.

He was, quite simply, perfect. He looked like he had stepped from the pages of a magazine ad—and not one of those oh-so-chic, androgynous ads that made women look like men and men look like little boys. This man was old Hollywood handsome, like Cary Grant or Clark Gable. Only he was blond and . . . her thoughts fragmented as she realized what else she was seeing, and she was mortified to hear a small giggle escape from her lips. He was blond and gorgeous and wearing something that looked like an ancient gladiator costume and left very little of his amazing body to the imagination! Pamela felt her face warm again, this time out of shock and secondhand embarrassment.

"What?" she asked, staring stupidly, having completely forgotten what he had said.

"Your finger," he pointed at the tissue-wrapped appendage. "I saw you cut it. I said I hope it doesn't cause you too much pain."

His smile made her stomach tighten with a ridiculous little nervous quiver. Dimples! The guy had dimples, which lent his masculine beauty an unexpectedly sweet boyishness. Boyish and breathtaking and very, very tall— a totally lethal combination.

"Oh, uh, yes . . ." She shook her head as if to clear the cobwebs from it. Oh, bloody buggering hell, she'd definitely had too much wine. "No . . . I mean, no, it's nothing. Just a silly mistake."

"Do you know that in the Ancient World people did not believe in mistakes? They thought every action carried with it a purpose, an omen, a meaning, and that the future could be foretold through things as simple as leaves of tea or smoke rising from a ceremonial fire."

Pamela could hardly believe what she was hearing. Her mind flitted from thought to thought like bubbles in a windstorm. Could a man who looked like that actually carry on an interesting conversation? Just exactly why *did* he look like that—not as in incredibly handsome, but as in bizarrely costumed? And that accent! It made his deep voice seductive . . . intriguing . . . It wrapped around her and slid down her spine like hot oil.

Pull yourself together! The rational part of her brain berated. *Sober up, girl! Weird outfit or not, this man is prime flirting material.* She needed to stop staring like a slack-jawed tourist and speak intelligibly.

"No, I didn't know that," she said in her best let's-pretend-I'm-sober voice. "It's been too long since my last college humanities class, and I'm ashamed to admit that the only part of history I really paid attention to was my art history class that focused on the elements of ancient architectural design." The words *ancient architectural design* slurred together alarmingly. Oh, God! She was babbling. She sounded like an inebriated egghead.

"Ancient architecture interests you?"

He seemed surprised, and even through her wine fog Pamela had to stifle her instant irritation. Just because she was pretty didn't mean that she was incapable of intelligence, and she truly hated the patronizing attitude that said the opposite . . . Wait . . . She studied his handsome face. Wasn't that just what she had thought about him? She was chagrined to remember that she had instantly been surprised to hear such a gorgeous man have something intelligent and interesting to say. When had she become a walking double standard? Actually, now that she was able to form a few coherent thoughts, she realized that he looked pleased, not patronizing. Maybe he hadn't meant to insult her. Maybe she had become too damn sensitive. Couldn't he simply be doing his part in carrying on a polite conversation? He did look genuinely interested in her answer. Maybe her knee-jerk annoyance reaction said more about her than about him, or even men in general. And she was still babbling—only this time (thankfully) it was internal babble. She cleared her throat and smiled.

"Yes it does, but I'm interested in all kinds of architecture. It's an important part of my business."

"You are an architect?" he asked.

This time the shock in his voice was so apparent that Pamela frowned and narrowed her eyes at him. "Do not tell me that you are one of those men who believe women should be relegated to certain roles. Please. It's the 2000s, not the '50s."

The annoyance in her voice and the cold, intelligent snap in her clear eyes suddenly reminded him very distinctly of his sister, and Apollo felt surprise begin to build within him. He had known countless mortal women, many of whom he had thought beautiful and tempting, but not one of them had ever reminded him of his willful, independent, outspoken twin. They had all been too busy worshiping him to remember to be very interesting. He had just begun speaking to her, yet this modern mortal was already proving a delightful change. He laughed, and shook his head. "I did not mean to insult you—it is just that you are so young. All of the architects I've known have been old, wizened men with gray thickening their beards." He leaned forward and pretended to study her cheeks. "I see no gray, hence my surprise."

"Ma'am should I bring another glass?" The waiter asked. He handed her a Band-Aid before he placed a new glass on the table and carefully filled it.

"I would be honored if you allowed me to join you."

He inclined his head to her in the kind of chivalrous half-bow that she imagined men used to execute to their "ladies" on a regular basis. That small, old-world affectation did something to the pit of her stomach. That and the fact that he was undeniably gorgeous was beginning to outweigh the weirdness of his costume. And anyway, why shouldn't she have a drink with him? He was probably paid to dress like that and to entertain vacationers at Caesars Palace. She'd just think of it as helping him out with his job, which was actually exceedingly considerate of her. Who said alcohol inhibits rational thought? Her thinking was perfectly clear. She nodded at the waiter.

"Yes, please bring us another glass."

The waiter hurried away. Pamela tore open the Band-Aid, but before she could wrap it around her finger, the tall man leaned forward and took it from her.

"Here," he said, "let me help you."

Apollo placed the small bandage securely around her

slim finger, and as he did, he sent a tiny sliver of his healing power through his hands and into her.

Pamela blinked in surprise at his gentle touch.

"Thank you. It feels better already." She grinned at him. Holding out her hand with the newly bandaged finger she said, "I'm Pamela Gray."

His hesitation was so brief that it was only much later that she thought about it at all.

"Phoebus," he said with a smooth smile. "Phoebus Delos." He took her hand and automatically shifted his grip so that he could raise it to his lips. Their eyes met as his mouth touched her skin. Hers were wide with surprise; his were impossibly blue.

Pamela felt the warmth of his lips tickle through her body. Her mouth went dry.

"So you're still in character?" she asked, pulling her hand from his and running it through her hair as if she didn't know what to do with it.

"Character?" He looked puzzled.

She wiggled her bandaged finger up and down at his outfit, cocked her head and let her eyes travel his body in blatant appraisal. The short tunic was made of the finest linen she had ever seen—and she had definitely seen her share of expensive fabrics. It was trimmed in heavy metallic embroidery and ended in pleats that left much of his incredibly well-shaped legs bare. Over the tunic, which tied above his left shoulder, was an ornately decorated breastplate that looked like it was made of hammered gold.

"It really is a great costume," she said, tapping her chin with her finger. "Let's see, the dancers were supposed to be nymphs, so my guess is that you're supposed to be a god." Pamela smiled impishly as she realized the irony of the situation. Hadn't she just asked for a god? And then, poof! Like magic, this guy showed up at her table looking like a living, breathing example of the real thing. It made her want to laugh. Only in Vegas . . .

"Your guess would be correct," he leaned back. He liked to watch her talk. She had obviously partaken of quite a bit of wine, but instead of thinking that she was silly, Apollo was intrigued by her. The flush became her honest, animated face. Her intelligent eyes sparkled an unusual hazel brown that reminded him of rich, sweet honeycomb. And her lips . . . there was a whole other world waiting to be explored there. He could already imagine her lips against his. She would taste of wine and woman . . .

He pulled his eyes from her mouth and refocused quickly on what she was saying.

"A god, huh? Well, you certainly look the part. I mean, besides the outfit, you are definitely ginormous enough to be a god. I say well done you!"

Ginormous? At least she appeared to be using the word in a flattering sense, whatever it meant. He brushed her odd compliment aside, not wanting to pursue the direction their conversation had taken. The waiter reappeared and filled his glass. When he left, Apollo raised it to her.

"I drink to you, Pamela, and to coincidence and fate."

"Would that mean that you believe in coincidence or fate?"

"I think I'm beginning to believe in both," he said.

CHAPTER 7

꧁

"So tell me how it is that you have become the most beautiful architect I have ever cast my eyes upon," Apollo said.

Pamela made a little hiccuping laugh. "You shouldn't have already described my competition as a bunch of old men if you wanted me to be complimented by that. Actually, I'm not an architect, but understanding architecture is an important part of my job. I'm an interior designer."

"An interior designer." Apollo repeated the strange title, searching for its meaning. What was it she designed the interiors of? He had no idea. And then Apollo, God of Light, master of music, healing, truth, and lover of innumerable mortals as well as goddesses, found himself doing something for the first time in his existence. He struggled to think of something to say to keep himself from sounding like an ignorant fool.

He blurted the first question that came into his mind. "Architecture is important to an interior designer?"

"Of course." The tiny frown lines were back between her brows. "It only makes sense that in order to properly decorate a space the designer must first understand the building's architecture. I mean, please. Me not understanding the structure of a building would be like a chef not understanding in what order to mix the ingredients to make a soufflé. Besides that, there are lots of times that I work directly with builders and am involved in the design of a project from the time the foundation of the home is laid all the way through to when my clients move in and host their fabulously successful housewarming party."

Apollo's mind swiftly sifted through the strange wording of her answer, focusing on familiar ideas. It seemed Pamela's job involved decorating mortals' homes. Perhaps she was like Zeus' sister, Hestia, Goddess of the Hearth. Ancient mortals invoked Hestia's aid when erecting a new home and in many villages women tended ever-burning flames dedicated to her as a symbol of their desire for safety and harmony within their households.

"You make home a pleasant place in which to live," he said thoughtfully. "That must be a rewarding job."

Pamela grinned. "Well, I try. I especially enjoy owning my business. I like to call the shots." Her smile faltered as her expression grew more serious. "I've decided that it's better to be in control of my life than to constantly try to live up to someone else's expectations."

Apollo nodded thoughtfully, thinking of how lately he had begun to feel stifled by the role he had played for eons. It seemed he was eternally viewed as the great God of Light, and never seen as himself. He met Pamela's eyes and surprised himself by speaking his thoughts aloud.

"I envy your independence. I know what it is to be restricted and controlled by what others expect of you."

"It's suffocating," Pamela said softly.

"Exactly," Apollo said.

They studied one another as they sipped their wine, pleasantly surprised at finding common ground so easily.

Pamela's smile returned. "Well, even though I own my business, some jobs allow me more independence than others. For instance, the job that brought me to Vegas is feeling like one of the others."

"You do not live here, in The Forum?"

"You mean Las Vegas?" She automatically corrected him. "No way. This is my first time in Vegas. I'm from Colorado." Her wry look took in the fountain and the area surrounding it. She shook her head. "Manitou Springs is about as different from Las Vegas as you can get. How about you? I don't recognize your accent, but it's obviously not from around here."

Wishing he'd given himself more time to fabricate answers to simple questions like who he was and where he was from, he took another drink of wine while his mind searched around for a response Pamela would find reasonable.

"I can not really say I am from only one place. I consider both Italy and Greece my home."

At least that accounted for his unusual name and the accent, she thought.

"It seems we have more than our love of independence in common. I am new to Las Vegas, too," he said. It was a stretch of the literal truth, but not by much. His two previous visits had been brief and confined to Caesars Palace. He had basically followed his sister's lead and tried to appear as if he was enjoying himself.

"So you don't usually pretend to be a god?"

Apollo's smile was slow and enigmatic. "I can assure you that I have never pretended to be a god."

"Really? Then how did all of this"—she gestured at his costume—"happen?"

Apollo's smile widened as he decided to tell the truth. "I blame it entirely on my sister. I believe she thought I had become too serious, so as a favor to her I came to Las Vegas. Hence, what you see before you."

Pamela's laughter delighted Apollo. It didn't have the perfectly musical sound of an amused goddess; instead it was filled with earthy joy and brought to mind images of hot firelit nights and slippery entwined limbs.

"Now that makes total sense. I have a brother myself. He's a big, tough fireman, and he never lets me forget the time I talked him into dressing up as a Star-Belly Sneetch and reading Seuss to some local preschool kids. How was I supposed to know the media would get wind of it and snap a picture of him climbing out of the fire truck in costume?" Remembering, Pamela laughed so hard that she snorted. "His buddies had the picture blown up, laminated and posted at all the fire stations. Sometimes I still call him Fireman Sneetch, but usually only when I am well out of reach." She giggled at her own rhyming minitribute to Seuss.

Apollo had no idea what she was talking about, but her laughter was incredibly infectious, and when she snorted he had a sudden, irrational desire to lean across the table and kiss her squarely on her adorable nose.

"So I understand perfectly the trials a sister can impose upon her brother." She wiped at her eyes and caught her breath. She really should slow down on the wine. "What do you do when your sister isn't torturing you?"

Apollo considered and discarded several answers before he replied. "I do many things, but I like to think of myself predominately as a healer and a musician."

He was a singing doctor? Was that anything like a singing cowboy? The giggles bubbled up through her chest again. She drowned them in a gulp of wine, which did absolutely nothing to help her teetering sobriety.

"What kind of doctor are you?" she finally asked when she was sure she could speak without dissolving into giggles.

"I believe I am an excellent one," he said, surprised at her question.

Laughter spilling over, she shook her head. "I think we have a translation glitch, and this"—she flicked a fingernail against her almost empty wineglass—"is definitely not helping."

"Perhaps, you would like to walk with me?" He pounced on the opportunity to guide the conversation away from questions about himself. "Taking in the night air would be an excellent way for you to clear your head."

She pointed to the perpetually daylight sky of The Forum. "But it's not night out there."

He leaned forward. "In a land such as this, can we not imagine it night?"

In a caress so soft that she felt the heat from his body more than the pressure of his touch, he stroked one finger down the back of her hand. It was only a brief meeting of skin, but the small, intimate gestured seemed to pull her forward. The world around them fell away, and Pamela submerged herself in his eyes. He was just so damn outrageously gorgeous. She was flooded with a sensation that it took her several heartbeats to identify. Desire. How long had it been since she had felt the hot pull of lust for a man? Years—it had been years. And she was only thirty. It was like she'd let herself become dried up and old and passionless. Well, no more. She loosed her breath in a rush.

"Okay. I'll take a walk with you," she proclaimed. "Are you staying at Caesars Palace? I can wait here while you change your clothes."

"No. I—I am . . ." He mentally flailed around. Thank the nine Titans that he managed a credible excuse. "I am staying with my sister."

"Oh." She frowned at his costume. "Well, I suppose you don't really need to change."

This was something he understood perfectly. Her words said one thing, but her body language said another. Mortal women and goddesses had this form of communication very much in common.

He glanced around The Forum. Modern mortals dressed so oddly. How had he not noticed earlier how out of place he was? Poorly carved statues were the only things in this world attired like him. He suddenly realized with a start of shock that he must look like a buffoon to her. A buffoon was unlikely to romance anyone, and he must romance her to grant her desire and to break the bond her invocation had forged. In the back of his mind a thought whispered that there was much more to this than the completion of an invocation—that he wanted her to take him seriously for an entirely different reason. The thought was strangely intriguing.

What was he going to do about it?

Then his eyes widened. The answer to his dilemma surrounded him.

"I will simply purchase the correct clothing," he said.

Pamela's lips quirked up in a surprised smile. "Just like that?"

"Of course! Are we not surrounded by shops?"

She raised her brows and nodded. "We are, indeed."

He stood, and then he realized he needed to do something he had never before had to do. Until that moment the God of Light had never had to ask a woman—mortal or

immortal—to wait for him. Gently, he touched the back of
her hand again. "I will not be long. Will you wait?"

Pamela took her time considering. A naughty smile
played at the corner of her well-shaped mouth. She ran one
finger around the rim of her crystal wineglass while her
eyes met his.

"I suppose I could wait. For a little while."

He smiled, took a couple of steps, stopped, frowned and
returned to the table.

"Which shop would you suggest?" he asked in a low
voice.

"Well," she said, dropping her voice to match his. "It's
lucky for you that I am a shopping expert. I have instant recall when it comes to couture." She squinted her eyes, considering. "I remember an Armani's just around the corner
there." She pointed to her right.

"Then I go to Armani." He took her hand in his and
lifted it to his lips. "Αντίο, γλυκιά Pamela," he spoke the
ancient language against her skin. Then he turned and
strode away around the corner.

As soon as he was gone, she bolted for the ladies' room
and quick-dialed V.

"Please tell me that you're calling because you just won
the million dollar jackpot," V said instead of hello.

"Oh my God! I think I have, but I'm not talking about
money."

"Get out of town! You actually sound giddy. Wait, let
me sit down. If you tell me you're speaking to a man, I
may faint."

"I'm not speaking, I'm *flirting* . . ." Pamela breathed
the word like a prayer, and then she dissolved into giggles
that ended in a snort.

"You're drunk," V said.

"I am not. I'm tipsy."

"Oh, good God."

"That's exactly what he looks like. V, you wouldn't believe it! I was wiping up the spilled wine, well, then I cut
my finger. Which hurt like hell, by the way. And I even
said it. Admitted it out loud. *I want romance in my life.*"
She enunciated the words slowly and distinctly before

gushing on. "And then there he was. He's dressed in some kind of Greek god costume, but that's because of his sister. You know, like Richard and the Star-Belly Sneetch. Anyway, we've been talking, and as soon as he buys new clothes we're—are you ready?—going for a *walk*."

"Uh, Pammy," V said. "Where are you right now?"

"In the ladies' room."

"And where is he?"

"Buying new clothes."

"Okay. Listen to me. Sober up. He might be a freak," V said.

"He's not a freak. He's a singing doctor."

"Has lack of sex completely deteriorated your brain? You're talking like a crazy woman." V wanted to reach through the phone and shake her.

"It's not as weird as it sounds," Pamela said, chewing at her bottom lip. "V, I like him. He makes me *feel* again. And . . . and I have some kind of connection with him. I know it sounds crazy, but there's a spark between us. It's like we understand each other."

Vernelle opened and closed her mouth. She stifled the litany of warnings that were running through her head. "Pammy, I think that's wonderful."

"So I'm not being stupid?"

"No, doll. You're being young and single. There's not a damn thing wrong with that," V assured her. "Go for a walk with the tripod. Flirt your cute little butt off. But no more wine tonight, okay?"

"I've already cut myself off."

"Good. And use a condom."

"*Vernelle!* I am not going to have sex with him."

"*Pamela!*" V mirrored her friend's shocked tone. "Here's a news flash—if you want to have sex with him, you can! What I want is a full report tomorrow. Good-bye, Pammy."

Pamela was picking at the Band-Aid *when* Phoebus *walked* back around the corner. She felt her eyes widen, and a thrill that was liquid and hot ran the length of her body to settle deep inside her thighs. In his god costume he had been handsome and exotic in an unbelievable kind of way, like an actor to be "fallen in love with" during a movie. In normal clothes he was no less gorgeous, but now he was suddenly real and no longer something unattainable. He had become a living fantasy. He was wearing cream-colored linen Armani slacks that hugged his sleek waist and hips, and a silk knit pullover that was the same amazing blue as his eyes. Those eyes locked with hers as he approached her. He stopped beside her stool. For a moment he didn't say anything. Then he pulled nervously at his shirt and smoothed both palms down the front of his pants. His smile seemed uncertain, which totally baffled Pamela. How could someone who looked like a Greek god be worried at all about his appearance? The silence stretched between them. He fidgeted with the collar of his shirt.

He was definitely nervous, which was undeniably adorable.

"Do you like the new clothing?" he finally asked.

"You look like a walking Armani ad."

"Is that a good or bad thing?"

"Good. Definitely good. What did you do with your outfit?"

The worry that had tightened his face relaxed. "I left it with the Armani servant. I will retrieve it later. As for now, shall we walk?"

He held out his arm for her to take, just like she was a princess. Or maybe, she thought, glancing up at his profile, a goddess. She placed her arm through his and slid off the stool. She could swear that she felt every nerve ending on her bare arm prickle where it touched his.

"The servant at the Armani shop told me that if we leave Caesars Palace, turn to the right and cross the street, we will come to pool of magnificent dancing fountains."

"The Bellagio fountains. I've heard about them, but I haven't seen them."

"He said it is but a short distance." He raised his eyebrows and looked expectantly at her.

What in the hell was she supposed to do? Of course she wanted to go with him, but would walking to the Bellagio fountains at—she glanced at her watch—at almost 11:00 P.M. be smart? Of course 11:00 P.M. Vegas time was like prime time anywhere else. The streets would be filled with people rushing from casino to casino. Wouldn't they? It should be okay.

On the other hand, she didn't want to make the mistake of being one of those women who acted too stupid to live. And she certainly didn't want to be hacked up into little pieces by a gorgeous but crazy serial killer and have a tragic CSI episode based on her last hours.

"Pamela," he unlinked their arms to take her hands in his. "You have nothing to fear from me." His eyes caught hers and held, and he read the indecision there. It pained him to think that she did not trust him. If only she knew who he was! He quickly cast aside the fleeting thought. If she truly knew who he was, she would also know his past and how he had seduced and discarded countless mortal women. If she knew the truth, she would surely turn from him. And he could not blame her for doing so. But she didn't know who he was; she thought he was a simple mortal healer. She had no reason to turn from him. His jaw tightened with resolve. This time he longed for it to be different. This time it would be different—he would make it so.

Apollo spoke before he could stop himself. "I would never harm you, nor would I allow anyone else to cause you pain. Σου δίνω τον όρκο μου."

The foreign words seemed to linger in the air around them, and for a moment Pamela imaged them as tinged with a bright golden light. Then she blinked, and the image dissipated like smoke in shadow.

"What did you say?" she asked.

"I said that I give you my oath. You should know that in my homeland, the giving of an oath is a sacred thing, broken only by one who has no honor."

His words touched her, but more than that, *he* touched her. His physical allure was obvious, but she was drawn to more than just the beauty of his body. There was something about him that tugged at her insides, something she recognized. Her heart skittered around in her chest as she realized what it was: she saw herself in him. In his eyes she saw the echo of something she had carried around within her for years, the longing for more . . . and the inability to find it.

"Why aren't you involved with some nice woman, instead of here asking a virtual stranger to go out with you?"

His smile was like dawn breaking the gloom of night. "I am with a nice woman. I am with you."

She sighed and slipped her arm back through his. "Then I suppose I have no choice but to go to the fountains with you."

"You do," he said, starting to walk, "but I do not think any other choice would be a wise one."

"Just so that you know, I'm holding you to that oath of yours."

He smiled down at her. "I would have it no other way, Pamela."

CHAPTER 8

With linked arms, they made their way through The Forum
Shops towards the main entrance to Caesars Palace. As
they walked, Pamela couldn't help but notice the looks
Phoebus drew; it was totally, nauseatingly obvious.
Women couldn't keep their eyes off him. But she also noticed something else: Phoebus paid no attention to other
women. He didn't return their smiles. His eyes didn't stray
to steal an "accidental" glance here and there.

What he did do was to walk slowly, matching his long
strides to her much shorter ones. He was attentive to whatever she said. His responses were witty as well as interesting. And he window-shopped. Really. Without being
coerced, tricked or bribed.

He actually seemed to enjoy it.

The thought was enough to sober her up. Or maybe she
was completely drunk, had passed out and was still at The
Lost Cellar, slumped on her stool in a damp, drooling pud-
dle pathetically passed out.

No, she was alliterating fluently. She couldn't be hallu-
cinating.

Was he gay? She glanced at him, caught his fabulous
blue eyes, and gave him a sexy smile. He returned the
smile with an inviting warmth that said that there was no
way he wasn't heterosexual. No. He definitely wasn't
gay . . . So what was wrong with him? There had to be
something . . .

"Are you married?" she asked abruptly.

His golden brows drew together as he frowned. "No. I have never been married."

"How about a live-in girlfriend or something?"

"No."

"So you're totally uninvolved."

"Yes," he said firmly.

Well, at least *that* wasn't what was wrong with him. In theory anyway.

Without any prodding from her at all, he paused in front of a shop called Jay Strongwater, which specialized in gem-encrusted picture frames.

"This really is excellent workmanship," he said thoughtfully. "The artisan has extraordinary talent."

"They are gorgeous." Pamela peered into the window and caught the reflection of a price tag on one of the very small frames. "Four hundred and fifty dollars! For a little picture frame! I don't think they're *that* gorgeous."

Apollo turned to her and put a finger gently under her chin, lifting her face. "I think there are some pictures that would be worthy of such a frame."

When he looked at her with that focused intensity (How could she have ever even considered that he might be gay?) she felt all jittery inside, like she was back in high school and he was her sweetheart. She certainly would have never admitted anything so sophomoric out loud, but that didn't make it any less true. They were standing so close that she could smell him—man mixed with the raw silk of his shirt, and something else . . . something as subtle as it was seductive. It reminded her of heat. Heat as in warm sun on a white beach where naked bodies basked in uninhibited . . .

She laughed a little too giddily, pulling her face from his grasp, and started walking again.

"Phoebus . . ." She ran her fingers through her hair, trying to calm the pounding of her heart. "I think you're a romantic."

His eyes glinted when he smiled at her. "Good."

She gave him an appraising look. "A lot of men wouldn't like being called a romantic. It's not macho enough."

"Quite often men are fools."

"I couldn't agree with you more," she said firmly.

Apollo laughed, enjoying her honesty. "You should know that I am not like most men. You should also know that it is my intention to thoroughly romance you."

"Oh . . ." She faltered, not sure how to respond to his announcement.

He laughed again, and nodded, but said nothing. Instead, he watched her. His words had flustered her, and he liked how her cheeks had instantly flushed a light rose. Her short hair made her neck look impossibly long. It invited the touch of his lips against the hollow of her delicate throat. The style of her dress was as foreign to him as was the clothing he now wore, but he liked the flattering, feminine lines of it and how it dipped down in a teardrop shape to reveal the tops of her softly rounded breasts. She was petite, but fully a woman. Her legs looked long and lean . . . How did she balance on those perilous shoes? They were little more than a swatch of fabric attached to spikes. Odd as they were, he did enjoy the way they caused her calves to stretch and flex, and her well-rounded buttocks to sway enticingly as she walked beside him.

She could feel him watching her, and it made her already jumpy insides turn into a pinball machine—*What's he looking at? God, he's handsome. He smells good enough to eat. Is he thinking I look fat? Please don't let him be a serial killer*—her thoughts pinged around and around. What was it about him that made her feel like each of her nerve endings had suddenly come screamingly alive? Maybe it wasn't him at all. Maybe it was just that she was so totally out of practice with men.

Don't be stupid, she told herself. She'd never had a hard time dating before Duane. She was the same person, just older and smarter. At least in theory. She paused in front of a Fred Leighton jewelry store where beautiful chandelier diamond earrings were showcased hanging from beveled mirrors. Pamela caught the reflection of his gaze in the glass.

All she had to do was to quit analyzing the situation so damn much. She was making this harder than it should be.

His steady gaze caught hers, and again she felt it, that wordless connection that sparked between them. She drew in a deep, relaxing breath.

"When you said that you gave me your oath that I would be safe with you, what language were you speaking?" she asked.

"Greek," he said.

"Is that the only other language you speak?"

He shook his head and hesitated before answering. "I have a gift for languages. I speak several."

"Really? I don't speak any other language. Well, I don't count my limited ability to order cheese dip, extra-hot salsa, and beer in Spanish. Actually, what I pretend to speak is probably more like Spanglish anyway."

In response to his questioning look she grinned and explained. "Spanglish—a bad mixture of Spanish and English. I am decidedly *not* good with languages, and I do envy people who are multilingual."

Her praise made Apollo uncomfortable. His "gift" with languages was nothing special—at least not for the God of Light. He was one of the Twelve Immortals; none of the languages of man were unknown to them.

"I am most fluent in Greek and Latin," he amended.

"What was it you said to me before you went to Armani's? Was that Greek, too?"

He loved how her tawny eyes reflected the faceted light of the diamond jewelry. "Yes, it was Greek. I said, 'Goodbye, sweet Pamela.' Did you know that in Greek your name means exactly that—all that is sweet? *Pan* is all, and *meli* is sweet, as in the honey, or the nectar of a flower."

She turned from the mirrors and looked directly up at him. "I had no idea. I've always thought that it was a boring, ordinary name."

"It is anything but that, *Pamela*."

When he said her name, his accent made it sound mysterious and beautiful. Of course, he could probably make the word *excrement* sound like a seduction, but, she admitted to herself, she loved knowing that what she had thought of as mundane for her entire life had really been hiding so much more.

"What about your name? What does Phoebus mean?"

"It means *light,*" he said.

Pamela looked up at his bright hair and his eyes that were bluer than a summer sky. "Light," she repeated. "It suits you."

"Now I have a question for you," he said, changing the subject smoothly. "What does the word *ginormous* mean?"

Her little burst of surprised laughter made her mouth look even more inviting.

"*Ginormous* is a word my friend, V, and I like to use, but I don't think you'd find it in any dictionaries. It's gigantic and enormous mixed together. Like *gihugic* is *gigantic* and *huge.*"

"The same as Spanish and English making Spanglish," he said.

She nodded. "Yep."

"So *ginormous* means bigger than large," he said as they both remembered that ginormous was how she had described him.

"Exactly," she smiled saucily. Well, there was something about him that went beyond height, that seemed to make him bigger than large. He *was* ginormous.

One of the multitudes of bellboys opened the glass doors for them, and they exited Caesars Palace. It was, of course, fully dark, but the night teemed with light and sound and excitement. Apollo and Pamela stood frozen, both awestruck by their surroundings. The entire front grounds of the Palace were filled with ostentatious, spurting fountains lit up like a beacon to the heavens. Stretch limos dropped well-dressed couples at the door, and uniformed valets scurried around like liveried mice.

"Ταριώτο!" Apollo breathed the Greek curse. He was thoroughly shaken by his first sight of automobiles. Zeus had insisted that before any of the immortals passed through the portal that Bacchus must first explain to them the details of modern day transportation, as well as the mortals' use of currency, electricity, and an extraordinary communication system called the Internet, so Apollo was able to logically identify the madness before him, but seeing the monstrous vehicles that appeared living, yet were actually devoid of all life, as well as the garish way the warm spring night had been illuminated with harnessed electricity, was far more overwhelming than he could have imagined. He focused on the most familiar of the bizarre visions—the fountain—and reminded himself that he was an Olympian god, one of the original Twelve Immortals. He could flatten everything around him with a thought.

One of the shiny black things blared and skidded to a stop as another monstrosity cut in front of it. Apollo moved quickly, placing himself between Pamela and the metal creatures and neatly retucking her from his left to his right arm.

"I know exactly what you're thinking," Pamela said softly.

Apollo's eyes jerked down to meet hers. Rationally he knew that she could not be reading his mind, but the thought of even the slightest possibility of her knowing what was going through his head was alarming.

"You don't have to tell me," she said, eyes sparkling puckishly. "You were thinking that the fountain is ginormous."

He hoped his relief wasn't too obvious. "Tragically, you are wrong," he returned her teasing tone. "I was thinking that it is gihugic."

"Well, that's only because you're confused about the correct usage of the word. Gihugic is not as big as ginormous; therefore, ginormous is the proper word to use when describing that"—she hesitated dramatically, casting her eyes the length of the Palace's front grounds—"that fountain."

He nodded his head in gracious acceptance of defeat. "I concede to you. Yonder monstrosity is definitely ginormous."

"So I wasn't really wrong," Pamela said.

When it came to women, Apollo was no fool in any world. He smiled. "How could anyone so beautiful ever really be wrong?"

"May I call a cab for you and the lovely lady?" One of the bellboys asked.

Apollo's *"No!"* was spoken with more passion than he

intended—and he was suddenly glad that night in this
world was already so filled with lights and sounds that the
bolt of lightning that flashed across the sky in response to
the God of Light's shout went unnoticed. Even so, he made
certain to tighten control of his voice. "No," he said with
considerably more calm. "The lady and I are walking."

"The Bellagio fountains are not far from here. Right?"
Pamela asked.

"Yes, madam," the bellboy pointed. "Follow the sidewalk down to street level, turn right and cross the next
street, and you'll be there. You can't miss it."

"Thank you," she squeezed Phoebus' arm. "Ready?"

Apollo was absolutely not ready. He would rather have
faced the mighty serpent Python again, alone in the black
caves of Parnassus, than to walk out into that alien night.
But the petite woman on his arm strode ahead with the
confidence of Hercules. Apollo gritted his teeth and
plunged forward, all his senses on high alert.

"It's so warm here, really a nice change from Colorado.
Even though it's May, we've had an unseasonably cold
spring—it snowed again last week." Pamela tilted her
head back and flung wide the arm that was not holding his.
Laughing, she breathed deeply, loving the warmth of the
desert day that still lingered in the air. "I didn't realize how
much I'd been craving spring until I got here."

Apollo grunted a vaguely affirmative response. His
gaze kept skipping from the enchanting woman at his side
to the vehicles that sped past on the crowded street, to the
huge glowing signs and towering buildings, many of which
had colorful, moving images flashing over them. The
thought came to him that he would have to make sure that
Zeus ordered the nymphs to stay within the confines of
Caesars Palace. Like beautiful little moths, they would be
overcome with excitement at all the sparkling, flashing
lights if they ventured outside. He hated to think about the
scene that would be caused by the fun-loving semideities,
drunk on light and sound.

"Careful!" Pamela's voice pulled him back to the modern world as her hand likewise tugged him to a halt.
"Whew, that was close. I was so busy gawking that I al-

most didn't see the street, and this traffic is terrible. We better wait for the light."

They were standing on the corner of a street that seethed with cars, and Apollo realized that if it hadn't been for Pamela, he would have stepped out into the flow of traffic. Of course he couldn't actually be harmed by the metal things, but he certainly didn't want to try to explain to Pamela why he hadn't been smashed to pieces by one of them. Daydreaming in the Kingdom of Las Vegas was not a wise thing for him to do.

"That must be where the fountain show is," she said, pointing across the street to lights reflected off a body of water.

He squinted over the stream of vehicles and people. "I do not see any fountains."

In front of them a red circle changed to a green circle, and the people around them moved forward. Apollo hesitated, but when Pamela stepped confidently into the street, he moved with her, keeping a close watch for any errant vehicles that might streak into their path.

"I don't think the fountains are active unless the show's going on. Here, I'll bet this will tell us about them." She led him to a small signpost giving iformation on displays. Reading, she nodded, "Yeah, the fountain show begins every quarter hour." She glanced at her watch. "It's eleven twenty-five, so we have five minutes."

Recollecting himself, Apollo tuned out the wash of distractions around him and refocused his attention on the lovely woman he was supposed to be romancing. "Would you like to walk, or would you rather sit and wait for the fountains to begin?" He gestured to one of several marble benches that dotted the wide sidewalk that ran the length of the minilake.

"Walk, definitely," she said, and they began strolling slowly along the bank.

After a small stretch of companionable silence, Pamela said, "This place is such an odd mixture of tacky and refined, don't you think?"

Apollo wanted to tell her she had no idea how odd Las Vegas seemed to him, but he was heartened by the fact that

Pamela obviously found their surroundings at least a little
unusual, too.

"I couldn't agree with you more," he said.

"I mean, look at that," she pointed towards the opposite
side of the street. "Over there it's nothing but one big
cheesy 'come spend your money here!' trap after another.
But over here it's different." She stopped and leaned
against the white marble railing that had been fashioned to
look like an old Italian balustrade. It ran the length of the
water, separating the sidewalk from the pool. "On this side
the street was built to make us believe that we are strolling
down a European walkway. The lights aren't neon adver-
tisements, they're lovely old-fashioned streetlamps separated by sweet little trees. And this"—she looked out
across the water at the shops and restaurants of the Bellagio—"reminds me of a chic Tuscan village. I know it's all
subterfuge, but the imagery works. As a designer I have to
applaud a successful masquerade."

Something in her tone called his gaze back to her face.
He was surprised to find that she looked sad, and it was
that unexpected melancholy that had been mirrored in her
voice. Until then she had seemed happy, even giddy, enjoying the evening and their shared conversation. What
had happened?

"Is a masquerade such a bad thing?"

"It's not really bad," she said, still looking out across
the water. "It's just that I sometimes wonder if anything is
really as it seems."

He knew she was speaking of much more than architecture and streetlights. He wanted to comfort her, to tell
her that she needn't be so sad. But how could he? *He*
wasn't what he seemed. Or was he? At that moment he felt
very much like a man who wanted nothing more than to
make a beautiful woman smile.

"Sometimes things are *more* than they seem, *better* than
they at first appear."

She turned to look at him and was caught in the impossible blue of his eyes.

"I wish that were true, but in my experience things

aren't usually better than they pretend to be—it's usually the other way around."

"Perhaps," he said, trailing his fingers lightly across her cheek and down the smooth side of her long neck, "that is because you have not yet had the right kind of experiences."

Pamela's stomach tensed. Apollo bent to brush his lips against hers in a brief, soft suggestion of a kiss. And as their mouths touched, the fountains came alive.

CHAPTER 9

Violins filled the air around them, and music enticed the water skyward, calling hidden lights to spotlight the liquid dance. Then the tenor began to sing. Pamela shivered as her body responded to the magnificence of his voice. It was so unexpected—so amazing. The arcs of water moved in perfect time to the rise and fall of the orchestra as if they had been choreographed by the hand of a master magician.

It was unbelievable and wonderful, like their kiss had been the cue that started it all.

At the sound of the first note, they had turned to face the fountains, and now Pamela stood very still, sheltered within Phoebus' arms while her emotions soared with the song.

"It's Italian, isn't it?" She leaned back against him, tilting her head up so that he could hear her question, without taking her eyes from the water.

"Yes," Apollo said. His eyes, too, were riveted on the incredible show before them. "He is singing of *la rondine*, the swallow," he murmured, using his voice as a backdrop to the beautiful music rather than a distraction. "He tells the story of the life of a little swallow who migrates far, far away to find love in a distant land. But of course he does not truly sing of a bird—he sings of his lover, who he is afraid has flown from him and is lost forever."

"I wish I could understand Italian," Pamela whispered.

Apollo tightened his arms around her. "Do you really

need to? Listen to the music with your heart, and you will understand the soul of the song."

Pamela listened with her heart. At the crescendo she felt her eyes fill with tears. She did understand—she understood the pain of lost love, of regrets, and the fear of forever being alone. When the song ended and the water went still and black, she stayed with her back pressed against Phoebus. She could feel the beat of his heart. The warmth of his body enveloped her.

"I did not expect to find such beauty here," he said softly, not wanting to break the spell the magical waters had cast.

"Neither did I." She drew a deep breath. "There's a lot about tonight that I didn't expect."

Apollo turned Pamela so that she was facing him. He kept her within a loose circle of his arms. He was reluctant to let her go, but he didn't want to frighten her or entrap her. The night had been filled with firsts for him. And now, for the first time in all the eons he had been in existence, he wanted a woman to come to him willingly, not as a bedazzled maiden overcome by the presence of Apollo, God of Light, and not as a seductive goddess, looking for a temporary partner with whom to dally. He wanted her to choose him, as a mortal woman would choose a man.

"I was not speaking only of the dancing waters," he said.

"Neither was I."

When he bent to kiss her, he couldn't stop himself from cupping the back of her head with his hand and letting his fingers splay through the short, tousled hair that he had so longed to touch since he had first glimpsed her. She didn't pull away from him, but she also didn't sink into the kiss. Her lips were warm and yielding under his, but they didn't open immediately in invitation. Instead it was as if they were posing a question for him to answer before he would be allowed to continue. *Think!* he ordered himself. *What is it women want?*

He realized shamefully that in spite of all of his experience, he wasn't sure how to answer that question. He concentrated, reading her body and through it trying to understand

what she desired of him. Moving slowly, he forced himself to
ignore the heady lust that touching her evoked. Instead of behaving like a boorish, arrogant god, Apollo held himself
tightly in control. He tenderly kissed her full bottom lip, and
then he took it gently between his teeth and pulled at it teasingly, but only for a moment. He moved from her lips to plant
a quick kiss on the tip of her nose, and was rewarded with her
smile, which he promptly kissed at the corners. His fingers
played in her short locks as he nuzzled her ear, and then whispered into it.

"I like your hair very much. It reminds me of the proud,
free race of Amazons." His lips traveled down. "And it
leaves your neck so enticingly bare."

He felt her shiver, and he raised his head so that he
could look into her eyes, which were still filled with the
emotions the music had made both of them feel.

"I want you to be what you seem," she said slowly. "I
don't want another man who pretends to be one thing, but
is really another."

He felt his heart go still.

"Earlier tonight I admitted something to myself that I
had been hiding from for a very long time. I admitted that
even though I am content, I am not actually happy. I have
locked myself away from even trying for happiness." A
small smile lightened her serious expression. "Then I made
a silly wish. Out loud. And what I think I was really wishing for was to be able to trust my instincts again."

"And what do your instincts tell you about me?" Apollo
asked.

She cocked her head and looked at him. "They tell me
that you really are different. I've never met a man like
you."

"I can assure you that your instincts are correct."

He bent to kiss her again, this time with all the passion
he was feeling, but just before his lips touched hers, the
sky opened, and a steady rain began to fall.

Pamela made a little shrieking noise and held her
ridiculously small purse over her head in a futile attempt
the shield herself from the rain.

Apollo scowled and looked fiercely around them. Rain

in the middle of a desert night? No matter how odd the modern world had become, it could not change the weather patterns. But Gods could. This rain was definitely suspicious. It had the mark of immortal interference. Probably that toad Bacchus at work causing mischief again.

People all around them were running towards the nearest buildings. Deftly, Apollo guided Pamela between the scampering mortals to the closest tree. With an almost imperceptible movement of his hand, he solidified the leaves above them into one frondlike mass so that they were sheltered from the rain. He encircled her with his arm, and they stood together, peering out through the downpour.

"This seems like weird weather," Pamela said, wiping water from her face. "I thought it hardly ever rained here. Ugh," she frowned down at her shoes. "I think I just ruined my fabulous Jimmy Choos."

Apollo smiled crookedly at her. "How do you walk on those daggers?"

Pamela swung her foot out. She admired her soggy shoe. He admired her shapely calf. "Walking on three-and-a-half-inch slides is the mark of a true woman." She ran her hand through her hair, causing it to stick up in adorably messy spikes. "You wouldn't think such a little tree would give so much protection." She glanced up. "It's like a green umbrella."

"Oh, there's some rain getting through," he said, pointing upwards in a small motion that instantly let a drop or two leak through his divine protection. "At least the rain has cleared away the crowd."

Not giving the tree another glance, she grinned and nodded. "It's like we're in our own little world."

He touched one short strand of her hair. "I think that we are."

And then through the veil of rain and intimacy the fountain came alive again, and Faith Hill's sexy voice swirled around them through the water:

"I don't want another heartbreak, I don't need another turn to cry.

*I don't want to learn the hard way, baby, hello, oh
       no, good-bye."*

This time they didn't watch the show.

"Are you doing this?" Pamela whispered. "Did you pay
them to play these songs?"

He shook his head and framed her face in his hands.
"They're about you, though, aren't they? The swallow is
you, and so is the woman who doesn't need another turn to
cry."

Pamela could only nod.

"This kiss, this kiss!"

As if the song played only for them, Apollo pulled her
into his arms and kissed her. He kissed her as a man wanting to keep his lover safe from pain and heartache and sadness.

Her lips parted and she accepted him, and as she did
Apollo felt something open within him, like a latch had
been unlocked and a trapdoor lifted, allowing what had
been missing to fill his soul. Her arms crept up to return his
embrace, and he forgot Mount Olympus; he forgot the
modern world of mortals. His reality tunneled down to the
taste and touch and scent of Pamela. Then she moaned and
shivered, and the world rushed back. The fountain was
dark again, and the wind and rain had intensified.

"You're cold!" He rubbed her arms, thinking himself an
insensitive clod. While he'd been lost in her, she'd become
waterlogged. "We need to get back. You could become ill
out here."

"Phoebus." She pulled on his arm, keeping him under
the little tree. "It's true that we should probably go back to
the hotel, but I wasn't shivering because of the rain. And
you should know that even though I might look a little"—
she wiped at a drop of rain that crept down her forehead
and grinned—"waterlogged, I'm not some delicate hot-
house flower. I won't melt, and I've loved every second of
kissing you in the rain."

He felt the tightness in his chest dissolve as his heart acknowledged the warmth of her gaze. He wasn't the only one who felt their connection—she was in it with him. And somewhere in the depths of his mind his instinct whispered to him that this is what men and women do . . . this was the mortal dance of love.

"But I am totally soaked, and it doesn't look like it's letting up," Pamela said, glancing out at the downpour that surrounded them.

Apollo followed her gaze. He could, of course, keep the rain from touching them all the way back to Caesars Palace—but there was no possible way he could explain such a feat to Pamela.

"I'll tell you what—I'll race you back to the Palace." Pamela grinned at him.

"You can not run in those shoes," he said, pointing to her feet.

"Well . . . we are in Las Vegas. What would you like to bet on that?"

Without waiting for his answer, she dashed, shrieking, out into the rain. Laughing, Apollo followed her, staying just far enough behind her so that he could watch the roundness of her buttocks jiggle as she ran with cute, feminine little steps.

Apollo couldn't recall the last time he had felt so young or so happy.

Neither of them were paying attention to the street. He was watching her. She kept glancing back over her shoulder at him.

"I'm winning the bet!" she shouted at him.

A sound made her look in front of her, and she gasped. The street! She'd completely misjudged how close it was. Trying to pull herself to a stop, her stiletto heel caught in a crack on the edge of the curb. Helplessly off-balanced, her arms windmilled as she tried to right herself. Twisting, Pamela felt a horrible, sickening pain in her ankle, and then she toppled forward.

Always before when terrible things had happened, like the death of Hector or when Artemis lost her temper with Actaeon, Apollo had noticed that time slowed, drawing out the event and letting it unfold before him like pine resin beading and then traveling in a tedious trail down the rough bark of a tree. Not so with Pamela's accident. Everything sped up with superhuman force. One instant she was smiling coquettishly over her shoulder at him, the next she was teetering at the edge of the street. She twisted forward towards the street surging with metal monsters. Apollo read her death in the air around them. There was no time for rational thought. His body acted on impulse guided by his immoral heart that had suddenly felt shattered at the thought of losing her.

"No!" Apollo leapt towards her with speed that was blinding to the moral eye. He flung out his hand, palm open. His shout caused an instant sonic blast, which created an audio tidal wave, buffeting the cars away from the path of Pamela's falling body.

She didn't touch the hard, wet concrete. He couldn't allow that. With superhuman speed, Apollo caught her in his arms and pulled her back onto the sidewalk.

Tires screeched to a halt. There was a vague crashing sound of one car hitting another. Honking horns blasted the night. But through the rain and wind, no one seemed to notice the god who had caused it all. The god who now knelt on the flooded pavement cradling a mortal woman close to his chest.

"My ankle," Pamela's voice shook with pain and shock. "I think it's broken."

Apollo gently pulled her slender foot from the ridiculous shoe. As he did so, he felt through her soft skin to the bone that had been twisted until it snapped, and he cringed, imagining her pain. Quickly, his hand brushed over her ankle, and he silently willed the nerve endings to cease their shooting agony. Almost instantly he felt her breathing deepen as she relaxed. In one smooth motion, Apollo lifted her into his arms, and the God of Light strode like a shaft of blazing sun through the rain and wrecked cars.

Later, witnesses of the bizarre pileup on the corner of Las Vegas and Flamingo would talk of a tall man they had glimpsed through the rain that night. They would say that they thought he carried a woman, but they couldn't be sure, because all that they could remember was the odd way his eyes had flashed. They would also all swear that they couldn't tell exactly what he looked like because his body was surrounded by a light that made him look like he was glowing with the fire of the sun.

CHAPTER 10

"*She must be taken to her room!*" Apollo barked at a bellboy who was staring with wide eyes at the golden apparition who had seemed to appear suddenly out of the rain-shrouded night. He was carrying the damp body of a petite woman who was wearing only one shoe.

"The elevators are just inside and around the corner, sir."

Apollo's confusion at his odd words (What exactly was an elevator?) changed to anger.

"Show me to her room, or I will flay the flesh from your living body!" he growled.

"Room number?" the bellboy squeaked.

"Eleven twenty-one," Pamela said into Apollo's shoulder.

Apollo glared at the bellboy. The youth nodded and scampered ahead of them through the swinging doors. The God of Light ground his teeth together as the metal box they stepped into closed. The boy punched a round button that read 11. It lit up as the box began to move. The god's stomach dropped, and he held Pamela more tightly against him. Bacchus had explained nothing about this particular mechanical form of transportation to them. Apollo definitely didn't like it. Not at all. Thankfully, the ride was short, and the doors parted smoothly. He followed the boy out into a plushly carpeted hallway. Statuettes decorated niches, and chandeliers hung from the ornately painted ceiling. They stopped in front of a door boasting the golden numbers 1121.

The bellboy looked at Apollo. Apollo looked at the bellboy. The god narrowed his eyes dangerously. The bellboy cleared his throat nervously.

Pamela stirred and handed the boy the purse she still clutched to her chest. "It's in there."

Swallowing audibly, the boy unclasped the little purse and extracted the card key, ran it through the lock, and opened the door. Apollo strode in and slammed the door behind him with one thought.

"You should have tipped him," Pamela said faintly.

"I should have skinned him," Apollo muttered. He hesitated at the entrance to the room, assessing his surroundings. There was one large room with a divan and two silk-covered side chairs, plus an overlarge armoire. Doors painted to look like marble were half open to reveal a glimpse of a large bed. Apollo headed in its direction.

Pamela moaned and as he lay her on top of the thick silk comforter. Her body spasmed, and her teeth chattered.

"I d-don't know why I'm s-suddenly s-so cold," she said.

Apollo knew why. She was in shock. He hadn't healed her ankle—he'd just temporarily blocked some of the pain. He sat gently on the edge of the bed and touched her face, willing her to relax.

"You must rest. Trust me to see to your pain."

He watched as his hypnotic suggestion caused her thick-lashed lids to begin to flutter over those wide amber eyes.

"I don't . . ." she began sleepily, and then lost the thread of her thought. Struggling against a drugged sense of lethargy, she blinked her eyes. "I'm wet . . . towels through there . . ." She made a weak gesture in the direction of the bathroom.

"Your ankle comes first," he said.

When her eyes closed and did not open, he rearranged himself at the end of the bed. He shook his head. The ankle was badly injured. It was already swollen to double its size and terribly discolored. He could see where the bone had snapped, causing the foot to hang at an awkward angle. He took her ankle between his hands and closed his eyes in concentration. Within his mind he mapped the skeleton of her foot and ankle. Taking his time, he envisioned the path of each bone, muscle and nerve. And he saw the break. Apollo's hands warmed. *Heal,* the God of Light commanded. *Suffering cease. Health return. Purge her of pain.*

The intensity of the glow between Apollo's hands would have blinded Pamela, had she been conscious to witness its splendor. But she did not awake. Instead she slept on as the golden Apollo used his vast powers to knit her broken bones together and end her pain. Much later, when he was finished, he rose and went into the small room just off the bedchamber. In there he found a quantity of towels and a thick, white robe. He brought them back to Pamela and hesitated. He could disrobe her easily. She would not awaken; he would be sure of that. The wet fabric of her dress molded to her, revealing her gentle curves and the roundness of her breasts. She was a lush land awaiting his exploration . . .

No, his mind shied away from the thought of seeing her naked body without her consent or knowledge.

"Pamela," he whispered. That within her, which slept at his suggestion, roused.

"Oh!" she said, sitting up and looking around. "What happened? My ankle!" She leaned forward and then stopped short, frowning at her leg. "But it felt terrible, like it was broken. I could have sworn it was already swelling. Now it looks perfectly normal." Testing, she flexed and then rolled her foot in a circular motion. "And it feels fine."

"You just needed to rest it. You strained it, that is all." He handed her a towel, and she dried her face absentmindedly.

"I feel kind of stupid. I mean, you actually carried me up here. In the rain."

"I am a doctor. Healing is my job."

She looked up at him. He was completely wet. His shirt clung to the muscular ridges of his chest as if it was liquid silk. His hair curled in damp tendrils around his forehead. And those eyes! She thought the lyrics of the Faith Hill song

described them perfectly: impossible . . . unstoppable . . .
unthinkable . . . unsinkable . . .

"Well, I guess it's a good thing that you were close by."
With an effort, she pulled her eyes from his and began
towel drying her hair with considerably more enthusiasm
than was necessary.

Apollo watched her. She looked bedraggled and sodden. Her hair was a limp mess. Her clothes were wet. She
only had on one shoe—and that one was leaking bright
dye colors onto the ivory comforter. His heart lurched. He
had never been so attracted to a woman, mortal or goddess,
in his life.

"I should leave," he said abruptly.

Pamela peeked up through a fold in the towel. "Oh?"
She looked at her soaked watch. (Thank God it was water-
proof.) It was past 4:00 A.M.! "I didn't realize it was so
late." She reminded herself that he was a strange man and
that, although the chances of him being a rapist or a serial
killer were slim, especially in light of the fact that he'd
"rescued" her, he was still a man alone with her in her
hotel room way past midnight. The situation had the mak-
ings of a Lifetime Movie of the Week, and they never
ended well.

"Yes, it is late." He definitely didn't want to leave,
which was why his conscience was telling him firmly he
must go.

"I suppose your sister will be wondering what happened
to you."

Apollo paled. "You have no idea."

His expression made Pamela smile. "Oh, but I do. My
brother would be pacing back and forth while he waited up
to yell at me for staying out so late and worrying him."

His lips quirked. "She will definitely want to know
what has taken me so long."

Pamela cocked her head to the side in a gesture that had
already become familiar and endearing to Apollo.

"And what will you tell her?" she asked.

"I will tell her that I was detained by an unexpected accident." He walked to her and with one graceful movement
knelt at the side of her bed. His hand touched her ankle

gently. Then he stroked it, letting his fingers travel a short way up her calf. He felt more than saw the slow intake of her breath. "A lovely, unexpected accident."

She could hardly breathe when he looked at her and touched her like that. She wanted to beg him not to leave, to ask him to stay the night with her . . . Pamela's stomach clenched. She shouldn't want him so much and so soon; he was a stranger. A handsome, sexy, wonderful, stranger . . .

Apollo watched the shifting emotions that were so clearly written on her face. That she desired him was obvious. He saw the soft, liquid wanting in her eyes. He could have her—he could take her in his arms and complete the seduction. That was what he was supposed to do. It was what Artemis expected and what he had planned. Pamela hadn't said that she wanted to be made love to when she had spoken aloud the desire of her heart and completed the invocation, but her need had been transparent in her words. He'd seen it, as had Artemis. So, in order to fulfill the invocation, he needed to make love to her.

And then what? A sudden thought blew through his mind like an unexpected winter storm. Perhaps the invocation had cast some kind of spell over her, and the desire he saw in her eyes was only a result of the powerful magic the nymphs had worked. If that were true, then once he made love to her, the spell would be broken. She would no longer desire him. She would no longer gaze at him with those intelligent, expressive eyes that turned the rich color of honey when he aroused her earthy passion. The thought left him feeling lost and sick. Abruptly he stood.

"I must go," he said. "No," he motioned for her to stay in bed when she moved to get up. "You should rest your ankle. Sleep with it elevated tonight. Tomorrow it will be as if the accident never happened."

Pamela's stomach dropped as he turned to the door. He'd said he would explain her to his sister as an accident. Was he saying that this was it? That after this one night they wouldn't see each other again?

"And tomorrow will it be like the accident never happened to you, too?"

She only realized she'd spoken her thought aloud when

her words stopped him. He turned, and his brilliant blue eyes seemed to glow. He lifted the hand that had so recently caressed her ankle and presented it to her, palm open.

"Tomorrow I will still feel your skin against mine. Tomorrow I will still taste the silk of your mouth. Tomorrow the breeze will still carry your scent to me. How could I possibly forget you?"

"Then I will see you again?" she asked breathlessly.

"I would not stay away from you, even if I wished it. And I do not wish it. I will be at our café again tomorrow evening at the same moment we met this night. Until then, my sweet Pamela, I will think of you."

When he left the room, Pamela felt as if the sun had suddenly fallen from the sky. She looked at the clock and began counting the hours until she would see him again.

Artemis waited in the obscure hallway that branched from an unadorned delivery entrance to Caesars Palace. She stood beside a door, which opened to an incongruous-looking closet that held a portal leading to another world. She crossed her arms and sighed. She had told Apollo that she would wait for him in Olympus, but as the night had waned she had become increasingly restless. It was late—almost dawn—and still she felt the chains that yoked her to the mortal woman. What could possibly be taking the God of Light so long to seduce her?

A tall man dressed in sodden clothes turned a corner and approached her. With hardly a thought she lifted her finger to force him to turn away and use a different exit.

The man surprised her by laughing.

"Your tricks do not work so well upon me, Sister," Apollo said.

Artemis' eyes widened in recognition. "Apollo? By Zeus' beard! What has happened to you?"

Apollo shrugged and pulled his wet shirt away from his body. "An accident."

"An accident! But what of the seduction?"

"It comes along well."

"Well!" Artemis almost shrieked in frustration. "How could it be coming along well if I can still feel the bond of the invocation upon me?"

"These things take time, Artemis. Pamela is not a city to be breached, or a fortress to be attacked and sacked. She is a mortal woman who desires romance."

"I understand that all too well. What I don't understand is why you have not yet bedded her."

"Because it is not truly what she desires," Apollo said.

Artemis' eyes narrowed at the odd, introspective tone of his voice. "Having the God of Light in her bed is not truly what she desires? I find that hard to believe, brother."

Apollo sighed. "What would you say if I told you that bedding her tonight is not what I desire?"

She would say that that was easier for her to understand. She had thought that her brother had found the mortal attractive, but apparently that had changed. "Well," she said slowly, "this really is Bacchus' fault. He's just going to have to be involved in fixing it. Perhaps he can use the most potent of his wines to drug her into a desirous state. He is a god; I supposed he has seduced mortal women before, no matter how repulsive it is to imagine him engaging in such an act."

"*No!*" The word exploded from him. "That toad will not touch her!"

Artemis' slender brows knit in confusion. "Apollo, be clear! One moment you say you do not desire the mortal, and the next you are ready to defend her against another god as if you were that fool Paris, and she your Helen."

"I simply said I did not wish to bed her tonight, not that I didn't desire her. She injured herself tonight," he blurted as his sister stared silently at him. "Of course I healed her. Without her knowledge," he added quickly before Artemis could speak. "But to take her to bed after that would have been an ignoble act."

Artemis' sharp eyes saw the veiled discomfort on her brother's face. He was not being entirely truthful—not with her and perhaps not even with himself. Either way, she could tell by the stubborn set of his jaw that he would admit no more to her.

"Tomorrow?"

Apollo nodded tightly. "Tomorrow."

"Good. Let us retire to Olympus. I find that I am weary of the mortal world."

Apollo opened the closet door and motioned for her to precede him through the shimmering, shell-colored portal. He was returning to their world, but he had no intention of retiring to Olympus. He bade his sister a distracted good night and then transported himself to the one place he knew in which he could find aid.

CHAPTER 11

It had been as much a surprise to Apollo as to the rest of the Olympians to discover that the goddess who had won Hades' supposedly cold heart wasn't really a goddess at all. That Demeter had instigated a swapping of her daughter Persephone's soul for the soul of Carolina Francesca Santoro, a mortal from the modern world. Demeter had wanted to tame her carefree daughter, and the trade had seemed an excellent opportunity to mature Persephone. It also presented the lovely side benefit of having the more mature mortal businesswoman bring a calming female presence to the Underworld. It had been a totally unexpected development for the Lord of the Underworld to fall hopelessly in love with the mortal masquerading as a goddess.

Although, Apollo thought, once he'd met Carolina, or Lina as Hades called her, it didn't take long for him to understand why the God of the Underworld had become so smitten with her. She was wise and filled with a kind of unique exuberance that shone like a beacon from within.

Apollo had always been drawn to Lina's laughter, and now he finally understood why. It carried the sound of her mortal soul within the voice of the body in which she temporarily inhabited—that of the Goddess Persephone. And within that mortal soul he heard the echo of Pamela's earthy joy.

"So this mortal woman has already driven you to Hell!"

"Carolina, do not torment him." Hades smiled fondly at his soul mate.

"You're showing your sensitive side again, my love," Lina said in the teasing tone that only she could use with the God of the Underworld.

Hades snorted. "It is not that I am sensitive, it is simply that I understand very well the havoc a modern mortal woman can wreak in a god's life."

Lina pointedly ignored her husband's words and turned her attention back to Apollo. The golden god had discarded the wet clothing he had arrived in and was now wrapped comfortably in one of Hades' robes. She and Hades lounged in their private chamber, sipping ambrosia. Apollo had visited them frequently since it had become common knowledge that a mortal woman had become Queen of the Underworld, and the three of them had grown into good friends. The God of Light should be relaxed and at home with them. Instead he looked like a wound spring. He couldn't sit still. He paced restlessly in front of the wide picture window that looked out upon the beautiful gardens in the rear of the palace. But Apollo paid no attention to the lovely view.

"I don't know what you're so worried about. From what you've told us, Pamela seems to be very interested in you," Lina said.

"That is exactly what I am not sure of! Is it me that interests her, or is it the damned power of the invocation spell?"

"That seems easy to determine," Hades said. "Simply make love to her. If she casts you from her sight afterwards, it is the spell that attracted her. If not, it is you."

Apollo frowned at him, not sure why he was so unwilling to test Pamela's affection. Wasn't it really just that simple? Why did the thought of it cause his stomach to roil?

"It's scary, isn't it?" Lina's soft voice interrupted the god's inner turmoil. "It's something we mortals know all too well—the fear of rejection. But in order to know true love, you must be willing to open yourself to the possibility of true hurt. I wish I had an easy answer for you, but I don't."

"So it's always this hard."

Lina smiled kindly at the golden god's pained expression. Sitting beside her, Hades slid his hand within hers, and for a moment they shared a secret look.

"It's only this hard when you really care," she said.

Apollo's face paled. "I might fall in love with her?" He spoke the words as if he had just given name to a new plague.

Lina nodded, careful to keep a clamp on the laughter that threatened to bubble over. Poor Apollo. He was just so adorably miserable. "I'm afraid you might."

"Cheer up!" Hades said. "Loving a mortal is not such a terrible thing."

"Well, I'm glad to hear you say so," Lina said sarcastically.

Hades just chuckled and kissed the top of her head.

"She doesn't know who I am!" Apollo blurted. "She thinks I'm a mortal man, a doctor and a musician. Perhaps it is not the spell. Perhaps she could fall in love with me, too. But won't that change when she finds out that I have been masquerading as someone I am not?"

"Do not allow her to turn from you." Hades' voice had gone flat and deadly serious. His hand tightened on Lina's as he remembered how he had almost lost her because of his own pride.

"Apollo, you have to be sure that you *are* showing her the real you," Lina said, choosing her words carefully. "That's the trickiest part about love. You have to bare yourself for it to work. And if you really bare yourself, all of a sudden you'll realize that you aren't a god or a doctor or a musician; you're just a man in love. If she loves you in return, she'll see that."

"If not?" Apollo asked.

Lina answered truthfully. "If not, you get hurt,"

"It is worth the cost," Hades said, looking into his lover's eyes. "The chance to know true love is worth any cost." In response Lina touched his face with a gentle caress.

Apollo watched Lina and Hades. At times they seemed to speak to one another in a secret language of their own.

They fit together as if they had been fashioned for each other. By all the gods, Hades had changed since Lina had come into his life! It was as if loving her had opened a new world to him. Where once the dark god had been brooding and withdrawn, now he seemed at peace, even affable. Lina had made Hades complete.

Apollo wanted that same completion.

"I will do it!" he proclaimed. "I will make love to her. If it is only a spell that draws her to me, I must know it."

Lina thought Apollo looked like a man who was getting ready to run a gauntlet. Then his face changed once again, and he rubbed a hand across his brow as if he wished he could wipe away his worries.

"But if it is not a spell, how do I keep her affection?" He blinked at Lina. "What is it that modern women desire?"

"That's no mystery, Apollo." Lina smiled. "We want the same thing you want, the same thing Hades wants. We want someone who will love who we really are—no masquerades—no pretenses—no games." She stood up and approached the golden god, laying her hand on his arm. "Can you do that, my friend? It's not like chasing after nymphs and goddesses. It's much less glamorous."

Apollo thought about how the world had disappeared as Pamela relaxed into his arms and how the growing trust in her eyes made him feel more godlike than all the glories of Olympus. And then he thought about the stab of terror he had felt as he watched her body crumple forward and into the path of the metal machines. If he hadn't used his powers, she would have been crushed . . . killed . . .

He rubbed his hand across his brow again.

"I've grown weary of glamour. I believe that I choose love," he said wearily.

"Good choice, honey." On tiptoes, Lina gave him a quick, sisterly kiss. "Uh, you might want to consider telling her who you really are as soon as possible." She slanted a sideways glance at Hades. "Take it from me, it's best to get the truth out and over with."

"Yes, yes, I shall." Distracted, Apollo didn't seem to hear her. "Thank you, my friends." He patted Lina's hand

and then stepped away from her, preparing to transport back to his Olympian palace. "Perhaps I should bring her a gift . . ." His words floated through the chamber as his body wavered and then disappeared.

"I think the heart of the God of Light will be gift enough," Lina said, sighing heavily.

Hades shrugged one shoulder. "Jewelry never hurts."

Pamela woke up in small degrees. She stretched and then hugged her pillow, sleepily thinking that something wonderful was going to happen today, but in the place between awake and asleep, she couldn't quite remember what it was. She felt wonderful. Her body was well-rested, yet she was filled with a tight hum of anticipation. A finger of daylight broke through the thickly brocaded drapes that were pulled just short of completely closed. The light tickled her closed eyelids. It brought to mind golden rays of sun . . . heat . . . eyes the color of brilliant aquamarines . . .

Last night . . . kisses in the rain . . . Phoebus . . . Her eyes snapped open. Oh. Shit. How could she have forgotten? She was meeting him tonight at 8:00. She looked at the bedside clock and sat straight up. It was almost noon! She was a morning person, and she'd slept until noon!

Well, she was also a woman who had avoided men and romance for the past several years, and last night she distinctly remembered melting into a practical stranger's arms. Pamela hugged her knees to her chest, feeling her heart beat with excitement. She wasn't a dried up old hag—she was young and alive. She'd taken a chance, and it had paid off. Big time. A delicious shiver ran through her body as she thought about how it had felt to be wrapped within Phoebus' arms. And his mouth! His kiss had seared from her lips to her toes. If he was that good at kissing, she could only imagine what else he could do with that fabulous mouth—

Her phone rang, jarring her out of the erotic daydream.

"Hello, V," she said without looking at the caller ID number.

"Are you alone?" V asked, using her best stage whisper.

"Yes," Pamela bit her lip and added, "unfortunately."

"Oh, nuh-uh! Listen to you, doll!"

"V, I feel alive again. It's like I'd become a desert, and he's a warm spring rain. And let me tell you, I'm ready to lap him up." She sighed happily.

"You're be-friggen-sotted."

"You're right! You're right! I *am* besotted—in lust—giddy! And holy shit, it feels good! Oh, let me just get this out of the way right now. Aloud and without coercion, I admit readily that you were right," she chanted joyfully.

"Wait, I'm pinching myself. Yes, it hurts. No, I'm not dreaming. Damn right I was right! You aren't still drunk, are you?"

Pamela laughed. "I was never drunk; I was just tipsy enough to do what you told me to do. And, ohhhh it was wonderful!"

"Gory details, please. Tell me everything."

"We went to the Bellagio fountains. First they played some insanely romantic song from an opera, which Phoebus—"

"Phoebus?" V broke in.

"That's his name. It's Greek. Or Roman. Or Latin. Or something. Hey—did you know that Pamela means 'all that is sweet' in Greek?"

"Pammy, you're losing focus. Again. Snap back. His name is Phoebus and . . ."

"Oh yeah. So first they play the song from the opera. He knew the words. God, it was romantic . . ." She sighed.

"You already said that. Fast forward."

"Then it started to rain and we ran under a tree. And you won't believe this part—we're standing there and—V, did I mention how gorgeous he is?"

"Focus, please."

"Sorry. Anyway, we're standing there, and the fountain comes on again—and it's Faith Hill singing 'This Kiss.'"

"You've got to be kidding," V said.

"Seriously. And then we did it."

"You copulated right there on the street?"

"No! It was on the sidewalk, and we didn't do *it;* we kissed."

"Then you went back to your room and copulated like naughty heterosexual bunnies?"

"Again, no!" Pamela cleared her throat and had the insane urge to whisper the rest of the story. "But he did carry me up to my room."

"You mean like Rhett and scrumptious Scarlett?"

"Exactly like that. Only I'd twisted my ankle, and it was raining."

"So you fell off your stilettos . . ."

"Which shows how distracted this guy makes me, because, as you know, I can jog over a sheet of ice in three-inch heels," Pamela said smugly.

"He played a knight in shining armor—a cliché I know you straight girls adore, by the by, and you still didn't copulate with the poor tripod?"

"Not yet," Pamela said breathlessly.

"Yet? Give up the rest of the story."

"We have a *date*. Tonight. Ta da!" she finished with a verbal flourish.

"Ya don't say?"

"I do say."

"Okay. What's the plan?" V, the consummate date-aholic, got straight to business.

"Well, I thought we might go to dinner," Pamela said.

"Pammy, you're in Vegas. You can do better than that."

"Please don't tell me we should gamble."

V's sigh was long-suffering. "Of course not. Vegas is a Mecca for fabulous shows. Go see one, a sexy one."

"That's a good idea, except . . . well . . . shouldn't I wait to see what he has planned?"

"Pammy, you know I'm your friend, so please don't take this the wrong way, but do you really want another relationship where you let the man always take the lead?" she asked gently.

"No!" The word came out in a flash of anger. "I don't want anything like what Duane and I had. I'm not that silly young girl he married anymore."

"You weren't silly, Pamela. You were just young and in love. You made a mistake. It happens to the best of us."

"Well, it's not going to happen to me again," Pamela said firmly.

"Which part? Being in love or being young?"

Pamela opened her mouth to say both, but then she remembered the soft blue of Phoebus' eyes and the way he looked at her with equal parts of interest and desire. And she remembered something else that she was almost sure she had recognized within his eyes and his voice and the way he touched her—a familiar searching that tugged at her heart as well as her soul. *Soul mates* . . . the thought wafted like the fragrance of spring flowers through her mind.

"I'm not young anymore," she said. "And there's no way I can fall in love in a weekend."

Vernelle laughed. "Keep telling yourself that, Pammy."

Pamela frowned. "I'm going now. I have a lot to do before tonight."

"Such as . . ."

"Such as I have to sketch that awful fountain so I can have something to send to the Fountain Boys." The Fountain Boys were what Pamela and V called the brothers who owned a huge fountain wholesale business that Ruby Slipper had used several times to fill orders for all types of water features. "I am here to do a job, remember?"

"I thought Faust said you were to loll about soaking up the ambience of The Forum this weekend."

"That doesn't mean that I can completely ignore work. Which reminds me, are you meeting with Mrs. Graham today?"

"Yes, of course. The crazy cat lady and I have a date this afternoon. We're going to discuss the color of her shutters. Pray for me."

Pamela laughed. "I'll see if I can find a candle to light."

"Okay, enough about unfinished jobs. You're supposed to be lolling, not working."

"Well, I've definitely soaked up enough tacky pretend Roman ambience. The sooner I get going on this job, the sooner I can be done with it."

"Fantasy and fun, remember?" V said.

"Vernelle, tonight I'm going out with a gorgeous

stranger named Phoebus. Isn't that enough fun fantasy for you?"

"Mix a little of that cheeky attitude in with this job without losing your sense of humor, and I think you'll have the perfect recipe for succeeding with E. D. Faust, as well as Phoebus. Have fun with both of them, Pammy."

Fun . . . her personal life had definitely stopped being fun. She was comfortable and secure, but fun . . . happy . . . joyous? No. Had her job stopped being fun, too? She liked what she did; it satisfied her. But when was the last time she had felt a sense of wonder or a rush of joy at the completion of a job? She couldn't remember . . . The thought brought her up short.

"Pammy? You still there?" V asked.

"Yeah, just thinking."

"How about this—you give the fountain an hour of your time, *after* you give the concierge a call and arrange for your show tickets," V said.

"Okay, okay. You're right," Pamela said.

"And tomorrow I want a full report."

"You'll get it."

"Good. Bye-bye, birdie," V quipped before hanging up.

Pamela rubbed the sleep from her eyes. She just hoped she'd have something worth reporting tomorrow. Then, before she changed her mind, she dialed nine for the concierge.

An efficient-sounding woman answered on the second ring. "Yes, Miss Gray. How may I help you?"

"I would like to see a show tonight." She paused, drawing a deep breath. "An erotic show. But nothing too nasty," she finished in a rush.

"Of course not, ma'am. I highly recommend a show that's currently playing at New York-New York. It's by the same company that produces Cirque du Soleil. Have you heard of them?"

"Yes, I've been to a Cirque du Soleil show when they came through Denver."

"Excellent. This production is called *Zumanity*. It is erotic but tasteful. I've seen it myself and enjoyed it very much. Actually, it's been selling out lately, but the hotel does have access to a few hard-to-find tickets."

"That sounds perfect," Pamela said, relieved that everything was falling into place so easily.

"And how many tickets will you require?"

Pamela's grin telegraphed through the phone lines. "Two, please."

CHAPTER 12

—✦—

Pamela shifted her weight and curled her feet under her, completely engrossed in sketching the fountain. Well, *her* version of the fountain. She kept its cloverleaf shape, but she shrank it and ignored the hideous statues of Artemis, Apollo, and Caesar, replacing them with pretty swirls meant to look like waves from the middle of which fish spouted water. She glanced up at the bulbous center statue and sighed. No matter how she "fixed" the rest of the gihugic thing, there was no way she could make Bacchus acceptable—especially if Eddie kept insisting that the thing be animated. Her fingers, which had been flying over the page of her sketchbook, slowed. She drew in the center pedestal, but left blank the area on top of it where Bacchus sat. Surely she could talk Eddie into something less . . . she frowned at the statue . . . less fat and hideous.

She checked her watch—three-thirty. Four and a half more hours until her date. She should get her camera and take pictures of the columns, as well as make notes about colors and textures. All this preliminary work would be needed Monday when she finally met with Eddie at his home. But instead of thinking about work, her mind wandered to thoughts of pleasure. The gilding of the overly ornate columns reminded her of the brightness of Phoebus' hair. Now that her concentration was no longer required to sketch the fountain, Pamela's mind circled back to him. The pretend sky from which fluffy clouds billowed reminded her of his eyes. Hell, even the tacky statue of Apollo was somehow beginning to look like him.

It was like he was one of those glowing bug lights, and she was a love-struck mosquito. She was obsessed. Pamela knew it, and was more than a little chagrined to realize that she really didn't care. On the contrary, she felt like she did when she was reading an exceptionally good book—like she was walking around in someone else's world and enjoying every second of it.

Her smile was self-satisfied and very, very sensual. Maybe she should gamble; she sure felt lucky.

As if echoing her thoughts, a slender young woman breezed up to the fountain, talking in excited little snatches to her friend.

"Can you believe our *amazing luck?* Oh. My. God. Stumbling into the Chanel sale of the year!"

A sale at Chanel? Pamela's ears perked.

"I thought I was going to faint when I saw how far that dress had been marked down."

Giggling and hefting their full shopping bags, the two women breezed past Pamela's bench.

It must be fate. Pamela gave the ugly fountain another look and almost laughed out loud. Or maybe it was ordained by the gods. She was going to buy a fabulous new Chanel dress to wear tonight. She was going to go to an erotic show with a gorgeous hunk of a man. And she might even have sex with him afterwards. Her stomach butterflied.

Okay, scratch that. She was getting ahead of herself. Big, deep breath.

How about . . . She might even make out with him afterwards. And heavy petting wasn't out of the question, either. She closed her sketchbook and slid it into her leather briefcase.

Red. She'd buy a red dress that showed just a little too much leg. She might even get a pedicure. Yes, she would get a pedicure. Red toes were definitely a necessity tonight. Humming softly to herself, she headed happily towards couture heaven.

*   *   *

Bacchus drummed his fingers on the top of the restaurant table. Things weren't going as he'd planned.

"Bring me another tequila!" he snarled at a passing waitress and then was instantly sorry when she cringed at the heat of the god's wrath and almost knocked over several chairs in her haste to get to the bar to place his order. It was bad enough that the young Olympians were annoying him. It was totally unacceptable that they were causing him to take out his annoyance on the innocent people in his kingdom.

And it was still *his* kingdom.

The waitress rushed up to his table with his tequila.

"I'm so sorry, sir. I should have been paying better attention to you. I didn't mean for you to have to wait for your drink."

Bacchus smiled kindly at her and touched her arm, transmitting a dose of magic into her body. Instantly her terrified look vanished. Her young cheeks flushed, and her lips parted seductively.

She thought how wrong she had been to have ever considered him a terrifying, obese stranger. His anger wasn't palpable. And he wasn't fat. He was just a big man. She liked big men—*really* liked them. Heat coursed from his fingers into her arm and all through her body, tingling her nerve endings and causing her most private parts to become wet and ready. She stared into his dark eyes and leaned closer to him, wishing he would take his hand from her arm and slide it down between her legs and . . .

Bacchus chuckled and stroked the firm flesh of her young arm. "Later this night you will come to my suite. Just think of me, and your desire will lead you to the correct room." Only after he was certain that his command had been firmly planted into her subconscious, did he break contact with her skin.

The waitress shivered with intense pleasure. "Yes." She moaned the word.

"Now be off." He gestured slightly with his hand, and a veil lifted from her eyes.

She blinked and smiled hesitantly at him.

"Is there anything else I can get you, sir?"

"Later, perhaps," he said.

She walked away slowly, still looking dazed. Bacchus studied her well-rounded buttocks and let himself imagine how she was going to feel beneath him later that night. She would be delightful and young and fresh and completely enamored with him. He was a god; he could easily be certain of her adoration. Modern mortals needed to worship him. He was actually doing the young woman a favor by adding the intoxicating magic of wine and fertility to her otherwise mundane life.

But he was the only god who had a right to use his power amidst them. Las Vegas had been his discovery. HE WOULD NOT SHARE HIS REALM! He especially would not share it with the golden twins. He had always loathed both of them with their perfection and their nonchalant arrogance about everything. They hadn't been content to remain within Caesars Palace and gamble alongside the mortals. They had actually found their way to his special place—the fountain in The Forum.

Yes, he had loosed his immortal power through the nymphs. He had meant to shock the twins. He had purposefully targeted that repressed little mortal and caused her to drink just enough of his wine to set into motion the sequence of events that would allow the invocation to be completed. He knew Artemis' temper—all of Olympus knew it. He had been certain that the goddess would act to prevent the invocation, especially when he used the caricature of the vain Huntress in such a blatantly disrespectful manner. And in acting against him, the godlings would have betrayed themselves as immortals to the modern world. What an intoxicating spectacle that would have been! Of course Zeus' anger would also have been great, but after the thunderclouds had cleared from Olympus, Bacchus could have slid through the discarded portal, alone once again in his magnificent Las Vegas to reign with no restrictions to bind his desires and no rules to follow.

But neither of the twins had interrupted the invocation, and the mortal had actually bound Artemis to fulfill her heart's desire. Apollo had begun wooing her! Bacchus had watched the two of them fawn over one another the rest of the evening. He was even fairly sure that the God of Light hadn't been using any of his immortal powers to seduce the woman.

Anger mushroomed within Bacchus. Apollo didn't need to use his immortal powers to seduce with magic. He had a muscular, golden body that held a masculine beauty far beyond mortal standards. What the God of Light had been gifted with wasn't fair; it had never been fair.

He'd coaxed the desert sky into sending a rainstorm to ruin the god's little tryst, but that hadn't worked. Then he'd nudged the unsuspecting mortal, causing her to catch her heel. The mortal should have fallen into traffic, and the golden god should have betrayed his presence to save her, but Apollo had managed to foil the accident Bacchus had orchestrated without the mortals of Las Vegas realizing there was a powerful immortal in their midst. It was insufferable.

He would not tolerate another god usurping his place.

Then Bacchus remembered the passionate kiss Apollo and the mortal had shared, and the way the God of Light had carried her through the rain as if he were her savior. She was what was keeping the god's interest focused on Las Vegas. Who could guess how long Apollo would enjoy toying with her? And what if, after Apollo tired of this particular mortal, he found he had developed a taste for modern women? Bacchus certainly had. He threw back the shot of potent liquor. No. That would never do. He would not tolerate Apollo's seduction of his mortals.

But how to rid himself of the God of Light? It would be difficult. He obviously wasn't going to betray himself as a god and bring down Zeus' wrath, and neither he nor his twin sister seemed to be in any rush to tell Zeus about the invocation rite he'd worked. Unfortunately, it was apparent that, after Apollo had begun the seduction of the mortal woman, he was, indeed, thoroughly enjoying himself. Bacchus ground his teeth together. Well, he had himself to blame for that, so it was up to him to discover a way to dampen Apollo's enjoyment of Las Vegas.

Bacchus wanted to shriek in rage. How could Apollo not enjoy Las Vegas? It was a playground fit for the gods, and Apollo had the power to command its dormant magic alive, as did Bacchus. Ha! Scorn twisted the god's face into a sneer. He would like to see Apollo survive in Vegas without his supernatural powers. He would be a child lost in a dark forest. Apollo thought himself so superior to Bacchus, but he didn't know the modern mortal world—he didn't have his reserves of money or his luxurious suite of rooms and vast knowledge of how to manipulate mortals to his will.

Suddenly, Bacchus sat up straighter in the seat that was far too narrow for his bulk. That was it! If he could contrive a way for Apollo to miss the closing of the portal tomorrow evening, the great God of Light would be trapped in the mortal world for the span of five days, *without* his formidable powers. He would be weak . . . helpless . . . miserable. And when the portal reopened, he would be only too happy to depart and never return. Then it was only a matter of time before the God of Light's dislike for Las Vegas would be mirrored in the rest of the snobbish Olympians.

He would do it. Apollo would be trapped in Las Vegas without his powers. Bacchus' smile was filled with awful glee.

CHAPTER 13

"*The garments are certainly odd, my Lord, but we still find* your form pleasing within them," the yellow-haired nymph said in her seductive, musical voice. The cluster of nymphs that had gathered around Apollo after he had emerged from his dressing room cooed their agreement.

Apollo studied his reflection in the large, ornately framed mirror. Last night he had been so distracted when he left Pamela that he had forgotten to retrieve his clothing from the Armani store, but this morning his rendezvous with Pamela had been the first thing on his waking mind, and with thoughts of her came problems like what should he wear and where should they go? His modern clothing had been ruined by the rain. He wondered as he had inspected the rumpled shirt how modern men kept up with the constant demand for new clothing. At least that explained the proliferation of shops hawking all types of garments. It must be time-consuming to be properly dressed in the Kingdom of Las Vegas. But Apollo was a god. He didn't desire to waste his time in the endless acquisition of clothing, so he had done what many of the immortals did; he'd sent nymphs to run his errands for him. The god brushed a small piece of lint from the butter-colored shirt, which was made in same style as the one he had ruined. It had almost imperceptible lines of light blue woven cunningly through it. The slacks were fashioned of well-made linen, a shade darker than the shirt. It was always wise to call upon the aid of nymphs when beauty and colors were

involved. The subtle shades they had chosen were like the
first soft rays of the sun mixing with the blushing blue of
the morning sky.

"You made an excellent choice." Apollo smiled his approval at the nymphs, who giggled and fluttered at his
praise.

The boldest of the group, a lovely auburn-haired dryad
with whom Apollo thought he remembered having a passionate fling several centuries before, approached him.
She shook her waist-length hair back, so that the sheer-
ness of her almost nonexistent gown was openly displayed
to him. Her nipples had been darkened, and as his eyes
were naturally drawn to them, they puckered enticingly in
an automatic response.

"Why not stay with us, God of Light?" she purred, running knowing hands over her body. "We can entertain you
much better than any mortal woman."

"Yes," said another nymph who moved closer, "and you
will not need to wear *any* garments for the entertainment
we provide."

The other nymphs laughed seductively and began a little impromptu dance around their favorite god. They
smiled clear invitations to him and beguiled him with their
blatantly sexual beauty.

He watched them, amused and flattered by their show
of affection. He had long been popular with the little semideities. They were like beautiful, erotic flowers, easily
plucked, their sweetness easily enjoyed. But this time he
was not tempted to taste their charms. If they were flowers,
Pamela was the Earth—sensuous and lush. What he desired foremost was to bury himself within her richness.

"Perhaps another time, my beauties," he told them.

"Begone!" A sharp voice that was the feminine version
of his own shot from the doorway. "The God of Light will
be otherwise occupied tonight."

The nymphs flitted from the room, casting nervous
glances at Artemis.

"There was no need to offend them," Apollo said,
pulling his fingers through his hair.

"Let's just say I am a little distracted right now, and I

have more things on my mind than the honey-sweet feelings of nymphs. For instance, right now I feel shackled to a mortal woman with chains that Prometheus would find heavy to bear. "

Apollo laughed. "It can not be as bad as all that."

His sister's face remained tense and serious. "I feel the weight of her need and desire. Both are great."

Her words stilled Apollo's laughter. "Has something happened to her? Is she well?"

"The silly mortal is perfectly fine. She's just filled with lust and need and desire and anticipation. It's overwhelming."

"Pamela isn't silly," Apollo said after the drowning sense of relief rushed through him. She was safe. There was nothing wrong with her . . . nothing except a fierce desire for him.

"I hope that the ridiculous grin on your face is because you will be taking the mortal to bed tonight—and ridding me of the burden of her invocation."

"That is my intention," Apollo said. He didn't bother to stop grinning. By all that was sacred, he was happy!

"I am exceedingly glad to hear it." She gave him a disgruntled look.

Apollo linked his arm with hers as they walked toward the Great Hall of Olympus and the portal to the modern world. "Have I thanked you for making me visit the Kingdom of Las Vegas with you?"

"I certainly never intended for all of this to happen." But she had to return her brother's smile. "Although I did sense that you needed a diversion."

Apollo was silent until they faced the portal. Then he looked at her with eyes that held an expression that Artemis couldn't quite identify.

"I believe you have provided me with much more than a diversion, Sister."

Hiding the unease his continued odd behavior made her feel, she said, "Just be certain that I'm unshackled. Soon."

"Not to worry, Sister," he said, voice and body fading as he stepped through the portal.

Artemis gazed after him, her smooth forehead wrinkled

in consternation. She sighed in disgust. She was going to have to check up on him. His head was definitely in the clouds. He needed a push to make sure what must be done was actually done. She shook her head and glared at the portal. Sometimes she simply did not understand her brother.

Pamela hadn't seen him yet, so he purposefully stayed in the shadow of the large column so that his eyes could devour her. She was sitting at the same table she'd been seated at the night before. She sipped from a crystal goblet of wine. She looked magnificent. Her dress was red, a rich, brilliant shade that complemented her dark hair and fair skin. Its design was simple and elegant. The sleeveless length of soft fabric hugged her body like a second skin, and it left a long, seductive length of leg exposed.

He smiled and shook his head. She had on those shoes again. Not the same pair as last night, of course. The ones she'd chosen to perch precariously on tonight were golden sandals melded to daggers. He could hardly wait to see what walking in them would do to her legs and her shapely buttocks. He felt his loins begin to become tight and heavy as he watched her. He wanted to take her right then—to sweep her away from the crowd and up to her room where he could show her what it is to be loved by a god. He even took half a step towards her before he stopped himself short.

No. He didn't want just to ravish her. He wanted more, and in order for him to have more, she had to know him, the real him. Whether she had been intoxicated by the invocation ritual or not, if all that was between them was sex, his relationship with Pamela would go the way of all of his other lovers. They would part when their bodies were sated.

Apollo thought about Hades and Lina and the happiness they had found together. He wanted his own happiness, and he would never find it if lust was his only focus. He stepped out of the concealing shadows, moving towards his future lover with strong, purposeful strides.

He knew the instant she saw him. Her eyes widened, and her luscious mouth curved up in a sweet smile of welcome. Apollo's heart thudded. What was it she made him feel beyond the white-hot lust and the yearning? Nerves? This petite modern mortal had to ability to make the God of Light nervous.

As he got closer to her, Pamela felt tension and excitement course through her. She was seriously glad she'd bought the new Chanel dress, and at that moment she didn't even care that it hadn't been on sale. At least she was sure she looked good. Now all she had to worry about was opening her mouth and babbling like a moron.

His eyes were more beautiful than she'd remembered; they were Paul Newman blue times five. And he was tall. So. Damn. Deliciously. Tall.

"Good evening, sweet Pamela," Apollo took her hand and raised it to his lips. He made sure his lips lingered against her skin for just a moment longer than necessary, but not long enough to make her feel uncomfortable, and was pleased by the response that flushed her cheeks. He was inexperienced with falling in love—but the God of Light was definitely not inexperienced with making love. "You look as if someone should paint a picture of you, or write a poem in honor of your unique comeliness."

"Thank you, I think," she said, trying to regain her equilibrium. "If being called uniquely comely is a compliment."

"It is indeed." He was still holding her hand.

"Then thank you for sure."

"You are most welcome." Reluctantly he released her hand and sat beside her. "You were never far from my thoughts today, Pamela." His gaze slid from her lovely face down her body to the long legs she had crossed and cocked to the side so that their sleek length was clearly visible. "Your ankle must be fully recovered if you chose to balance on blades again tonight."

She smiled and wiggled her foot. "It feels perfect. And these are not blades. These are this season's new Pradas, which cost me a fortune, but I fell in love them, so I had no other choice but to take them home with me."

"Fortunate shoes," he said in a voice turned husky. Apollo reached down and caught her ankle in one hand, running a thumb across her skin while he felt for the bones and tendons he had healed just the night before, double-checking that all was well with her. But he was finding it difficult to focus on healing. Her ankle and foot looked incredibly sexy in the little slip of a shoe—and her toes had been painted a bright red to match her dress. There was something indescribably sexy about those almost naked feet and those scarlet-colored toes.

Pamela felt his touch travel from her ankle through her thighs to coil in the pit of her stomach like a long, intoxicating drink of expensive scotch. She was very sorry when he released her foot.

Apollo motioned for the servant to bring him a glass of wine before returning his attention to Pamela. "You already know what I did today—I thought of you. Tell me what you did here in Las Vegas while time passed slowly until we were to meet again."

Good, she thought, conversation was good. They needed to converse, because she needed time and mundane talk to get her raging hormones under control. Please, please, please don't let her babble like a boob.

"First, I did something I rarely do. I slept late."

He raised one quizzical, golden eyebrow.

"I'm definitely a morning person. I usually get up in time to drink a leisurely cup of coffee while I watch a beautiful Colorado sunrise."

"You like sunrises?"

She smiled, relaxing into the familiar subject of the conversation. "I adore them! Actually, sunrises are one of my absolute favorite things."

Her answer resonated within his soul. Suddenly he longed to bare himself to her, to tell her who he was and to share his world and his life with her. She loved sunrise. Didn't it stand to reason that she would love the God of Light? He actually opened his mouth to tell her his true name, but his rational mind caught up with his impulse. He didn't want her to automatically "love" him as a god. He wanted her to fall in love with Phoebus, the man inside the God. Still, he couldn't mask the intense desire that filled his voice when he spoke. "Sunrise is also very important to me. Perhaps someday soon you and I will experience the sun climbing the sky together."

Pamela blushed and didn't know what to say. She couldn't even stutter. Hell, this was definitely more than just being out of practice with dating and flirting in general. He made her feel like she couldn't catch her breath. She wanted . . . she wanted . . . Bloody buggering hell! She wanted so many things when he looked at her like that. But she'd wanted so many things when she'd first met Duane, too. He had seemed to hold the key to the rest of her life within his firm, capable hands. Reality had shown that the only thing he'd held within his hands had been emotional ropes with which he wanted to bind her to him—to choke the spirit from her and to make her into something she wasn't, his ideal of a perfect wife. She could still feel the rope burns from that stifling relationship.

So, slow and easy . . . she needed to slow down and take it easy with Phoebus. He seemed wonderful, but her intuition kept screaming that things were rarely as they seem. Having fun this weekend was one thing. Getting tangled in the ropes of another relationship was certainly another.

Within Pamela's expressive eyes Apollo read her struggle and then her subsequent withdrawal from him, and it pained him more then he would have imagined. But he had no intention of giving up so easily. His smile was warm and open.

"Good," he said as if he hadn't just issued an invitation that she had ignored. "It pleases me that we have the appreciation of sunrise in common, but you said you overslept, so you missed the rising of the sun this morning. What else did your day hold?"

Pamela met his eyes. They were so warm and so incredibly blue. They made her think of the summer sky over the Mediterranean Sea . . .

Hell! She was doing it again—falling into his good looks like an f-ing teenager.

"Pamela?"

"Oh, sorry." She took a sip of her wine. "My mind was wandering. Sometimes I lack focus. Not with my job," she amended hastily. "There I'm totally single-minded. Like this afternoon. I started sketching my version of that horrible fountain. I thought I'd been there maybe twenty minutes or so, but when I finally checked my watch and took a breath, two hours had passed." Pamela paused and squinted her eyes. "I just did it again, didn't I?"

"It?"

"Lost focus, shifted subjects." *Babbled,* she thought.

"Definitely."

"Sorry again, Phoebus."

Apollo smiled. He enjoyed her bright thoughts and the way expressions danced across her face, especially when she spoke about her work. She wasn't a vixen trying to entrap the God of Light, nor was she a maiden, dazzled by his immortal powers. Pamela was real. Her responses to him were honest and true—and that was more of an aphrodisiac than he could ever have imagined.

"I don't mind. I like to hear your mind flitting about."

"Well, that's"—she paused, watched him carefully for signs that he was being sarcastic or making fun of her— "unusual of you. Most men find it distracting."

"Really?" He shook his head. "I think I have already said that quite often men are fools."

"And I have already agreed with you on that point."

They smiled at each other. On impulse, she raised her glass to him.

"To a man who is *not* a fool."

"That is a toast I am pleased to join you in." He laughed and touched his glass to hers. "Now tell me about this sketch you created. Are you an artist, too? Or is it like understanding architecture—you must have a working ability of it to properly do your job?"

His question pleased her—it showed that he'd actually listened to what she'd said yesterday—as did the attentive way he waited for her to answer.

"I love to sketch, and I'm even passable with watercolors, but I'm definitely not good enough to be considered an

artist. But you're right. It is like the importance of understanding the rudiments of architecture in my job. It's also
important that I am competent enough artistically that I can
create mock-ups for carpenters or upholsters, or even
sculptors so that they can get a tangible grasp of what my
clients want."

Slowly, both of Apollo's brows raised, and his gaze
turned to the monstrous fountain in the courtyard before
them.

Pamela followed his gaze, breathed a long-suffering
sigh, and nodded. "Yes, you guessed it. This particular
client wants a reproduction of *that* in the courtyard of his
vacation home."

"Are you quite certain you heard him correctly?"
Apollo stared at the gushing monolith. His eyes kept being
drawn back to the atrocious copy of himself.

"More than quite. Actually, what I was doing today was
trying to come up with a more tasteful compromise, but he
insists that I keep Bacchus as the center statue." She shuddered. "I'm going to have to figure out some way to
change his mind. I did manage to get rid of the awful side
statues, though."

Apollo looked quickly back at her.

"You mean the statues of Caesar and Artemis and . . ."
His voice faltered on his own name.

"Apollo," Pamela offered. "That one with the big head
and the harp is supposed to be the Sun God."

Apollo was careful to keep his expression neutral. "Actually, Apollo is more accurately called the God of Light,
and the instrument he is holding is a lyre, not a harp."

"Huh," Pamela said, studying the statue. "I didn't know
there was a difference. That's right, you're a musician,
aren't you? All I know is that it glows neon green when the
horrid thing comes alive."

"Yes." He tried not to cringe. "So I've heard."

Eyes still focused on the statue, Pamela said, "I didn't
know Apollo was called the God of Light. I thought he was
the Sun God."

"That is what the Romans insisted upon calling him, but

to the Greeks he will forever be their God of Light, bringer of medicine, music, poetry, and truth."

"Truth?"

"Yes, truth was very important to Apollo. He was one of the few Olympians who found dissembling and subterfuge offensive."

"I had no idea. I thought all of the mythological gods were supposed to be impulsive and self-serving. I think I remember one of my English teachers describing them as playboys and womanizers."

Apollo cleared his throat and shifted in his chair uncomfortably. "The gods are . . . were certainly passionate, and passion can sometimes lead to impulsive, self-serving acts. Also, you must remember that in the Ancient World it was considered a privilege to be loved by a god, particularly the God of Light."

"Oh, so what you mean is just because Apollo told the truth, that doesn't mean that he knew how to be faithful."

Apollo frowned and wasn't sure what to say. He wanted to defend himself, but he couldn't. Pamela was right. He'd been truthful but never faithful. He had never before had any desire to be.

"So, is mythology one of your hobbies?"

"I think you would call it more of a passion than a hobby," Apollo said with a slight smile. "I do know enough about it to assure you that the God of Light's lyre did not glow green when he played it, and his head was not that big."

Pamela grinned. "I'm glad to hear it. I don't know how he could possibly have been a womanizer looking like that."

"Did you know that some ancient texts report that Apollo found love?" He spoke quickly, before common sense caught up with his voice. "And that afterwards he was entirely faithful to his lover."

"I had no idea. Who was she? Some fabulous goddess?"

"No, he found the mate of his soul within a mortal woman."

"A mortal? Huh. I guess that's why they call it mythology. I can't imagine a real woman who would be stupid enough to take a chance on loving a god."

Apollo felt his chest tighten. "But look at what she gained. She took the chance and won her soul mate."

Pamela's smile was slow and sweet. "You really are a romantic."

"Yes," he said more fiercely than he'd intended and had to stop and take a breath to settle his raging emotions. "I haven't always been. Actually, I have been much like Apollo, content to find love where it seemed convenient or enjoyable and to think nothing more of it. But I feel myself changing." He shrugged and purposefully lightened his tone. "Perhaps that's why I understand the tales told about the God of Light so well."

Pamela silently studied her wineglass. She didn't know what to say to him. She was definitely attracted to him, and what he was saying touched her heart. He seemed so open and honest. But she was afraid. Thinking of having a weekend fling made her nervous and giddy. Thinking of beginning a relationship terrified her.

She glanced up at his handsome face. He was watching her intently. She took a deep breath, but instead of mouthing some offhanded quip about romantic reformed playboys, she heard the truth slipping out.

"I'm divorced. I had a bad marriage. No, scratch that. I had an awful marriage. I haven't really even dated since then. You're being honest with me, so I need to be honest with you. Just thinking about the possibility of a new relationship scares me. I don't think I'm ready for anything more than . . ." She hesitated, not wanting to sound like a slut or a dolt.

"You must heal." Apollo spoke into her hesitation.

"Yes, exactly," she said, grateful that he had put words to what she was bumbling around trying to say.

"And you shall heal, sweet Pamela," he said.

"Thank you for understanding," she said, resting her hand on his. "I know it sounds crazy. I've only known you for a couple of days, but there's something about you that makes me feel like you honestly do understand what I mean."

"It's true, sweet Pamela. And you have no idea how rare it is to find that connection between two people." He had literally lived eons without it.

Pamela stroked her thumb slowly over his hand and fell into the blue of his spectacular eyes. "Oh, I think I might have some idea."

The knot that had been building within Apollo's chest suddenly loosened. It wasn't that she was unwilling to give herself to love, it was that she had been hurt. Terribly hurt. She needed to heal, and that was one thing that Apollo, God of Light, could do for her.

"I brought something for you tonight. I think now is the perfect time to gift you with it." Apollo reached into his pocket and pulled out the delicate gold chain. He held it up so that the light glinted off a small coin, mounted in a thin circle of gold, which dangled from it. On the face of the coin was stamped the strong profile of a Greek god.

"Oh, it's beautiful," Pamela breathed. The coin was gold but imperfectly formed, its shape more of a chipped-at circle than a regular coin, and she realized that its irregular shape marked it as being very old. "I can't accept it, though. It's way too expensive."

"I can assure you that it cost me nothing. I have had it a very long time. Please, it would give me great pleasure if you would wear it. After all, we were just discussing the god who is depicted on the coin."

"Really? It's Apollo?" Intrigued, Pamela leaned forward and cupped the piece of gold in her hands, studying the handsome profile.

"It's a better likeness than the fountain statue," Apollo said, smiling wryly.

"You know," she said, glancing from the coin to Phoebus, "it looks like you. I mean, not exactly like you. But the profile is similar."

"That is indeed a compliment." His smile widened. "At least it is a compliment as long as you don't say that I resemble yonder statue, too." He pointed his chin at the big-headed fountain Apollo.

"No." Pamela laughed. "You look nothing like that statue."

He chuckled, appreciating the irony of the situation. "If you wear the coin you could think of Apollo as your own personal god," he coaxed. "Apollo could be your talisman. Perhaps the God of Light will help you to solve the problems you're having with your client's unusual request."

Pamela looked back and forth from the coin to Phoebus, ready to tell him no thank you. But she hesitated. What was so inherently wrong about accepting a gift from a handsome man? She liked him; he liked her. Okay, she didn't believe for an instant that it hadn't cost him anything, but he was a doctor. It wasn't like he couldn't afford it. And it was an interesting coincidence that they had just been talking about Apollo, the god who had supposedly fallen in love with a mortal woman. It was also silly and romantic and out of character for her to . . .

"Thank you, Phoebus. I accept it."

Before she could change her mind, he stood and moved behind her so that he could fasten it around her long, slender neck. But first he held it in the palm of his hand and concentrated his vast, immortal powers on the little piece of gold.

"May it bring you everything Apollo represents: light and truth, music and poetry, and, most of all, healing." Then placed the gold chain around her neck.

"That was a beautiful thing to say," she looked up at him, touching the coin. She could almost swear that it felt warm against her body.

Apollo smiled and bent so that he could brush his lips against hers. He hadn't meant for the kiss to be anything more than a quick gesture of affection, but her mouth opened beneath his, and one of her hands slid up to press against his chest. Automatically, he deepened the kiss. Her mouth was sweet and slick. He wanted to taste more of her, all of her. He wanted . . .

"Ur, uh, excuse me."

The waiter's voice broke through the red haze of lust that had enveloped Apollo. The god snarled dangerously at the hapless servant, who was quick to step back and apologize.

"Sorry, sir. It just gets kinda crowded in here, and I was trying to move around your table."

"Find another pathway," Apollo growled.

The servant nodded and hastily retreated. When Apollo turned back to Pamela, her face was blazing, and her hands were covering her cheeks.

"I can't believe it. I'm making out in public, and I'm a sober adult."

"Then let us go somewhere more private," he said, stroking the hand that covered one of her flaming cheeks.

Pamela opened her mouth, looked at him, sputtered something incomprehensible, closed her mouth, and looked at her watch.

"Oh, bloody buggering hell!" she gasped.

"What is it?"

"It's almost nine," Pamela grabbed her little gold purse and leapt up from the table. "Oh, God . . . I've forgotten. Which way is it to the front of Caesars Palace?"

Apollo pointed in the correct direction, wondering what was wrong with her. She started to hurry off, then she stopped, drew a long breath, and came back to where he was still standing. She ran her hand through her short hair as she spoke.

"I'm sorry. It's just so unlike me to kiss you like that, right there in front of everyone." She blushed again as she remembered how it had felt to meet his tongue and return his passion. "That freaked me out. Then I suddenly remembered that I managed to get tickets for us to a show that has been selling out, and that show starts in"—she glanced at her watch again—"fifteen minutes. So that's why I rushed off like an idiot. Accidentally without you." *And without any sense,* she added silently to herself.

"A show?" he asked.

"Yes, it's called *Zumanity.* It's . . . it's supposed to be erotic but tasteful." Her eyes skittered away from his. "It's by the same people who do Cirque du Soleil."

When she finally met his eyes again, they were smiling.

"An erotic circus of the sun? Fascinating." He took her hand and linked it through his arm. "We had better hurry."

CHAPTER 14

*Apollo couldn't believe that the Zumanity players were mor-*tal. The women moved with the grace and seduction of nymphs. The men were all beautiful of body and face. And the music! The music was ethereal. It was the perfect back-drop to the parade of sensuality performed on and above the stage. He and Pamela had been quietly ushered to their intimate seating on the balcony in a lushly upholstered couch that was fashioned like a chaise lounge. The per-formance had already begun. In the middle of the round stage there was an enormous glass, made to look like a wine goblet filled with water. Within the glass were two nubile young women, who wore very little except nude-colored loincloths. In time to the pulsing tempo of the se-ductive music the girls swam a dance of innocent seduction, personifying the awakening of uniquely femi-nine passion and desire. Though the golden god was much more interested in the woman who sat close to his side, his body stirred in appreciation. He glanced sideways at Pamela, gauging her reaction. She was watching with eyes that were large and round. When the scene was over, she applauded enthusiastically. Then she looked away from the stage and caught Apollo watching her. Her already flushed cheeks blushed even pinker.

"Did you find the young women pleasing?" he whis-pered as the stage temporarily darkened.

"I did. I mean, I'm definitely not a lesbian, but they were so beautiful." Her voice was breathy, and her laugh was a sensual purr. She'd have to remember to tell V that she finally understood her attraction to women.

Apollo leaned into her, drawn by her earthy response to the show. "There is nothing wrong with appreciating the beauty of the female body. You would have to be made of stone not to be moved by them."

She had been about to whisper back that it was definite that she wasn't made of stone when the spotlights illuminated the stage again and the appreciative audience fell silent. This time an exquisitely muscled man with black velvet skin appeared on the stage through a trapdoor in the floor. He, too, had almost nothing on. He moved in time with the music as he was joined by a woman who was as blond as he was dark. She was covered in sheer layers of a filmy dress, and as the two met in the center of the stage and began an erotic version of the lover's scene from the ballet *Romeo and Juliet*, he slowly unwound piece after piece of her covering, until they both wore only the briefest of G-strings.

They moved with a fluid, sensual grace and a passion for each other that Pamela could not believe was feigned. The scene ended, and this time Pamela readily met Phoebus' gaze.

"They must really be in love. No one can act that well. I swear I could feel the sexual tension between them up here."

"Now who's the romantic?" he said, putting his arm around her and pulling her close to him.

For the rest of the performance, that's where she stayed, tucked against Phoebus' body. About midway through the show, her hand found his thigh. It rested there, against the soft fabric of his slacks, through which she could feel the heat and hardness of his leg. His fingers traced a lazy pattern over the bare skin of her arm, caressing the smooth indention inside her elbow and causing gooseflesh to rise up and down her body.

Zumanity was, indeed, an adventure in eroticism. It titillated and teased, seduced and sensitized. When Phoebus' hand traced its way up her arm to slowly caress her neck, she had to bite her lip to keep from moaning aloud.

A tall, stunning redhead, who reminded Pamela very much of Nicole Kidman, left the stage after performing an incredibly sexy version of autoerotic masturbation, and before the audience's applause had died, the lights flashed on a thick length of red silk that dropped from the darkened ceiling of the theater as if an inattentive giantess had haphazardly thrown her scarf from a bedroom window. It unrolled to expose a woman whose waist-length hair shined golden in the spotlight. Her arms remained cunningly twisted in the scarf so that only the tips of her bare, gracefully pointed toes touched the stage. Beneath her, the end of the scarf pooled like wine on the slick onyx stage. Her beauty was blinding, and as the audience caught sight of her, the theater let out a collective murmur of awe. At first it seemed that she was nude except for body glitter, but as the lights flashed and changed, Pamela could tell she was really wearing a sheer body leotard, nude-colored and covered with brilliant, diamondlike sparkles. The music began, and the scarf was pulled up, and along with it up went the glistening golden woman. She spun and twisted in a sensual dance, all the while dangling over the stage. It was breathtaking.

"She's a goddess," Pamela whispered to Phoebus.

"She is indeed," he murmured, glad that Pamela was so transfixed by the performance that she hadn't glanced up to register the shock on his face. He sat very still, trying to school his expression into a mask of polite appreciation for the show his sister was putting on.

And he'd known it! The entire performance had felt snared in an Olympian web of eroticism. Now he understood clearly why—the modern mortals were being honored by the presence of the Huntress Goddess herself. Though she usually preferred her forest and her freedom, the rumor that had been proliferated by her independent ways was false. Artemis was no virgin goddess. She was, whenever she chose to be, an exquisite temptress. What she was up to tonight was obvious. She wanted to be certain that he fulfilled the invocation, so with her immortal kiss of power, she had generously blessed the mortal actors—their allure had been heightened, as had the sexual tension in the audience. He had to admit, it was clever of her—annoying, but clever.

Suddenly, the audience gasped once more as a small, muscular shape ran onto the stage. Apollo's eyes widened in surprise. A satyr! Though his cloven hooves were camouflaged by boots and the magic of the goddess, and the fur that covered his legs not visible beneath the silken pants he wore, his identity was obvious to Apollo. The top of the creature's blond head came no higher than Artemis' waist, but his bare chest and arms were so powerfully muscled that as he raised his arms to beckon the goddess to him, it appeared that he was one of the Titans. The satyr wound his arms in the end of the scarlet scarf, and he, too, was lifted into the air over the stage—and there commenced an erotic chase, which took place not just over the stage, but the two swung out and over the raptly watching audience, where the fey creature enticed and coaxed, stroked and seduced, until finally the goddess deigned to be "captured," and the two of them were gently lowered to the stage. Shocked, Apollo watched his sister allow the woodland creature to wrap her within his arms, and the Huntress melted into the satyr's kiss in a public display of sexuality he knew she would never allow had they been in Olympus. The two exquisite immortals exited, arms still around each other. The audience was totally silent. All eyes were still staring at the spot on the stage where the goddess had last been seen. Apollo was the first to break his sister's seductive spell, and his applause was soon joined by riotous shouts and cheers.

The house lights came up, but before the audience could begin to get to their feet, the cast of actors, led by Artemis herself, came back onstage. The Huntress Goddess addressed the audience.

"We greet you, lovers and friends, and hope that you have enjoyed our little offering to the shrine of love." Her voice was like honey, and it drew the mortals close in a sweet trail of words. "Before you depart, I would like to meet some of you—if you would be so kind."

Clarion bells rang a warning in Apollo's mind, but ex-

citement soughed through the listening crowd like wind
through a forest of trees.

The goddess smiled beatifically, as if she addressed
crowds of modern mortals every day. Then she began
speaking to them, asking them their names, choosing
blushing young married couples and newlyweds, sprin-
kling the magic of her seductive voice throughout the theater. Just once, Artemis glanced up at the balcony where
Apollo sat with Pamela close to his side. She met her
brother's eyes only briefly, but it was long enough for
Apollo to clearly see amusement flash within their cool
blue depths. Almost imperceptively, she made a motion
with her hand, and Apollo felt the warm shower of her
magic rain on him. It tingled over his skin, causing his
body to feel flushed and heavy. Pamela's reaction was
much more elemental. Almost unconsciously, her hand
gripped Apollo's thigh. She leaned into his body and
looked up into his eyes. Her breathing deepened, and her
lips parted with a moan that was an open invitation.

Apollo cursed silently under his breath, tightened his
arm around Pamela, and forced his attention back to the
stage. He couldn't kiss her. Under the spell of his sister's
immoral magic, neither of them would be able to stop
there. *It will pass,* he reminded himself, and even as the
thought came to him, he felt the grip of Artemis' meddling
magic loosen. He glared down at his sister, who was neatly
ignoring him. Within the circle of his arm he felt Pamela
shiver and knew that the glittering spell had begun blow-
ing from her skin, too, and he breathed easier. He was not
using his powers to seduce Pamela—he wanted her response to him to be honest. Artemis' foolery was no more
welcome than his own magic. Neither brought about love,
only lust—a temporary desire, which was too easily sated.
He wanted more.

"Oh, look," Pamela said, pointing down at the stage and
trying to get her breathing to return to normal. She must be
hornier than she thought because this show was driving her
completely crazy. Just minutes before if Phoebus had so
much as smiled at her, she would have straddled him right
there. V had obviously been right; going without sex for

too long made a girl lose her mind. "That couple just said that they're here for their fiftieth wedding anniversary."

"Fifty years!" the lovely Artemis repeated, and the crowd clapped politely. One of the actors rushed over to the goddess and whispered in her ear. Artemis smiled, nodded and addressed the old couple again. "Would you come up on stage and close our little performance with a special dance for just the two of you?"

Apollo leaned forward to get a better view as an elderly couple rose slowly to their feet, and with a smattering of encouraging applause, they walked up the stairs to the stage. The lights dimmed, and a soft waltz began to play. At first the couple moved awkwardly together, before eventually falling into a rhythm that was fluid and familiar. The silver-haired man turned his wife, catching the end of her long, cloaklike dress, and the audience let out their breath in surprise as she twirled, and her dress unwound until she was standing onstage in only a dancer's body leotard and a flowing, wraparound skirt. She curtsied to the theater like a lovely ballerina, and then she and her husband resumed their waltz. This time they moved with the grace of professional dancers. Effortlessly, the old man lifted her still-vibrant body to his shoulder, then turned, dipped, and with a flourish she spun down into his arms once more. The dance ended as they kissed in the middle of the stage.

"And thus we celebrate love. At any age—in any way—it is truly magical and carries with it a touch of immortality. Go with my blessing tonight, lovers, and take pleasure where you will. Love, laugh and be merry!" the goddess proclaimed, and in a blaze of shooting sparks, the entire company disappeared through a trapdoor in the floor of the stage.

The applause continued for a long time, but when none of the actors returned for an encore, the theater began to empty. The audience was almost exclusively made up of couples, and as they left there were many linked hands, intimate conversations and lingering touches.

When the other couples sitting around them in the balcony began to file out, Pamela hesitated. She and Phoebus were standing beside their love seat, and for a moment the two of them were completely alone, as if they had discovered a pocket of intimacy within the darkening theater. Pamela thought it was a little like the night before when they'd kissed in the rain. She looked up at him, overwhelmed by the mixture of lust and longing that was coursing through her body in time with the beating of her heart. And in that moment she knew she would make love to him. She was tired of settling for contentment rather than joy. Pamela spoke in a sudden burst, as if the words had to break through a wall of inhibitions and caution.

"You make me feel like we're in a world alone, all to ourselves. Sometimes when I look at you I think second chances are possible."

"Believe that," he said fiercely. "And believe that I would never do anything to hurt you. Think of me as you do your talisman, Apollo. I, too, want you to heal and be whole so that you can love and trust again."

He touched the coin she wore around her neck, and she imagined that she could feel the healing warmth of that touch all the way through the metal and into her heart. Tired of hesitation and second thoughts, she slid her hands up his chest and pressed herself close to him.

"Would you do something for me, Phoebus?"

"Anything within my power," he said solemnly.

"Would you take me back to my room and make love to me?" she asked breathlessly.

"It would be my great honor, sweet Pamela," he said, and bent to kiss her upturned lips.

CHAPTER 15

In *a warm mist of anticipation, they walked back to Pamela's* suite. They spoke little but touched each other constantly. Apollo was already becoming familiar with the curves and lines of her body, and he stopped often to pull her into a shadow and kiss her with a tenderness that did nothing to mask his growing desire. He wanted her with an intensity that was a white fire building within him, and to his eternal delight, Pamela was responding with matching passion. She felt so right pressed against him, as if she had always been there. As they walked, he thought about the old couple who had closed the theatrical production. Obviously, they, too, had been actors, planted amidst the crowd, but that didn't mean that they hadn't truly been lovers. Apollo remembered the way the old man's eyes had radiated love and pride as he led his lifelong bride in their special waltz. Apollo knew he would never experience growing old by Pamela's side, but he wanted her with him—and he wanted it with an intensity that filled him with purpose. They would be together, he promised himself.

Pamela slid the key card into the door, and with a green light and a click, she entered the suite ahead of him. Her hesitation was gone. She knew what she wanted. She wanted Phoebus. Forget past mistakes. Never mind about what may or may not happen in the future. Something had happened to her tonight while she was watching *Zumanity*'s magical sexuality. She realized that she had been

wrong. Duane hadn't killed romance or fun or even sex for
her. He had just caused that part of her to hibernate. And
now it that it had awakened, she was ravenous.

When Apollo closed the door, she turned and stepped
into his arms. He kissed her, wanting to take his time to
taste her thoroughly now that they were finally alone, but
when she moaned into his mouth he bent and cupped her
well-rounded buttocks and lifted her, so that the hot core of
her pressed firmly against his arousal. She moved restlessly against him and with a gasp he broke the kiss, struggling for control.

"I'm losing my mind with desire for you," he moaned
as her tongue and lips made a hot trail down the side of his
neck.

"Put me down, and I'll take off these clothes." Her
warm breath whispered against his skin.

He almost dropped her, and her laughter was deep and
throaty. Pamela stepped teasingly away from him, and then
began to walk backwards towards the bed, while she used
one hand to reach behind her and unzip her little red dress.
She shrugged her shoulder. It slid free, and she stepped
delicately out of the scarlet heap it made around her heels.
Apollo's eyes drank in her body. She was wearing something black and lacy that did next to nothing to cover her
breasts, but it lifted them and pointed them enticingly at
him, and a matching swatch of lace that barely hid the dark
triangle between her legs. The golden dagger-heeled sandals did something incredibly sexy to her long, bare legs.
As she reached behind her again to unlatch the lingerie, he
closed the distance between them.

He kissed her again and against his mouth she said, "I
want to feel you naked against me."

Breathing hard, he broke the kiss long enough to
roughly yank the shirt over his head. While he fumbled
with the unfamiliar fastening of his pants, Pamela slid back
on the bed, watching him with sparkling eyes. And she still
had on those incredibly sexy shoes.

Finally, he managed to make himself naked, but before
he could join her on the bed, she half sat up and halted him
with her raised hand.

"Wait. Just stand there, and let me look at you." Her gaze traveled down from his eyes that had darkened to sapphire over the rest of his body. Her tongue flicked over her lips before she spoke again. "Phoebus, you are the most beautiful man I have ever seen. God! Look at your skin. It covers your muscles like liquid gold." She shook her head and gave a small, breathless laugh. "Artists should paint you. Sculptors should sculpt you. How can you be real?"

He sat on the bed beside her. "I am real, and what is happening between us is real. How I look is nothing unusual or extraordinary to me." He paused, considering. He had made love to countless women, goddess and mortal alike. Always before he had used the magic of his immortal power to heighten his own pleasure during the act of lovemaking. This time was different. Pamela was different. He hadn't wanted to use his powers to seduce or entrap her, but he wanted very much for her to feel the depth of his passion. He wanted her to know him in a way no other woman had. He touched her as he continued speaking. "What is new and wonderful to me is what is happening within, and the only way I know of sharing that feeling with you is to love you." Gently, he caressed her long neck and let his fingers move up and through the short locks of hair. As he touched her, he allowed some of his immortal power to escape from his hand and to lick through her body. She shivered under his touch. "Let me love you, sweet Pamela. Let me make this real for you."

"Yes." She breathed the word into his mouth.

His hands moved over her body as their lips met again. Her skin hummed under his touch. Pamela had never before felt so sensitized. It was like she had become a living conduit for all of the hot, intense, mind-blowingly erotic sensations she had been missing for years.

His hands moved down her leg, until they came to her foot. His eyes flashed up at her, and then kissed the ankle she had injured the night before.

"I wanted to do that then, you know," his voice was rough with desire.

"You should have," she panted. "I wanted you to."

Phoebus undid the little gold buckle that held the small strap of leather around her ankle, and slid the shoe off. Then he kissed the delicate arch of her foot. Electricity danced up her leg to settle deep in her moist center.

"I'm glad you like it," he said, moving to her other foot. "Tonight I want you to believe that you are a goddess being loved by a god."

She moaned and bit her lip as his mouth moved from the arch of her foot to her calf. He had to be a musician, she thought, when he stroked the inside of her thigh and his lips found the hollow behind her knee. Only a musician could have hands that talented. His touch felt hot, and she melted under his caresses. As his lips followed the path his hands traced up the inside of her thigh, she arched to meet him, gasping in pleasure when his hot tongue delved into her. Her orgasm was so quick and explosive that her entire body jerked in response. Somewhere in the violet haze of passion she acknowledged that it had never happened like that before—never so fast or so intense. Feeling dizzy, she reached out for him, and Phoebus gathered her to him.

"Yes, yes, I'm here, my sweet Pamela," he murmured.

She could feel his heart pounding against her breast. The erratic pace of his pulse matched her own. She opened her mouth and his tongue met hers. She tasted her sex on him—salty and sweet at the same time. Pamela deepened the kiss, lifting herself so that her wet heat was pressed against the hard length of his erection. She reached between them to guide him to her. But she didn't sheath him within her—not yet. Instead she held him there, rubbing his engorged tip against her velvet folds while she stroked him with her hand.

Until she began stroking him, Apollo had been in complete control. He had reveled in the uninhibited way Pamela responded to him, and he had carefully used his immortal power to heighten her sensitivity. He made love to her with his body and his magic. When she found release, he drank in the honey of her ecstasy. But she had a magic of her own, that of a woman's allure intensified by the desire of a god's heart and soul.

"I can not wait any longer." His voice was raw with lust.

"Phoebus . . ." She breathed his name as she finally guided him inside her and then rose to meet his thrusts so that he buried his entire length within her over and over and over.

Apollo lifted himself so that he could look into her eyes. *Heal,* the God of Light's soul spoke to hers. *Believe that you can love again.*

His eyes captured her. She couldn't look away from him. She was consumed by his touch and his scent and the hard heat of him. She responded to him on a level that was deeper than physical. He was touching her, not just with his body, but with his mind, his heart and maybe even his soul. When his orgasm began, he took her with him. She closed her eyes against the intensity of her pleasure, and it seemed that a flash of pure yellow light burst against her closed lids as she heard Phoebus cry her name aloud.

Artemis froze, midsip of the delightful martini she was sharing with the satyr who had served her so well earlier that evening. Like the vanquished Gordian knot, she felt the ties that bound her suddenly slice away. Apollo had done it. The ritual was completed. The goddess smiled and drew a deep breath, pleased that she was unhampered by the clinging emotions of a . . .

"No." Artemis ground the word through clenched teeth. "This can not be."

"Is anything amiss, my Lady?" The satyr's eyes were wide with concern.

"Be still!" Artemis commanded.

The woodland creature looked wounded but instantly obeyed his goddess. Artemis narrowed her eyes and concentrated. There! She hadn't imagined it. The overwhelming pressure that bound her to the mortal woman had lifted, but in its place was a single thread, thin and almost insubstantial. What was this? What had happened? Apollo must have made love to the mortal. That should have fulfilled the invocation. The mortal had asked to have romance in her life. How could being made love to by the God of Light *not* satisfy the woman's ideal of romance? Especially after she had been primed for him by the magic Artemis had used during the wonderfully erotic theater presentation. Her immortal eavesdropping on Pamela's conversation with the concierge had been fruitful; joining the erotic show herself was an inspired idea. The Huntress's full lips tilted up. She was discovering that there were things about the modern world that she enjoyed. She'd had no idea how much fun it would be to take a little sojourn as an adored star of the theater. She'd have to do so again very soon . . .

Artemis cringed as the thread that still bound her to the mortal woman tugged at her. It was just a slight pressure, like a very small burr that had worked its way into her slipper. At first it was only a minor annoyance, but left alone it could cause much irritation.

The goddess blew out a frustrated breath. There was nothing she could do about it right now. She couldn't very well chase down her brother and burst in on his lovemaking, demanding to know why his performance hadn't been romantic enough. That certainly wouldn't help. She twirled the thin, cold stem of her martini glass between her fingers. It was still early. Perhaps by morning Apollo would have managed to do whatever it was that the ridiculous mortal woman required to satisfy her romantic desires. Until then it was pointless to brood about it. She needed a diversion.

She glanced slyly at the young satyr who still sat quietly beside her. He really was a handsome beast.

"Darling," she purred, and his ears literally perked in her direction. "Remember how exciting it was when you pursued me through the air earlier tonight?"

"Of course, Goddess," his voice was eager. "An eternity can pass, and I will still remember."

"I'm not ready as yet to return to Olympus. Pay for our drinks, and then let us go back to that lovely theater. You shall practice your aerial pursuit, and this time perhaps you will be more fully rewarded when you finally capture me."

She ran one finger down his muscular arm and his fawn-like eyes dilated in response.

"I live to serve your needs, Goddess," he said.

"That is exactly what I am counting on," Artemis murmured to herself as the satyr rushed off to pay the servant.

CHAPTER 16

Oh, bloody buggering hell. She'd forgotten to use a condom. And not just for the first time. For the second, as well as the third. She rolled her eyes. What. A. Moron. How could she have forgotten? Especially after she'd swallowed down the knot of embarrassment that had threatened to choke her and bought a brand new box of Trojans from the hotel gift shop after her pedicure. And thank God she'd gotten that pedicure. Phoebus had kissed and caressed and even sucked her toes. Just thinking about it made her feel all flushed and weak-kneed, again.

Focus! Her internal monitor chastised her. Not using condoms had nothing to do with toe-sucking. Or did it?

A movement to her right drew her eyes. Pamela turned her head and looked at Phoebus. He was so beautiful. When she wasn't looking at him, she could think of him as just an ordinarily nice-looking man. And then she'd see him and realize that there was nothing ordinary about him. Nothing at all.

Her body still glowed from his touch. She should be sore and tired and probably battling a raging urinary tract infection from too much sex. Instead she felt marvelous. Lazy and lethargic and very, very well-satisfied.

But she'd still forgotten to use a condom.

"I can feel you frowning," he said without opening his eyes.

"That's impossible," she said, forcing a smile on her face. "And anyway, I'm not frowning.

Still without opening his eyes Phoebus said, "Not any-more you aren't." He opened his eyes then and turned his golden head so that he could look directly at her. His smile was tender. "Good morning, my sweet Pamela."

"I forgot to use a condom last night." She blushed. "And this morning."

His brow wrinkled. "Condom?" He tried out the unfamiliar word.

"Yeah," she said, her face getting hotter by the second. She grabbed the sheet, which had come completely untucked, thanks to their aerobics last night, wound it around her naked body, and retreated to the bathroom. Over her shoulder she said, "You know—condom, prophylactic, rubber. I'm not on the pill or anything. You're the doctor. I shouldn't have to tell you how easy it would be for me to get pregnant."

A condom was something that kept a mortal woman from getting pregnant? How very interesting. Although he didn't think it would stop a god from impregnating a mortal, should he desire her to become with child. Apollo had not impregnated Pamela. He stretched and smiled. He would like to, though, but not until she knew she was his, and she had agreed to spend her life with him.

"You could not have become pregnant from our love-making, Pamela," he said.

She stuck her head out of the bathroom, her toothbrush in her hand. "You've had a vasectomy?"

He had no idea what she was talking about, but it seemed the thought relieved her, so he nodded and smiled.

"Oh, well. That's good." Her head disappeared for a moment, and then reappeared, toothbrush still in hand. "But what about, uh," she faltered, and then she felt ridiculous. She'd just been more intimate with this man than she had ever been with anyone, including her ex, and asking about STDs was making her stutter? Besides that, he was a doctor, for God's sake. She tried again. "But what about sexually transmitted diseases?"

His golden brows drew together. "I have no diseases."

"Oh, well. Again, that's good. Neither do I. Good," she repeated for the third time, feeling like a total and utter boob. She ducked back into the bathroom, turned on the water and shut the door.

Apollo listened to her busy herself in the other room. It took a great effort of will for him not to join her. He wanted to pull that sheet away from her and lift her onto the counter; then he could plunge into her while he stared into her honey-colored eyes until, once again, he saw the reflection of his own soul within their depths. His body stirred, already becoming heavy and hard at the thought of her. Time . . . he reminded himself . . . there would be plenty of time for lovemaking in the years they would have together. He closed his eyes and drew a long breath of relief. It hadn't been the invocation ritual that had caused her to desire him. If that had been the case, her desire for him would have waned after their initial lovemaking. It most definitely had not—if anything, Pamela's passion had grown each time they joined. She had slept in his arms, fingers entwined with his. Even in her sleep she had nuzzled ever closer to him. He adored that about her, another thing that truly surprised him. Never before had Apollo nuzzled and cuddled afterwards with a lover—or if he had, it had only been as an impetus to begin another round of sex. He felt so different with her. He actually wanted her close to him, even when they weren't making love.

Now he understood why Hades and Lina often sat near enough to each other so that their bodies would be sure to touch, and why their fingers lingered during simple, ordinary activities, like passing a goblet or a platter of fruit. They wanted that connection. No, he amended. They *craved* that connection. Just as he craved Pamela.

She emerged from the bathroom with the sheet still wrapped around her, face freshly washed and hair damp.

"What shall we do today?" Apollo asked, holding out his hand to her.

Pamela took his hand and curled up against his chest. What an incredible rush of pleasure such simple words made her feel! He wanted to know what "we" would do today.

"Well, since we've missed breakfast"—she looked at the digital clock whose red numbers said it was already

2:05 P.M.—"and lunch, I think food should be on the agenda." She kissed the strong line of his jaw, wondering briefly why no day-old stubble bristled against her lips. "And I hate to mention it, but I really have to do some work to prepare for tomorrow's meeting with my client."

Apollo touched the wet hair that stuck out around her head in adorable messy tufts. "What kind of work?"

"Eddie wants a pool built based on the one here at the Palace. I, of course, have never even seen the Caesars Palace pool. So I really have to check it out, maybe do a few sketches so that I have some preliminary ideas to show him." She frowned. "I've already read through his notes, which were more than a little confusing. It seems he wants a pool, outside, but covered—like the 'authentic Roman bath downstairs.' I can only hope that it's less 'authentic' than that wretched fountain."

"Perhaps I can help. I do know something about authentic Roman baths."

"I forget that you know all about this old-world mythology stuff. You're a handy guy to have around, aren't you?" she teased, leaning into him.

"You have no idea . . ." He smiled and kissed her.

"Gihugic?" Apollo said, shaking his head.

"Hunormic," Pamela said. "How in the bloody buggering hell am I going to translate this into a backyard pool?"

"I think that would depend upon the size of his grounds."

Pamela made a snorting noise.

"You are right." Apollo said, not taking his eyes from the wide expanse of water and marble and fountains that stretched before them. "This . . ." He broke off, unsure of what to call it.

"Man-made lake?" Pamela supplied.

Apollo tired to hide his smile at Pamela's aghast tone. "Yes, man-made lake does aptly describe it. This man-made lake would appear ostentatious even on Mount Olympus."

"Huh! I'd like to think that the gods would have better taste."

The God of Light thought about Aphrodite's pink-and-gilt-covered palace with its ever-flowing fountain that rained blush-colored ambrosia instead of water. "One can only hope so," he mumbled.

Pamela was still gaping around them. "At least now I know what his notes meant. He wants it outside, but covered, like that." She pointed at the center of the massive pool. It was a gigantic circular marble dais, which rose several feet out of the water. Marble columns, at least fifty feet tall, supported a copper dome affording shade to the many bikini-clad bathers who swam to, and then lounged beneath it, as well as the bigger-than-life-sized waving statue of Caesar. "But his notes say that he wants the entire pool covered by the dome. And he wrote that he wants the thrones copied exactly, too. That must be what he means." She nodded at a lifeguard's station not far from where they stood. It was marble and had been built in the shape of a large throne flanked by two winged lions.

"Does he want to keep the seahorses, too?" Apollo asked, highly amused by the whole experience.

Pamela squinted at the massive statues of marble horses whose hindquarters morphed into mermaidlike tails. "Oh, God. I hope not." She ran her hand through her hair. "This together with the fountain is going to do me in. It's awful. Tacky. The whole thing screams, 'I have lots of money but no taste!' "

"And," Apollo said, studying the winged lions mounted on rectangular pillars, which flanked the smaller, more distant wading pool, "it is definitely not anything like an authentic Roman bath."

She shuddered. "I hope not. Any country that ruled the world as long as Rome did should know better than to create this mess."

"It's not just the decorations. The ancient Roman baths weren't bathing pools like this. They were a series of heated rooms built in succession, beginning with an area where bathers were oiled and massaged. The next rooms grew warmer, and were often filled with soothing steam."

He grinned at her. "They did not hold great pools of water; instead they were built around small, ever-flowing fountains, which were used to refresh the bathers. Of course the rooms did culminate in actual bathing pools, usually one that was heated and one that was kept refreshingly cold."

Pamela's expression changed instantly from horrified to hopeful. "Do you think you could describe the Roman baths to me well enough for me to sketch up something? I mean, I would have to incorporate some of this, of course," she flipped her fingers at their surroundings, "but maybe I can tame it down and make it more authentic—and sell the idea to Eddie. I mean, he already said he wants it covered. I'll just give him a series of lovely covered rooms, each with its own water element, all surrounding a less offensive-looking pool."

"It is an interesting idea," Apollo said.

"Great! Let's get to work." She started to march towards one of the least occupied rows of white lounge chairs. Then she stopped short. "Food," she said. "I have to have food to work." Her gaze slid across the pool to a marble building that had a short line of people queuing in front of it. She read the gilded, Romanesque letters and rolled her eyes heavenward.

This time Apollo made no attempt to cover his amusement. He threw back his head and laughed heartily. She scowled at him and headed towards the building. Over her shoulder she called, "You know, Snackous Maximus is just not that damn funny."

Apollo closed his eyes and inhaled the golden heat of the desert sun. It caressed his skin lovingly and filled him with power and contentment. He felt indescribably good. The soft sound of Pamela's busy charcoal pencil created a soothing background for his thoughts. They fit well together, he and his sweet Pamela. Her quick wit and impish smile had made spending the afternoon working with her a wonderfully pleasurable experience. She joked easily with him— she even teased him about simple things, like how curly his hair was after one of his dips in the pool, and his sur-

prising obsession with a delightfully salty snack called
French fries. He'd had three helpings of them. Women
didn't tease the God of Light, but Pamela did. When he
made her laugh, her sparkling eyes made him feel truly
godlike.

And he had quickly discovered that she was a much
more talented artist than she realized. He could already en-
vision their future together. She would never again have to
work for rich bores like this writer who obviously thought
of himself as a mortal god. Perhaps he would build for her
a grand gallery within his temple at Delphi. She could
spend her days sketching the wonders of Olympus, and her
nights sharing his bed.

Love was so much easier than he had imagined. He
could hardly remember why he had been so distraught
when he had rushed to Lina and Hades for advice. What
had he been so worried about? He had found his soul mate;
now all that was left to do was to adore her, and loving
Pamela was a delight. True, he had yet to tell her his true
identity, but wasn't that just a rather incidental detail? She
already knew the real him; he was the man who loved her.
And a part of his ego whispered that she would probably
be pleased to discover that she had won the love of an immortal.

His lips tilted up, and his mind drifted lazily. Life was
good.

"Don't you worry about burning?" Pamela peered at
him over the top of her sunglasses. He was stretched out
beside her on a lounge chair just like hers, except his chair
was situated directly in the still-blazing sun of the desert
evening. Pamela had pulled her chair over into the shade
provided by a scalloped-edged pool umbrella. Even her
bare legs, which were bent so that she could use them as a
rest for her sketch pad, were carefully out of the direct sunlight, and still she was feeling a little flushed and over-
cooked. She had been working at the bathhouse sketch for
hours, and for the entire time Phoebus had been lounging
beside her, explaining details of ancient Roman baths and
giving insightful input about the small, separate rooms and
the general layout—while stretched out in full sunlight.

"Burning?" His brow wrinkled.

"Yeah, you've been lying out there in next to nothing all day. I'd be fried to a crisp." But Phoebus didn't even look hot. On the contrary, he looked outrageously handsome in his hastily purchased swim shorts and nothing else. He was one long expanse of golden tan skin and luscious muscles.

"You mean burned by the sunlight?" He chuckled as if he found the idea new and amusing. "No. I do not worry about burning. The sun and I are old friends." He shifted up on one elbow and turned towards her. "Have you finished?"

She chewed her lip as she studied the sketch. "I think so. I actually like it, but I don't know if Eddie will go for it. What do you think?" She handed him the sketchpad.

He studied it carefully. Nodding, he said, "I do think it was a wise choice to make the small fountains in each of the heated rooms more ornate than you originally intended."

"Yeah, I'll just be sure to keep the walls plain marble, then the effect won't be so overwhelming. If he wants more decoration, I'll try to steer him towards the mosaic flooring you suggested."

"You said that he keeps mentioning the importance of authenticity. You can assure him that this sketch is based entirely upon the ancient plans of a working Roman bath. Of course the throne at the edge of the central pool is not exactly . . ." He paused, glancing up at Pamela. And the smile in his eyes died as something behind her caught his attention.

"Here you are. Finally!"

The woman's voice, filled with frustration, cut over Pamela's shoulder. Before she could turn to see who was speaking Phoebus had leaped to his feet.

"What an unexpected pleasure," he said.

Pleasure? Pamela thought he sounded way more annoyed than pleased. She looked over her shoulder, and had to hold her hand up to shield her eyes from the bright orange light of the setting sun, which perfectly silhouetted the curvaceous shape of a tall woman. She could vaguely make out the flowing lines of a short dress and the fact that the woman's hair was piled up around her head in a style that looked very much like a crown. She didn't spare Pamela a glance. Instead, she launched immediately into a tight-lipped chastisement of Phoebus.

"I waited and waited for you. You didn't come and you didn't come and still you didn't come. So I was forced to come to you."

Phoebus frowned. "I do not believe I specified a time at which I would return."

"I assumed you would return after you—"

"Forgive my rudeness, Pamela," Phoebus interrupted her as he reached forward, snagging the woman's wrist and pulling her around the chaise to face Pamela. "Allow me to present you to my sister. Pamela Gray, this is my twin sister," he hesitated and gave the woman a sharp look, "Diana."

Pamela stood up, smiling brightly with her hand extended. "It's wonderful to meet you, Diana. And please, don't blame Phoebus if he's late for something. It's entirely my fault. When I found out how much he knows about ancient Rome, I couldn't stop picking his brain."

Artemis looked from the mortal's friendly smile to her outstretched hand. She could feel her brother's censoring glare almost as surely as she could feel the invocation thread that still bound her to this woman. Reluctantly, she took Pamela's hand in her own and was surprised by the firm confidence in the woman's grip.

"Wait!" Pamela said, eyes widening in surprise. "I know who you are! You're the beautiful woman from the *Zumanity* show." Her eyes sliced over to Phoebus. "I can't believe you didn't tell me she was your sister."

"Perhaps he was embarrassed by my performance," Artemis said with a haughty lift of her chin.

"That's ridiculous," Pamela said, giving Phoebus a perplexed look. "Your performance was amazing—athletic, and seductive and incredibly romantic."

One of Artemis' perfectly shaped golden brows arched. "You found it romantic?"

"Definitely!" Pamela said, nodding her head enthusiastically.

"Diana knows that her performance did not embarrass me," Apollo said quickly. "I just hadn't realized she would be appearing last night, so it did surprise me. I would have mentioned it, but after the show I had more on my mind than my sister's theatrics."

He shared an intimate smile with Pamela.

"Tell me, Pamela," Artemis said, as if her brother had not spoken. "Has Phoebus been romancing you properly?"

Pamela's face blazed from pink to scarlet. Her mouth opened and then closed.

"Diana!" Apollo barked. "That question was unnecessary as well as inappropriate."

"Was it?" she hurled back at him. "I think not, *Phoebus*." She enunciated his name distinctly. "The chain is still there! Less than before, but not gone."

Diana's words made no sense to Pamela, but she saw Phoebus' expression change instantly from anger to shock.

"I want it gone," Diana continued in a hard voice. "Need I remind you that our stay here is only temporary? We must leave before dawn."

Pamela felt her stomach tighten. What they were arguing about might make no sense to her, but the word *temporary* was crystal clear. They were leaving. Soon. Of course she would only be in Vegas for a week herself, but she had been honest about it, telling him up front that she was only visiting to do a job for a client. Phoebus had made love to her and spent the entire day with her, and hadn't once mentioned that he had to leave in the morning. She was an f-ing fool. What had she thought she'd been doing, playing house? Shit. Shit. Shit. She should know better than this. Her inexperience in the dating world was showing. She shouldn't have expected more than fun and temporary games from a one-night stand.

"Ya know," Pamela broke into the sibling rivalry using her brisk, matter-of-fact businesswoman's voice, "if there's one thing I understand, and understand well, it's that sometimes brothers and sisters need to battle things out. In private." She picked up her sketchpad from where Phoebus had discarded it on the lounge chair and stuffed it into her leather bag while she hastily slid her feet into her

Mizrahi flats. "Actually, Diana, your timing is excellent. I was just thinking that I really should get back to my room and do some more prep work for tomorrow."

"No, Pamela! Please don't—" Phoebus sputtered.

She barely glanced at him. "I've spent too much time playing this weekend as it is. Good-bye, Phoebus."

Artemis was shocked. The mortal was actually *walking away* from her brother. Through their invisible connection the goddess could feel much of what was going on inside of the woman. She was . . . Artemis concentrated, sifting through the emotions pouring through the bond that linked them. Pamela was very upset. And embarrassed. And hurt. She was certain that Apollo had used her. The mortal was breaking into little pieces on the inside, but on the outside she was showing only cool annoyance. Had Artemis not been linked to her, she would never have guessed the turmoil taking place within the mortal woman. How odd. Could this woman's hidden strength have something to do with why the invocation had yet to be fulfilled? Could it be that this young mortal saw through their charade? Diana looked at her with new respect. Apollo had been right about one thing. Pamela certainly was not a simple, silly woman.

"Pamela, my brother is correct. I am being insufferably rude."

Diana's voice stopped Pamela's retreat. She looked at her lover's sister, who smiled at her. Pamela suddenly saw Phoebus' dazzling good looks reflected on her beautiful face.

"I have been experiencing some"—she hesitated and glanced at her brother before continuing—"difficulties of a personal nature of late. I haven't been myself. Please believe me that the last thing I desire is to drive you from my brother."

Pamela met Diana's aquamarine eyes. "Whether I go now or later really doesn't make that much difference, does it? You just said you're leaving in the morning."

"But not forever!" Apollo said hastily, moving to Pamela's side and taking her hand. "You can not believe that I would walk away from you and never return."

Pamela pulled her hand from his grasp. She shook her head and even managed to smile.

"Look, we had fun. Let's leave it at that. You don't need to make a big thing out of it."

Artemis stared at her brother's shocked face. Why didn't he say something? The mortal was leaving him! She obviously didn't want to—not only could Artemis feel Pamela's pain screaming within her own head, but it was apparent in the stiff, mechanical way she held herself. Pamela was hurt and upset. She wanted comfort, not speechless ineptitude.

Apollo, however, was being silently inept.

"We did not mean to offend you," Artemis quickly said. "This is just a misunderstanding. Please. Don't go away upset."

"I'm not upset," Pamela responded.

"I would be." Apollo finally found his voice. This time he didn't touch her. He stood very still and tried to convey everything he was feeling through his words. "I would be upset and angry if I thought that you were planning to leave me before dawn, and you hadn't told me. I should have told you. I meant to. But you must understand, my sweet Pamela, that I knew I would be returning, so to taint our day together by telling you that I must leave soon seemed a cruel thing to do. I can see now that I was wrong. Can you forgive me?"

She should tell him that it was no big deal. She should say that she didn't expect any damn thing from him. And keep walking. She could call V and they'd have a great girlfriend talk about how men are shitheads. Then tomorrow she'd go back to work and forget about him. She'd just slept with him; it wasn't like she'd married him or anything too crazy like that.

But those eyes caught her. Again. She could swear that she saw an echo of herself there, deep within them. He had that same "somethin's missin'" about him, and he'd touched her—body, heart and soul. If Duane had embalmed her, Phoebus had brought her alive again. She didn't want to go back to her tomb of complacency, and she knew herself well enough that she understood that this weekend had been a turning point. Pamela wouldn't go back to being satisfied with the safety of her life. She'd get out there; she'd flirt and take more chances—with or without Phoebus. But everything within her was screaming that she wanted to take those chances *with* him.

"Okay," she said, biting the word off. "I forgive you." And then crossed her arms and waited. The ball was in his court. Surprisingly, it was his sister who fielded and returned it.

"My brother and I must speak. It is a family matter, and I—"

"Not a problem," Pamela snapped. "I'm out of here."

"Pamela, is it correct that you have a brother, too?" Artemis' gaze was calculating.

Caught again in the motion of turning away, Pamela nodded tightly.

"Then you understand that sometimes family problems can overrule our individual desires. We are needed at home. Please do not judge my brother harshly because of that."

Pamela answered her with equal candor. "I'm not judging your brother harshly; I'm protecting myself."

"You do not need protection from me," Apollo said. Unable to stop himself from touching her, he brushed her long, bare neck with his fingertips. When she shivered, he was unsure whether it was because she desired or rejected him. "Meet me tonight. Let me see you again before I must leave. You have my oath that I will return."

She shouldn't. He made her feel too much. Pamela opened her mouth to tell him no, and then she thought about the night without him. It would be like the morning sky without sunlight—bleak . . . empty . . . like her life had become. She wouldn't go back to that, even if it meant taking a chance on getting her heart broken. At least now she knew that her heart was working again.

"Fine," she said, making sure her voice remained neutral. "You can take me to dinner. Snackous Maximous doesn't count as a real meal anyway."

"He will choose the place," Artemis said with a satisfied smile.

"Fine," Pamela repeated. "If we meet at eight o'clock, will that give you enough time to get your family business straight?"

Artemis nodded slightly at her brother.

"Yes," he said. "I will call for you at your room."

"No!" Pamela said too quickly. She cleared her throat and gave a little cough like the word explosion had been a tickle and not a knee-jerk. "I'll meet you at the wine bar. Just like before." Then she instantly regretted saying "just like before." Just like the night before . . . when they'd ended up in her bed making love until past noon . . .

His smile was a caress as he remembered all too well what the previous night had held. "I will meet you, sweet Pamela, at our wine bar. Just like before."

This time nothing prevented her retreat.

CHAPTER 17

⟞

The insubstantial opaque of the portal shimmered as the twin deities stepped from the modern world back to Olympus. Apollo's square jaw was set, and his eyes flashed with unspoken rage. With a brusque gesture he motioned for his sister to follow him out of the crowded banquet hall.

"I did not intend—" Artemis hissed a whisper, but Apollo's dark look was enough to make her hold her tongue.

"Not until we are in my temple. Alone," he said through his teeth, smiling and shaking his head in a polite no to Aphrodite, who tried to wave him over to the chaise on which she reclined. The Goddess of Love was surrounded by a flock of giggling Napaean glen nymphs who had shed their wisps of clothing and were practicing a fertility dance that involved intricate belly undulations.

"Napaeans are terrible gossips," Artemis whispered conspiratorially.

Apollo shot her a disgusted glance. "They all are. You all are."

"What is that supposed to mean?"

He took her elbow. "Not here. Not now."

Brother and sister continued to make their way through the Olympian gardens, responding with polite hellos and regretfully declining the myriad invitations for fun and frolic offered them, until they walked through the golden doors of Apollo's Temple.

As soon as they were within the god's private chambers, he rounded on his sister. "I can not believe the foolish scene you created with Pamela! What were you thinking? Or were you simply not thinking at all! You almost ruined everything."

"Ruined everything?" she said mockingly. "And what *everything* do you mean? The earth-moving romance you're having? The bond still exists, Apollo! I can feel the chains of the invocation. I'm still bound to her. What is wrong? Why have you not yet made love to her?"

Apollo looked away from his sister's piercing gaze.

The Huntress's eyes widened. "You *have* made love to her," she breathed. "And it didn't work. It didn't fulfill her heart's desire."

Apollo's nod was a single, tight jerk. He walked over to a glass-topped table carved in the image of his plunging chariot of light and helped himself to the waiting goblet of ever-ready wine.

"You had no idea you hadn't fulfilled the invocation ritual."

It wasn't a question, but after taking a long drink, Apollo answered her. "None whatsoever."

"I don't understand what's happening," she said. "Did your lovemaking go well? Did she respond to you?"

He glared over the top of the goblet at her. "Of course it went well! I'm not an inexperienced youth."

"So you satisfied her?"

Apollo scowled. "Yes."

"You're quite certain? You know, often men only believe they have brought a woman to completion, when in fact—"

"She did not pretend with me!" Apollo bellowed.

The walls of his temple flashed with the blinding light of an exploding star. Artemis hastily covered her eyes, waiting for his tantrum to pass.

"Well, something went wrong." She checked carefully from between her fingers before lowering her hand. She sincerely hated it when her brother's light leaked out. "Perhaps her desire could not be fulfilled by making love to her just once."

"It wasn't just once," Apollo said, rubbing his hand

across his face. "We made love all night and past morning. She was as satisfied as I."

"There is another possibility. What if Pamela's true heart's desire has little to do with the act of lovemaking?" Artemis paced restlessly as she worked through the problem aloud. "Although, it's tied to lovemaking—because I felt the bond between us loosen during the night—but the connection forged by the invocation is undeniably still in place between us, so there's more to her heart's desire than sex." Considering, the goddess paused while she poured herself some more wine. "I could sense her feelings, especially as she was trying to leave you at the pool."

Apollo's eyes fastened on his sister. "What was she feeling?" he demanded.

"She was hurt and confused and embarrassed."

He sank into a chair and groaned. His sister watched him carefully.

"You care for her, don't you?" she asked quietly.

He raised his head and met her eyes. "I think I am falling in love with her."

"In love?" Artemis shook her head. "You can't be. She's a mortal. And, as if that's not impossible enough, she's a mortal from the modern world."

"I am aware of that," he said between clenched teeth.

"How would you know, anyway?" Artemis scoffed. "You have never been in love."

"That is exactly why I believe I am falling in love! I have lived eons and never experienced this feeling until now."

"What? What feeling is so overpowering that it must be love?" Artemis asked.

"I care more for her than I do for myself. Her happiness is mine. Her pain causes me despair."

The goddess looked at him as if he had just broken out in a mystifying rash. "Perhaps it will pass, or fade completely with time."

"The problem with that, my dear Sister, is that I don't want it to." He smiled, but the expression lacked humor. "This morning I was so smug. I thought love was so incredibly simple. I'd found my soul mate. I'd made love to her, and she must feel the same for me. I was an arrogant imbecile."

"You believe she is your soul mate?"

"I'm afraid that she might very well be the mate of my soul."

"Then, if she is, by the very nature of the bond she must love you, too," Artemis said, trying to make sense out of her brother's bizarre proclamations.

"You would think so," he said miserably.

Artemis drummed her chin with her fingers. "Well, she is a mortal. We really should not be surprised at the confusion. Perhaps that's it! Pamela's heart's desire was for her soul mate to come into her life—she just named it romance, but couldn't it all mean the same thing? Romance . . . love . . . true desire . . . soul mates . . . Are they not all words that could be used to describe the same phenomenon? And if I'm right, it would make sense that the invocation has not been fulfilled."

"How does that make sense? If the desire of her heart was for her soul mate to come into her life, and I am her soul mate, then why hasn't the invocation been fulfilled?"

"She has to recognize and accept you as the mate of her soul. Obviously, she has not." Artemis rested her hand on his shoulder. "The emotions I felt through our bond were not filled with love and contentment. Pamela felt hurt and confused; she did not feel loved."

Apollo's eyes were haunted. "I know she has been wounded by a man in the past. I was arrogant enough to believe that a little touch of my immortal power and the passion of my body had healed her."

"You were wrong, Brother. There is more to Pamela."

"There is also more to love," he muttered.

She clapped his back. "Your misery makes me glad that I haven't experienced it."

"I think I'm beginning to understand that love is misery and wonder all wrapped together in the soft skin of a woman," Apollo said, staring off into the distance.

"Why not simply reveal who you are? Whisk her away to Olympus tonight—use your immortal powers to coax her love to the surface."

Apollo looked horrified. "That wouldn't be love! That would be abject worship, or fear mixed with adoration."

"Now this is an excellent example of how you and I differ. You won't use your powers to win her; I think it only makes sense. What mortal wouldn't want to win the love of a god?"

Hearing the arrogant thoughts he'd had early spoken aloud, Apollo was disgusted with himself. Little wonder Pamela was reluctant to recognize him as her soul mate.

"Something tells me that Pamela would not be overjoyed to learn my true identity."

Artemis snorted.

"Modern mortals are not like the people of the Ancient World. They command metal creatures to obey their will. Information passes between them through machinery, not through the power of magic and ritual. We are dead to them. No, she must find her love for me as a man, first. After that I will persuade her to accept the god."

"And how do you plan to do that?"

"I have to love her as a man loves a woman."

Artemis raised both brows questioningly.

"With my heart and not my powers," he said.

"Which means exactly what?"

"When I understand that, I will have gained something priceless. Her love," said the God of Light.

"Do you think you can win her love before dawn tomorrow?"

"It seems doubtful," he said.

Artemis sighed. "I suppose I should be grateful that the bond between Pamela and me has loosened. Now it is more like an itch that is difficult to scratch than a constant, jabbing annoyance. Bacchus certainly set a great deal of mischief afoot with his little prank."

"Have you spoken to him at all?"

"No, he has been conspicuously absent from Olympus these past days." She shrugged. "Although it's not as if he ever spent much time here. He has long preferred the company of mortals. When this ordeal is over, we must remember to deal harshly with his impertinence."

Apollo was silent. How could he tell his sister that "this

ordeal" would never be over? He knew little of love, but he was already certain of one thing. Love couldn't be ordered around—it didn't begin and end on demand. Unfortunately.

"Apollo? Pay attention. I asked for your plan of action tonight."

"I don't know!" The walls glowed dangerously, and the God of Light reined in his frustration. "Dinner—she asked that I take her to dinner. You heard her."

Artemis' smooth brow wrinkled as she thought about what Pamela had said, "Snackus Maximus? What type of name is that?"

"A poorly chosen one."

"I still think you should bring her here tonight. Woo her in Olympus, in your very own temple. What could be more romantic?"

"Artemis, I already explained to you that I refuse to use my powers to win her love."

"Then don't use your powers, stubborn! But this is your home, and it's certainly much more beautiful than anything the Kingdom of Vegas has to offer."

Apollo considered his sister's words. "She does appreciate ancient architecture."

"So bring her here. Tell her it's an exclusive part of Caesars Palace. At least you'll be assured privacy."

"I supposed I could use my powers just enough to veil her senses as we cross through the portal."

"Then transport her here quickly, before any of the other Twelve glimpse her."

Apollo was beginning to enjoy the idea. "I wouldn't have to worry about accidents, or metal monsters, or any of the other distractions of the modern world. I could focus on assuring her of my love." And he honestly wanted to show Pamela his home and to witness her reaction to its beauty—even if he couldn't claim it as his own.

"I'll plan the meal myself, and have my own hand-maidens wait upon you. The nymphs can't be trusted."

"Excellent!" Apollo said. "Be certain that you remind them not to call me Apollo."

"Yes, yes, my maidens will continue your charade, *Phoebus*," she said.

"I am in your debt, *Diana*," he said, smiling.

She returned his smile, thinking how charming and handsome her brother was. Pamela would not be able to resist him, especially if Artemis had anything to do with it—which she would make sure she did.

"Then we've decided, and there is much to do to prepare. Time is short. By dawn Pamela must be returned to the Kingdom of Vegas. Hopefully, completely enamored with Phoebus," Artemis said. Then she clapped her hands together twice, and in the commanding voice of the Huntress of Olympus, called, "Handmaidens, attend me!"

Before a breath could pass, twelve beautiful young women materialized in a puff of glittering silver dust that looked like it had been borrowed from the light of the moon.

"Ladies, my brother has need of our aid. Here is what we must do . . ."

Apollo watched the flurry of activity until his sister shooed him from the room, reminding him that it was almost time for him to meet with his lover. The God of Light smiled as he readied himself. He was bringing his true love to his home. He would woo her and love her here, where he was most comfortable. She would see that she need not fear being hurt again. Safe within his realm, he was certain that nothing could go wrong.

CHAPTER 18

~

"I don't have a clue what to wear," Pamela sighed into her cell phone.

"Something hot, but not too hot," V said. "He has some explaining to do before you fall on your back, legs all akimbo again."

"My legs were not akimbo."

V's silence weighed heavily against Pamela's guilt-ridden ear.

"Okay, okay. Maybe they were a little akimbo," she admitted.

"Pammy. There's no such thing as 'a little akimbo.' That's like being a little pregnant, or engaging in a little nuclear war."

"Oh, God. I'm a slut." She covered her eyes with her hand.

"Please. You've had sex with two men in, what, eight or nine years? That absolutely does not even begin to qualify you for slutdom."

"But I slept with him on what was barely our second date," she whispered.

"You don't have to whisper. You're alone. And you're making your case to the wrong woman here. Let us review the old joke. What does a lesbian take with her on a second date?" She paused expectantly.

"A U-Haul trailer so she can move in," Pamela provided.

"Right you are. So you see, from my point of view I think you've shown amazing discretion."

"You're right. I'm talking to the wrong woman," Pamela said.

V ignored her. "Which does not mean that you shouldn't play it cool. At least for a little while tonight until Young Jedi Phoebus explains why he's cutting out on you in the morning and, more importantly, why he failed to mention that little fact before, during, or after your legs were akimbo."

"I really wish you wouldn't call him that."

"Why? I mean it as a compliment. Besides, according to your gushing descriptions, it fits him perfectly."

"He's not like a Jedi. If you want the truth, he's more like a young god."

"Oh, get a grip on yourself. Nothing trumps a Jedi Knight except Princess Leia."

"Vernelle! You're so not helping."

"Sorry. Okay, what to wear . . . How about that adorable little butter-colored silk dress, you know, the one with the spaghetti straps. It's a spring fashion staple and always a hit with the masses. You did bring it with you, didn't you?"

"Yes I did. And do you remember how low it's cut? Hello! It has spaghetti straps! Bare shoulders and cleavage do not add up to hot without being hot," Pamela said.

"True. Okay. Did you bring those black slacks with you? The ones with the little slits that show a pretty glimpse of your calves?"

"Yeah, I think I did."

"Wear those with one of your sleeveless shells. Just be sure it's a shell that's also high-necked. That way he gets to see a little of your legs and a little of your arms, and just the outline of everything else. Then if he's a good boy, he can unwrap the rest of the package after he's made amends."

"V, you're incorrigible," Pamela said.

"Yes, I am, but I also know what looks good on women."

"You've got me there. Okay. I'll wear the slacks. And I won't sleep with him. Again."

"Sleep with? You didn't say anything about *sleeping* with the Jedi. I may not be hetero, but even I know no one *sleeps* with Jedi Knights."

"Stop it. You know I'm talking about sex."

"Pammy, you can have sex with him. Just make him miserable first."

Pamela started to say something, and then changed her mind. "Okay. Maybe."

"Don't *okay maybe* me. I know that tone. What's wrong? Give, girl."

"I like him," Pamela said softly.

"Yes, you've made that more than clear. So what's wrong with that?"

"No, I mean I *really* like him. And I don't want to. It's just not very smart."

"Pammy, listen to me. What's not very smart is letting Mr. Control Freak Duane poison your future. This Phoebus guy might not be *the one*. He might just be someone to have a fun Vegas fling with, and you will forever remember him as the man who got you out there again. But you'll never find out what he is, or what any other guy is, if you aren't willing to take a chance. Love's like that. You have to chance losing to win."

"I don't know if I can," Pamela said. "We've already established that I'm not a very good gambler."

"You can," V said firmly.

"How can you be so sure?"

"If you were meant to be alone, you wouldn't agonize over the should I or shouldn't I's. You'd accept the shouldn't I as what feels best for you and move on with your life. Be honest. Can you really tell me that it felt better before you met Phoebus?"

"It felt easier," Pamela said dryly.

"Well, doll, it's easier to make bedroom window treatments out of the same material as the bedspread. Does that make it better?"

Pamela grimaced, visions of perfectly matched floral prints assailing her. "Definitely not."

"Please take a chance, Pammy. You deserve to be able to really live again."

"I love you, V," Pamela said.

"That's what all the girls say. Have fun tonight. And try not to overanalyze the poor tripod. Remember, you can be smart without being uptight."

"Huh?"

"Never mind. Go get dressed."

"Okay, I'll call you tomorrow," Pamela said.

"By the way, you do realize that this is the second phone call in a row during which you haven't once mentioned work, don't ya?"

"Bloody buggering hell! I am losing my mind. How did it go with Mrs.—" she began, but V's laughter cut her off.

"Pammy! Stop. It's a *good thing* that you actually have something besides Ruby Slipper on your mind."

"Yeah, but—"

"Yeah, but everything's fine. As usual. You have no worries. Call me tomorrow after you meet with Faust. And remember—fun and fantasy, Pamela, fun and fantasy . . ."

"You look beautiful as well as amazingly seductive tonight," Apollo said, kissing her hand with his lips lingering on her skin almost as suggestively as his eyes.

Great, she thought as her stomach pitched and rolled at the sight of him, *the exact opposite of the look I was going for.*

"I'll bet you say that to all the girls," Pamela quipped, borrowing V's line.

"Not lately, I haven't," he said, his summer-sky eyes going all dark and serious, "and never with as much sincerity."

"Then thank you," Pamela said, trying unsuccessfully not to fall under the blue spell his eyes cast. Like a cat ridding itself of water, she shook herself mentally and neatly changed the subject. "How's your sister?"

"She is well. Still troubled, but well." He kept Pamela's hand enclosed in his own as he propped one foot up on the bottom rung of the tall chair next to her. He wanted to pull her into his arms and kiss her soundly right there in front of their café, but her body language told him clearly that he needed to take it slow and easy. "Diana did not mean to offend you this afternoon. As she said, she has not been herself lately."

Pamela started to shrug an offhanded "no big deal" comment when she stopped herself. Instead, she squared her shoulders and looked directly into his bottomless eyes. "I'm not going to pretend that it didn't hurt my feelings to find out you're leaving so soon and you didn't say anything to me about it. To tell you the truth, it made me want to run away from you."

"Ah, truth . . ." He nodded his head thoughtfully, thinking how very much he appreciated her honesty, and at the same time realizing how few women had ever been honest with him. They had adored him—worshiped him—vied for his attentions. But he didn't think any of them had ever really been honest with him.

"It caused you pain to think that I would leave you without an explanation. And I am sorry for that." He touched her cheek. "The last thing I desire is that you feel that you have to run from me to protect yourself." He let his finger touch the gold coin that dangled around her neck. "Please trust that your feelings are safe with me."

Again, she answered him with total frankness. "I'll try to trust you, but I can't promise you anything yet."

He lifted her hand to his lips again. "Then I'll settle for your honesty and the opportunity to win your trust."

"Can you tell me why you're leaving?"

"Would you mind very much if we talked about it over dinner? I have something rather special planned for you tonight."

"Oh, okay," Pamela felt a flush of pleasure that she wished she could control better. "I am hungry." She stood up, very aware that Phoebus still held her hand, but unwilling to pull it from his warm grasp. "Where are we going?"

"Mount Olympus," he said, eyes shinning.

"That sounds like a restaurant that would fit right in

around here, but I don't remember seeing it while I was walking around The Forum. Is it in Caesars Palace?"

"It can be entered through Caesars Palace, but it is very exclusive. Few people know of it."

"Just the gods, right?" Pamela kidded.

"Just the gods," Apollo agreed, grinning at her.

They strolled hand in hand through The Forum towards the casino. Their arms brushed together intimately, and Pamela remembered how wonderful it had felt to be wrapped in his arms, pressed against his naked chest. She could smell his unique scent. It wasn't some trendy, oh-so-manly department store cologne smell. Phoebus' scent was clean and natural and male. It made her want to inhale him.

"Did you finish the sketch of the baths?" Apollo asked.

"Yes, I did," she said, jerking her thoughts away from remembrances of his naked skin. "And I like it, too. I've never designed anything similar to it. It's exciting to do something totally new. Well, that is, it will be if I can talk Eddie into it."

"I think you'll persuade him."

"I really hope so, I—*OHMYGOD!*" Pamela stopped as if she'd run into an invisible wall. She was staring at a glittering display of purses that sat on a marble pillar inside a locked glass case in front of a sassy little accessory store. "I can not believe how perfect it is!"

Transfixed, Pamela dropped Phoebus' hand and approached the display case. Three jeweled purses were placed on small crystal boxes. One purse looked just like a child's piggy bank, another was a lovely dragonfly, and the third—the third was the one she gravitated to. It was an exact replica of one of Dorothy's ruby slippers. It winked and glistened with red beads and semiprecious stones under the display spotlight, looking magical and familiar and very, very *Wizard of Oz.*

"I have to have it." Pamela crooked her finger at an attentive salesman within the store.

Apollo watched as Pamela, completely entranced by the purse that looked like a red slipper perched on one of the daggerlike heels she was so fond of, waited impatiently for the servant to unlock the case and carefully lift out the shoe purse. Pamela handled it reverently. She flipped over the gold-embossed tag that hung from the clasp. And her face paled.

"Let me be sure that I'm reading this correctly. Does it say four *thousand* dollars and not four *hundred* dollars?" she asked the clerk.

"Yes madam, you are correct. The purse is a Judith Leiber original." His tone said that was explanation enough for the price.

"It's beautiful." Reluctantly, Pamela returned the purse to the clerk, who placed it back in the case.

"May I show you anything else, madam?"

"No, thank you."

The employee closed and locked the case. "Just call if I can be of further assistance." He executed an abrupt about-face and returned to the posh interior of the boutique.

"Are you not going to purchase it?" Apollo asked, hating the forlorn look on Pamela's face.

"Are you kidding? It's four thousand dollars. I can't spend that kind of money on a purse."

"But you said that it was perfect."

"It is! Four thousand dollars worth of perfect." She sighed and slid her arm through his, steering him away from the front of the store. "Let's go before I cry."

"You don't have four thousand dollars?" Apollo asked as they walked.

"Yeah, I have four grand. But I don't have four *extra* grand—or at least not extra enough that I can justify spending it on an extravagance like a jeweled purse. Even if it is a ruby slipper jeweled purse. Oh, well," she said wistfully. "Maybe someday."

Apollo thought about the roll of currency he carried in his pocket. He couldn't remember exactly how much he'd brought with him. He'd just skimmed some off the top of the pile of bills Zeus had commanded Bacchus leave in a golden bowl near the portal. He did a quick mental calculation, and was pretty sure it wouldn't add up to four thousand dollars. Pamela seemed to consider it a great deal of money anyway, probably more than she would accept as a gift. He glanced down at his gold coin that nestled just above the valley of her breasts. She almost hadn't accepted that from him, and she had had no idea of even a fraction of its worth. No, Pamela definitely would not allow him to gift her with the purse.

The faux stone floor gave way to an opulent carpet as they left The Forum Shops and entered Caesars Palace.

"It's this way," Apollo said, turning to their right and winding past several rows of busily blinking slot machines . . . and his steps slowed and then stopped.

"Did we take a wrong turn?" Pamela asked him.

He smiled. "No, but I just had a thought. Would you like to take a small chance?"

Her pretty face was a question mark.

"You want the purse, but you don't want to spend your four thousand of dollars. But what if you won the money? Would you purchase the purse then?"

"I suppose . . ."

Apollo tilted his head at the nearest row of slot machines. "I feel that luck is with us tonight."

Pamela chewed on the side of her lip. "I'm not really a very good gambler. I like knowing that I'm getting something back when I let my money loose."

"Then allow me to provide the money." He reached into his pocket and pulled out his roll of currency and flipped it open, shuffling quickly through the dozen or so bills, most of which had 50 or 100 printed on them.

"Good lord, Phoebus, do you not believe in credit cards?"

He tried to keep the confusion out of his voice. Bacchus had mentioned something about other ways modern mortals paid for their purchases, but Phoebus couldn't remember exactly what he had said.

"I like this currency," he paused, trying to decide what else he could say. "It's not very colorful, but it's interesting looking." He handed her a hundred dollar bill. "Take this one and feed it into one of the machines, and let us see what happens."

Pamela screwed up her face and looked at him like he was crazy. "I can't just blow a hundred dollars like that, even if it is yours. And really, I never gamble. I don't think I have the right attitude to be lucky at it."

"I think you are lucky. You're lucky for me."

That drew a reluctant smile from her. "I can't throw one hundred dollars away."

"Then use this one." He shuffled the money until he found a fifty dollar bill. "Remember, you might win enough money to buy your slipper purse." At the mention of the much-coveted purse, Apollo saw a light come into her eyes and he knew he'd won.

"Okay, here's the deal." She didn't take the fifty dollar bill. Instead, she rifled through the wad of money until she found a twenty. "I'll play this, and only this. If I win, you get half. If I lose, I owe you ten dollars."

"I'll take your deal," Apollo said. "Which machine shall we try?"

Pamela studied the rows of blinking, bonging, blaring machines, feeling a little intimidated by their slick foreign appearance. It was after eight o'clock on Sunday night, but still at least half of the machines were occupied by gamblers who were pressing buttons and pulling metal arms with a single-minded intensity.

"You're the one feeling lucky. You pick," she said.

Apollo rubbed his chin, pretending to carefully consider the rows of machines. "I like the way this one looks." He took her hand and pulled her to a machine not far from where they were standing. There were only two other people in that row, and they sat several seats down from the one he stopped in front of.

"Wheel of Fortune. Are you sure you want this one? I think it might be a bad omen that I never liked the show. I'm not a particularly good speller." She shrugged. "Hated it."

"You're nervous." Apollo didn't understand all of her words, but he certainly recognized the tone of her voice and her body language.

"Yep," she said, feeling foolish. "You're right. I am. I told you I've never gambled before."

"Don't think of it as gambling. Think of it as purse shopping."

Pamela visibly perked up. "Purse shopping is definitely

something I can do." She sat on the little padded seat and searched the front of the gaudy machine. "I guess the money goes in here," she said, sliding the twenty into a little slot. The money disappeared, and the machine clicked and clanged, digitally displaying a credit of twenty dollars. She looked up at Phoebus. "Ready?"

"Ready."

Pamela grasped the red ball at the end of the silver arm, and pulled. Her attention was totally focused on the three-panel window, and she didn't notice the small, commanding gesture Apollo made with his hand.

"Bar . . ." Pamela said as the first scroll clunked to a stop inside the window. *"Bar . . ."* she said when the next one halted, excitement growing in her voice, until *"BAR!"* she shouted as the third black picture stopped. The machine exploded in lights and sirens and began vomiting money from its mechanical mouth as Pamela shrieked and leaped up to throw her arms around Apollo, who hugged her back, laughing joyously.

Sometimes it was really good to be a god.

CHAPTER 19

The strap of the ruby slipper purse was made of a filigree gold chain that reminded Pamela of something a 1920s flapper would have worn as a long, sultry necklace. She slid it over her shoulder and had the insanely childish urge to skip like Dorothy down the Yellow Brick Road. She couldn't believe it was hers! V was going to shit monkeys when she saw it.

"I can not believe the jackpot was exactly eight thousand dollars," she gushed, doing a little twirl as she watched the purse wink and glitter in her reflection in the store windows they passed.

"I told you I was feeling lucky tonight," Apollo said, delighted at the uninhibited exuberance of Pamela's reaction to winning the money.

"I would never have let myself buy something so outrageously expensive." She squeezed his hand and lowered her voice. "Not even a pair of fabulous, beginning-of-season designer shoes — not for four thousand dollars."

"But you love the purse." Apollo smiled down at her, thoroughly pleased that he had been able to orchestrate such joy for her. And, oddly enough, he didn't even care that he couldn't tell her that he had commanded the machine to spurt out the money she required. That he got the credit wasn't the point. The point was that Pamela was so incredibly happy. It made his heart feel light and carefree.

"I love the purse. I adore the purse. I'm totally enamored with the purse!" She laughed. "I don't care how shallow and materialistic it sounds. I'm only going to carry it on special occasions. When I get back to my shop, I'm going to mount it under glass in the front picture window, the one with our logo painted in red script on it: Ruby Slipper Design Studio . . . We Make Sure That There's No Place Like Home."

They retraced their way back through Caesars Palace as Apollo listened to Pamela's excited chatter. He believed her design studio's motto. Without Pamela, there was no home. He knew it was true—he'd already proven it. The Kingdom of Vegas was a foreign, strange place, but when he had passed through the portal that night and made his way to The Lost Cellar and Pamela, he felt as if he was coming home. However improbable, Apollo, God of Light, one of the original Twelve Olympians, was falling in love with Pamela Gray, a very modern mortal woman.

"Hey! What are you going to do with your four thousand dollars?"

Apollo raised her hand to his lips. "I have no idea. Perhaps you would help me decide. I believe I distinctly remember you saying that you've never purchased a four thousand dollar pair of designer shoes . . ." His voice trailed off as his gaze drifted down her body to the dangerous-looking black stiletto sandals she was wearing. "And I find that I have grown very fond of your daggerlike shoes."

"You definitely know the way to a girl's heart." She grinned.

"By all the gods, I hope so," Apollo said earnestly.

He turned down a small side hallway and after just a few feet stopped in front of a plain-looking white door.

"This can't be it," Pamela said, looking around. "This isn't marked at all. It's not even near the other restaurants." She gave the door, and then Phoebus, a suspicious glance. "I think you've gotten turned around somewhere."

His smile was surreptitious. "I told you it was exclusive."

"But . . ." she began.

Apollo turned her to face him. He'd have to do this quickly. He didn't like using his powers to fog her mind, but he needed to get her through the portal and then instantly transport her to his temple—without her being aware of what was happening.

"I promise tonight's dinner will be like none other you have ever eaten." He didn't bother to search the area around them; the little service hallway had been charmed by the power of Olympus. There would be no mortal intruders to stumble upon him using his immortal magic on Pamela. "But before we go in, I must do something I have been waiting to do since my sister so abruptly interrupted us earlier today."

Apollo drew her into his arms. As his hands skimmed down the soft curve of her body and his lips met hers, he concentrated on sending a mist of his golden power into her mind. He commanded the light-filled mist to gently blanket her thoughts so that, for just the space of a few breaths, her precious mortal soul would be dizzy and disoriented.

"Oh," she breathed, swaying slightly.

In one swift movement, Apollo picked Pamela up, cradling her in his arms as he opened the door and stepped through the portal. He only had a brief glimpse of the Great Hall of Olympus, but it was enough for him to see that Artemis had done as she had promised. The room was empty. There was not a single immortal to witness the God of Light reentering Olympus carrying a modern mortal carefully in his arms. Apollo silently commanded that the two of them be transported to his temple, and they disappeared in a shower of displaced sunlight.

Bacchus' smile was sly as he stepped from the mouth of the hallway and approached the door that held the Olympic portal. This was going to be laughably easy. As always, Apollo was too self-assured and arrogant. He hadn't noticed that Bacchus had been following him since he'd met the mortal woman at the wine bar. Actually, Apollo had not noticed anything except the modern mortal with whom he was quite obviously thoroughly obsessed. Apollo had played the unsung hero, manipulating the slot machine and

gifting the mortal with the means to purchase the object of
her whim. He could hardly wait until the woman witnessed
how helpless and pathetic the golden god would become
without his powers. Bacchus was looking forward to seeing the God of Light's arrogance extinguished, even if it
was only for the span of five days.

Bacchus strode through the portal. Just as he had anticipated, the Great Hall of Olympus was empty. And if he
knew the golden twins, they would make certain that the
hall stayed empty so that Apollo's little tryst with the mortal would go unnoticed by the other immortals. How convenient. He almost laughed aloud, but with an effort
controlled himself. There would be time aplenty to gloat
afterwards; now he needed to concentrate.

The Wine God faced the portal and lifted his arms over
his head, calling forth the intoxicating power of his realm,
and beginning the ritualistic spell.

> *"Powers of wine, rich and heady*
> *cling to this portal, make it ready*
> *the mortal may pass through unchanged*
> *but if she returns she must become what she was*
>   *named.*
> *Linger for only a moment, gentle powers*
> *then fade, as Apollo's light burns away morning*
>   *showers."*

Bacchus paused to stifle the glee he felt at using the ref-
erence to the God of Light in his spell. Refocusing on the
business at hand, Bacchus completed the words of his trap.

> *"The lesson I desire the Sun God to learn*
> *is that there is more than one way to be burned."*

Bacchus flung his hands towards the portal, and for an
instant it shimmered in liquid light the color of chilled rosé
wine. Then the blush tint faded, and all appeared to be normal once again.

"Step one completed," Bacchus murmured to himself.
"Step two awaits."

The God of the Vine uttered a soft command. His body disappeared, and then re-formed in the rear garden of Apollo's temple. He peered around a well-manicured bush. Just as he had anticipated, the grounds were deserted. Usually, bright nymphs clustered around their favorite god's temple, vying for Apollo's attention.

"The adoration of nymphs must not be convenient when entertaining a modern mortal," Bacchus said under his breath. "So much the better for me."

For a large god, Bacchus moved with surprising stealth. He entered through one of the rear doors of the temple and made his way silently down the marble hall until he came to a cavernous room in which a dozen of Artemis' virgin handmaidens were tittering and laughing as they arranged food and pitchers of wine on platters. Yes, he was in time. He waited, impatient for the handmaiden who seemed to be in charge of the wine to turn her head as she replied to a giggling question from one of her friends, and then with a swift, sure movement, he flicked his fingers at the pitchers of wine, whispering,

> *"Intoxicate . . . arouse . . . flame their desire . . . fog inhibitions . . . set them afire."*

The wine glowed briefly with an unnatural, pale pink light. Unseen by anyone, Bacchus backed out of the room and melted into the night. Now all that was left for him to do was to wait and watch . . . wait and watch . . .

Bacchus' self-satisfied laughter echoed eerily through the empty gardens.

*Artemis rushed into the room, and her handmaidens respect*fully silenced their chatter.

"They have arrived."

Excited whispers ceased with one motion of the goddess's hand.

"Tonight by serving my brother you serve me." The handmaidens bowed their heads. "Play your parts well."

"Yes, Goddess," their sweet voices intoned.

"Take them wine," Artemis commanded, and two of the handmaidens hurried to do her bidding. After they left, the goddess drifted over to the platters laden with delicacies. She glanced at her attentive handmaidens and said mischievously, "Shall I aid the God of Light in achieving his desire?"

Her maidens giggled and nodded. Artemis spread her hands over her brother's feast.

> *"Intoxicate . . . arouse . . . flame their desire . . . fog inhibitions . . . set them afire."*

Power showered from the goddess's hands to settle over the food. There it glowed for a moment before settling back into the appearance of normalcy.

"Serve them and then leave them alone. Privacy is what Apollo will wish for tonight."

Feeling very satisfied, Artemis left her brother's temple and walked slowly in the direction of the Great Hall. It would be deserted; she had made certain of that. Aphrodite and Eros had returned earlier from their weekend foray in the Kingdom of Las Vegas, and they were resting in their temples. Artemis herself had made it clear to the nymphs still fluttering about Las Vegas that it was time they returned to Olympus, and with a few sharp words she had sent them scattering back to the forests and glens where they belonged. Silly creatures. The rest of the Twelve Immortals were making themselves scarce. Artemis had begun a rumor that Hera and Zeus were fighting again. Neither mortal nor god wished to get in the middle of that. So she would wait for her brother in the empty hall and hope that before dawn she would feel the bond between herself and the mortal dissolve. She'd certainly done all that she could. The rest was up to Apollo.

"This is absolutely spectacular." Pamela gazed around her in awe. "I can't believe that plain little door was hiding all of this."

"Does it please you?"

"Please me? Are you kidding? This place is magnificent!" Pamela tilted her head back, trying to see to the top of the domed ceiling on which she could just make out some kind of fabulous fresco, but the dizziness that had struck her earlier caused her to stumble back. Phoebus' strong arm was there to catch her.

"Maybe you should sit down," he said, guiding her over to one of two exquisitely upholstered chaise lounges that rested on either side of a marble table.

She sank down on the chaise and rubbed her forehead. "I must have gotten too much sun today. My head feels woozy."

As if on cue, two young women entered the room. They were wearing short, diaphanous tunics made of white silk trimmed with silver thread embroidered in the shapes of forest creatures. One was carrying a tray that held a golden pitcher and two golden goblets. The women smiled shyly at Phoebus and Pamela.

"Wine?" they asked in perfect unison.

"Of course," Apollo said.

With graceful movements that were lovely to watch, the waitresses served them.

"Your feast is prepared," one girl said melodically.

"Shall we serve you now?" the other asked.

"Yes," Apollo said.

The two women curtsied deeply and hurried out the way they had come.

"But we haven't even ordered," Pamela said. She had a terrible headache, and she felt disorientated and slightly uneasy.

"I specified what we required for the feast earlier." He thought for a moment. "I think you would call it preordering." When Pamela's perplexed expression changed into a frown, he added, "I hope you don't mind. I wanted to surprise you with Greek delicacies."

"Surprise Greek delicacies? That sounds intriguing. Almost as intriguing as this restaurant," she rubbed her hand down the side of the chaise. "Silk velvet—my personal favorite upholstery fabric." As if the familiar touch of the velvet was grounding, the thick feeling in her head began to clear. Her fingers lingered on the beautiful fabric. "Silk velvet always reminds me of water; it's so slick and soft. I adore it."

"I am glad you approve," Apollo said, relieved that she seemed to be recovering from the power he had sprinkled over her.

Pamela looked around the dimly lit room. Not only were they the only patrons, but their table was the only one set up in the whole place. It was obviously a big space, but unlike the rest of Caesars Palace and The Forum, someone with taste and style had decorated it. Which meant that it wasn't loaded from floor to ceiling with gaudy pseudo-Roman opulence. The flooring was incredible. It appeared to have been fashioned from a single sheet of marble, even though she knew that was not possible.

"This flooring is amazing. It looks like fine Carrara marble, but I've never seen Carrara with veins of gold going through it like this has." Her eyes traveled from the floor to the walls, and they widened. "They've used the same marble for the walls and the columns. And I really like the minimalist style. The decorator was right on here; the marble is too beautiful to cover with a bunch of paintings. The single tapestry adds the perfect touch," she gestured at a large hanging that covered most of the wall in front of them. It was of a naked man. A gorgeous, young, naked man. She squinted, trying to see it better in the dim lighting. He was standing beside a chariot, and he was holding a harp in his hand.

"He looks familiar," Pamela said.

"Probably because you're wearing his likeness around your neck," Apollo said quickly.

She touched the gold coin and smiled. "That's right, you did say that the name of this restaurant is Mount Olympus. I guess this must be Apollo again. You know, I really can see a resemblance between you and him, especially how he looks in that tapestry. It's kind of weird."

"Coincidence," Apollo said nonchalantly. "Shall we drink?" He handed her one of the goblets and then raised his own. "To feeling lucky."

Pamela grinned and patted the sparkling purse that

rested by her side. "To feeling lucky." She sipped. "This wine is delicious! I usually don't like white." She looked into her goblet. "But this isn't exactly white." The color of the wine was as unusual as its taste. If Pamela had been asked to describe it for one of those wine-tasting magazines, she would have said that it was light and crisp on the pallet, like the scent of pears or melons, and the color of sunlight. "What is it, a Pinot Gris?"

Apollo shrugged. "I'm not certain. I asked them to serve us the house's finest." And about that, he was telling the truth. Artemis had planned the dinner, along with the wine. Apollo took another long drink. He would have to ask Artemis about the wine—it was delicious as well as unusual. It was chilled, but as he drank he could feel it fill his body with warmth that seemed to radiate from his core. He looked at Pamela. Her cheeks were flushed, and she had quit inspecting the design of the room. She was smiling softly at him. Her lips were gently parted. They looked full and inviting.

"I did not like being away from you this evening," he said.

"I missed you, too."

"How will I bear being apart from you for the next five days?"

"Five days?" That would make it the weekend again when he returned to Vegas. Wasn't she planning on flying back to Colorado then? This job was only supposed to take a week. Five days without him . . . Her thoughts were suddenly sluggish and disjointed . . . The time seemed at once interminable and unimportant. She didn't want him to leave, she knew that, but he was here now, almost close enough to touch. How could any man be so handsome? She had to force herself to stay on her chaise, when what she really wanted to do was to join him on his . . . to pull off his shirt . . . and begin licking her way down his body.

"Yes, I . . ." he faltered. What was it he and Artemis had decided to tell Pamela about his "trip"? He was finding it difficult to concentrate on anything except her lips.

The stream of maidens carrying food-filled platters interrupted his impulse to push aside the table and devour her mouth.

On golden plates Apollo and Pamela were served food of the gods.

"The finest grape leaves, stuffed with morsels of meat and cheese," one of Artemis' handmaidens proclaimed in a soft, hypnotic voice as Pamela bit into the fragrant bundle.

"Lamb, from a beast raised on honey and milk," another maiden murmured.

Apollo tasted the meat, then smiled, eating with relish. His sister was usually not at all domestic, but tonight she had outdone herself.

"Cheese from goats that nymphs care for as if they were beloved children."

"Olives and figs picked from Mount Olympus by the smooth, knowing hands of Aphrodite's priestesses."

They were undoubtedly the best waitresses Pamela had ever had. She wanted to ask Phoebus how he had managed this evening. He must have reserved the entire restaurant for their private use, which meant—amongst other things—that he must be an incredibly successful doctor. And he looked so young! She meant to ask him exactly how old his was, when was his birthday, and where had he been born—not that it really mattered. She was just curious. She should also ask him about . . . about . . . about . . . what? She couldn't concentrate . . .

. . . Because the food was so completely, absorbingly delicious. The taste filled her senses. It was more than food. It reminded her of summer sunlight and heat and desire . . . her eyes lifted from her plate to find Phoebus watching her with a sapphire intensity that made her breath catch.

"We leave you alone; for the night we retire . . ." the handmaidens sang. And as they faded from the room their sweet voices whispered an almost inaudible prayer: ". . . Intoxicate . . . arouse . . . flame their desire . . . fog inhibitions . . . set them afire."

Apollo and Pamela barely noticed the handmaidens' departure. They stared at each other, and everything else in the room, in the world, faded. Their skin tingled with growing heat and desire.

"I need you to love me," Apollo's voice was thick with lust and longing. Somewhere in the recesses of his mind, where common sense still lurked, he knew his reaction to her was too raw, too uninhibited, but he couldn't stop it— he didn't want to stop it.

"Yes." She breathed the word.

With a feral, liquid movement that Pamela thought made him look like a large, tawny lion, he stood. He hurled the table separating them out of the way. Pamela realized that the table flew away from Phoebus' touch with an inhuman force, but the thought was vague and only partially formed. When he ripped off his shirt and roughly tore his pants from his body, all she could think of was her body's reaction to the guttural sound of her name on his lips and how magnificent he looked stalking towards her naked.

"Yes," she moaned again, coming off the chaise and into his arms. His mouth devoured her. She slid one hand around his shoulders, feeling his muscles tremble with the force of his desire. With her free hand she yanked her shirt over her head and then quickly unzipped her slacks, which slid fluidly from her body. Phoebus found the hook of her bra, struggling to open it.

"I can't . . . I need . . ." he groaned in frustration. "I must feel you against me." He tore the strip of lace from her back, and her breasts came free. She rubbed them against his chest as she kissed a hot path down the side of his neck.

A curse wrenched from his throat as Apollo tried to control his lust. Then Pamela took his hand that was kneading her breast and guided it to her panties, and all thoughts of control flew from his mind.

"These, too." She tugged at his bottom lip with her teeth, pulling it into the slick den of her mouth and sucking enticingly. "I want you to rip these off, too."

With a growl he obeyed her. Then he splayed his hands around her naked waist, and with the strength of a god, he lifted her and impaled her on his throbbing shaft.

Pamela was incredibly slick and ready for him. She

wrapped her legs around his waist and dug her fingernails
into his shoulders. Throwing her head back, she arched
into him, totally consumed by the overwhelming need to
sate herself in his touch . . . in his fire.

He was fire. Under her hands his body actually glowed.
Her senses acknowledged it, but her mind could not hold
the thought. It seemed that the light that glistened from his
sweat-damp skin was just another part of his arousal; it
tempted her and teased her and goaded on her own passion.
His hair curled around his face, thick and golden and glo-
rious. And his eyes . . . his eyes burned her. She wanted to
be burned by him; she wanted to be licked by the flames of
his lust.

She felt gloriously, wondrously out of control.

"Harder . . ." she gasped into his mouth, hardly recognizing her own voice. Phoebus lunged forward, and
Pamela felt the cool smoothness of one of the marble
columns against her naked back. She used the strength of
the column to brace herself, so that she could meet his
thrusts with her own inflamed passion. "Don't stop . . . not
yet . . . don't stop," she panted, feeling herself tip over the
edge of the world. Her orgasm was like nothing she had
ever experienced. It engulfed her, rippling through her
body with an intensity that verged on pain.

And then she was no longer being pressed against the
column. His erection still impaling her, Phoebus carried
her from the room. They passed through an arched doorway that led to a chamber adjacent to the dining room. In
the center of the new room was a large, canopied bed. Logically, Pamela understood that they had entered a bedroom
and that that shouldn't make any sense, but her mind was
as filled with Phoebus as was her body—nothing was real
except his touch, taste and smell.

"What's happening?" she whispered as he lay her on the
bed beneath him.

"I am loving you. Forever, Pamela. This is what it is to
be loved by me."

He began moving against her in the ancient dance of
lovemaking, withdrawing his hard length from her body,
and then plunging into her—again and again. Pamela ran

her hands across his slick chest as he lifted himself over her. His skin was a golden glow. Dazed, yet ultrasensitized, she gazed down at where their bodies joined. They were both glowing . . . on fire . . . flames were licking their skin . . . driving them on . . . engulfing them . . .

"Look at me, Pamela." His voice was raw.

She locked her eyes with his.

"See me," he said. "This time really see me."

As they joined together she looked at him. He was power and beauty and love all melded into one being. How had she ever believed that he was just a man? Her mind struggled to grasp the elusive truth of what she was seeing as their bodies flamed in his blinding, immortal light. What was he? What was happening to her?

Apollo saw panic flicker in her eyes, and he framed her face with his hands, forcing her gaze to remain locked with his. With an enormous effort of will, he commanded his body to still.

"Look deeper," he said. "Look beyond the strangeness that you fear. Can't you see your reflection in my soul?"

The blue of his eyes held her even more intimately than their joined bodies. She was trembling with the intensity of her emotions. And there, beneath the new power that radiated from him, she found Phoebus—the heart of the man she knew. In that heart she saw the reflection of her own longing and need and emptiness, and she suddenly knew that by filling him, she would complete herself, too.

"What are you?" she whispered.

"Your soul mate."

His voice shook, and despite the awesome power that so clearly radiated from him, Pamela thought he suddenly looked very young and vulnerable.

"Yes," she breathed, feeling the fire begin to reignite deep within her. "You are my soul mate."

She pulled him down to her, and with a wrenching moan he thrust into her again, unable to hold back any longer. When the world began to explode, she buried her face in his glowing shoulder and hung on.

*   *   *

In the Great Hall, Artemis suddenly sat straight up. She drew a deep, cleansing breath. Gone! The bond with the mortal was gone. Apparently, her magic had tipped the scales in her brother's favor. And it was about time. She stretched luxuriously, enjoying the absence of the ever-annoying itch that had been Pamela's unfulfilled heart's desire. Then she settled back on her well-stuffed chaise. She would have liked to have retired to her forest—a run in the moonlight would be refreshing—but, no, Apollo still needed her to ensure no nymphs would glimpse him returning the mortal to her own world. It was really of little consequence; their dealings with the mortal were almost completed. Now that Apollo had won her heart, Artemis predicted that he would tire of Pamela quickly. Soon everything would return to normal, and their escapade in the Kingdom of Las Vegas would be nothing more than a semiamusing memory . . .

Artemis ignored the prickle of doubt that niggled at her mind as she remembered her brother's earnest proclamation of love. Apollo's soul mate was a mortal woman? It was simply not possible.

Hidden in the shadows, Bacchus smiled and waited.

CHAPTER 20

~~

Something was wrong. Apollo knew it in the same way he knew the many languages of man, or the voices of musical instruments—innately, on the most elemental level of his being. The warm shape in his arms stirred. Automatically, he tightened his arms around her. Pamela . . .

Apollo's eyes shot open. What had happened last night? They were naked on his bed. *Think!* he commanded his addled brain. *Remember!* And the events of the evening rushed through his memory. He stifled a groan. He had lost all control. How? Why had he not been able to—

He knew the answer before he finished the thought. The feast had been filled with the intoxicating power of a goddess. And he knew who that particular goddess had to be. Artemis!

"Apollo!"

As if his thoughts had conjured her, the goddess's impatient whisper sizzled through the room.

He turned his head and glared.

"What are you doing?" she hissed. "You know dawn is close to breaking. Do you want the mortal to be trapped here?"

Shocked, Apollo sat up. That was what was amiss. As always, the God of Light had felt the coming of the blazing chariot that ushered dawn into the sky. Instinctively he had known that it was past time for Pamela to be returned to her world. Last night he had revealed too much. How would her mortal mind ever grasp what it had gleaned

from their uninhibited lovemaking, as well as accept that
she was trapped in Mount Olympus? He remembered the
fear that had flickered through her eyes when he had revealed himself to her.

She wouldn't be able to understand it, not truly. Or if
she did, he could only imagine how it would change her
feelings for him. No, it was too soon. He must get her out
of Olympus. By the time the portal reopened, he would
have an explanation for the unusual night. He would spend
more time with her and solidify her feelings for him, feelings she had only admitted under the influence of his sister's magic. He scowled at Artemis again.

"Go!" he whispered back at her. "Make sure the Great
Hall is empty. I will follow with Pamela."

"Hurry . . ." she said as her body dissipated.

"Phoebus?" Pamela's voice was groggy. She blinked
sleepily and rubbed her eyes. "Where . . ."

He clenched his teeth and reluctantly passed his hand
over her face, instantly fogging her mind and dulling her
senses.

"You must dress. We have to leave," he said, leading
her gently by the hand into the adjoining room where he
found their discarded clothes.

Numbly, she complied. He hated himself as he hastily
tugged on his own pants while Pamela mechanically
dressed herself. Her underthings, like his shirt, were totally
ruined. The memory of the passion he had felt when he
tore the clothes from their bodies shivered through him,
causing his loins to stir. How was he going to live without
her touch for five days? His will wavered. He did have a
choice. He could bespell her and keep her with him until
the portal opened again. He touched her face and, even
with her mind shrouded by his magic, she swayed towards
him. It would only be a week . . .

No! He shook himself. She would loathe him for doing
such a thing. How could she not? He loathed himself even
for the thought.

"Come, I will take you home, my sweet Pamela."

He wrapped his arms around her, and they disappeared,
re-forming almost instantly beside the portal in the Great

Hall. Artemis was there, arms crossed, tapping her foot restlessly. She took in his bare-chested appearance and Pamela's zombielike expression and shook her head. The sooner they were finished with the modern world of the mortals, the better.

"Quickly, the sun is rising," Artemis said.

"I know it!" Apollo snapped. "Or now that my senses are no longer numbed by a goddess's magic, I know it."

Artemis had the good grace to look uncomfortable.

"I will take her through and then return."

The goddess sighed but didn't argue with him. Apollo put his arm around Pamela and led her through the portal.

They stepped into Vegas, and Apollo opened the door to the little closet. In the deserted hallway he straightened Pamela's clothes. He touched her face gently. Apollo felt like a thief. He'd stolen her love, and now he was skulking back before the light of day could reveal his crime. He had no choice, but still he hated himself for allowing it to happen like this.

"I love you, my sweet Pamela. Remember that, and remember to trust me. I will return to you. I will make this right." He bent to her and commanded silently, *With my kiss, awaken.*

He kissed her deeply, and while she blinked and her dazed expression began to clear, he backed into the closet, closed the door and returned to Olympus.

Pamela rubbed her eyes. Ugh, she felt dizzy and a little sick. How much had she had to drink at dinner? She looked around her. Where the hell was she? The plain-looking little door and the empty hallway registered in her woozy brain. Where was Phoebus? She ran her hand through her hair, and the motion of raising her arm jiggled her breasts. Jiggled her breasts? Where was her bra? A thread of panic trailed down her spine. Think! What did she remember?

Phoebus had met her at the café. They'd gone to dinner at a wonderful, exclusive restaurant . . . but her memory of the meal itself was sketchy. Weird, dreamlike flashes of hot, slick skin and the salty taste of the remnants of passion assailed her. She had a brief image of ripping clothes, and then another of Phoebus leading her from a bedroom so she could get dressed—in only some of her clothes. Her panic swelled, and her headache spiked. *Breathe,* she ordered herself. She was fine; she'd just had too much to drink.

But where the hell was Phoebus!

Okay, her last really clear memory was her happiness at buying the fabulous ruby slipper purse—

"Bloody buggering hell! My purse!"

She looked at the little white door. What had happened at dinner? She couldn't wrap her mind around the memory, even though she knew it was there. For some reason it hovered just beyond her reach. Had she been drugged? By Phoebus? But why would he?

To keep her fear at bay she latched onto one small bit of normalcy. She'd left her brand new four thousand dollar ruby slipper purse in the restaurant. Phoebus or no Phoebus, she was going to go back and get it.

Pamela opened the door and stepped into . . . A closet? In the middle of the closet was a door-sized disk that shimmered and glowed. A memory stirred. She had gone into this disk/door with Phoebus. It was the entrance to the restaurant. Squaring her shoulders, she walked into the bizarre entryway.

She felt a funny, tickly sensation like feathers brushing over her skin, and the light changed from the closet's single yellow bulb to a soft, rose-colored luminescence. But she didn't enter the fabulous restaurant she half remembered. Instead, she seemed to have stepped into the middle of a magnificent ballroom. The impression she got was of enormous size and incredible beauty. The huge room was empty, except for two people who were shouting at each other. As she emerged from the entrance, they turned toward her. Phoebus, minus a shirt, stared at her with blank-eyed shock. His sister at first looked enraged, and then her expressed changed as—

Pain sliced through Pamela. She opened her mouth to scream, but as change rippled down her body, the scream had to echo through her mind because she had no mouth left with which to give it voice. Helplessly, she reached toward Phoebus as her body folded, then morphed into something not human. At the same instant, the pain dissipated the fog in her mind, and her memories came rushing back. Phoebus. His skin glowing with an unearthly passion. Taking her in his arms. Making her his own. He wasn't human. No human man could be made of fire. What had he done to her? What was he doing to her now? She remembered his fire licking her and stroking her and . . . Another scream ripped through her mind.

Apollo's back had been to the portal. He had been chastising his sister for being an interfering, meddlesome—

His barrage had been sliced in two when he felt his soul mate enter Olympus. The moment her mortal feet passed through the portal, her body began to change. Helplessly, Apollo watched as his Pamela faded, melted, and then reformed as a beautiful, fragrant jasmine flower.

"Get her back through before the sun rises!" his sister shouted. "When the portal closes, the spell will fade."

Then she would be Pamela once more. Her words worked on him like a prod. He lunged forward, feeling Artemis close behind him. Grabbing the delicate jasmine flower, he pulled it from where it had already begun embedding its roots along the marble floor. Whispering a broken apology, Apollo leapt through the portal with Pamela's changed body clasped tightly in his hands.

Artemis hesitated in front of the portal, glancing quickly over her shoulder at the floor-to-ceiling windows that showed dawn beginning to lighten the already blush-tinged sky.

"No, fool!" she yelled into the madly swirling disk. "You weren't supposed to go through with her!" The goddess leaned forward, trying to see within the glowing passageway.

From the shadows Bacchus moved swiftly on silent feet. With one decisive motion, he rammed his shoulder into the center of the Huntress's back. Artemis shrieked and fell into the disk just seconds before the portal went dark, slamming firmly shut as dawn broke over Mount Olympus.

Bacchus' laughter was filled with terrible triumph.

CHAPTER 21

Pamela was on her hands and knees. Her breath came in ragged sobs, and her teeth chattered in time with her body's trembling. *Her* body! Frantically, she felt her arms and face. She'd turned into something—something green and growing and decidedly not normal. But now she was normal again. Human again.

"All is well now, my sweet," Apollo said, reaching out to her.

She flinched away from his touch. "You!" she gasped, but before she could say anything else, Phoebus' sister fell headfirst into the small room just before the swirling pearl-colored disk disappeared.

Artemis sputtered a foreign curse as she picked herself up from the floor. Her brother stared slack-jawed at her. "I will make Bacchus sorry Zeus saved him when his foolish human mother—" Her tirade broke off as she realized the portal was closed. "No," she breathed the word. "We can not be trapped here."

"What the hell are you?" the words exploded from Pamela.

Apollo and Artemis turned to the little mortal who crouched on the floor. Pamela had scuttled backward until she was pressed against the closed door. Her eyes were huge and looked impossibly dark against the whiteness of her face.

"Pamela," Apollo spoke in a soothing tone, holding his hand out to her again. "You know who I am."

"No!" she said sharply, recoiling from his touch. "I didn't ask *who* you are. I asked *what* you are."

"You're going to have to make her forget," Artemis said, completely ignoring Pamela. "She has seen too much. Look at her—she remembers." The goddess raised her slender hand. "Oh, I'll do it for you; I know you've become entirely too attached to her. Sleep and forget," she flicked her fingers at Pamela, who automatically flinched back.

"Stop!" Apollo shouted. "I don't want you to tamper with her."

"What in the hell is going on?" Pamela's legs worked just well enough for her to stand up, but there she stayed with her back to the door, pressing her hands flat against solid wood to stop their trembling.

"Why isn't she sleeping?" Artemis asked her brother. She shook her hand and studied her fingers.

"The portal is closed," Apollo said.

His sister scowled at him. "I can see that."

Apollo simply kept gazing at her. Then his sister's eyes widened. "When the portal closed . . ." Her words faded.

"When the portal closed, it severed us from our powers," Apollo finished for her.

Artemis' hand flew to cover her mouth as she gasped in horror.

"Okay. That's it. I'm leaving." Pamela jerked open the closet door and left the room on legs that felt like rubber.

"Look what you've done now," Apollo growled at his sister before he hurried after Pamela.

"Me?" Artemis sniffed indignantly. Reluctantly, she followed her brother. She didn't want to. She wanted the portal to reopen. She wanted to return to Olympus and have a long soak in her mineral spring. She wanted her immortal powers returned to her and . . . She sighed and stepped into the hall.

Apollo had caught Pamela by the elbow just a few feet from the closet door. She was trying to pull her arm from his grasp as he murmured reassurances to her. Artemis shook her head. How the mighty had fallen. She marched up to the two of them.

"Be still, mortal," she said in disgust. "It is really very simple." She pointed at her brother. "His true name is Phoebus Apollo, God of Light, Music and Healing. My name is Diana, but only if you are of ancient Roman descent. Otherwise I prefer to be called Artemis, the Huntress Goddess. I also have an affinity for the moon, just as my brother is allied with the sun, but I certainly wouldn't want to give you so much information that I confuse you," she finished sarcastically.

"You're gods?" Pamela hoped fervently that she would wake up very soon.

"Yes. Immortals. Or at least we were until the portal trapped us in this wretched world. Now I suspect we are just extremely attractive mortals," she said dryly.

"Apollo and Artemis," Pamela looked from brother to sister.

"I told you it was simple."

"You're fucking crazy!" she said.

"I didn't want you to find out like this," Apollo said. "But you know Artemis is telling you the truth." He frowned at his sister. "Even if she is doing a poor job of it."

"What?" Artemis said. "If you wanted soft music and the scent of flowers, I'm sorry, but I won't be able to oblige you—at least until the portal reopens."

"You're not helping," Apollo told his sister.

"But there's no such thing as the gods. It's just mythology," Pamela said.

"I thought you said she was smart," Artemis scoffed.

Pamela's gaze took in the beautiful young woman who looked so much like her lover, and she felt some of the numb horror that had overwhelmed her thaw. Through that thaw she began to become pissed off.

"You don't have to be so rude," Pamela said.

"Rude?" Artemis' eyes narrowed. "You call *me* rude when *you* deny my existence? Yet you're standing in the middle of a structure built because ancient people honored me and the other eleven like me so well that I have been remembered for thousands of years. Does that sound particularly intelligent to you?"

"It doesn't sound smart or dumb. It just sounds incredible. This whole thing is incredible. It can't be true."

Apollo took her other elbow and turned her to face him. Tried to ignore how she continued to pull away from him. He spoke in a quiet, calm voice. "You know the truth, Pamela. You've experienced it. All you have to do is accept it."

She looked at him—really looked at him. He was the same tall, handsome man he had been the night before. Yet he wasn't. There was something . . . *missing* about him. He was still unusually attractive, but the spectacular blue of his eyes had dimmed to a more . . . she gulped . . . a more *human* shade. And there was something else, too. He had less presence. That was the only way she could describe it. Technically he looked the same; yet he didn't. The specifics hadn't changed. His shoulders weren't any less broad, and his chest wasn't any less muscular—as she could easily see because he was wearing no shirt. Yet he was changed . . . altered . . . less.

And Artemis had been right; Pamela did remember. Little things, like the fact that Phoebus could lie in the desert sun all afternoon and not even sweat. Big things, like the fact that he had turned into flame last night as they were making love. And then there was the undeniable fact that she had stepped through a glowing door and been turned into something that definitely was not human . . .

It couldn't be. It wasn't possible. But in her gut she knew they were telling the truth. They were gods.

"What was that thing in the closet?" she whispered.

"It was a portal Zeus opened from Mount Olympus into the Kingdom of Las Vegas," Apollo said.

"Why?"

Apollo shrugged and attempted a half-smile. "Who knows the mind of the Supreme Ruler of Olympus?"

"If I remember correctly, he said something about wanting us to observe and delight in your world," Artemis said.

Pamela's eyes snapped to hers. "You mean a kind of experiment? Like a sick *Star Trek* episode?"

"Do you know what she means?" Artemis asked her brother.

"No, but I do know that, again, *you are not helping!*" he said through gritted teeth.

Pamela stared at him. "What happened to me when I went back through that portal? Something happened to my body—something terrible. What did you do to me?"

"No! It wasn't me. You can't believe I would do anything to hurt you."

Pamela turned her face away from him. "You already have."

"It was that toad Bacchus. He must have bespelled the portal." Artemis paused as she thought about what had been happening to Pamela. "You were changing into a flower."

"A jasmine flower, as her name suggests," Apollo said. "The sweetest of all flowers."

Artemis snorted. "Very romantic, and what it tells us is that Bacchus bespelled the portal so that if she came through without you, she'd revert to the most basic form of her name."

Pamela's heart felt like it had gone numb. "It's just like in the myths. You use humans, and when you discard them, you turn them into something . . . something *not* human."

"I wouldn't say that's quite accurate." Artemis looked offended.

Apollo turned his back to his sister. "Let me explain," he told Pamela. "It isn't like that at all with you and me."

"No. I'm done being experimented on," she sent Artemis a disgusted look. "And I don't want you to explain. I just want you to go back to where you came from and leave me alone."

"We would like nothing more, but it appears we are stuck here until your weekend comes around again," Artemis said.

Apollo shook his head. "No, *she* would like nothing more. I want nothing more than to be with you—to explain to you."

"I'm not interested in—" she began, trying again to pull her arms from Apollo's strong grasp, but a sharp voice interrupted her.

"Is there a problem here?"

A blue-uniformed security guard was standing in the entrance to the hallway. He was short and chubby, but he had a badge and a gun and an expression that said that he took his job very seriously.

"Oh, begone," Artemis said, automatically flicking her fingers in his direction. Then her disdainful expression turned blank as she remembered she was powerless.

"What did you say?" the guard said, narrowing his eyes at the beautiful woman dressed in a short toga-like tunic.

Apollo dropped Pamela's arms and stepped in front of her and his sister. Pamela looked at the darkening expression on his face and realized that with or without immortal powers he had the potential to be a very dangerous man.

"There's no problem here, Officer," Pamela said quickly, stepping up beside Apollo. "It's just that my"— she paused, glanced at Apollo's naked chest and discarded trite words like boyfriend and date, which she was sure would make her sound like a candidate for the *Jerry Springer Show*—"my fiancé and I had a lover's tiff, and, well . . ." She shrugged and smiled sheepishly. But the man was not looking at her or the half-naked man beside her; he was staring at Artemis.

"Wait!" the officer said, his small eyes glittering. "Don't I recognize you as one of the stars of *Zumanity*?"

Pamela held her breath while Artemis raised one slender eyebrow.

"I am *the* star of *Zumanity*," she said.

"This is Diana, my fiancé's sister," Pamela said. She didn't look at Apollo, but she could feel the tension in his body as he stood there silently beside her.

"You know, I caught the show for the first time just the other night." He rocked back and forth on his feet. Sweat popped out over his upper lip. "It was really something. You were really something."

"I suppose it is rewarding to know that I pleased the masses," Artemis said.

Pamela grabbed her elbow and took Apollo's hand and began leading them both past the officer. "Well, we really should be getting back to our rooms. I can't imagine how we took a wrong turn and ended up here."

"Next time be sure you're dressed properly when you leave your rooms," the officer said to Apollo as Pamela rushed him past. Then he tipped his hat to Artemis. "Pleasure to meet you, Diana. I can't wait to see the show again."

Pamela could feel the growl that rumbled through Apollo's body.

None of them spoke until they turned the corner and were walking through the casino's lobby. Then Pamela let loose Artemis' arm. She tried to pull her hand from Apollo, but he just tightened his grip on her. She frowned at him.

"I want you to let me go." She lowered her voice so that the people who were nearby wouldn't overhear her.

"I don't plan on ever letting you go," Apollo said.

Artemis sighed dramatically.

"Stay out of this," Apollo ordered his sister. "You don't understand what it's like to be in love."

"In love! Oh, please. I realize that I'm just a human, but I'm not a moron. No matter what your sister thinks." She glared at Artemis, who curled her lip back at her.

Pamela met Apollo's gaze again. Her eyes were no longer glassy with shock. Instead they glittered with outrage.

"How can you possibly say you're in love with me? You pretended to be someone you're not. You used me as some kind of observation experiment. And I suspect you worked some kind of weird spell on me!"

Several people turned and looked curiously in her direction.

"Let me explain," Apollo said.

Pamela started to shake her head, but the god touched the side of her face. She froze.

"Please," he whispered, hating that when he touched her fear suddenly overpowered the anger in her eyes. "You must. I already told you that I won't let you go. Once given, I never break my oath." His hand left her face and briefly touched the coin she still wore around her neck. "I've pledged my protection to you. You have nothing to fear from me."

"Excuse me, sir," a casino worker approached them.

"I'm afraid I'm going to have to ask you to put your shirt on."

"We're just on our way to our room," Pamela said, pulling Apollo toward the hotel elevators.

"Such fuss over a little bare flesh," Artemis said, following her brother.

"I want everything explained to me," Pamela said as they entered the elevator.

"It will be," Apollo assured her, still holding her hand.

"It will be *boring*," Artemis muttered.

"You're not helping," Apollo and Pamela said together.

CHAPTER 22

"So you're telling me that the whole thing was nothing more than a misdirected spell?"

Pamela was sitting in one of the chairs in the living room area of her suite. Artemis lounged across the couch, and Apollo, who couldn't seem to sit still, was currently pacing up and down in front of the picture window.

"It's technically not a spell. It's an invocation ritual. Very ancient and very powerful. As Apollo said, it shouldn't have been possible for all of the required elements to come together as they did—"

"Except that Bacchus obviously had his hand in it. He must have manipulated events," Apollo finished for his sister.

"Manipulated—that is an excellent way to describe it." Pamela's look clearly said that she wasn't thinking of the invocation.

"No! It's not like that. Our feelings weren't manipulated, only the events that brought us together were."

"You lied to me," Pamela said.

"I didn't. I am a healer and a musician."

"Actually, he is *the* healer and *the* musician of the ancient world," Artemis chimed in.

Pamela drew in a sharp breath. "My ankle! You did something to my ankle that night in the rain."

"It was broken. I simply healed it."

Pamela stared at him like he'd suddenly sprouted horns and a tail.

"And the slot machine jackpot?" she asked.

"Your desire for the purse was great; it pleased me to grant that desire."

She thought his smile made him look like a little boy whose hand had been caught fisted full of cookies and trapped inside the jar. She automatically wanted to smile back at him—he seemed so normal. Then she remembered how it had felt to have her flesh twist and melt into something not human, and her resolve hardened. Her next question erased the little-boy smile.

"And the sex? What kind of magic did you use to get me in bed with you?"

"None," he said sharply. "I did not woo you as the god Apollo. I wooed you and made love to you as Phoebus, a mortal man like any other."

It was Pamela's turn to snort. "Please! I was there. It was different with you than it had been with any other man. And it's so not like me to jump in bed with a weekend fling. You had to have done something to me."

Apollo stopped his pacing and walked over to her chair. "I used no immortal power to seduce you, and what we experienced was not a weekend fling."

Pamela's mouth felt dry and her stomach tightened at his closeness. "You're doing it again," she hissed. "I want you to stop."

Apollo's boyishly endearing smile came back in full force. "Sweet Pamela, that is an impossibility. As my sister has already discovered, when the portal closed, we were cut off from our immortal powers. Until Friday at dusk, I have no more power to touch your heart than any other mortal man."

"And if you want to be angry at someone for bespelling you, be angry at me," Artemis said, studying her fingernails. "I sprinkled some of my magic on you the night of my performance. I also filled last night's feast with the power of seduction."

"Why would you do that?" Pamela asked.

"We already explained to you about the invocation ritual. Until Apollo satisfied the desire of your heart, I was bound to you." The goddess brushed a golden curl from her face. "And I was supremely tired of being bound to you. You needed a little nudge to admit to yourself that Apollo was your heart's desire. So I nudged. Thank the Nine Muses it worked."

"You're not very nice, are you?" Pamela said to the goddess.

Artemis didn't appear in the least bit offended by the question. "Nice? Why would I need to be nice?"

The phone rang. Shaking her head at Artemis, Pamela answered it.

"Pamela, this is Mr. Faust's assistant, James," said a male voice.

"Oh, yes. Hello, James." Pamela's stomach sank. It was Monday morning. She was supposed to begin work today—this morning. She'd totally forgotten about E. D. Faust and the job she was there to complete.

"I wanted to remind you that Robert will be there with the car to pick you up at the entrance to Caesars Palace in exactly thirty minutes.

"Thank you for the call, James. Of course I'll be ready."

"Wonderful! Mr. Faust is looking forward to beginning the work on his villa."

Pamela responded woodenly with an appropriate reply and hung up the phone. She stared at Apollo and Artemis, who were watching her.

"I have to go to work," she said.

"Of course—the author's home. The one with the Roman bathhouse and the fountain," Apollo said.

"Yeah, he's sending his car for me." She glanced in the mirror and grimaced at how terrible she looked. "In exactly thirty minutes. I have to get ready to go." She started to hurry towards the bedroom.

"Excellent!" Artemis said. "Where is it we're going?"

Pamela stopped short. *"We're* not going anywhere."

"Well I'm certainly not staying here in this little hovel. It's dreadfully boring."

"Well you certainly aren't coming with me," she mimicked the goddess' regal tone.

Artemis narrowed her eyes. "Do not forget to whom you speak, mortal."

Pamela planted her hands on her hips and raised her chin. "Look, goddess or not, you're going to have to learn to not be such a bitch. And you can threaten me all you want." She pointed at the gold coin that dangled from around her neck. "I have Apollo's oath that I am under his protection." She heard Apollo's chuckle, but she refused to look at him. "Just stay here and order room service, dial up a movie, learn about the Internet . . . or something. Oh, hell. I'll figure out what to do with you two when I get back."

"Pamela."

Apollo's voice stopped her retreat into her room. She turned to face him.

"We could help you," he said.

"Help me what?"

"I could help you to persuade Faust to build the bathhouse. And," he added with a little smile, "Artemis could help you to persuade him to use her as the model for the statue in the center of the fountain."

Pamela sent a doubtful look Artemis' way.

"Throughout the ages men have worshiped images of my beauty," she said flippantly. "They are easily enamored with me."

"That may be true, but it's only because they're seeing your statues and your paintings; they don't have to actually be subjected to your hateful presence."

Artemis opened her mouth to snarl at Pamela, but Apollo cut her off.

"My sister will give her oath that she will be polite."

"I will not!"

"Faust is a modern bard, and he wants the statue in the center of his fountain to be dedicated to Bacchus. Think of the tales he will spin dedicated to the God of the Vine," Apollo told his sister.

"That fat toad should not be worshiped in the modern world!" Artemis said.

He shrugged. "It's up to you."

The goddess cleared her throat and reluctantly met Pamela's eyes. "I give you my oath that I will be polite. For today."

"I don't know . . ."

"Please, Pamela," Apollo said. "Let me show you I am no different today than I was yesterday. The god Apollo and the mortal Phoebus are the same man."

She shouldn't. She knew she shouldn't. She didn't want to be loved by a god. She had liked things the way they were before he had suddenly become an all-powerful immortal. She wanted her Phoebus back . . .

"Fine," she said suddenly. "We'll have to buy you a shirt on the way out," she glanced at Artemis. "At least you're okay dressed like that. We'll just say you're in costume." She faltered, "Just . . . just stay there. I'll hurry."

She closed her bedroom door and rested her head against it. He was Apollo. Her insides shivered as the reality of it settled into her. Her lover was the Greek god, Apollo. He had lived for eons. Temples had been built to honor him. Songs had been sung of him. His hands, which had stroked every part of her body, were the same hands that had brought music to the ancient world. And he said he loved her. She pressed a trembling hand to her mouth, overwhelmed by a sudden surge of shock and disbelief and awe.

She should tell Faust she didn't want the job, get on a plane and fly directly back to Colorado. She should forget this weekend ever happened. That was the smart thing to do. But she already knew she wasn't going to do the smart thing.

The God of Light said he was in love with her.

"I'm probably making the most gihugic mistake of my life," she whispered.

They were standing outside the revolving doors that swished into Caesars Palace exactly twenty-five minutes later while Pamela's stomach churned like she was just getting ready to bungee jump.

"Remember, you're Phoebus Delos, a specialist in ancient Roman architecture. I called you in to help advise me on this project. And you're his sister, Diana. You—"

"Have the beauty of a goddess," she broke off Pamela's

nervous repetition of instructions. "Yes, yes. We know our parts. We're immortals, not imbeciles."

"I was going to say that you are to remember to be nice," Pamela said.

"My words will be so sweet that they could make honey in my mouth like the brown bees of Greece," Artemis with an innocent bat of her long eyelashes.

"Okay, you're giving me a headache," Pamela told her. "Just be normal. Is that too much to ask?"

"She will keep her oath. You need not worry, sweet Pamela," Apollo said.

"Don't call me that. You're just supposed to be my employee," she said, and then hated the hurt that she saw flash across the god's handsome face. The *god* . . . How in the hell had she gotten herself into this situation? She was dating Apollo.

She was doomed.

She'd read the literature. Even though she didn't remember it too exactly or too well, she knew what happened to mortals who caught the attention of the gods—especially mortals were also happened to be females. Never a good ending, especially for the woman. Besides that, what was she going to do with him all week? She already knew the two of them had no money. She'd found that out when he'd reached into his pocket to pay the cashier for the shirt he'd worn out of the store and discovered that somehow (possibly during the hasty extraction of his clothes last night right before he screwed her against the marble column) he'd lost the four thousand dollars he'd filched from the slot machine. So he didn't have a dime. Neither did Artemis. And the portal wouldn't reopen for five really long days.

"Good morning, Miss Gray."

Pamela jumped. She hadn't even noticed that the silver vintage limo had pulled up in front of them.

"Oh, good morning Robert." He opened the door for her, and she paused, cleared her throat, and put on her best businesswoman's smile. "These two will be joining us today. They are my assistants."

Robert looked down his slender nose at the golden twins. He sniffed once.

"Very good, madam," he said, holding the door open and helping first Pamela and then the costumed woman to enter the limo. When the tall man hesitated, Robert gave him a very British look (cool and polite without being overly concerned). "Is something amiss, sir?"

If Apollo still had his powers he would have used them at that moment to open the ground beneath him so that he could be swallowed out of sight. From the inside of the metal beast Pamela and Artemis were watching him with mirrored expressions of curiosity. Then his sister suddenly seemed to understand.

"It really is very nice in here," she called out to him. "It's nothing to be worried about." She patted the seat next to her.

"I am not worried," Apollo spoke with tight control. He took a deep breath and entered the maw of the thing.

"Please help yourselves to the mimosas. The trip to Mr. Faust's estate in Red Rock Canyon will take approximately thirty minutes." Robert closed the door.

To Apollo it seemed that he had only taken a couple of short breaths, and then they were moving forward, gliding like a smooth-limbed reptile out into the street. There was an awful rolling feeling in his stomach, and his ears were ringing. He couldn't stop staring at the world outside as it whizzed by at a dizzying pace.

"Are you okay? You look pale," Pamela said.

"She's right, you do," Artemis said. "Perhaps something to drink would help." She started to reach for the ice bucket, which held a bottle of champagne and a slender glass pitcher of orange juice.

"No! I don't want anything to drink." He had the oddest feeling inside of him, and he was afraid if he tried to drink something, it would come right back up.

"Carsick. I think you're carsick," Pamela said. "You might feel better if you sat up front with Robert. My friend V gets violently sick if she sits in the backseat of a car. Want me to have Robert stop so you can move?"

"I am a god," he said slowly from between clenched teeth. "I do not get sick."

"Suit yourself, but if you puke in Eddie's car, I can promise you as your employer I am going to be very pissed."

Apollo closed his eyes and tried to ignore the fact that they were hurtling across the earth inside a metal monster that could smash itself into something and disintegrate at any moment.

"What exactly is a mimosa?" Artemis asked.

"It's champagne and orange juice mixed together. It's pretty good, actually."

"Well," she glanced at her brother's strangely pale face and then shrugged her shapely shoulders, "I'm going to try one. Would you care to join me, Pamela?"

"No, thank you," Pamela said.

Artemis helped herself to one of the champagne flutes. "See how polite I'm being?"

"It's truly a miracle," Pamela muttered.

"Just wait. The best is yet to come." The goddess sipped her mimosa and gave Pamela a wicked little smile.

Pamela decided Apollo had the best idea. She closed her eyes and prayed the trip, the day—hell, the week— would be over soon. But not before she slipped her hand within his and squeezed.

CHAPTER 23

E. D. Faust's *vacation home had been built to look like a* charming Tuscan villa. Pamela was relieved. Yes, she'd seen the blueprints and read through the architectural notes James had given her, but after Eddie's bizarre request to make the interior look like The Forum, she had been leery about what to expect. Of course as they got out of the limo and approached the impressive double wrought-iron doors within which was set outrageously expensive, hand-blown, etched and beveled glass, she remembered that she'd thought that the outside of The Forum meant that the inside was modestly styled and classically tasteful. Please. Talk about mistaken first impressions.

She glanced at Artemis, who looked cool and beautiful in the morning sunlight. Her cheeks were attractively flushed, and one long curl of bright blond hair had escaped her elaborate coiffure.

The goddess smoothed down the skirt of her short tunic, hiccupped, and then giggled slightly. Pamela scrutinized her more closely. Oh, crap! She looked tipsy. Why in the bloody buggering hell had she not thought to keep her eyes open and on Artemis? Just exactly how many mimosas had she slurped down in thirty minutes on an empty stomach while she'd been sitting there obliviously clutching Apollo's carsick hand?

"Are you drunk?" she hissed.

Artemis gave her a bleary frown. "Immortals do not get

drunk. Only mortals get drunk. Don't be a silly little flower." She shook her finger at Pamela.

Pamela rolled her eyes. "You're not immortal right now, remember!" She squelched the sudden urge to scream. Instead, she looked at Apollo for help. His face was an odd shade somewhere between white and green. She watched him wipe sweat from his brow with the back of his hand. "Are you okay?"

He nodded tightly. "Better now that we're out of that . . ." He shuddered and looked off in the direction the car had taken.

"Limo," she said. "It's a limo." She was stuck in a revolving nightmare. "All right. Here's what we do. You two try not to speak unless you're asked a question directly, and even then, I'll do most of the talking. Let's go. We might as well get this over with."

Pamela adjusted the strap on her shoulder briefcase and started purposefully up the lovely curving marble stairs. The twins followed her less purposefully. Just before she touched the antique doorbell, she heard a scuffling sound behind her and Artemis' very out-of-character giggle. She glanced over her shoulder to see that Apollo had his sister's elbow.

"She almost fell," he said under his breath.

"Impossssable," Artemis slurred.

"Oh, God," Pamela muttered.

The double doors opened, and James's smiling face greeted them.

"Please come in, Pamela. Eddie is in the courtyard waiting for you." His smile shifted to polite curiosity as Apollo and Artemis followed Pamela into the foyer.

"These are two assistants I've hired. Experts, really," Pamela said quickly.

"I'm sure Eddie will be pleased by your initiative. He has been eagerly anticipating your meeting all weekend. Come this way, please."

James led them across the foyer, a mammoth space from which two curving staircases with old-world marble railings ran up to a second level of the villa. But the marble railings were the only finished aspect of the interior.

Everything else was bare. The walls were still Sheetrock; the floor was still cement. The entire back wall, which they were approaching, was fitted with floor-to-ceiling windows, so new that they still had their orange factory stickers on them. But Pamela didn't see the rawness as she walked slowly through the unfinished space. She gazed around her, seeing only its unlimited potential.

"It is horrible," Apollo said under his breath to her. "There is no floor, no walls, no decoration whatsoever."

"No, it's perfect," she whispered hastily back to him. "The foundation is here, but the floors and walls are all unfinished; most of the fixtures have not even been installed. It's like a blank canvas. It's my job to choose wisely and to make sure this is turned into a masterpiece."

James was waiting patiently beside the glass door that led to what Pamela already knew from the blueprints to be the central feature of the mansion—the amazing courtyard around which the rest of the villa had been built in an open-ended square shape. When they reached him, James opened the door and motioned them through. It was only then that Pamela noticed the crowd of people who were gathered in the courtyard. In answer to her questioning look, James only smiled and pointed to the middle of the crowd where E. D. Faust was seated at a marble bench piled high with swatches of material.

"Ah, Pamela!" he cried when he caught sight of her.

Rising to his feet, he reminded Pamela of a movable mountain. Again today he was dressed exclusively in black, from his well-tailored slacks to his silk dress shirt, the sleeves of which had been fashioned to mimic the fullness of a painter's smock. Or, she thought as she noted the twinkle in his dark eyes, a pirate's shirt.

"Good morning, Eddie," Pamela said. "This is quite a crowd."

"All for you, Pamela!" He laughed heartily, his great girth shaking like a rumbling earthquake. "I've brought all the artisans to you. I thought it would save us time to have them here at our beck and call. They simply await our commands."

Pamela couldn't believe it. She looked around the

group, and her eyes widened as she noticed that each little cluster of people had beside them mounds of what were obviously samples of everything from more fabric swatches to pieces of marble and other raw stone and paint boards that held paint and faux finish samples. Eddie had turned his courtyard into an interior designer's mini-market. It was mind-boggling and more than a little intimidating. Then she remembered she'd brought her own entourage. Well, such as they were.

"Good." She recovered control of her vocal cords semi-smoothly. "You're right. That will definitely save us some time. And let me introduce the assistants I brought with me today."

She angled her body so that Apollo stepped up beside her. Artemis, who had been standing behind her brother staring with tipsy focus at a speck of lint on the back of his shirt, suddenly realized that there was an audience to play to, and she moved languidly to the other side of Pamela.

At the appearance of the golden twins, the gathering let out a collective sigh of appreciation.

"This is Phoebus Delos, an expert in ancient Roman architecture."

Pamela was pleased to see Apollo incline his head politely at Faust, but the author barely glanced in his direction. His eyes were blind to everything except the beautiful goddess who stood at her other side. Pamela drew a deep breath, mentally crossing her fingers.

"And this is his sister, Diana. She is a model who is renowned for her beauty throughout Greece and Italy. I realize that you told me that you preferred to retain Bacchus as the model for the central figure of your fountain, but I thought that perhaps—"

Her words were broken off when Artemis moved forward with a loose-hipped, languid stride until she stood an arm's length from the bulky author. There she stopped, raised one perfect hand to the elaborate twisting crown of her hair, and with a slight pull she freed its golden length so that it spilled in a thick wave to wash around her waist. She shook her head, and it glistened hypnotically in the morning light

"Pamela thought that perhaps you would rather model your statue after a goddess," she purred.

Pamela had to hand it to her—Artemis was one excellent actress. Just like during her performance in *Zumanity*, she had the crowd totally enamored. Faust looked like he'd been knocked over the head, then he blinked, and his face was transformed into a wide smile. He executed an amazingly graceful bow, flourishing his arm rakishly.

"Well met, Diana!" he boomed. "My home is honored to be graced by the presence of the Goddess of the Moon, Forests and Glens." He spared a glance for Apollo. "And you, my fine fellow, must be the God of Light. How divertingly entertaining that your mother thought to name you after the immortal twins."

Pamela's stomach twisted. Of course a man who made his career out of writing fantasy would instantly recognize the poorly hidden truth in their names. What the hell should she say? Could Faust possibly realize who they really were?

Apollo smiled and spoke smoothly. "You have found us out, sir."

"Please, there is no sir here. Call me Eddie." His eyes swung back to the woman who still stood in front of him. "Pamela, already you have proven that you are the genius I thought you to be. Now that I am face-to-face with a goddess, I heartily agree with you. The center statue of my fountain shall be changed. Bacchus is banished, and the beauty of the Goddess Diana embraced in his stead."

Pamela breathed a sigh of relief, and Artemis performed a liquidly graceful curtsy.

"No! It is not seemly for a goddess to bow," Faust reached quickly forward and pulled Artemis up from her deep curtsy.

"Finally," Artemis said breathily, "a mortal who knows how to treat a goddess."

Pamela bit her lip, but Eddie chuckled with good humor, took the goddess's hand, and raised it briefly to his lips.

"But of course I do." He looked over the crowd of workers gathered around them. "Which of you has the talent to sketch this lovely goddess so that a stone master can then carve her immortal image into marble?"

"Wouldn't it be easier to have some digital pictures taken of her in different poses, and then the sculptor could work from them?" Pamela asked hastily.

"Easier, perhaps, but it feels wrong to me. Too cold. Too impersonal."

"But Diana will only be available until Friday. After that she has a . . . uh . . . prior commitment that she can not break," Pamela said.

"Then we must work quickly, because I wish to have my goddess immortalized in the ancient way. Phoebus, you're an expert in ancient Rome. How would it have been done then?"

"You are quite correct. The sculptor would have sketched his model and then worked from his sketches." Apollo paused and quirked one eyebrow up. "That is, unless you have hired Pygmalion. I believed he worked from the image of the woman he saw only in his heart." He suddenly shifted his gaze to Pamela and sent her a scorching look. "But few of us are lucky enough to have our heart's desire granted."

Pamela forced herself not to squirm. He said he was cut off from his immortal powers, but when Apollo looked at her like that, she felt hot and cold and tingly all at once.

Faust didn't seem to notice the byplay going on between his designer and her assistant; his attention had been captured by his own immortal. "Ah, but we have Diana with us, not Galatea, so a sketch of the model it shall be."

"Galatea was not a goddess. She was only stone brought to life by one," Artemis said, sounding vaguely annoyed.

"How true! How true!" Eddie exclaimed. "Pygmalion was not as fortunate as I."

"I can sketch your goddess, sir." A young man disengaged himself from the crowd.

"Excellent," Eddie said. "We have our artist; we have our model. I believe I have some photographs of the original fountain in The Forum. I suppose the artisans can work from that whilst our goddess is being sketched."

"Actually," Pamela said as she opened her briefcase and hurriedly pulled out her sketch book, "I thought that you might like something unique, so I worked up some preliminary sketches of a new fountain—based, of course, on the one you like so much in The Forum. I just didn't want to fill in the central statue without your approval. I think you'll be quite happy with them."

"Pamela conferred with me on the sketches, and I can assure you that the fountain she has created is one that even the gods would have welcomed on Mount Olympus," Apollo said.

"Well done, Pamela!" Eddie took the sketchbook from her and nodded appreciatively. "Mount Olympus." He chuckled, "I would expect no less for a fountain boasting a sculpture of our Diana. Please, share these sketches with our artist." He glanced expectantly at the young man.

"Matthew," he supplied. "My name is Matthew Land."

"Come, Matthew, Pamela, Phoebus and my lovely Diana. Let us sit and decide upon the details of my home." Eddie offered Artemis his arm. She smiled sweetly and rested her fingertips on the top of his silken sleeve. "Is there anything you require, Diana?" he asked as he led her around the marble bench.

"Yes. I have recently developed a liking for something called a mimosa."

Pamela tried not to groan as Eddie shouted for James to have his chef prepare mimosas for everyone.

Pamela glanced at her watch. She could hardly believe that it was after 4:00 P.M. The day had passed in a busy blur. It had certainly gone worlds better than she had anticipated. Ironically and irritatingly enough, she knew she had Artemis to thank for that. Pamela looked up from the glossy catalogue page of old-world-styled lighting fixtures the representative from Shonbeck was showing her. Eddie was pretending to pay attention as Apollo and the architect went over the latest version of the bathhouse sketch they had been working on for most of the day. In truth, Eddie

was doing what he had done for the past several hours—
he was gazing in rapt adoration at Artemis.

Artemis was incredibly beautiful. Even the flamingly
gay fabric representatives had sighed wistfully over the
perfection of her hair and her breasts and the lean lines of
her legs. Currently, she was standing on a raised platform
that Eddie had ordered erected, holding a large vase
against one hip from which water would eventually pour
when the sketch was turned into a sculpture turned into a
fountain. It made Pamela dizzy just to think about it—and
that was without figuring the expense Eddie would be in-
curring for this original piece of art. But her client seemed
happy, and the fountain was actually going to be very
beautiful. Plus, it was definitely going to be minus the
awful animation. One horrified gasp from Artemis in response to the mention of animation, and Eddie had quickly
vetoed the idea. Just like a frown from the goddess had
been enough to talk Eddie out of building the horrid gi-
normic swimming pool and instead going with the tasteful,
unique Roman bathhouse idea.

Those two issues dealt with, everything else was turning out to be a breeze. Eddie's taste wasn't as atrocious as
Pamela had at first thought. It was just that his whole aura
was so damn big. His ideas were big, and not just in his
epic-length best-selling novels. E. D. Faust filled the world
around him with the largess of life. Yes, he was eccentric.
Actually, Pamela thought that he seemed like a character
from one of his novels, larger than life and constantly
ready for a new adventure. She smiled to herself. His flam-
boyance took a little getting used to, but she understood
why people gravitated to him. Eddie was as generous as his
size. The truth was, E. D. Faust was honestly a nice guy.

It had taken a little gentle nudging, with the help of
Artemis and Apollo, but Pamela had convinced him to shift
the design of his villa from the tacky pretend Romanesque
Forum, to something that was beginning to remind her of
the set of Elizabeth Taylor's *Cleopatra*. The design emerg-
ing was no less opulent than Caesars Palace and The
Forum, it was just much more chic.

Her gaze shifted from Eddie's bulk to Apollo. His

golden head was bent and his expression intent as he nodded at something the architect had just drawn in on the
sketch. As if he knew she was looking at him, his eyes
lifted to hers. She looked hastily away, but not before she
saw his lips tilt up in the barest hint of a smile. He'd caught
her again. And it hadn't been a difficult thing for him to do.
She'd been sneaking glances at him all day. He knew it.
She knew it. And she couldn't help it. He'd just been so
damned wonderful! He'd meticulously described the
workings of the ancient bathhouses of Rome in detail to
Eddie and his architect. He'd been more than patient with
their endless questions. He'd answered them intelligently
and with such focus that even to Pamela he sounded like an
enthusiastic expert. And not once had he exhibited the obnoxious arrogance Pamela thought of when she imagined
what the real Apollo should act like.

She couldn't say the same for Artemis. Even though she
was definitely on her best behavior today, she was still
maddeningly demanding and conceited. Fortunately, Eddie
seemed to enjoy playing along with her goddess "charade." It was a good thing that Eddie had insisted the
kitchen be completed before he'd called Pamela to design
the rest of the villa, because all that day Artemis had kept
the chef busy with her demands for drinks and delicacies.
And Eddie, who obviously enjoyed good drink and food
himself, had been delighted to indulge his "goddess's"
every whim.

Apollo seemed so different than his sister. Pamela had
to admit it to herself, he was the same attentive, intelligent
man today he had been all weekend. But he wasn't really a
man; he was a god. No woman with any sense wanted to
entangle her life with one of the ancient gods . . . She
sighed and forced her attention back to the page of fixtures.

"Eddie," Artemis sounded like a pouty little girl. "My
arm is dreadfully tired of holding this silly vase. And I believe I'm hot. I think I might perish if I don't sit down."

"Of course, of course, my goddess!" Eddie lurched to
his feet and hurried to take the vase from Artemis. Brushing aside the young artist when he tried to help his model

from the platform, Eddie took Artemis' elbow and supported her as she stepped delicately from the makeshift altar. "Look at the time! How unthinking of me. We have been at this for hours. Much too long for a goddess to labor, much too long." He raised his large hand, and his deep voice silenced even the workers who had been busy with the interior of the villa. "I proclaim that we are all finished for the day!" he called. "We shall meet again at the same time on the morrow."

There were sighs all around at Eddie's command. It had been a hard but productive day, and Pamela hated to admit it, but for what felt like the zillionth time, she was thankful that she had let Apollo talk her into bringing them along. She was rubbing the back of her neck and trying to work out a kink that had settled there, when Eddie's booming, "Pamela!" summoned her to his bench.

"Ah, there you are, my dear." He motioned for her to take a seat next to where Apollo was sitting across from him. Artemis was, of course, seated beside him, fanning herself with a feathered fan that Eddie had produced. Pamela noted that the goddess was currently sipping straight champagne from an iced crystal flute. It was a good thing Artemis would be immortal again in a few days. At the rate she was going, it was either immortality or alcoholism.

"I've been discussing our new arrangements with the lovely Diana and her brother, and I believe we are all in agreement."

Pamela felt an all-too-familiar sinking in her stomach. "Arrangements? What arrangements?"

"It's quite simple, really. There is no need for the three of you to drive all the way back to Vegas when you can all stay with me," Eddie beamed.

"But the only room that's finished is the kitchen."

Eddie chuckled. "Not here. I have reserved the Spring Mountain Ranch House at the Red Rock Canyon Resort. It has rather modest accommodations, but it's much closer to the villa than Caesars Palace. There really is no point in your returning there anyway. We no longer need The

Forum as our example of ancient Rome. We have Phoebus."

"But my clothes . . . and, uh, Diana and Phoebus didn't bring much with them."

Pamela's eyes darted to Artemis. The goddess serenely sipped her champagne and then winked slyly at her.

Eddie waved away her worries. "James will take care of fetching your things, and Diana has already explained to me that she and her brother had only planned to stay the day, but they have graciously accepted my offer to extend their stay for the week. Anything our goddess needs I would be honored to purchase for her at the resort."

"Dinner, Eddie, dinner," Artemis sighed. "I can not believe how positively famished I am."

"Of course," he patted her hand. "It has been a tiring day. Let us retire to the ranch and sup and be merry." Eddie rose ponderously from the bench. Artemis lifted one hand so that he could help her to her feet. And then, moving with a decidedly more wobbly step than her usual graceful stride, she clung to the big man's arm as he lumbered from the courtyard, bellowing for Robert to bring the car.

"I guess we have little choice in this," Pamela said, hesitant to look directly at Apollo now that they were alone for the first time that day.

"I have already made my choice, sweet Pamela," he said.

She looked at him then. He smiled his familiar, endearing smile at her, and her chest tightened.

"Sometimes it's easy to forget who you really are," she said softly.

He touched her face. "You already know who I really am. You've known since the night we met."

"But you're not just a man," she said.

"I am for the next five days."

Then he mimicked Eddie's actions by standing and taking her hand and helping her to her feet. She let him thread her arm through his as they walked through the emptying courtyard. He felt warm and normal and right beside her. And that scared her so much that she started to pull her arm from his, but he suddenly stopped in the middle of the foyer. She felt a tremor go through his body, and she looked up at him. His face had gone pale. She followed his staring gaze. James was holding the front doors of the villa open for them, and through them Pamela could see Robert helping first Artemis then Eddie into the waiting limo.

"I'd completely forgotten about that metal creature," Apollo said.

"Come on, I'll make sure you sit up front this time."

Pamela tightened her grip on his arm and pulled him forward. He was Apollo, God of Light, Music and Healing, an immortal who had lived for eons and about whom stories and poems and songs had been written. But he was also wretchedly carsick.

CHAPTER 24

Eddie's idea of "rather modest accommodations" was to lease the entire nine-bedroom adobe-style mansion that had been lavishly built in the 1920s and lovingly restored with antiques and modern plumbing and lighting in 2003. It was situated at the edge of the Red Rock Canyon Spa and Resort, which was a lovely oasis of natural springs and verdant foliage that looked bizarre and beautifully out of place in the middle of the jutting rust-colored rocks and starkly intriguing desert landscape of Red Rock Canyon. Pamela stood at one set of three double doors, which led from the lodge-style den out to the huge wooden deck where uniformed waiters were hastily putting the finishing touches of fresh flowers and candles on the dinner table, while a trio of musicians were tuning their instruments. Music, candles, flowers and fine china—she was relieved that she had chosen her little black dress instead of something more casual. Outdoor lighting suddenly clicked on, watercoloring the clear Nevada night in soft splotches of color.

She breathed in the cooling desert air. Sitting with carsick Apollo in the front seat (He'd insisted she stay with him, and he'd looked so pathetic that she sighed and squeezed in the front seat, thoroughly annoying Robert) had been an eye-opening experience. Pamela loved Colorado. Though she had been born and raised there, she never tired of the majesty of Pikes Peak and the green, mountainous beauty of her home. She considered herself fairly well-traveled, especially within the United States, and she had seen many lovely states, but no place had ever filled her senses and soothed her soul like her home. So it was a surprise that she was so drawn to the desert. The short ride from Eddie's estate on the edge of Red Rock Canyon to the ranch had been filled with scenery that was both stark and spectacular. There was something mysterious and wonderful about the desert. It made her imagination run wild with girlish fantasies of Old West cowboys and leather and sweat. She grinned to herself at her silly romantic imaginings.

"I love your smile."

Apollo's deep voice startled her. She turned. He was standing so close behind her that she could feel the heat of his body. It was just normal body heat and not the immortal power of the God of Light, but it made her remember the night before, and how flames had licked her body in time with his thrusts.

She ran her hand nervously through her short hair. "I didn't hear you come in."

"I didn't mean to startle you."

If only he knew. His very presence made her stomach tighten and her face flush. And that was before she'd found out that he was the bloody God of Light! She was being wooed and pursued by immortal Apollo. It was a little like being caught up in an old *Star Trek* episode without the ability to be beamed the hell out of a tight situation.

But she didn't want to be beamed away from him, and the truth of that was driving her crazy. He was Apollo! She couldn't stop the thrill of wonderment that coursed through her at the thought. It was heady and maddening and terribly frightening.

Instead of babbling like the crazy woman she thought she might be becoming, she nodded out at the desert night with what she hoped was at least semi-nonchalance.

"It's not your fault; I was preoccupied by the scenery. It's so much prettier here than I expected."

"Yes, I know exactly what you mean. The Kingdom of Las Vegas has surprised me with its beauty, too," he smiled and brushed a short tendril of dark hair from her forehead.

His eyes caught and reflected the deck lighting, and for a moment they seemed to shimmer again with immortal blue. She moved a step away from him.

"Why?" he asked wearily. "Why do you shun my touch?"

One of the waiters looked up with obvious curiosity at his question, and Pamela motioned for Apollo to follow her out to the far edge of the deck where they were less likely to be overheard. She lowered her voice and tried not to fidget.

"I'm not shunning your touch. I-I'm being careful," she stuttered, not looking directly into his eyes.

"I don't understand." He wiped a hand across his face and sighed. "You see, Pamela, this has never before happened to me. You must explain the rules of love."

Her heart beat into her throat, and she had to swallow carefully before she answered him.

"I don't know the rules. I don't know how to love a god." Reluctantly, she met his eyes. "The truth is it was different when I thought you were just Phoebus."

"I am Phoebus, Pamela."

"No you're not! My God, Apollo—" she broke off, pressing her lips together. "See! I can't even say normal things around you anymore. My God . . . you are a god! I don't know what to say . . . what to do . . ." She rubbed her forehead. The musicians began playing a waltz, which only increased the surreal feel of the night. It was like Apollo had conspired to add a soundtrack to their conversation. "I don't want to be in love," she said softly. "I didn't want to before I knew about you, and now it just seems too much—too impossible."

He shook his head. "No, it's not impossible. It's just that the way you found out was wrong. I should have told you sooner, made it easier for you to accept."

"How could it be easier? You are an ancient god, and I am just a mortal woman. We weren't meant to be together." Saying the words that had been haunting her all day made her stomach feel sick.

"I fulfilled your heart's desire." He spoke in a low, tight voice.

"Of course you did! It's not that I don't desire you. I do. You're perfect. I asked for romance, and you are most definitely a romantic dream come true." She wanted to shut up, to stop the words that vomited from her mouth, but she couldn't. She was afraid if she did, she would throw herself into his arms and want to stay there forever. And then what would become of her? What would happen to her heart when he left her world and returned to his own?

He grimaced and shook his head. "I am more than a romantic dream, and you asked for more than a dalliance with a god."

"Apollo, I know what I asked for," she said tightly.

"Do you really? Then perhaps you would be interested to know that the invocation bond between you and my sister did not break until you admitted last night that I am your soul mate."

"Your soul mate . . ." She whispered the words, shaking her head. "No!" He couldn't be. If he was her soul mate, how would she survive without him?

All expression left his handsome face. "Perhaps I have been lucky all these eons not to have known love. I am discovering it is a painful emotion." He bowed formally to her, turned on his heels and walked away.

But instead of making it through the doors and back to his room as he had intended, he almost ran over his sister and Eddie as they surged out onto the patio, followed closely by the ever-present James.

"Good! Good! You're here already," Eddie said, clapping Apollo on the shoulders. Then he caught sight of Pamela. "Excellent! We are all here. James, you may tell them to begin the feast. Come, my goddess. The fare here may be simple, but I promise that you will not be disappointed by its quality."

"Eddie, I want more of that lovely champagne."

"Of course, of course," he murmured, helping her into one of the chairs.

Pamela watched the big man cluck and fuss over the goddess like a gihugic hen. Apollo was standing across the table from the two of them. She could feel his gaze on her. She blinked away the tears that had been pooling in her

eyes, squared her shoulders, plastered a professionally cor-
dial smile on her face and joined the small group at the
table. Eddie, of course, insisted she sit next to "Phoebus."
Thankfully, as soon as her butt touched the chair, a swarm
of waiters converged upon the table.

Eddie had described the dinner fare as "simple," which
made Pamela wonder what he considered extravagant. The
food wasn't served in courses, as one might expect from an
expensive catered meal in the middle of an exclusive resort; instead, Eddie ordered that everything come out at
once. It was like a food explosion. The salads of wild field
greens, exotic fresh mushrooms and ripe bursts of tiny
tomatoes had been fashioned to look like miniature bird's
nests. The bowtie pasta was divine and smelled of fresh
garlic and white wine. Thick salmon steaks had been
grilled to perfection, as had long slices of halved zucchini
squash covered in melted provolone cheese and sprinkled
with cracked pepper and sea salt. Throughout the entire
meal, attentive waiters poured glasses of icy champagne.

Everything was delicious, and Pamela felt herself relaxing as Eddie and Apollo chatted easily about the daily
bathing traditions of ancient Rome. Actually, Pamela was
intrigued by the living details Apollo was divulging about
a world considered long dead.

"So bathing really became a social activity," Eddie said
through bites of salmon.

Apollo nodded. "Do not think of it as simply something
done to cleanse one self. The Roman baths were much
more than that. In the same bathing complex it was not un-
common for there to be exercise areas, masseurs, barbers,
restaurants, shops and libraries. It was a place of cama-
raderie; a life vein into the happenings of the city. There
were private rooms set aside in which matters were dis-
cussed that should not be made public. Some say that even
the gods themselves frequented the bathhouses of Rome to
listen in to the intrigue of the day."

"Ha! Might the plot to kill Caesar not have started in
one of Rome's baths?" Eddie said.

Artemis scoffed. "Caesar! Proclaiming himself a god
was only one of his many mistakes. He should have lis-

tened to his wife. Calpurnia warned him. Too often Rome did not listen to the voices of its women," she finished fiercely.

Eddie's eyes widened. "I have it, my lovely! I have been pondering it since this morning when first we met. Something was off—not precisely right—and now I understand what it is. You are not Diana at all, but now I recognize your true nature."

Artemis raised one golden eyebrow at him and nibbled at her second piece of salmon. "Do you?"

"Yes! You are too fiery to be the wan and ethereal Diana. You flame and sparkle, not just with the light of a full moon. You carry within you the nature of a huntress. Tomorrow we shall doff the silly vase you held today and replace it with a bow and a quiver of arrows. Diana's meekness has set, and the goddess Artemis has risen."

Pamela choked midswallow of bowtie pasta and a waiter hurried to bring her a glass of water. Between sputters she shared a secret look of surprise with Apollo, but Eddie was not finished. He placed his hand over his heart, and in a deep, resonant baritone his a cappella voice, rising and falling like one of The 3 Tenors, filled the desert night.

*"I sing of Artemis of the golden shafts, who loves the
        din of the hunt
and shoots volleys of arrows at stags. She delights in
        the chase
as she stretches her golden bow to shoot the bitter
        arrows.
Hers is a mighty heart; she roams all over
        destroying the brood of wild beasts."*

Artemis stopped eating when Eddie began to sing. She stared at him in obvious amazement. The big man paused, gesturing at the trio of musicians who had been playing soft background music throughout dinner. Their playing stopped, but when Eddie began singing again, the harpist caught the melody of his song, and the magical sound of liquid strings accompanied him.

> *"But when the arrow-pouring goddess has taken her*
> *   pleasure,*
> *after slacking her well-taut bow, she comes to the*
> *   great house of her brother,*
> *Phoebus Apollon, to the opulent district of*
> *   Delphi . . ."*

He nodded at Apollo, who tilted his head in regal acknowledgment.

> *". . . to set up a beautiful dance of the Muses and the*
> *   Graces.*
> *There she hangs her resilient bow and her arrows,*
> *   and wearing her graceful*
> *jewelry, she is their leader in the dance. Divine is*
> *   the sound they utter*
> *as they sing of how fair-ankled Leto gave birth to*
> *   children,*
> *who among the gods are by far the best in deeds and*
> *   counsel.*
> *Hail, O daughter of Zeus and lovely-haired Leto!*
> *I shall praise and remember you . . ."*

Eddie's voice held the last note while the harpist improvised a fantastic flourish. And then the night became very quiet as the song faded. Pamela's gaze shifted from Eddie to Artemis. And there it stayed. Totally shocked, Pamela watched Artemis' stunningly blue eyes fill with shimmering tears. Then the goddess leaned forward and kissed Eddie lingeringly on the lips.

"You know the Homeric hymns," the goddess whispered, only a hand's length from the big man's face.

"I know the Homeric hymns," Eddie replied solemnly.

"You have surprised me, Eddie."

The goddess's smile of honest delight made Pamela's breath catch with its beauty.

"Brother," she said without taking her gaze from Eddie, "I wish to reward our host for his keen powers of observation. Will you play for me?"

"Of course," Apollo said. "But I have no instrument."

Eddie's distinctive voice boomed across the deck. "That is enough music for the evening. You may depart. But leave your instruments. My assistant will be certain they are returned to you on the morrow."

The three women left quickly and discreetly, and Pamela wondered just exactly how much money Eddie was paying them so that they didn't so much as blink at leaving behind their instruments.

Apollo took the harpist's vacated seat and put his hands on the instrument without showing any of the trepidation he was feeling. He was the God of Music. Harpists had worshiped him and sang his praises for uncounted centuries. The Muses revered him. Since the day he had talked the newborn Hermes into gifting him with the very first lyre known to mankind, he had taken his immortal power over his chosen instrument for granted. It was like the air he breathed and the wine he drank—unquestionably, always there. But today he was not the immortal Apollo. He was only a man. He knew the notes. The feel of the harp was familiar. Still, his stomach churned. What if his talent had fled with his powers? What if he played the wrong notes? Or worse, played the right notes so poorly that they seemed wrong.

He looked up. Artemis had stood and was backing gracefully away from the table so that she would have room to begin her dance. Eddie's eyes never left her face. The author was completely enamored with his sister. Apollo pressed his hand against the taut strings. He understood how the big man felt. Reluctantly, the god turned his gaze to Pamela. She was watching him intently, no doubt waiting to hear the brilliance with which the God of Light played. At that instant he sincerely wished that he had his immortal powers—or that he was in reality the mortal man, Phoebus. He suddenly wanted very much to be one or the other. Being stuck between two worlds was like being thrust into a battlefield with only the memory of weapons.

"Play Terpsichore's favorite melody," his sister said imperiously.

Apollo knew the melody. He'd been there when the Muse of the Dance created it, and he had played it for her when she performed it at one of Zeus' great banquets. He closed his eyes and concentrated. His first notes were tentative, soft, almost inaudible, but his fingers had more confidence than the god. They knew the feel of the silver strings, and they traveled up and down the length of the instrument like old friends returning each other's greeting.

He opened his eyes. Artemis floated across the deck, recreating Terpsichore's masterpiece. He smiled fondly at his sister. Tonight she had no immortal powers, but she needed none. The little silk slip of a dress Eddie must have purchased for her swirled gracefully around her body. Her movements were languid and filled with a unique, hypnotic suppleness. His fingers flew over the strings, increasing the tempo of the tune. Artemis matched him, twirling and undulating in perfect time with the music until the crescendo, after which she collapsed in an elegant heap near Eddie's feet.

"No!" Eddie cried, pulling her up so that she stood beside him breathing heavily. "It is I who should be at your feet, my goddess."

Artemis laughed breathlessly. "Then you liked your reward?"

"I will cherish the memory of your dance even unto my dying day."

The goddess's expression instantly sobered. "I do not wish to think of you dying."

It was Eddie's turn to laugh, and he did so heartily. "Then think not of it, for that day is far off, my goddess!"

Artemis' smile returned. "Eddie, will you walk with me? I know it is dark, and night has fallen, but—"

"Your wish is my command," he proclaimed. "Come, the grounds are well lit and it is my great honor to escort you."

Without so much as a glance at Pamela or Apollo, the two of them left the deck, heads already bent together as Eddie began asking her about the origins of her dance. Still dazzled by the goddess's incredible performance, Pamela watched them leave. She couldn't believe it. Artemis had danced for Eddie as if she really meant it, as if she really cared for him and wanted to thank him. What a difference a single day had made. This morning Artemis had been arrogant and impossible. Granted, the goddess was still impossibly arrogant, thoroughly spoiled and ridiculously self-indulgent and vain. But when she looked at Eddie there was no doubt about the softness that came into her eyes. Could Artemis really have a heart?

Two soft, magical chords waterfalled over one another, calling Pamela's attention back to her immortal. *Her immortal.* The thought shivered through her. Before tonight she would have imagined that a man playing a harp would look, at the very least effeminate, at the most, definitely gay. Apollo was neither. He was magnificently masculine. He didn't just play the harp; he stroked it with a lover's touch, coaxing beautiful music from it as if his caress had brought it to life. With his golden, well-muscled body and his sun-colored hair, he looked like an ancient warrior who had paused between battles to rest and recite heroic deeds. She met his eyes as he began to sing while his fingers teased a sensuous, rhythmic hum from the strings.

> *"I am that man who sits opposite you*
> *and, while close to you, listens to*
> *you sweetly speaking*
> *and laughing with love—things which cause*
> *the heart in my breast to tremble."*

His voice was so perfect it was almost indescribable, and Pamela tried to imagine how he must sound when he was able to use his immortal powers. No wonder generations of people had built temples and carved statues in his honor. And now here he was, singing just for her. At that moment she wanted him so much that the force of it almost choked her. Without conscious thought she stood and walked to him.

> *"When I look at you,*
> *I can speak no more.*
> *My tongue freezes silent and stiff,*
> *light flame trickles under my skin,*
> *I no longer see with my eyes,*

my ears hear whirring,
cold sweat covers me,
shivering takes me captive,
I become more green than the grass,
near to death to myself I seem."

She stopped in front of him. The only power he had at his command was that of a man in love, but still he entranced her. She shivered as he repeated the chorus and blanketed her with the warmth of his emotions.

"I am that man who sits opposite you
and, while close to you, listens to
you sweetly speaking
and laughing with love—things which cause
the heart in my breast to tremble."

When the little night breeze blew the last note away, she reached out tentatively and with one finger stroked the back of his hand that rested against the strings of the harp.

"Did you write that?"

He smiled and took her hand in his. "No. It was written by Sappho. She was a Greek poetess, and a passionate lover of women. I borrowed her words. She had a caustic sense of humor and a sharp wit. I think she would find our situation sublimely entertaining, and I do not believe she would mind the small changes I made to her verse."

"It was very beautiful. Your voice is . . ." She paused, trying to find words to describe what she had heard. "Your voice is like a half-forgotten dream. Something too fantastic to be real."

"But it is real. I am real." He pulled her towards him. She came hesitantly, and so he looped his arm around her waist, drawing her against him. "What you feel for me is real." Apollo pressed his lips gently against hers. He hungered for the taste and feel of her, but she was so stiff and unyielding that he contented himself with an almost chaste kiss—first on her mouth, and then on her cheek. Finally, she relaxed enough that her head rested against his shoulder, and he breathed in the clean scent of her hair. When he bent to kiss her again, she lifted her hand and pressed her fingers against his lips.

"I'm going to ask you to give me time," she said.

"Time?"

"I need time to think about what's happening between us, and I can't think when you touch me and kiss me. So I'm asking you for some thinking space. Will you do that for me?"

He wanted to say no—to toss the harp aside and take her into his arms and make slow, passionate love to her until she could not think at all. He knew he could persuade her to give in to him; he felt it in the way her body gravitated to him and the liquid way her eyes stared into his. He knew the passion that smoldered within her, and he knew how to awaken and use it. And then what? In the morning she would just retreat from him again. He wanted her to come to him freely, with no morning-after regrets.

Apollo took his arm from around her. Instead of trying to kiss her again, he brushed back the little tendril of dark hair that habitually fell over her forehead.

"I will give you your thinking space."

He smiled sadly, kissed her hand, and walked slowly from the deck. Alone.

CHAPTER 25

The 7:30 wake-up call from the perky-sounding young lady who announced that breakfast would be served on the deck at 8:15 came entirely too early for Pamela. What the hell was happening to her? Her internal clock usually woke her right around dawn. To her normal schedule, 7:30 A.M. was sleeping late. But this morning she rubbed her eyes and felt thick-headed, wishing she could curl up and sleep for a couple more hours.

It was Apollo's fault. Knowing that the God of Light was sleeping alone just down that hall from her had kept her tossing and turning most of the night. So had that damn liquid voice of his. It seemed to tumble around and around inside her head. And his touch. Every time she closed her eyes, she could feel his lips burning against hers. Apparently it didn't matter that he was minus his immortal powers. To her his touch still felt like fire and light and sweat and . . .

Bloody buggering hell! She really needed to get a grip on her hormones. She rubbed at her eyes again and reminded herself that Eddie was bound to have excellent coffee all brewed and waiting for them.

Which reminded her that she was certain she'd heard Eddie and Artemis giggle their way back to *one* of their rooms at practically 2:00 A.M. They might have even had sex, as gross as that was to think about. Would Artemis do that? Wasn't she supposed to be one of the virgin goddesses? Pamela thought about her erotic stint with *Zuman-*

ity and the sexy way she walked and talked. She seemed as virginlike as Madonna (the singer, not the other one); the exact opposite of an aloof, untouched and untouchable goddess.

Pamela groaned again as she got out of bed. She washed her face and brushed her teeth and reminded herself that it was Tuesday. Not counting today, there were only three more days till the portal reopened and Artemis and Apollo returned to their world to leave her to get back to normal in her own. Her stomach rolled. No, she wouldn't be naive enough to even hope that Apollo would actually stick around long enough to have a real relationship with her. He would leave. And she would return to her normal, boring, dateless life . . .

No. She'd already been over this with herself. She wasn't going to crawl back into her sexless, manless, romanceless shell. She had to think of Apollo as her beginning foray into the world of dating. It had been a successful reconnoiter. She would change her mission when she got back home. No longer would she be all work and no play. She. Would. Date.

"Bloody buggering hell," she told her frazzled-looking reflection in the bathroom mirror. "I'm thinking like a kooky member of a dating militia. V is going to be so ashamed of me—" She broke off, smacking herself on the forehead. "V! I haven't even checked in with her." She rummaged through her purse until she found her cell phone and punched in V's number.

"Are you tiring of me? You never call me anymore. Say it ain't so," V said instead of hello.

"It ain't so," Pamela said. "God, V, I'm so damn sorry I didn't call you. Things here have been more than a little on the gihugically insane side."

"The author is terminally crazy?"

"No. Actually, Eddie is a pretty good guy, and the job is even turning out to be almost semitasteful. You know, like something Elizabeth Taylor and Richard Burton would have liked."

"Shut up! Do not tell me you've talked him into creating scrumptious Cleopatra's palace!"

"Well, kinda."

"What does that mean?"

"Yes, I'm creating something like the set from *Cleopatra*. But it's not me who was responsible for the talking-into part."

"He has a lesbian assistant with an Elizabeth Taylor obsession, too? God, the world's a small and miraculous place," V sighed happily. "Are you fixing me up?"

"Again, no. His assistant is a guy, and I'm pretty sure he's straight. It's my assistants who have persuaded him into changing his focus, and it was just a happy accident that it's looking like an MGM set."

"Wait, wait, *wait!* You only have one assistant. She is me. And I am definitely not there because I am here dealing with crazy old cat lady Graham—who, by the bye, has finally let me talk her out of the plum-colored velvet settee. We're looking at chintz today. I told her it would show less cat hair. Regardless of the cat lady story, there is still the very important fact that your one assistant is *moi,* and I am here. Explain."

What could Pamela tell her? If she admitted that she believed Apollo and his sister were immortals stuck in Vegas, V would be on the next plane out there with a carry-on filled with valium and a reservation for her to spend a nice little "vacation" at the nearest psychiatric resting facility. Not to mention that she would needlessly worry her best friend. She definitely couldn't tell her the truth. She drew a deep breath. She wouldn't think of it as lying; she'd think of it as fictionalizing. It's what Eddie did for a living, and no one called him a crazy person. Okay, well, not to his face, they didn't.

"I hired Phoebus and his sister to be my assistants until Friday. Phoebus is an expert in ancient Roman architecture, and his sister is, well, so drop-dead that Eddie changed his mind about insisting the stupid center statue of his fountain be fashioned after horrid Bacchus and is using her as a goddess model instead." She finished, breathed, and waited for the storm.

"You hired your boyfriend?"

"He is not my boyfriend."

"And his sister?" V continued as if Pamela hadn't spoken.

"Yeah, well, his sister just kinda came with the deal. Phoebus really is an expert on ancient Rome. He's helped me convince Eddie to build an authentic Roman bathhouse instead of a tacky replica of the Caesar's Palace pool. Did you know that ancient Romans used their public bathhouses as country clubs?"

"Okay, focus. I'm not through with the boyfriend questions."

"He's not my boyfriend."

"Whatever. And I thought you said he was a doctor and a musician," V said. "And wasn't he supposed to be high-tailing it out of Vegas early Monday morning?"

"He *is* a doctor and a musician. He's also an expert on ancient Rome. And, yes, he was supposed to leave, but he, uh, missed his flight, so he decided to stay," Pamela said, trying to keep her voice light and unliar sounding.

"Sounds too curiously convenient to me. And I thought he was a young Jedi Knight. How the hell old is he, anyway?"

"Older than I thought at first," Pamela said, grateful she could answer one of her friend's questions truthfully.

"Are you still boinking him?"

"No! At least I didn't last night."

"His idea or yours not to boink?" V asked.

"Mine," Pamela said miserably.

"Oh, nuh-uh. You're totally stuck on him. Please tell me you didn't hire him just so you could keep him around and torture yourself with your growing obsession. It sets up a sick soap opera scenario, Pammy."

"It's not like that. I hired him—and his bitch sister—because I could use their help."

"So the beauty is a beast?"

Pamela smiled. She knew the red herring bitch tidbit would work.

"She's awful. Gorgeous, haughty, total goddess complex. You'd love her."

"You're such a tease." V sighed.

"I'm also a design genius. Hiring Phoebus and Diana

has totally taken the pressure off me to produce something tasteful out of something impossibly tacky. Eddie is completely gone on Diana. One smile or pout from her, and he instantly changes his mind."

"And you, of course, have briefed her on what you want Eddie to like?" V said.

"Of course," Pamela lied. Again. Artemis couldn't be told to do much of anything. It was just a good thing that the goddess had excellent, if exceedingly extravagant, taste.

"So what is your handsome tripod doing besides standing around looking male?"

"He's not mine. And he's working with the architects on the bathhouse. It's really pretty interesting to find out about—" A knock on her door interrupted her. "Hang on, someone's at the door."

"Pamela?" Apollo's deep voice carried easily through the door. "I need your help."

"Uh, V, I gotta go."

"Okay—call me later. And remember, don't overanalyze everything, but be careful."

Pamela grunted a bye and closed the little flip phone before she cracked the door. One look at Apollo, and the door widened, along with her eyes. He was naked from his waist up. His hair was a wild curling mass, and his chin and cheeks were covered with blood.

"Oh my god! What did you do?"

"I shaved," he said. "And I'm bleeding!"

"Get in here," she pulled him into the room and closed the door. Under the splotches of blood that speckled his face his skin was pale. She shook her head at him and pointed at a chair. "Sit down before you fall down. You don't look so good."

Apollo dropped into the chair. He touched one of the blood drops, looked at his reddened finger, and swallowed convulsively.

"It's my blood," he said.

Pamela frowned at him. "Of course it is. It looks like you nicked the shit out of yourself shaving." She headed into the bathroom to get a wet washcloth, glancing over her shoulder at him. "Haven't you ever shaved before?"

He shook his head woodenly. "No."

She came back in the room with the wet washcloth, remembering now that she had noticed how smooth and stubble-free his face had been the morning they'd woken up together.

"You've really *never* shaved before?"

He looked up at her. "I never had to. My face never grew a beard."

She bent in front of him and examined his face, touching him gently on the cheek. "It's really not so bad. You only cut yourself a few times. It's just that the face bleeds easily."

"I didn't know," he said, looking even paler.

She straightened. "Is bleeding something else you haven't done before?"

"No," he said, then frowned, "I mean yes. Bleeding is something I have never done before."

Pamela opened her mouth and then closed it. He was a god. Gods didn't die, so it was only logical that they didn't bleed, either. She didn't know what the hell to say. Before she could formulate an intelligent response, two knocks beat against the door, followed by the faint sound of her name.

"Hang on," she told Apollo. "Who is it?" she asked through the door.

"Me!" the word was a whimper.

"Artemis?" Pamela said, opening the door.

Dressed in her short tunic once more, the goddess swept into the room, looking like an ancient Greek tragedy come to life with one hand dramatically stretched out before her, the other clutching her throat.

"Pamela! Something is terribly wrong with—" She caught sight of her brother sitting in the chair, face speckled with blood, and her hand went from her throat to her mouth.

Pamela slammed the door shut and grabbed the goddess's elbow.

"Do. Not. Scream," she said slowly and distinctly.

"Oh! Oh!" Artemis wobbled, and Pamela guided her to the bed where she collapsed, still staring with huge glassy eyes at her brother. "Is he dying?" she gasped.

"Oh, good Lord. Of course not. He just cut himself shaving." Pamela rubbed her right temple, feeling the twinge that signaled the beginning of a pounding headache.

"Apollo?" Artemis asked in a shaky voice.

"I am not good with the . . ." He made a shaving motion.

"Razor," Pamela said. "No, you're not good with the razor." She walked over to him and bent down again. "This might sting a little." She touched the wet washcloth to the nicks. Apollo's only movement was a hitched breath. His sister watched in horror.

"He's bleeding," Artemis exclaimed.

"Yeah, that's what happens when you cut yourself with a razor. You bleed." She rolled her eyes at the goddess before turning back to Apollo. "Okay, now you need to take some tissue and press little pieces of it against these cuts. Pretty soon they'll coagulate and stop bleeding, and you'll be good as new."

"Tissue?" Apollo said.

"Coagulate?" Artemis squeaked.

"Never mind. I'll do it." Pamela sighed, went into the bathroom, grabbed a couple of Kleenexes and came back to crouch beside Apollo's chair. The twins watched her with amazed expressions as she tore tiny round pieces of the tissue and pressed one each against his shaving nicks. "There," she said, straightening up and assessing her work. "That should stop the bleeding soon. By the time you put your shirt on and comb your hair, you should be able to take them off without the cuts opening up again."

"Opening up again?" he asked.

"Apollo, aren't you the God of Healing or whatever? How can this be so shocking to you?" Pamela was exasperated. She didn't know whether she wanted to hug him or shake him.

Abruptly, the god stood. "You are quite right. I . . . I

feel rather foolish. I will get dressed and join you soon."
He made a very hasty exit.

"That was not very nice," Artemis said.

Pamela put her hands on her hips and turned to the goddess. "Oh, look who's suddenly concerned about not very nice. Might I remind you that you've made it clear that you consider me no more than the little mortal experiment gone wrong? I seem to distinctly remember that you said something about being supremely tired of being shackled to me as your excuse for zapping me with some kind of sex magic so I'd like your brother."

Artemis cringed back from her. "You're hurting my head."

"Good!"

"Again, that's not very nice. Especially in light of the fact that I think I might be dying."

"And why would you think that?"

"Just look at me! Something is terribly wrong. My eyes are all red and there are horrid puffy bruises under them. My stomach feels very, very ill. And I think my head may burst open at any moment!" she said, falling back dramatically on Pamela's pillows.

"Please. There's nothing wrong with you except that you're hungover," Pamela said, trying not to laugh.

"Will it kill me?" Artemis asked, sitting straight up and then grimacing and holding her head.

"No. But I'd lay off the mimosas and champagne today."

The goddess blanched. "Do not even mention those drinks."

Pamela couldn't help smiling at her. "I'll bet you're thirsty."

"Absolutely parched. How did you know? Have you had this sickness yourself?"

Pamela went over to the minibar refrigerator and took out a bottle of water, cracked the seal, and handed it to Artemis. "More times that I'm willing to admit. You drank too much alcohol yesterday. Your body—your temporarily mortal body—is telling you that's not a good idea." She watched as Artemis guzzled the bottle of water. "Wait, don't drink it all. You'll need something to take the Tylenol with," she said, rummaging through her purse until she came up with her little emergency travel pill box, and picked through the Benadryl and Xanax until she found two Tylenol. "Here, take these and have a bland breakfast—maybe some toast or muffins." Noting Artemis' blank look she said, "Oh, all right. I'll show you what to eat. But make sure you have some coffee and some more water. You'll feel better soon."

"Will I look better? I can not believe the wretched sight that greeted me in the mirror."

Pamela studied the goddess's face as she had her brother's before her. She was, of course, still amazingly beautiful, but this morning Artemis definitely looked haggard. "Come on in the bathroom and let me see what I can do about those dark circles." She paused and gave Artemis an appraising look. "Wait. I'll make a deal with you. I'll do something about your face, if you promise to be nice to Eddie again today."

At the mention of the author's name Artemis' face changed. It seemed to soften, and her cheeks flushed a delicate pink.

"Oh. My. God! You really like him," Pamela said.

"He . . . he reminds me of someone," Artemis whispered.

"You like him because he reminds you of someone? Who?"

The goddess's eyes flashed, and she looked more like her usual haughty self. "It is my concern not yours who Eddie reminds me of, and I do not like him simply because of that. He recognized me. He is a mortal from a modern world that no longer honors the gods and goddesses, yet he knows me and worships me. That pleases me."

"Huh," Pamela said.

She motioned for Artemis to sit on the bathroom counter while she looked through her makeup bag for her concealer. For a while she worked silently on the goddess's face, covering the dark circles under her eyes and brushing some bronzing power over her face to help bring back some of her natural color. Then, just because Artemis was so damn beautiful, she highlighted her eyes with some shimmery shadow. It was like touching up a painting that had already been completed by a master, she thought.

"Hippolytus," Artemis murmured.

"What's that?" Pamela said.

"Hippolytus wasn't a what—he was a who. Eddie reminds me of him."

"Was he an author, too?" Pamela asked, adding just a touch of blush to the goddess's high cheekbones.

"No. He was a warrior. Son of Theseus. He was tall, strong, and almost as beautiful as a god. Eddie's body does not remind me of my Hippolytus. It is in his devotion that I find the similarity."

"You talk about Hippolytus in the past tense. Is he dead?"

"Yes," Artemis said shortly. "Killed mistakenly because of his devotion to me. I was the only woman he could ever love."

"I'm sorry," Pamela said.

Artemis met the mortal woman's gaze. She was surprised to recognize understanding there. "You've lost a love, too."

"He didn't die physically. It was just that I found out that the man I believed in didn't actually exist."

Artemis nodded thoughtfully. "In a way, that would be even more difficult to bear. At least Hippolytus no longer walks the ancient earth. It would be a painful burden to see him and to know that he is only the shell of what I believed him to be."

"You do understand," Pamela said.

"Yes." Artemis smiled sadly. Then she turned and looked in the mirror and her smiled widened and became authentically happy. "You have performed a miracle!"

Pamela laughed. "Absolutely. It's called Borghese, Mac, and a little Chanel added in for good measure. The modern woman's miracle workers."

"Thank you, Pamela," she said sincerely.

"You are welcome, Artemis." She looked at her own still-rumpled reflection. "Now I'm going to have to perform a similar miracle on myself. And I'm going to have to hurry."

Artemis slid from the counter. "I will tell Eddie I detained you. He will not be upset at having some time alone with me before you join us."

"Artemis," Pamela called. With her hand on the doorknob the goddess turned to look at her. "May I ask you one question? Even if it is a little personal?"

The goddess shrugged one smooth shoulder. "You deserve a boon for the miracle you worked. I have no powers with which to thank you, so I will gladly answer your question."

"I admit I don't know my mythology very well, but everything I remember ever reading about you, about Artemis, said that you are a virgin goddess, totally untouched by any man or god. I was just wondering if it's true."

For a moment Artemis looked shocked, then perplexed, and then she began to laugh.

"Well, I didn't mean it to be funny," Pamela muttered, a little embarrassed by the goddess's reaction to her question.

"It is the storytelling of men at which I laugh, not you. They branded me as the virgin goddess because I refused to shackle myself to one mate. I take love where I will. I decide who and where and when. My real pleasure comes from my freedom. My favorite lover is the forest, my oldest companions my handmaiden nymphs. But I can assure you that I am no virgin." She left the room, and her musical laugher floated after her.

CHAPTER 26

Pamela was surprised to realize that Apollo was avoiding her. She was also surprised to realize how much his avoidance bothered her. She still caught him looking at her, but the moment she tried to meet his gaze, he turned from her and became very busy with whatever workman was near. He even avoided her during their lunch break. She sat with Eddie and Artemis and watched them flirt outrageously while she gobbled down one of the excellent gourmet sandwiches Eddie's genius cook made for everyone. Apollo had only paused long enough to grab a sandwich and send her a brief, distracted smile before he rejoined the architect over near the site where workers had already begun staking out the ground for the bathhouse.

Not that she wasn't busy herself. Today they were choosing the flooring, and it had turned out to be a major event. At first Eddie had wanted a horrid reproduction of the tacky fake stone flooring that was so nauseatingly abundant at The Forum. Thankfully, from her perch atop the dais where she stood regally, holding a bow in her hand instead of yesterday's vase, Artemis shook her head and said a quick, "Oh, no, Eddie. It is dreadful." And that was that. The laminated fake stone was instantly vetoed. Then Pamela had told the three representatives from the natural stone manufacturers to bring forward samples of their best marbles. And the deluge began. Eddie had been instantly enthralled with the different colors and varieties of the stone, and he kept moving from one outrageous sample to another, becoming more and more infatuated with each one and insisting that they choose a different color scheme for each room.

All in all, he was giving Pamela a pounding headache.

She tried to explain to him that with the open floor plan of his villa, abruptly going from Santiago marble, which was veined with reds, golds, siennas and greens, to Verde Fire, which was filled predominately with wild chartreuse, yellow and black, to Golden Alexandra, which was, well, golden, would be a terrible design error.

Artemis, again, saved the day.

"I like that one," she'd said, pointing one slender finger at a square of forgotten tile, lying well apart from the others.

"Do you, my goddess?" Eddie had said, instantly attentive.

Pamela had practically sprinted over to the tile. It was an understated creamy color, with slight buttercup variations which ran softly from a hint of yellow to a blush of gold. Pamela smiled. "It's lovely, but it's not marble. It's tumbled limestone." She carried it over to Artemis, who ran a caressing hand over its smooth surface.

"It's soft and perfect." Artemis looked at the author and purred. "Eddie, I would very much like to feel it pressed against my naked skin."

Eddie's eyes darkened. "Then allow me to fulfill your desire, my goddess. I choose this limestone to cover the floor of my humble home."

Humble home? Oh, brother! Pamela wanted to roll her eyes. Instead, she winked a quick thank-you at Artemis and then began going over the specifics of the order with the delighted stone merchant. Somewhere in the middle of the weighty order she was struck with inspiration. She told the salesman to wait a second and, grinning, she rejoined Eddie on the bench near Artemis' dais.

"I have an idea you might find interesting," she said.

"Do tell us, Pamela!" Eddie said.

"Well, what would you think of putting the limestone in all the rooms of the villa, *except* the bathrooms. In them you get to go wild—choose a different marble for each of them, and then we'll create the color scheme and personality of that particular bathroom to reflect its own individual, distinct marble. It would be like an adventure to enter each powder room. And in the case of the bathrooms that are attached to suites, like the master suite and the five guest suites, we would take one color from the chosen marble and use it as the accent in the adjoining room."

"What a marvelous idea, Pamela!" Artemis said with what appeared to be genuine enthusiasm. "And what fun we'll have choosing each one."

Eddie's booming laugh caused several heads to turn. "Well done, Pamela!"

Pamela smiled at the big man. "Your home is going to be truly unique, Eddie." And for the first time she meant the words as a compliment. Then she called for the stone reps to bring out their most outlandish marble samples.

She was just sipping a bottle of icy sparkling water and studying a square of marble that reminded her of a kaleidoscope, when she felt Apollo's eyes on her. Again. She looked up. He must have been taking a break, because he was standing across the courtyard from her, looking over the artist's shoulder at the sketch being created of his sister. His head was still tilted down towards the sketch, but his eyes were on her. Automatically, her stomach tightened. *Please don't let him look away,* her errant thoughts whispered. She smiled tentatively at him. He returned her smile, and then his expression shifted, as if he remembered himself, and he dropped his eyes back to the sketch. Pamela sighed.

"Why do you punish him?"

Eddie's voice, uncharacteristically low, came from beside her. She jumped and wondered how the hell he'd gotten so close to her without being heard. Pamela glanced up at the big man, ready to insist that she didn't know what he was talking about . . . and the honest concern on his face stopped her dismissive words.

"I don't want to punish him. I just don't know what to do about him," she said.

"You do know that he loves you?"

Pamela blinked in surprise, and Eddie rumbled a low, subdued version of his laugh.

"You should always remember that I am an author, which is really just a storyteller who observes the world and then reshapes it into his own vision to entertain and amuse. Besides that, Phoebus does not attempt to hide his feelings for you—it is *you* who masks what your heart feels for him. Is that not so?"

"Yes," she said softly.

"I know it is presumptuous of me to ask, but why? He seems a man of excellent character."

She hesitated, unsure of whether she could tell him any part of the truth.

"You are safe talking to me, Pamela. What you say will not affect our business relationship. And I would like you to think of me as your friend. I have always considered it sublimely ridiculous when people say that they never mix business with pleasure. How colorless their lives must be as they trudge alone under the burden of such restrictive rules. So tell me, what is it that is keeping you from accepting Phoebus?"

She studied Eddie's eyes. They were guileless and filled with warm concern. "If I tell you the truth, do I need to be afraid that it will appear in one of your books?" she asked, only half in jest.

This time his laugh boomed throughout the courtyard. "That is always the danger when befriending an author." He leaned in and lowered his voice to a stage whisper, "but I give you my oath that I will change your name."

Making a decision based entirely upon what her gut was telling her, she blurted, "I'm scared of getting hurt. Aren't you?"

Eddie's gaze went from her to Artemis. For a moment sadness shadowed his face, then he drew a deep breath, and it was gone, replaced by a knowing smile. Without taking his gaze from the goddess, he said, "You will remember that when first we met I wanted the center statue of my fountain to be fashioned after an image of the god, Bacchus?"

"Yes," Pamela nodded, hoping like hell she hadn't said something to make him reconsider that horrid idea.

"Bacchus has long been a favorite of mine. He is not typically Olympian. Mythology reports that he was the last god to enter Olympus—Homer did not acknowledge him at all. His nature was alien to the other gods; they who loved order and beauty did not always appreciate the unique character of Bacchus or his worshipers. I understand that. I know what it is to be titled as one thing and thought of as another." He shook his head and looked fondly at Pamela. "But I digress. It is not Bacchus' story I want you to hear, but his mother's."

The big man motioned for one of the workers to bring chairs for them. She sat beside him, waiting while the author settled his girth and called for a cold glass of mead. When he asked if she would join him, she shrugged and nodded. Why not? When one worked for Eddie, one definitely colored outside the lines. After their mead arrived, Eddie took a long drink before launching into his story.

"Semele was a beautiful Theban princess. Born of mortal parents, she had the face and figure of a goddess. Unfortunately, she caught the eye of Zeus, the Supreme Ruler of Olympus. Zeus dallied with many mortal maidens, as did most of the gods and goddesses."

Here Pamela blew out a puff of disgruntled air and recrossed her legs. Eddie smiled.

"Remember, my dear. It was a different world then. Pretend, for just a moment, that you are a lovely young girl living in ancient Greece. Born into a hardworking merchant family, you are dissatisfied with the role in life fate had allotted you. Do you cast aside your secret aspirations and quietly marry as your family chooses? What if, say, a handsome man looked your way? Perhaps the eldest son of a wealthy landowner. He is out of your reach, but you find love in his arms. Suddenly you discover that you are with child. Are you driven from your household in shame as your betrothal is broken? Or do you describe how, one day while you were gathering flowers in a meadow outside the walls of the city a god appeared to you, seduced you, and fathered your child—a child who is then birthed with much ado and whose life is surrounded by mystery and magic?"

"I get your point," Pamela muttered.

"May I continue with my tale?"

"Sorry," she said, settling back in her chair and sipping her mead.

"As I was saying, Semele became one of Zeus' many mortal lovers. But she was different, and in more ways than just her extraordinary beauty. Mythology reports that Zeus was completely enamored with his young mistress, so much so that when she told him she was to bear his child he swore an oath by the River Styx that he would give her anything she asked of him." Eddie paused, sipping his mead in slow contemplation.

"Well? Then what happened?"

"Semele's heart's desire was to see Zeus in his full splendor as King of Olympus and Lord of the Thunderbolt. Zeus pleaded with his lover to take back her request. He knew that no mortal could behold him thus and live, but she would not recant her heart's desire. The Lord of Gods had sworn an oath by the River Styx, and not even he could break that bond. So, with his cheeks washed in tears of foreknowledge, he came to her one last time and revealed himself as she had asked, and before that awful, beautiful glory of his burning light, she died."

"But that can't be right. If she was dead, how was Bacchus born?"

"Because of his love for her, Zeus snatched his son from her womb as she perished and carried the child within his own thigh until it was time for the God of the Vine to be born."

Before yesterday Pamela would have reacted to Eddie's retelling of an ancient myth as little more than an amusing story. Now she knew too well that the possibility that it was much more than simple fiction was pretty good. She ached for the bittersweet tragedy of Semele, who had died because she refused to cast aside her heart's desire . . .

"I had no idea," Pamela said.

"Do you think Semele regretted her wish?" Eddie asked.

"Well, it killed her."

"But do you think she regretted it? Do you think she would have traded that moment of wonderful, awful fulfillment—fulfillment so great that her mortal body could not contain it—for a lifetime of safety bereft of that blinding instant of splendor?"

"I'm not sure I can answer that. What do you think, Eddie?"

"You must decide for yourself." His gaze turned from her and found Artemis. His smile was no longer tinged with sadness. "I have made my own decision."

"Aren't you scared?" Pamela found she could barely form the words.

"Of course. There are no guarantees in love, Pamela, just endless opportunities—for hurt and for happiness. But I can say without any misgivings that I would rather touch her for one instant and be burned, than to live my life in the darkness bereft of her light."

At his words something changed inside Pamela. Something within her that had been sleeping finally did more than stir and stretch. It came fully awake. She knew what living in the darkness felt like, and she also knew what it was to touch the light.

"I don't want a life bereft of his light, either," Pamela said through the catch in her throat.

Eddie looked at her and beamed. "Well done, Pamela! Well done." Abruptly, he stood, and his deep voice blasted throughout the villa. "Phoebus! Come to me!"

Pamela tried to say something—something like, "Wait, Eddie! I didn't mean I was ready to touch the blood buggering light right now!" but the author totally ignored her frantic whispers. When Apollo hurried up to them, she was mortified to realize that her face felt fiery. She was blushing like a schoolgirl. Great.

"There you are, my boy! I have a request of you."

"What can I do for you, Eddie?"

"I believe Pamela has been working too hard. I have one strict rule: always mix business with pleasure. Our Pamela is new to this rule," Eddie said as if Pamela wasn't sitting less than a foot from him with a bright red face.

"I have noticed that about our Pamela, too," Apollo said, trying to keep his expression neutral.

"Good! Then you understand exactly what has to be done." At the golden twin's blank expression, Eddie rose and clapped him on the shoulder. "Why,. take her out of here, man! Stroll with her about the resort. Visit the springs and refresh yourselves. I'll instruct James to make sure he packs a lovely dinner for you, and we won't expect to see you again until dark."

Apollo looked as stunned as Pamela felt.

"James!" Eddie bellowed, and his assistant, as usual, miraculously appeared. "Tell Robert to take Pamela and Phoebus back to the resort. Have the staff pack them an old-fashioned picnic dinner. The two of them need some time to rest and to"—he hesitated and winked at Phoebus—"rejuvenate."

"Of course, Eddie," James said before hurrying off.

"Off you go," Eddie told them. "And don't worry, Pamela, Diana and I shall finish choosing the marble for the bathrooms."

"Are you sure you don't need me to double-check things with the limestone rep?"

"No, no, no," Eddie brushed away her concern. "The man has the blueprints. Now off with you!"

Seeing no other choice, Pamela got up and began walking with Apollo through the courtyard. The doors were open, and the sun reflected off the silver hood of the limo as it pulled up and braked in front of the villa. Apollo stopped.

"Remember, Phoebus, you must slay the dragon before you win the fair maid!" Eddie shouted from behind them.

The God of Light lifted a hand and waved back at Eddie with good humor, but Pamela heard his miserable sigh and noticed how his face had instantly paled at the sight of the limo. Apollo squared his shoulders and started forward again.

"Do they have dragons in the ancient world?" Pamela whispered, walking beside him.

"Yes, but they do not have cars. I can promise you that I'd rather face the dragons."

"I'll sit in the front seat with you."

"I can't slay it?"

"I don't think that would be a good idea." Pamela tried unsuccessfully not to laugh.

CHAPTER 27

‸

Hiking in and around Pikes Peak had long been one of Pamela's favorite hobbies as well as her main form of exercise. Why should she work out in the stuffy confines of a man-made gym when she had the splendor of the Colorado Rocky Mountains surrounding her? Not that she was one of those hard-core, backpacking, camping, shunning-the-conveniences-of-modern-life hikers. Scaling up the side of a sheer rock had never, ever appealed to her. Nor did sleeping on the ground and peeing in the woods. But taking a trail that wound up and around the mountain, especially early in the morning when everything was clean and still and private, was something she had been shifting her schedule to include at least four times a week ever since she had left Duane. Hiking was synonymous with freedom to her. And it didn't matter how sluggish or stressed out she was feeling at the beginning of her trek; an hour later when she returned she was relaxed and rejuvenated. V called it her "attitude adjustment time."

So the brand-new shorts, T-shirt and hiking shoes that had been set out on her bed for her brought a definite smile to her lips. She changed clothes quickly and emerged from her room in time to see Apollo, in a male version of her attire, walking down the hall towards her.

"I do not know how Eddie performs all of this magic without any immortal power," Apollo said, smiling wryly.

"The power Eddie has is called money. Lots of it. Coupled with his imagination, it equates to the modern world's version of magic. James called my room and said for us to meet him in the den."

"After you," Apollo gestured gallantly for her to precede him down the hall.

Pamela noticed that, just as in the short ride in the car, he was very careful not to touch her. She reminded herself that he was only giving her what she had asked of him, space and time, which didn't help to dispel the crappy, knotted feeling in the pit of her stomach.

James was waiting for them with a smile, a picnic basket and a map.

"I have marked a trail nearby that I thought you might particularly enjoy exploring. It begins north of the ranch house, winds through First Creek Canyon to a lovely spring-fed pool." He pointed at the end of his yellow highlighted trail. "The perfect place for a leisurely dinner. In the basket you will find plenty of water as well as sunscreen. And, though you probably won't need it, I also included a cell phone, which is programmed back to the spa information desk. Just hit star sixty-two in the unlikely event you get lost or need assistance."

"You're very thorough, James," Pamela said.

"Thank you, ma'am. Just keep in mind that night falls quickly in the desert. I believe sunset is scheduled today for 8:05 P.M." He handed Apollo the basket, bowed neatly and left the two of them alone.

They stood awkwardly in silence. Apollo was the first to speak.

"I suppose we should go."

Pamela cleared her throat. It was ridiculous that she was feeling nervous about being alone with him. She'd had sex with him. More than once. There was no reason for her stomach to feel sick and her palms to be so sweaty. None at all. She needed to get a grip.

"Okay," she pointed at the basket. "Sunscreen first."

Apollo raised an eyebrow at her.

She sighed and undid the clasp on the top of the picnic basket. So much for behaving normally. The situation was definitely not normal. The man standing before her didn't know what the hell sunscreen was because he was Apollo,

God of Light. Jangled nerves were probably the only normal thing about this situation. She peeked into the basket.
Organized as well as always prepared, James had placed
the tube of forty-plus sunblock right on top. With an open,
curious expression, Apollo watched her spread the creamy
lotion on her arms and face.

"It smells of coconut. What it is?" he asked.

"It's sunscreen. It blocks the harmful rays of the sun
from our skin."

He looked utterly baffled.

"Mortals can be burned by too much light. Remember
Semele?"

Apollo blinked in surprise.

"Eddie's been giving me lessons in mythology."

Apollo raised both of his golden brows. "Be careful
what you believe of the stories told and retold in your
world. I have it on excellent authority that many of them
are highly inaccurate."

"Yeah, I've already figured that out. They say Artemis
is a virgin."

He barked a laugh. "Which proves my point. Now tell
me truly, does this lotion that smells of coconut have the
power to block the light of an immortal?"

"I doubt it, but it will save you from getting a nasty
sunburn."

"Sunburn?"

"Think of it like shaving. It should be simple to understand, but it can mess you up if you're not used to everything that goes with it. Sunlight is like that for mortals."

Looking grim, he took the tube from her, squeezed
some into his hand, sniffed it and then spread it on his arms
and shoulders. Pamela watched him, and she felt suddenly,
inexplicably sad. Apollo, God of Light, should not have to
protect himself against the sun. A vision of the last time
they made love flashed through her mind. He had been a
flame, burning with immortal passion. He *was* the sun.

Apollo didn't belong here. She could give in to the desire of her heart and allow herself to love him, but she
could not delude herself into thinking that their story

would have an ending any happier than Semele's mythic love for Zeus.

"Don't forget your face," she whispered.

"Thank you," he smiled, drenching his face in the white liquid, "I would have forgotten. This is all rather new to me."

Her stomach clenched again, but she returned his smile. "I think that will do." Pamela recapped the tube and put it back in the basket, which Apollo picked up, and together they walked out the front door of the lodge.

"Do you know which way is north?" Apollo paused to ask her. When she gave him a startled look, he grinned like a little boy. "I am only teasing you. I'm without my powers, not without my brain."

"Well, that's comforting," she mumbled but grinned back at him as they crunched down the pebble-covered drive and angled to their left, weaving between the scattered adobe buildings that made up the rest of the chic little spa, restaurant, and well-supplied gift shop. It was hard to believe that just outside the resort the oasis gave way to the brutal beauty of the desert. Their trail was flanked by wild tufts of long-armed orange flowers, interspersed between fragrant purple plants that reminded her of lavender, as well as the familiar pointed, rubbery leaves of yucca clumps. It was cooler here in the canyon, and much greener, as if the desert had saved up all its softness and sweetness and focused it here.

They said little as they made their way through the heart of the resort. Apollo didn't take her hand or link her arm through his. When he spoke to her he was polite, even witty, but the passionate undercurrent that had been an almost tangible part of everything he said or did since they had met at the little café table at The Lost Cellar was gone, or at least well-subdued—and Pamela felt its loss keenly.

She thought about what Eddie had said to her, and the way his face changed whenever his gaze rested on Artemis. The big man knew the hurt he chanced, but he believed what he gained was more valuable than what he might lose. *There are no guarantees in love, Pamela, just endless opportunities—for hurt and for happiness.* It was a new and frightening concept for Pamela, but she had never been a coward, and she had rarely taken the easy way out.

Apollo spotted the little wooden sign made in the shape of an arrow on which was carved First Creek Canyon.

"I prophesy that First Creek Canyon is this way," Apollo said, dramatically holding one hand to his temple.

"Watch it," she smiled at him. "You're gonna get struck by lightning or something."

"Zeus," Apollo grunted.

"So do you think you're in trouble with him?"

"I'm afraid that Artemis and I will have much to explain. He is our father, and he loves us, but regardless of that fact, the God of Thunder will not be amused that we allowed ourselves to become trapped in the Kingdom of Las Vegas."

"Uh, it's not really called a kingdom. It's just Las Vegas, located in the state of Nevada. Like Rome is a city located in the country of Italy." *At least it's kind of like that,* she thought, not wanting to launch into a whole United States of America geography lecture.

"Not a kingdom?"

"Absolutely not."

They walked on down the red dirt path several paces before Apollo spoke again. "I probably appear very foolish to you, calling Las Vegas a kingdom, getting carsick, cutting myself shaving, not knowing about sunscreen," he said, not looking at her.

"Not half as foolish as I would be if I was suddenly plopped down in the middle of Olympus."

He glanced over at her. "You have been to Olympus, and you did not make a fool of yourself."

"No," she snorted. "I was too busy being drugged with your sister's magic and then turning into a flower."

Apollo stopped and faced her. He lifted his hand, as if he meant to touch her, but he didn't follow through with the gesture; instead, his fisted hand returned to his side. "I am ashamed that both of those things happened to you. I should have been able to protect you from them. My only defense is that I am new to this emotion, this being in love,

and I find it"—he paused; his gaze met hers and held—
"distracting."

Pamela drew a deep breath. "I know exactly what you
mean."

Apollo's expression shifted subtly, but he said nothing
more than, "Do you?"

"Yes," she started walking again. She wanted to talk to
him; she needed to talk to him, but she couldn't do it standing still.

"I already told you that I was married, and that it was a
bad marriage."

"Yes," he said.

"I want you to know the reason it was bad, and then I
think you'll understand why this has been so hard for me,
why I've resisted loving you."

"I'm listening."

"I met Duane while I was in college. He's ten years
older than I am, and he was already a successful professional. I thought he was dashing and smart, and he seemed
so kind. He wanted to take care of me. I understand now
that I didn't fall in love with who he really was; I fell in
love with the fantasy of the life we were supposed to make
together. But love is love." She lifted one shoulder, as if
trying to shrug off the uncomfortable admission, "and we
married the month I graduated from college. From the day
of our wedding on, things changed. We bought a house
together." She laughed humorlessly. "No, scratch that.
Duane bought the house. He insisted that it would be better if the title was in his name alone. He said it would be
quicker and easier. Just like my new car was a 'gift' he surprised me with. Again, the title was only in his name. I remember one day just a week or so after our wedding. He
was out of town, and he called. He liked to call. A lot." She
paused. Just the memory of Duane's constant checks on
her, how he had sent members of his family and the small
group of selected friends he approved of to "keep her company" so that he always knew where she was and what she
was doing made her feel edgy and frustrated. Her boots bit
into the trail with a satisfying crunch as she picked up their
pace in an attempt to vent the old frustration. It was in the

past, she reminded herself; she had escaped it, and it would never happen to her again.

Apollo watched silently as Pamela struggled with the emotions reliving the past caused her. He wanted to help her—he wanted to wipe away the hurt—but he knew that the past was a battlefield each individual had to fight. If Pamela couldn't vanquish her old demons, they would forever haunt her future. Their future.

"Anyway," she continued, "that day he asked what I was doing, as he always did. I said hanging a new picture. I'll never forget how his voice changed. 'Don't you think I'd like to be there with you to do that?' he'd snapped. I hadn't even considered that hanging a picture without him would be a big deal. It was. We had been married less than one month, and it was that day that I began to feel trapped." She couldn't repress a shudder.

It had gotten worse—so much worse. She had almost given up and let Duane consume her, but from somewhere deep within her she had found the strength to fight. Slowly and quietly she had worked to establish herself in her field. And to secretly put away money so that she could buy her way free of him. People think leaving an abuser is all about growing a backbone. Pamela knew how wrong they were. Leaving an abuser is about having a plan, and then having the means to follow through with it. Her plan included a kick-ass lawyer and a business of her own. She drew her spine up straighter and finished her story.

"I don't want to go into all the gory details. Suffice it to say that he smothered me for almost seven years before I finally got free of him. Then it was almost two more years before he stopped calling and coming by and showing up places he knew I frequented. Always there . . . he was always there, waiting, as if I were an errant child who would soon realize the error of her ways and come back home." She glanced at him. "It has just been during the last six months that he has left me alone."

"He hurt you." Apollo's voice was low and tight as he entertained thoughts of what he would like to do to this Duane after his immortal powers were returned to him.

"Yes, he hurt me, but that's not the part that still affects me. The hurt died with the love. What lived on was self-doubt. I didn't see it coming. I dated him for almost two years. If someone would have told me—at any time before we were married—that this man who seems so wonderful, so perfect, is really a vindictive, angry, control freak who is going to try to cage you and break you and make you a frightened wreck of yourself, I would have laughed in his face. I would never have believed it. He pretended to be something he wasn't to trap me, and I didn't see through it . . ." She ended in a whisper.

"The masquerade you were talking about the night we watched the fountain dance. It was your marriage."

She nodded.

"And when you found out that I was Apollo masquerading as Phoebus, you thought you had made yet another mistake in giving yourself to me."

"It's not just that. You're the only man I've been with since Duane. I've been working and keeping busy and—" She broke off, not sure of her next words.

"And you have been avoiding love," Apollo finished for her.

She gave him a quick, sideways look. "Yes."

"Which makes finding out about my subterfuge even more disturbing."

"Yes," she said again.

Apollo considered what she had told him as they followed the twisting path in silence. It made sense now, her continual withdraw from him, and why she couldn't let herself admit her love for him until she was under the intoxicating influence of his sister's power. How surprising to realize that her reticence was more about her past than his—and how refreshing. He suspected that his being a god made less difference to her than his being dishonest with her.

They turned an abrupt corner in the trail and then climbed up an unexpectedly steep incline to find themselves standing atop lumps of sand-colored boulders, worn smooth by time, from the center of which a waterfall poured down into a large, clear pool.

"James was right. This is the perfect spot for a picnic," Pamela said, looking around her in awe as she wiped the sweat from her face with her sleeve. The desert heat was tamer in the canyon, but still the hike had caused a sheen of sweat to break on both of them. Pamela breathed in the watered-cooled air and turned her face to catch the little breeze that lifted from the pool.

"I have a feeling James is usually right," Apollo said. Then he motioned to a flat-topped rock that perched nearby. "Sit with me a moment?"

The climb had served to help rid her of much of the nervous tension that recounting the past had stirred up, and Pamela sat on the sun-warmed rock, curling her legs up under her. She stared down at the sparkling pool, allowing the sound and scent of the gently falling water to soothe her. Apollo sat beside her, close enough that she could feel the heat of his body, but still he didn't touch her.

"I will not tell you that I understand what you must feel. I do not. How can I? I cannot even understand why a man would want to cage a woman. I have faults, but wanting to dominate and control women is not one of them." He pointed to the golden coin bearing his image that still danged between her breasts. "Remember that, whatever happens between the two of us, I have pledged my protection to you. You may rest assured that this Duane will not harass you again.

"Thanks," she said, "but I prefer to clean up my messes myself."

"Now you sound like my sister."

"I'll take that as a scary compliment."

"It was meant as one." Apollo grinned. Pamela met his gaze and returned his grin. He thought how much he loved her face. It was so open, and her emotions were so honest. He could watch her smile forever. And with a start he realized that she had become his sun, and the God of Light swallowed through a suddenly dry throat. He loved her dearly, and that gave her a power over him that was frightening. If she turned from him . . .

He looked away from her, collecting his thoughts and

reining in his emotions. If she turned from him, he would let her go. He would not haunt her life as Duane had. His jaw clenched. She hadn't turned from him yet. And she loved him—he knew she loved him. He turned on the rock so that he could face her and spoke slowly and distinctly.

"I do not understand Duane, and what it was to live under his control and to struggle for your release, but from the first night we met I recognized within your eyes an emotion that I do understand. I know what it is like to wish for more and to feel incomplete without it. What if we were fated to be together? What if everything that has happened in our lives has served one purpose—and that is to prepare us for one another. I am a god, one of the Twelve Olympians. Who would know better the intricate threads the Fates can weave?"

Her eyes sharpened on his, and Apollo chose his words carefully. "I have existed for a very long time, and for most of that existence I have lived in a bright blaze of passion and frivolity. Yes, I have done some good. I brought healing and song and light to the ancient world, but those things were almost an afterthought to me. I always felt hungry. I tried to slake that hunger in the way many men do, be they mortal or immortal. I loved and warred to great excess. It was like I was trying to fill an unending void within me."

"Apollo, I—" Pamela began, but he shook his head.

"No, these are things you should know. I will not masquerade to win you. I want no falseness between us. You must see me as I am if you are to accept me. I have told you that I did not know love until I knew you. It was more than that. I did not believe in the existence of love. After all, I had lived for eons without it, yet I had sampled all types of pleasures of the flesh. Love was obviously nothing more than a sham to which mortals clung. The God of Light had no use for such a sham. I could not feel it. I did not need it. I did not believe in it."

He paused and finally allowed himself to touch her briefly as he brushed aside the dark lock of her short, glossy hair which habitually fell over her forehead.

"Then something happened to change how I viewed my life and my world. And it happened before I met you. What do you know of the god Hades?"

Surprised by the sudden question, Pamela said, "Isn't he the God of the Underworld or something like that?"

Apollo smiled, wishing his friend could hear Pamela's response. "He is Lord of the Underworld. Hades' realm is not filled with misery and torture, like your modern version of hell. It is a place of incredible beauty. I know—I visit there often."

"You go to Hell?"

Apollo laughed. "I go to the opulent palace of Hades, which is built on the edge of the Elysian Fields. You would like Hades. The two of you have much in common. He designed and built his palace himself."

"Not like Caesars Palace?" she asked leerily.

"Absolutely nothing like it. I give you my word."

"That's good to know."

"But I didn't mention Hades because of his design expertise. I tell you about him because it is important how he and I became friends. My friendship with the God of the Underworld came about because of his wife."

"Wait! I remember this one. Hades is married to Persephone." Then her brow wrinkled. "But didn't he abduct her and trick her into marrying him?"

"I doubt anyone could abduct Lina."

"Lina? So he's not married to Persephone?"

"Hades is married to his soul mate. His soul mate just happens to be a mortal woman from a place in your modern world called Tulsa. Her name is Carolina Francesca Santoro."

"Tulsa? As in Oklahoma? How is that possible? And what about Persephone?"

"It is a rather long and complicated story. Persephone and Lina share their bodies and their identities. What began as a manipulation by an outside force, in this instance Persephone's mother, Demeter, ended with Hades finding his soul mate in Lina. But how they found each other is not important. What is important is what I watched happen to Hades as he allowed himself to love."

"Hades didn't want to love a mortal woman?" Pamela asked.

Apollo's lips turned up in the hint of a smile. "Hades didn't want to love anyone, mortal or immortal. He had walled himself away from love, taken the possibility of it from his life. He chose his duties—you would say his job—instead."

"He and I do seem to have a lot in common," Pamela said softly.

"Yes, only he had longer than you to perfect his choice. You should know what a loveless life was costing him, Pamela. He had become a shadow of a god, living a numb, emotionless existence."

"But he was safe," Pamela whispered. "He didn't feel hurt."

"You're right. He didn't feel hurt. He didn't feel anything. I said that he and I became friends because of his wife. That is because his love for Lina changed him, it awakened something within him. He went from a dour, humorless shadow to a vibrant god. And their love changed me, too. I watched it unfold, and as I did I began to recognize what it was that I had spent an eternity seeking." Apollo paused and took Pamela's hand in his. "Hades says Lina is his soul mate, and that in finding her he found his place in the world. Ironically, it is the Lord of the Dead who showed me how it is I want to live." Apollo raised her hand to his lips. "What I recognized within your eyes was that same seeking hunger I felt within my own soul before you came into my life. Our souls are mirrors, Pamela, because you are my soul mate. And whatever has happened in our lives before now has readied us for one another. I am no longer the heartless god who is able to care for nothing except his own pleasure. You are no longer the naive young woman who would rather love a fantasy than a man."

"If only I can accept it," Pamela said.

"Not *it*, sweet Pamela, *me*. You need only accept me."

She looked into his blue eyes and drew a deep, steadying breath. "I have already accepted you. I just don't know what to do next."

Then she smiled at him—that open, honest smile he had come to love so much. Apollo felt a bright blaze of joy. She was his soul mate! Mortal or immortal, to him she would always be his partner, his love, his own Goddess of Light. The brilliance of her smile rivaled anything his immortal power could produce. He cupped her face between his hands.

"Next you simply kiss me." He bent and brushed his lips against hers. "Then we will eat the excellent meal James packed for us." He kissed her again, this time nibbling gently at her bottom lip. "Then I believe I will make love to you in the pool below us." This time his kiss lasted long enough to cause Pamela to sigh softly and lean into him. "Tonight when we return to the ranch house, we will spend the night in each other's arms." He teased her mouth again, thinking that she tasted like sweet wine, except that she was much more intoxicating. "And tomorrow—"

"Shhh," Pamela cut off his words as she slid into his arms and fitted herself against him. She would not think of the eternity that waited just beyond tonight. She would only think of him. "Do you think we could skip the dinner part and go right to the making love in the water part?"

Apollo laughed happily and stood, scooping her up in his arms. He kissed her thoroughly once more before setting her down. Executing a quick bow, he said with a flash of his brilliant smile, "If you insist."

This time Pamela took his hand and raised it to her lips before she tugged him in the direction of path that led down to the level of the pool.

"Wait," she said after only a few feet. "I'm going to grab the picnic basket. I have a feeling that we're going to work up a gihugic appetite. And anyway . . ." She grinned over her shoulder at him as she scrambled quickly back up the trail to the ledge and bent to retrieve the basket from where Apollo had discarded it. "We shouldn't take James's hard work for—"

The rattling sliced off her words as Pamela's body turned to cold, immovable stone. Somewhere in her mind the thought flashed that it sounded more like the hiss of meat being seared in frying grease than the child's toy after which it was named. A terrible sinking sensation overwhelmed her, and she fought against a flood of vertigo when her eyes followed the path of the sound to find the snake coiled beside the picnic basket just inches from her outstretched hand.

CHAPTER 28

Apollo knew something had gone horribly wrong before he saw the serpent. Pamela froze, midsentence, and through the silent space between them, he heard the deadly sound of the viper's warning. The god's actions were automatic. He lunged forward with his hand up, focusing all of his immortal powers on destroying that which threatened his love.

Nothing happened. He cursed himself for being an impotent, powerless god. No! It wasn't that he was powerless—it was only that he was now a man. It was as a man that he must protect Pamela. As quickly and quietly as possible, he moved into position behind her. The snake was coiled into a huge rope of anger. Its triangular head was raised and staring slit-eyed at Pamela's hand, which was well within striking distance.

"When I move forward, you must leap to the side," Apollo said in a low, calm voice.

The snake's rattling increased, and Pamela opened her mouth to protest—to warn him away—to scream—to anything . . . but it was too late, Apollo was already moving. He shoved her aside, and with superhuman speed, he met the snake's strike. Pamela screamed as she watched the rattler imbed its fangs into the meaty part of Apollo's hand. And then, snarling an ancient curse, the God of Light grasped the snake's thick body with his other hand. Powerfully, he jerked the snake, wrenching it from his hand. Before it could strike again, Apollo spun his body, whirling the snake with him so that he could crack its head, like the deadly end of a whip, against the rocky ledge. It exploded in a shower of blood, but still the Sun God wasn't satisfied. He cracked it again and again against the rock before hurling its lifeless body over the edge of the cliff and down into the waiting pool.

Gulping air, his head snapped around to find Pamela. She was crouched not far from him, eyes wide with shock. "Did it harm you?"

"No," she shook her head in two shaky movements.

Relief washed over him just before the pain sliced through him, driving him to his knees. His hand! He hadn't even felt the viper's strike—he'd felt only blinding fury and the need to protect Pamela. He turned his burning hand over. The agony was racing up his arm from two bloody puncture wounds near his wrist below his thumb.

"Here, let me see it." Pamela was on her knees beside him, reaching blindly for the picnic basket. Her face was ghostly, and her hands were shaking, but her voice was firm. He gave her his hand and she sucked in her breath. "Oh, God. I knew it got you." She stared up into his face, cradling his bloody hand against her body while she groped through the basket. "What are you feeling?"

"Fire," he said shortly, surprised to find that he was still struggling for breath. He tried to laugh, but the sound came out as a groan. "It feels like my hand is on fire."

"You'll be fine. You'll be fine. Here, sit back and lean against the rock." She helped guide his shoulders until they rested against the smooth stone as he almost fell back from his knees, telling herself all the while that she had to stay calm . . . she could not panic. "Keep sitting up." She lay his wounded hand, palm up, gently on his thigh, trying desperately to remember everything she'd ever heard about poisonous snakebites. V had forced her to read an article not long ago about hiker safety. *Think!* "Make sure your hand stays below the level of your heart," she told Apollo, who nodded weakly. Then she turned her full attention to the basket. "Where is the fucking cell phone!" she said through teeth that kept wanting to chatter. "Ah!" Victorious, she hastily punched star sixty-two. "Come on . . .

come on . . ." she muttered. Looking back through the basket, she jerked out the two bottles of water. While she spoke into the phone, she unscrewed one of the bottles and handed it to Apollo, who drained half of it in one swallow.

"Yes, this is Pamela Gray. I'm a guest of E. D. Faust. My assistant and I are at the top of the pool in First Creek Canyon, and he has just been bitten by a rattlesnake," she spoke quickly and clearly, as if she wasn't riding on the edge of panic.

"First, are you certain it was a rattlesnake, ma'am?" the dispatcher asked in a calm, professional voice.

"Yes, I'm sure. Triangular head, dull brown body. Rattles."

"I'm sending an EMT team to you right now, Pamela."

She could hear the clicks and squawks of the dispatcher's radio in the background. Then he began firing specific questions at her.

"Where was he bit?"

"On his right hand. Below his thumb right around his wrist."

"Be sure he is sitting or lying down and that his hand is below the level of his heart."

"Already did that."

"Is he conscious?"

Pamela's eyes met Apollo's. "Yes," she said.

"In a great deal of pain?"

"Yes, he says it feels like fire." Her voice broke.

"Pamela, it is very important that you keep him calm. Do not let him panic. He needs to stay as quiet as possible."

"I understand." *Get control!* she ordered herself. If she fell apart, he had no one.

"Okay, do you have water?"

"Yes."

"Wash the wound, but be careful not to move his hand or arm around too much."

"I'll do that now, hang on." She put the phone on the ground next to her and grabbed the other bottle of water. "There's help on the way, but the bite needs to be washed out right away. I hope it doesn't hurt, but it might. You're

supposed to stay as quiet as you can, so even if it hurts try
not to jerk away."

"Do what you must. I will not pull away from you."

When she cupped his hand gently in hers, he closed his
eyes, and as she poured the bottled water over the deep
fang marks, the only movement he made was the rapid rise
and fall of his chest.

She wiped the blood-tinged water from her hands onto
her shorts and picked up the phone.

"That's done. What else?"

"Remove any rings, bracelets or watch he has on that
hand or arm."

"He's not wearing any."

"Good. Now all you can do is keep him calm and treat
him for shock."

"Shouldn't I make a tourniquet or something?"

"No, the bite is too close to his wrist joint. Keeping him
quiet and making sure that he doesn't lose any body heat
will help him more. Do not let him sleep. He may have a
rapid pulse or labored breathing. He may also go into
seizures, or even become unconscious. Rattlesnake venom
is extremely painful. Be prepared for his reaction to the
pain."

"When will the paramedics get here?" It was hard for
her to speak through the fear beating around inside her
breast.

"They will be there in less than twenty minutes. Stay
calm, Pamela. A rattlesnake bite is a serious event, but it
does not have to be fatal."

The word *fatal* knifed her heart.

"I—I am feeling—" Apollo began, but broke off as he
tilted sideways, eyes fluttering.

"Gotta go," Pamela told the dispatcher before tossing
the phone aside and scrambling over to Apollo. "No!" she
said, straightening him back against the boulder. "You
can't pass out." She touched his face. His skin felt hot.
"Don't leave me!"

His eyes fluttered once more, and then opened. He
blinked rapidly, as if he was having trouble focusing on her
face.

"Pamela," he said faintly.

"Apollo, stay with me," she said. Reaching into the basket, she pulled out one of the linen napkins, wet it with a little of the water left in his bottle, and gently wiped the sweat from his face.

"That feels good," he murmured, "cool . . . nice." He grimaced as another tide of molten lava rolled up through his arm. "So this is what it feels like to be burned. Ironic, isn't it, that it should happen to me?" he panted.

"It'll be okay," she said, wiping his brow. "The paramedics will be here any second. They'll bring the antivenin. You'll be okay. You have to be okay."

Apollo blinked again, trying to clear his vision. "You're crying." His unwounded hand tried to brush the tears from her cheeks but ended up falling weakly back to his side. "Don't cry, sweet Pamela. I already told you that the Greek Underworld is a rare and beautiful place. Like you, my soul mate, are a rare and beautiful woman."

"Don't talk about the Underworld!" Fresh tears rolled soundlessly down her face. "You can't die. You're Apollo, God of Light!"

"At this moment the God of Light is very much a mortal man." He paused. His panting was making it difficult to talk. The fire in his arm was spreading quickly. He could feel it clawing up his shoulder and spilling like hot tar into his chest. "Pamela, listen to me. Hades told me that soul mates always find each other. Life after life, they circle back together. Remember that . . ." The burning in his chest seemed to explode, and his face convulsed in pain. As he crumpled in on himself, Apollo closed his eyes against the agony and he slipped into black nothingness.

"No!" Pamela cried. With hands that shook so hard she could barely control them, she touched his face. Seconds ago it had felt hot; now it was cool and damp. She felt for his pulse and found nothing. No! It couldn't happen like this. It couldn't be allowed to happen like this. She stood up and threw back her head and screamed her rage to the heavens.

"Zeus! Your son is dying! Where are you? Save him—

open your damn precious portal and take him home. What kind of father are you?"

Above her, the air suddenly shimmered and then, like the fold of an invisible curtain being opened, a section of the sky parted, and a young man stepped through to hover over her. He was wearing a short tunic, much like the one Apollo had worn the night they met, and golden sandals that had gilded wings flapping at his heels—the same wings that were on his helmetlike hat and the crystal wand he held. His short, curly hair was white-blond, and his handsome face looked mildly amused.

"What? Are you suddenly struck wordless now that your shrieking has actually roused Olympus?"

Pamela narrowed her eyes at him, recognizing the same arrogant tone she'd heard countless times in Artemis' voice. "First save him," she demanded. "Then you're free to bully me."

The god raised his brows in surprise. "Do you realize to whom you speak, mortal?"

"Yes." She spat the word in frustration. "Your flying feet mean you must be Hermes. Talk later. Save him now."

Hermes huffed out a puff of indignant air. "Impertinent!" He glanced at the still body of Apollo and shook his head in disgust. "I believe he must be spoiling you."

Pamela wanted to wrap her fingers around his throat.

"Oh, there's no need for such a passionate show of concern. Zeus would not let Apollo die."

As he spoke he waved his crystal wand in Apollo's direction, and light showered down on his body like a Forth of July sparkler. The instant the first of the sparks touched him, Apollo's chest lifted as he drew in a long breath, and then his eyes shot open. He looked around in obvious confusion, but when his gaze found Hermes, he frowned.

"Oh, I know, I know," the hovering god said. "You were expecting Hades or Charon or someone equally as dreary."

"I have explained to you that Hades is my friend. Watch how you speak of him." Apollo's voice sounded rough, as if he had to struggle to speak through a raw throat. "What are you doing here, Hermes?"

"Being underappreciated." Hermes waggled his fingers

delicately at Pamela. "Your mortal shrieked for Zeus. Apparently, you were dying." He sighed and looked bored.

"Zeus sent you," Apollo said.

"Of course Zeus sent me. Your father is angry with you and the delectable Artemis, but he would hardly allow you to die."

Pamela's knees felt suddenly very wobbly, and she plopped down beside Apollo, who automatically pulled her closer to him. She wanted to sob with relief at the strength she felt in the arm he put around her.

Hermes watched Apollo's show of obvious affection for the mortal woman and decided that the God of Light had more to worry about than just the anger of his father. When a god loved a mortal, there was always a price to be paid.

"You should know that although Zeus is not going to allow you to die, he has decided that you need to be taught a lesson for disobeying him. Your wound will not kill you, nor will it actually damage your body, but your father is allowing you to feel the pain of the venom. *All* of the pain of the venom," he finished gleefully.

"Hermes, you would do well to remember that I am only temporarily without my immortal powers." Apollo's raw voice had gone flat and dangerous.

"Obviously you're temporarily without your sense of humor, too," Hermes huffed. "Nevertheless, I'm not finished delivering the Storm God's message. Zeus will open the portal at sunset on the mortal world's Friday. He expects you and your sister to appear before him directly after that. Have I mentioned that our Supreme Ruler is not pleased?"

"It was Bacchus' scheming that caused us to be trapped here. Take that message back to my father, and tell him that Artemis and I will be *pleased* to formally confront the God of the Vine with his misdeeds in the Great Hall."

Hermes rolled his pale eyes. "Zeus knows all about Bacchus and his incompetent plan to wreck divine havoc in the modern world in an attempt to keep the mortal kingdom to himself, which is why it is his decision that the portal to Las Vegas be closed. Permanently. With the corpulent Bacchus banished from the modern world as a part of his punishment."

Apollo ground his teeth against the pounding pain in his body and rasped, "Zeus is closing the portal? No, he cannot. That would mean—"

"That would mean," Hermes interrupted smoothly, "that you have until Friday to decide if you want your little mortal to join you in Olympus. *Unless*"—he drew the word out, tapping his temple in mock contemplation—"you would rather remain here as a mortal man." Hermes made a tisking sound. "And it doesn't appear that mortality agrees with you." Then the hovering god grinned mischievously and brushed his hands together as if he had just rid himself of a bothersome task. "Well, I have delivered my message and done my good deed for the day. Rumor has it that Aphrodite is hosting a gambling party, and I am planning on losing big to her."

With a flick of his delicate wrists, the flying god disappeared back through the fold in the sky.

Hugging his pulsing hand close to his body, Apollo shifted so that he could look into Pamela's face. Her cheeks were still wet with tears.

"I wish you wouldn't cry, sweet Pamela. All is well."

"Was he telling the truth? Are you really going to be okay?" Pamela said, brushing at her wet face.

"Hermes is Zeus' messenger. His manner is caustic, but his words are true."

She sagged with relief against him. And then she suddenly straightened, took his face between her hands and kissed him with ferocity. Ignoring the blazing pain in his body, he kissed her back, tightening his arm around her so that he could feel the curve of her breast and her soft hip pressing into him.

"Don't ever scare me like that again," she said against his mouth. She started to kiss him again but pulled abruptly away when she heard the scrambling of booted feet coming quickly up the trail. She straightened her shirt and ran a hand though her short hair. "I'm supposed to be keeping you calm."

Apollo managed a fairly credible smile. "You heard

Hermes. The venom can not truly harm me. So you may
kiss me, and whatever else, as often as you desire."

"I may take you up on that, Mr. God of Light. Later.
First things first." Pamela stood up and called down the
trail, "Over here! We're over here!"

"Yes ma'am! We're coming," the disembodied yell
replied.

She looked back at Apollo. His bloody hand was red
and already swollen. "I think it would be a little tough to
explain to them that it can't kill you; it just hurts like hell."

Apollo's handsome face twisted as another white-hot
wave of pain pulsed up his arm. "It doesn't hurt like hell.
It hurts like bloody buggering hell."

CHAPTER 29

Pamela decided that money could buy a lot more than anything. It bought attention and a definitely freaked-out level
of concern, although she liked to pretend that the paramedics would have been equally as wonderful with anyone, regardless of their patron's wallet. They'd opened up
an IV line of antivenin and fluids before they'd even tried
to move Apollo. Pamela stepped back and let them work.
Now that she knew Apollo was in no actual danger, she
could appreciate the efficiency of the EMTs as they
cleaned, dressed and immobilized his wound without sob-
bing hysterically or clutching at Apollo's unwounded
hand.

She did notice that there was a lot of discussion about
how good his vital signs looked, especially for a bite so
close to an artery. That made Pamela's stomach tighten
again, and she shut out the thought of how she had not
been able to feel his pulse before Hermes had shown up.

"Snake must've not been loaded," one of the paramedics said as they helped Apollo walk the short distance
down the trail and into the flatbed jeep that had been con-
verted into an ambulance. The God of Light had, of course,
refused to be lifted onto a stretcher. Insisting he could walk
on his own, he stood up and began striding towards the
trail, IV line in tow, when they tried to argue with him.

"Loaded?" Apollo asked.

"Yeah, poisonous snakes can control how much venom
they shoot when they bite. You must have just startled this

one and not pissed it off. Probably gave you a small dose. Close as it was to that major artery, a big, pissed-off rattler could have killed you."

Pamela felt like throwing up.

Apollo seemed intrigued by the paramedic's information, and the ride back to the resort was filled with lovely little tidbits of snakebite trivia she could have gone a lifetime without knowing. For instance, until then Pamela had had no idea that more than 8,000 poisonous snakebites happened in the United States each year, and that, on an average, about 10 deaths due to snakebites are reported. She also found out that horses get bitten regularly by snakes, and that they don't usually fare as well as humans because most horses are bitten on the nose when they lower their heads to investigate the snake. This is by far the most dangerous site for a bite because the resulting swelling often closes both nostrils and causes suffocation.

Pamela held Apollo's hand and tried unsuccessfully to tune out the entire conversation. *Ten deaths due to snakebites* kept playing around and around inside her head.

"Sir, your sister and Mr. Faust will meet us in front of the ranch house. From there they will follow us to the hospital," one of the paramedics said as the jeep crunched onto the resort's pebbled drive.

"Hospital?" Apollo frowned and shook his head. "I can assure you that there is no need for that."

"But sir, the full dose of antivenin takes several hours to be administered and monitored. It would be best if you went to the hospital and stayed the night for observation. Sometimes snakebite symptoms take several hours or more to appear."

Apollo looked out of the jeep's side window and caught sight of Artemis and Eddie standing beside the limo.

"Just take me there." He pointed.

The paramedic frowned his disapproval, but the jeep followed the driveway to pull up beside the limo. Before the EMT could touch the back doors, Eddie wrenched them open, and white-faced Artemis rushed up. She took one look at her brother, who was hooked up to an IV, had an oxygen line at his nose, and one hand splinted and bandaged, and her eyes promptly rolled up and she fainted in a full-out, gasping swoon of diva proportions.

"Great," Pamela muttered as each and every one of the paramedics flew out of the ambulance and swarmed around the fallen goddess.

"She's never swooned before," Apollo said, watching with open curiosity as Eddie batted away the men, scooped Artemis up in his arms and carried her to the ranch house. The paramedics hurried after him.

"For her first swoon I think she did very well." Apollo started to laugh and then closed his eyes against the jab of pain in his arm.

Pamela hated the way his face paled and tightened if he moved too much. "What can I do?"

Eyes still closed, he shook his head in tight jerks.

Feeling truly helpless, Pamela said, "Okay, well. Your sister is most definitely a drama queen." She tried to keep her tone light.

After only a few breaths, Apollo opened his eyes and smiled weakly at her. "She is that."

"Hurts like bloody buggering hell?" she offered.

"Yes, but I can tell you truly that I'm glad the paramedics have trailed away after Artemis. I don't want to go to a hospital, Pamela. I can tolerate the pain that my father has decreed as my punishment. I cannot tolerate being poked and prodded by strangers." He jabbed his chin in the direction of the IV needle that stuck out of his arm.

"Then let's see what we can do about getting E. D. Faust to throw his considerable weight around and have his appropriately eccentric guest treated here," she said, taking the oxygen line from his nose and unhooking the IV bag from its holder. "It's a damn good thing that I'm an *ER* addict." She studied him uneasily. She'd not noticed the lines of strain on his face before. "It's really awful, isn't it?"

"Zeus has been true to his word. I am enjoying all of the symptoms of snakebite." He rolled his right shoulder and flinched, as if the pain was crawling up his arm.

"Come on, let's get you inside and settled in your room. I don't suppose they'd give painkillers to a snakebite victim, but I think I have something in my emergency pill pack that will work wonders. I can promise you that after a couple of Tylenol threes and a glass of wine, you'll be feeling considerably less stress and possibly no pain."

"Tylenol three?" He asked.

"Trust me on this one," she said.

He grunted and held his bandaged hand close to his body as they climbed slowly from the back of the jeep, walked up the sidewalk and entered the ranch house—an easy thing to do because no one had bothered to close the front door.

Artemis was lying fluidly across one of the couches in the den. Eddie had knelt beside her. One paramedic was taking her pulse, another was waving a small vial in front of her nose.

"Oh!" she sputtered. "Get that wretched-smelling thing away from me!"

"Now, now . . . be calm, my goddess," Eddie crooned.

"Hey, that's okay," Pamela called, shaking her head in disgust. "The snakebite victim is just fine, thanks."

Artemis sat straight up. Her blue eyes were wide and pooling with luminous tears as she peered over the top of the couch at Apollo.

"My brother!" she gasped. "Oh, my poor brother!"

She wobbled, flailing her hands in his direction. Apollo went to the couch, and Eddie shifted his bulk so that he could sit beside his sister. Tears spilled from the goddess's eyes, and she hesitantly reached out to touch the bandage wrapped around his hand.

"They said a venomous serpent attacked you. I was so frightened. I thought that you actually might—" Artemis broke off, biting her lip.

Apollo put his arm around his sister and let her cry into his shoulder.

"All is well. All is well."

"What am I thinking?" Eddie seemed to suddenly grasp the entire situation. "You should be on your way to the hospital. Post haste!"

"No!" Apollo said abruptly. "Eddie, I have a boon to ask of you."

"You may have anything within my power to grant," the author said solemnly.

"Arrange it so that I may stay here until Friday."

"Oh, no! You should be surrounded by the finest healers in the land!" Artemis said, looking like she was going to faint again at any moment.

While everyone was focused—once again—on the soothing the goddess, Pamela managed to catch her eye and mouth a single word: *Hermes.* Artemis blinked in surprise, interrupting her own distressed sobs. During the break in her hysterics, Apollo's voice sounded calm and logical.

"The snake venom does not threaten my life; even these men will attest to the fact that my life signs are steady and strong. I simply need to rest, which I will do better here than in a place where I am surrounded by strangers."

Like a confused child, Artemis looked up at her brother. "You will not be . . . *damaged?*" She said the word as if it left a vile taste in her mouth.

Even though Pamela could see that he was still cradling his wounded hand close against his body and she knew he was in terrible pain, Apollo shook his head and smiled reassuringly at his sister. "I will not·be damaged."

Artemis managed to control her sobs long enough to take Eddie's hand. "Oh, please. Do not send him away," the goddess pleaded.

"I wouldn't think of it," the big man replied, patting her hand. "Transfer the equipment you need to his bedroom. I shall call in my personal physician to attend Phoebus," Eddie ordered the paramedics.

In awe, Pamela watched the paramedics jump to obey Eddie, who took the ever-vigilant James aside to explain to him who should be called and what should happen when and how and why. As if they existed in the eye of a storm, Pamela, Artemis and Apollo were left in momentary privacy.

"Hermes?" Artemis whispered the question to Pamela.

Pamela answered in the same low tone. "He showed up when Apollo was . . ." She hesitated, met Apollo's eyes and saw the slight shake of his head. "When he was snake bitten," she amended. "He took the poison from his body, but left the pain—thanks to your pissed-off father."

"We are to appear before Zeus after dusk on Friday. He has decided to close the portal then. Permanently."

Pamela saw surprise on the goddess's face, and then, when Eddie hurried back over to them, she was almost certain she saw something else. Something that might have been sadness.

"It is all being arranged, my friend," Eddie said to Apollo.

"Thank you, Eddie. I will remember your kindness," the god said solemnly.

Eddie put his hand on Apollo's shoulder. "It is my pleasure to follow the ancient ways. In my household the bond between guest and host is still a sacred one."

Apollo dipped his head in acknowledgment. "If the gods still listen to the modern world, may you be blessed for it."

"I have already been richly blessed," Eddie said, taking Artemis' hand and raising it to his lips.

CHAPTER 30

"So, the general consensus is that the snake bit you with little to no venom," Pamela said, sitting beside him on his bed. "Congratulations. You fooled them all."

Apollo shifted his weight restlessly and rolled his right shoulder. "I thought they would never leave."

"Hey, I liked Eddie's doctor."

"Dr. Kevin Glenn was too young and too smart. He could tell I was hiding something from his prying eyes; he just couldn't tell what."

"That's because you're not quite as good an actor as your sister is an actress."

Apollo grimaced. "I didn't think she would ever leave, either."

"Artemis is just worried about you."

He sighed and tried to find a more comfortable position for his bandaged hand. "I have never liked serpents. I know Demeter would be distressed to hear it, but ever since I battled Python, I have been uneasy in their presence."

"Was Python poisonous?" Now that they were finally alone, she dug through her purse for her emergency pill-box.

"No, but he was big enough to swallow a man."

She looked up at him. "You're kidding, aren't you?"

"Not at all."

Pamela shuddered. "That's gross." She picked out two large white pills and handed them to Apollo. "Hang on.

This will help." She crossed to the minibar and pulled out an expensive bottle of chilled Pinot Grigio—none of those cheap little airplane bottles for guests of E. D. Faust—opened it, and poured them both a glass. She waited until he'd popped the two pills in his mouth and then gave him his glass of wine.

"Perhaps you should bring over the bottle," he said after draining the glass in three swallows.

She did as he asked, refilling his glass quickly. With just her in the room, Apollo didn't feel the need to mask his struggle against pain, and every time he grimaced or rubbed his shoulder, she wanted to shriek in rage at the heavens. Again.

"He shouldn't have left you in such pain," Pamela said, unable to keep the thought to herself any longer.

Apollo took a long drink and then patted the side of the bed. "Sit here by me, and I will try to explain my father to you. Zeus is our Supreme Ruler. He is generous and compassionate, kind and protective of his children. He never aids liars or oath-breakers. His voice can be heard in the rustling of the branches on the ancient oak trees. He is majestic and good. But he is also Lord of the Sky, the Rain God and Cloud Gatherer, who wields the awful thunderbolt. He is a passionate, jealous god, and when his temper is aroused his anger is a terrible thing to behold."

"He sounds like a paradox."

"He is what all of us are, not simply one thing or another, but a mixture of many."

"That doesn't sound like a god of gods; it sounds like a man," Pamela said.

"Exactly," Apollo said. "In the Ancient World the gods did not create the universe. It was the other way about; the universe created the gods. Think of the universe—the heavens and the earth, the sun and the moon. Are they all one thing or another? It's much like the serpent today. It aroused my anger—so much so that I killed it—but it wasn't truly evil, though its venom feels like the burning fires of your world's hell."

"So what you're saying is that Zeus isn't evil, he's just imperfect."

Apollo smiled and lifted his glass to her in answer. Pamela watched him as he drained his second glass of wine. The day had taken its toll on his temporarily mortal body. Even if he wasn't in danger of dying, the dark circles under his eyes, the pallor of his skin, and the new lines of strain on his face were disturbing.

While Eddie's doctor had been examining him, Apollo had changed into a pair of drawstring pajamas. He'd left his top unbuttoned and loose so that the medical team that had hovered at his bedside for the past several hours could keep a constant check on his vital signs. Thankfully, they had all gone and taken with them their IVs, monitors, frowns of disapproval and the distinctive hospital smell that seems to cling to scrubs. Now Apollo looked like a normal, handsome man who had just been through a very difficult and long day.

And that's all she wanted to think of him as. Sure, they could discuss gods and the ancient world, but that all felt very abstract and surreal in the reality of his warm flesh and his kind smile.

But the truth was that on Friday he would return to Olympus. The portal would close, and he would leave her life. Her heart felt suddenly very heavy in her chest.

"What is it?" Apollo asked.

Her eyes met his. He looked so tired. She couldn't add to his pain, not tonight. She made herself smile at him.

"I just realized that I haven't thanked you for saving my life."

Apollo leaned forward and brushed his fingers against the gold coin she wore around her neck.

"I am pledged to protect you. I never break an oath." His touched moved from the coin to lightly caress the side of her long, bare neck.

She shivered.

"Are you cold, sweet Pamela," he murmured.

"How could I be cold with you touching me?"

His smile was filled with sunlight. "There, you see—I am the same whether I am mortal or immortal. You still feel my heat." He leaned closer to her and captured her lips with his. When she tried to soften the kiss and resist its erotic tug, he whispered against her mouth, "Help me to forget the pain. Let me lose myself in you."

How could she resist him? She burned for him.

She loved him.

But she pressed her hand against his chest, and he broke their kiss, giving her a baffled look.

"Tonight I want to make love to you. Let me give you this, Apollo."

When she pressed his shoulders back on the down pillows, he didn't resist. She stood and pulled her shirt fluidly over her head. Then she peeled her shorts and shoes off. Then, instead of joining him on the bed, she took a couple of steps back, so that he had a clear view of her entire body.

She loved the way his eyes devoured her. He made her feel beautiful and desirable and powerful. *This must be how a goddess feels,* she thought. Accepting Apollo's love had transformed her. Choosing to open herself to him had taken her from the darkness of Duane's shadow and breathed light into her world. He was a god, and she was a mortal, but with his love she became her own Goddess of Light.

Slowly, she reached back and unsnapped her simple, white lace bra. As she took it off, she let her hands glide over her breasts, taking her time to tease her nipples into blushing hardness. Caressingly, her hands traveled down her body, peeling her panties from her sleek hips. All the while, Apollo's eyes devoured her.

Naked, she approached the bed.

"No," she said teasingly when he tried to sit up to meet her. "Tonight it's my turn."

"You are so beautiful, my sweet Pamela," he said. "I— I hope I—" he began and then gave a shaky laugh.

What had she been thinking? He was in terrible pain, and she was acting like a stripper when he really needed a nurse. Pamela rested her fingers lightly on his arm above the bandage. "I can just lie here beside you. We don't have to do anything."

"It's not that," he said quickly. "I want you; I want you to make love to me. I just hope I don't disappoint you. I know I told you that I didn't use any of my immortal powers to seduce you, and I didn't. But when I loved you . . ." He moved his shoulders restlessly, "I could not help but touch you with my magic. Tonight I have no magic, no powers. I am just a man."

"You will never be *just* a man, Apollo. You will always be *the* man I love."

"My sweet Pamela . . ." Her name changed to a groan of sweet pleasure when she slipped her hands into his shirt, opened it, and rubbed the tips of her nipples against his muscular chest. She nipped lightly at his bottom lip and the firm line of his jaw. Then she nibbled a hot trail down his body, deftly unlacing the tie that held his pants closed. She could hear him gasp when she took him in her hands and rubbed the softness of her breasts against his pulsing shaft. And then her mouth was on him. First she used her lips and tongue up and down the thick, hard girth of him, loving the way his body trembled and strained beneath her touch and how he moaned her name over and over. She swallowed him, sucking and teasing until she heard his ragged cry.

"I can not wait!"

In one swift movement she straddled him. Holding herself up on her knees, she rested his tip against her wet heat. She locked her eyes with his blue-hot gaze. *Let me take away his pain, if only for a moment.* She prayed silently to any god or goddess who might be listening. Then she impaled herself on him, slowly, deliciously, taking his length within her. With a deliberately teasing motion, she lifted herself back up on her knees, so that his tip was throbbing against her opening. Then she slid down again. Slowly. She sheathed him within her, until the exquisite tension built beyond her bearing. Only then did she guide his hand to her hips and let him increase their tempo. They moved together urgently, the white light of mortal passion filling their bodies with exquisite heat that built and built until the sweetness of it was unbearable. When she felt his body gather beneath her, she rocked forward, pulsing down against him so that when he spilled his hot seed within her, she exploded around him.

Collapsing against him, she felt the slickness of their

bodies join and his arm tightened around her. "I love you," he gasped, kissing her gently.

She nestled her head into his shoulder, careful to keep her weight well away from his right arm. As she shifted her position to draw the sheet up around them, her contented smile widened to a happy grin. Eyes closed, his face was finally free of pain—relaxed and peaceful. Apollo had fallen into a deep sleep.

"Thank you," she whispered to the listening air.

"I don't know, Apollo. I just don't feel right about leaving you." Pamela stood near the bed, fidgeting with the leather strap of her briefcase. At his insistence, she'd gotten dressed and ready to go back to work on the villa. After all, he'd reminded her, there was really nothing wrong with him. And she still had a job to do.

"All will be well. I have this." He picked up the remote. "And this." He tapped his finger on the channel guide. "And you have explained to me all about cable television. I will be well entertained."

Pamela frowned. "Don't forget the phone. My number is—"

"Yes, yes, your number is written on the paper near the phone. Be off now. Eddie will be waiting."

"Okay." She leaned down to kiss him. "But I feel like I'm doing something wrong."

"Tonight when you return to my bed, I promise that I will allow you to make up for leaving me."

"I don't want to leave you!"

He laughed and then grimaced and rubbed his still-painful arm. "I only tease you, sweet Pamela. Actually, I envy you. I will miss the job site today. Are you quite certain there is no way that I—"

"You've already been all over this with Eddie. He totally refuses to let you leave this room to do more than to have dinner on the deck until Friday."

Apollo's annoyed response was interrupted by a knock at the door. Pamela opened it to find Eddie's bulk filling the doorway.

"I believe I have a compromise in which Phoebus will be interested." The author stepped aside and made an imperious gesture. Two men carried into the room a small drafting table, followed by the architect Apollo had been working with on the bathhouse. "Behold, if you cannot come to the mountain, the mountain will come to you!"

"Brad! Shouldn't you be at the villa?" Apollo said.

"I should, but so should you, except I hear that a snake decided to change our plans." The architect clapped him on the shoulder and then apologized when he saw Apollo grit his teeth against the pain the abrupt movement had caused. "Sorry, Phoebus. Rattlesnake bit my brother-in-law last year. He said it hurt like hell, and it put him flat on his back for a week." He glanced up at Eddie. "Maybe we should take up where we left off tomorrow."

"No! Whatever you have in mind, I can assure you that I am up for it." Apollo said hastily.

"Ah, but only if you promise that you will not literally be 'up' for it." Eddie stepped into the room. "Bradley has the blueprints of the bathhouse to finalize with your help—but only if you stay abed and continue to rest."

"You have my oath," Apollo said, already sitting up straighter, his attention caught by the long, slick papers Bradley was unrolling and laying out on the drafting table.

"Come, Pamela," Eddie said. "We shall leave the bathhouse to the experts. The goddess awaits us in the car."

As they left the room, Apollo's gruff "The car is something that I will not miss today . . ." followed them down the hallway.

"Thank you, Eddie," Pamela said, squeezing the big man's arm.

He smiled down at her. "You are quite welcome, my dear. Phoebus does not strike me as a man who is comfortable with inactivity."

"You're right about that. Actually you're right about more than just that."

His smile turned contemplative. "You look happy this morning, Pamela."

"Yes, I am. I have decided that Semele didn't regret her choice," she said softly.

CHAPTER 31

Pamela glanced at her watch and gasped. "Eddie! It's four! Didn't you say our dinner reservations are for six?"

"Quite right you are, Pamela!" Eddie bellowed from across the chaotic courtyard. He lurched up from his bench and lumbered over to stand behind Matthew, who was hastily putting the finishing strokes on the fountain sketch. Artemis stepped delicately from her perch and joined him. Pamela could hear them both congratulating Matthew on a job well done.

A job well done . . .

It was Friday afternoon, and this job was anything but done. How had two and a half days passed so quickly? Pamela ran a hand through her hair. She was exhausted and stressed beyond belief. Her days had been filled with the intricacies of designing Eddie's dream villa: juggling painters and stone layers, solving fixture problems and fabric glitches. Her nights had been filled with Apollo and the sun's love. She'd had very little sleep, and had been working her butt off. And they were still behind schedule.

She wouldn't have traded one single instant of it.

"Pamela, how is this for the faux design on the home theater room walls?" The faux finisher flamboyantly pointed the tip of his feathered pen at a mock-up board that had been covered with a deep burgundy paint marbled with delicate webs of onyx and gold.

"Absolutely perfect this time, Steve!" she said with relief. "This is the exact finish I meant for the room."

"Fabulous! It's going to be just fabulous, dahling." He waved the feather in triumph. "I'll start on it first thing Monday morning," Steve gushed.

"I'll be here," Pamela said.

Steve nodded and fluttered back into the house to happily clean up and leave for the weekend. Much more grimly, Pamela began arranging the day's notes neatly into her briefcase. She would be here Monday. In Las Vegas. The modern mortal world. And Apollo and Artemis would be in Olympus.

There would be no more dinners for them on the deck with the fantastically entertaining Eddie. No more late-night discussions with Apollo about the new marble that had just arrived for the master bathroom—and had been completely the wrong color. No more sketches that the two of them created together, which would soon become stone mosaics on the floors of Eddie's new bathhouse.

But still her lips tilted up in a secret smile as she thought about the past couple days. Besides working with the architect, in person and then later through the phone and a lovely little laptop Eddie had provided, which the god had taken to with remarkable ease, Apollo was becoming quite the movie buff. Ancient god or not, there were certain things that were very like a modern man about him. Like the way he enjoyed learning about electronics, and how he had taken to the remote control and channel surfing. When she came in from working at the villa last night, he had been totally engrossed in the second movie of the Lord of the Rings trilogy.

"Aragon reminds me of Hector. And the little hobbit— the little hobbit has the heart of Achilles' faithful Patroclus."

"Frodo is like someone named Patroclus?" she'd asked.

"No. I was not thinking of Frodo. I was thinking of Samwise. But I hope in the end they fare better than Hector and Patroclus," he'd said solemnly.

Pamela couldn't remember enough mythology to know what he was talking about, but she assured him Aragon and Sam had happy endings.

He'd grunted at her and held up his good hand. "Do not tell me the ending. It will spoil it for me."

She'd almost told him anyway. It was a long movie, and he was running short on time. He may never see *Return of the King*.

They had made their decision late that night. No, she corrected herself, *she* had made the decision. She remembered the tension that had radiated through Apollo's body as he realized that she wouldn't, couldn't return to Olympus with him.

"I would be useless there, Apollo," she'd said.

"Useless? How can you even think such a thing?" He'd gestured in frustration with his still-bandaged hand and then sucked in a breath at the sharp pain he caused himself. "By the gods, I will be pleased to be rid of this affliction!" he rasped.

Pamela shifted her position so that instead of being stretched out beside him, she lay across his body facing him. Gently, she rubbed his right shoulder, feeling him relax under her hands.

"Better?"

He nodded and kissed her palm. "Your touch soothes me. It has been the only thing that has the power to relieve this unending pain. Do you see how much I need you with me?"

She smiled sadly at him. "Apollo, snakes can't hurt you in Olympus."

"No, but your absence will hurt me."

"I know." She bit her bottom lip. "It will hurt me to be without you, too."

"Then come with me. You are my soul mate; I am asking that you also be my wife."

Pamela swallowed down the sharp taste of a future devoid of him. If only it were that easy. "What would I do there on Mount Olympus in the middle of all you gods?" She shook her head and barely paused to take a breath when he opened his mouth to protest. "No matter how much you want it, I'm not an artist. I don't want some kind of divine studio where I could pretend I'm talented and interested in creating pieces of whatever for whomever." She shook her head again and sighed. "Apollo, do any mortals live there? Any at all?"

"Many of the nymphs and handmaidens are semi-deities," he said quickly. "And often a priestess or priest is allowed to visit his or her immortal patron."

"Semideities are not mortals. Priestesses and priests *visit;* then they go back to live their mortal lives," she said sadly.

"You will be my wife. I will ask Zeus to make you immortal."

Pamela pulled her hand from his. "So let's say that I marry you and that I am made an immortal. Then for the rest of eternity, what do I do? I have no realm, like your sister. I have no job, Apollo. I have nothing, other than what I am allowed to have through you."

She saw the flash of understanding in his eyes.

"It would be another cage," he said slowly. "I am not Duane, but that matters little. To you it would feel like just another cage, larger, more powerful, and better gilded, but . . ."

"Still a cage," she finished.

He took her hand in his again. "Then I choose to stay with you."

Pamela's eyes widened, and she shook her head violently. "No! You can't! You are Apollo, the God of Light. You can't leave your world—not permanently—you know you can't. What would happen to the people there? Wouldn't you be condemning them to darkness?"

"The sun can make its way across the ancient sky without me. My mares know the path my golden chariot must take; they follow it often without me guiding them."

"Apollo, it wouldn't be right. You can't leave Olympus. You can not be a mortal man."

"I have been a mortal man for this week. I can be one for a lifetime."

"And how long would that be? Just look at what happened—on your very first mortal day. You died!" The words burst from her lips. "No matter what you tell your sister or Eddie or yourself, I was there. I watched it happen. You saved my life, and then you lost yours. If Hermes hadn't shown up, you'd be dead right now." She took a breath, feeling herself tremble as she clutched his hand. "I couldn't stand that, Apollo. I can't watch you die again."

"Shhh," he murmured, pulling her into his arms. "There must be a way. We will simply find it."

"How?" she said against the warmth of his chest.

"I will take our case to my father. Ask that I be allowed access to your world."

"What if he says no?"

"I do not know, but Demeter and Persephone found a compromise. So, too, will we." He put a finger under her chin and tilted her face up. "I will not be separated from my soul mate. You have my oath on that, Pamèla."

His mouth had closed on hers with such a fierce protectiveness that she could still feel his lips against hers there in the courtyard. She shivered and focused her attention back on the papers that she was clutching numbly in her hands. It was Friday. The sun would set in just a few hours, and Apollo and Artemis would go through the portal and return to Olympus. She might never see him again. The wash of pain the thought sent through her was her own personal poison.

"Pamela?"

She looked up over the open lid of her briefcase and into Artemis' eyes. The goddess looked like she'd slept very little last night, and even though she had painted on a bright face, thanks to the magic of modern makeup, Pamela could still see the circles that shadowed her eyes.

"You look tired," Pamela told her.

"My thoughts will not let me rest."

"Thoughts?"

"I worry for you. And for Eddie." The goddess's eyes found where the author was talking with his usual animation to one of the fabric representatives. "I find that as dusk approaches I am not as eager as I once thought I would be to leave your world."

Pamela smiled at her. Artemis was no less conceited or spoiled or bossy, but her relationship with Eddie had definitely softened her. She was warmer; less like cold, perfect marble, she had become a real woman.

"I'll miss you, Artemis."

"Then come with us," the goddess said. "If you tire of Olympus, you may visit my realm. My forests will always welcome my brother's wife."

"I can't," Pamela whispered, incredibly touched by the goddess's words. "I don't belong there."

"You belong with Apollo," she said firmly.

"If I go with him, I will lose myself. Eventually, there would be nothing left of me for him to love."

Artemis tilted her head and studied Pamela. "You have great wisdom, my friend. You would have made an excellent goddess."

"Ladies!" like one of the Titans, Eddie's presence shadowed them. "We must hurry. Phoebus awaits, as does our dinner. I have promised to leave you at the entrance of Caesars Palace at exactly eight o'clock tonight so that your own driver can take you from there to the airport."

Eddie frowned his displeasure at the story they had concocted so that the big man wouldn't follow Artemis into Caesars Palace. Artemis had told Eddie that their wealthy Greek family would send its own car for her brother and her promptly at eight o'clock (sunset, according to Pamela's Internet inquiry) at the Palace, and that she couldn't bear to say good-bye at airports. Apollo had, of course, blanched totally white when Pamela had explained to him that a plane was a lot like a big, flying car.

Eddie had been very unhappy about the arrangement, but, as usual, he could not say no to Artemis' divalike demands. The author drew a deep breath, and Pamela thought suddenly how old he looked. "I have agreed to your wishes, but you must agree to be timely. I have a spectacular farewell dinner planned for us."

"Eddie." Artemis pouted prettily, sliding her arm through his and smoothly distracting him from more arguments about limos and rides to the airport. "I do hope you have remembered to find us a restaurant with a good view. I have become overly fond of our splendid dining on that wonderful deck, and I cannot bear to think of how much I will miss it."

"The view will always be waiting here for you when you tire of your travels. But tonight, my Goddess, it seems it is wise that we try something new." The author touched the goddess's cheek, and she nuzzled his hand. Eddie's smile almost hid the sad resignation that haunted his face.

Pamela followed them across the courtyard, thinking that Eddie might very well be an even better actor than Artemis.

"I sincerely and thoroughly loathe those metal creatures," Apollo said through gritted teeth after he climbed awkwardly from the front seat of the limo.

"Sir?" the Bellagio doorman looked confused.

"He gets carsick," Pamela said.

The very British-sounding doorman took one look at Apollo's green-tinged face and his bandaged hand, sniffed his disapproval and stepped quickly out of the way.

She took Apollo's uninjured arm and steered him to the sidewalk. He wiped a hand across his brow and tried to command his stomach down from his throat while they waited during the lengthy process involved in extracting Eddie and Artemis from what he liked to think of as the limo's evil maw.

"Promise me," he said into her ear, "that when it is time for us to return to Caesars Palace you and I will walk there from here."

His words reminded her again of the short time they had left together. As if she needed a reminder. Ironically, it seemed the sun mocked them as it rushed towards the horizon. She tried unsuccessfully to smile at Apollo.

"I promise."

He met her eyes. "I will not live without you. All will be well. Remember that you have my oath."

Pamela nodded quickly. *He is Apollo, the God of Light. He can make it happen! He can find a way for us to be together!* she told herself sternly while she blinked back a sudden rush of tears. She needed to focus on her surroundings and keep herself together. No matter what, she didn't want his last memory of her to be of tears and heartache. She wanted him to know she believed in him—in his power and in his love.

The entrance of the Bellagio was an ornate circle drive that faced a balcony that looked down on the edge of the quiet, dark pool that she knew was just waiting for the musical cue for it to spring into light and life.

"The fountains," Apollo said, following her gaze. Putting his arm around her, he pressed her intimately against his body. "Our fountains."

Pamela looked up at him, and this time she did smile. He was so strong and sure of himself—so real. She couldn't doubt him. She had been given the oath of the God of Light. He wouldn't let her down. More importantly, he wouldn't let *them* down.

"Yes, our fountains," she said.

"Let us not dally! I have a surprise for my goddess for which we must be on time."

Eddie and Artemis swept past them and into the Bellagio. Pamela and Apollo followed more slowly. Inside the entryway Pamela stopped completely. Totally starstruck, she stared up at the ceiling.

"Dale Chichuly," she said reverently, gazing up at the incredible work of art that was the Bellagio's foyer chandelier. "I'd forgotten that he designed this."

Curious, Apollo studied the ceiling. "It is a most unusual chandelier."

"It's amazing. Look at the intricacy of the blown glass and the brilliance of the colors. It's like a field of jellyfish poppies. It's too bad Eddie didn't fixate on this décor instead of tacky Caesars Palace," she said under her breath with a little laugh.

"I don't know . . ." He hugged her and kissed the top of her head. "I've grown quite fond of Eddie's eccentric tastes. It is, after all, what brought us together."

"Dallying! You're dallying," Artemis said, grabbing her brother's sleeve and pulling them over to where Eddie waited impatiently in front of a restaurant whose gold filigree sign said Olives.

"E. D. Faust and party. I have a special reservation," Eddie told the maitre d'.

"Of course, Mr. Faust. This way, please."

They followed the maitre d' through the opulent restau-

rant, which was literally packed with people on the busy
Friday night, to a wall of beveled windows, in the middle
of which was a floor-to-ceiling glass door a waiter opened
for them, and stepped out onto a large, curving marble balcony that directly overlooked the middle of the famous
Bellagio fountains. The maitre d' led them to the single
table set with linens and china and crystal. He bowed first
Artemis and then Pamela into well-padded velvet chairs.

"As you instructed, Mr. Faust, the balcony has been reserved exclusively for you."

"It is perfection. You may now pour the Dom
Perignon."

"Oh, Eddie! How did you know that I have been craving some of that lovely champagne again?" Artemis said.

"I read it in your beautiful eyes, my Goddess," Eddie
said.

Pamela rolled her own eyes and shared an amused look
with Apollo. The waiter popped the cork, and as he poured
the champagne, the first notes of the theme song from *Chorus Line* brought the fountains to life.

"One! Singular sensation . . ."

As the song played and the waters danced, Eddie raised
his crystal flute to Artemis. "To you, my Goddess. A singular sensation."

"Oh, Eddie!" she said, touching her glass against his
and blinking quickly to clear the sudden tears that filled
her eyes. "You have dazzled me."

"It has been my very great pleasure to do so," he said,
his eyes suspiciously bright, too. Then he cleared his throat
and motioned for the waiter to bring menus.

They were served a spectacular dinner against the back-
drop of singing fountains and a desert sky that slowly
faded from blue to purple. Alone on their balcony, the
night felt filled with magic and mystery. Though they were
in the heart of Vegas on a bustling Friday night, they had
privacy and pageantry. To Pamela it was as if they had
been granted a special box seat from the gods of the city.

And, who knew? They might have been. Odder things had certainly happened.

When the last of many sets of fountain songs ended, Eddie glanced at his watch. Grimly, he lifted his bulk from the chair and stood facing the table.

"It is nearing the hour of eight. We have shared wine and food, friendship and music." His kind eyes looked from Pamela to Apollo before they came to rest on Artemis. "Now, I am sad to say, I must bid you farewell. I told you earlier that I had a surprise for you." His gaze remained on Artemis' beautiful face. "Especially for you, my Goddess." He gestured around them. "Part of the surprise was this setting and this dinner. The other part is that I would like to formally announce that I have decided upon the subject of my next epic trilogy. This morning my editor agreed with my proposal for the three books. They will tell the story of a warrior who is sent on a seemingly unattainable quest by his dying people to win the heart of a goddess who, in turn, will promise to return to his people, live by his side, and save their world. The cover of each hardback book will hold an image that will be sacred throughout the hero's journey, the image of his goddess. That image will be none other than the one our Matthew has been sketching of you." He ended his speech with a flourish, bowing to the woman he had proclaimed his goddess.

Artemis didn't speak. Instead, she stood and walked slowly to Eddie.

"Thank you, my warrior."

Gracefully, Artemis sank into a low curtsy. When she raised her supple body and linked her arm through his, Pamela could see that her cheeks were wet. The author took a silk handkerchief from his breast pocket and dabbed at her face; then, in a familiar gesture, Eddie patted her hand where it rested on his wide arm.

"Come then, and let us finish our journey."

Silently, the four of them retraced their path through the restaurant and out to the Bellagio's foyer. This time the Chichuly masterpiece didn't draw Pamela's eyes. Her heart felt too heavy; she couldn't look up. The only thing she could think to do was to keep holding Apollo's hand and keep believing that this wouldn't be the last time she touched him. It was through his hand that she felt the instant hum of tension when their limo pulled up to the circle drive, reminding her of her promise.

"Eddie, do you mind if Phoebus and I walk? You know how he is about cars," she said, wondering, in an abstract kind of detached way, at how normal her voice sounded. Like her heart wasn't breaking. Like her life wasn't dissolving with the setting sun.

"Of course! We shall meet you in front of Caesars Palace. It will give all of us time to say our private goodbyes." The author managed a strained smile before he ducked into the limo.

In his palace on Mount Olympus, Bacchus sat on his throne. He closed his eyes and focused his will. Sweat beaded his wide brow. His cheeks were florid with strain. Between his flaccid lips a line of white foam moved in and out with his breathing.

Where is it?

He increased his concentration. He would not panic. He would not despair. It would be found.

Where! Where is it?

He had felt it these past days. The portal's closing had weakened it, but he knew it was still there. All he had to do was to find it—then she would be his again. Bacchus raised his thick hands, holding his palms outward as if he was feeling the air in front of his dais. And something tickled against his skin. With all of his immortal might, his hands closed, and his mind grasp the faint sliver of the bond.

He had found it! He had found her . . .

Like a fisherman pulling in a rare catch, Bacchus clutched the thread of the mortal's soul to him, tightening and strengthening their connection until he could see her clearly in his mind. She was at work, little more than a slave, really, doomed to a life of drudgery as she carried drinks to men with groping hands, and then ducked into dark corners to raise a glass to her own lips.

Bacchus tugged harder at the bond, and the mortal woman drained the glass of fiery liquor.

Yes . . . drink me in . . . take me . . . let me ease your pain . . . his mind whispered to her through their bond, and he felt her sway, as if she, too, physically felt their connection.

That was how she had come to him, and that was how he had bound her, through her need for drink. It obsessed her, consumed her . . . it only followed logically that he could obsess and consume her. He had really done nothing wrong. He had simply granted the mortal woman her heart's desire. The delicious irony of it made him want to shriek with glee. He would use the mortal bound to him through her heart's desire to destroy that which had been bound to the golden Artemis, and in doing so, he would force both twins to feel a taste of the pain that losing his kingdom caused him.

The agony of the separation still raged within him. They thought they had beaten him. It was Apollo's fault. He and his golden sister. But would Zeus punish them? Of course not. They were his darlings, his favorites. It was insufferable.

The abuse heaped upon him must be redressed. This time there would be no reprieve. No mistakes would be made.

Bacchus channeled his power into the mortal. He drank in her soul, laughing at how freely she gave herself over to him. Through her, his spirit reentered the mortal world, spreading like a deadly, invisible fog from Caesars Palace. He searched . . . searched . . . and then with a triumphant shout he found what he sought. Perfect. They were so unaware—so caught up in their own little dramas they would not sense his presence.

Satisfied, he again concentrated his powers on the all-too-willing mortal. He was within her, coursing through her veins and filling her mind with his dark urgings.

Yes, you are doing so well! He coaxed as she left her workstation carrying only her keys. *Quickly now, time grows short. Let me tell you exactly what you must do . . .*

CHAPTER 32

Without speaking, Apollo and Pamela walked slowly, hand in hand, along the sidewalk that framed the Bellagio fountains. At the moment, the water was quiet and dark, but the walkway around it was crowded with bright, chattering mortals, and the adjacent street was filled with swiftly moving cars. Apollo thought that their brazen honking and squealing was much more distracting than the glittering acropolis of buildings that lined the opposite side of the street. He ignored the ever-present pain that radiated from his hand up through his arm. It was unimportant—something that would soon end. And it was of little consequence when compared with the heaviness in his heart.

It was almost time for the sun to set. This wasn't his world, but he was eternally linked to the light in the sky. He could feel it as it awakened the morning, and he always knew exactly when it slipped beneath the horizon. His time was short.

He should stay. He could. It would be a simple thing. With the reopening of the portal his powers would return to him. He could fog Pamela's mind and then insert the suggestion that she had asked him to stay . . . Like an evil sprite, his mind spoke other possibilities to his heart . . . He could take her with him. Gods had been stealing away their mortal lovers for eons. Mount Olympus was a place filled with incredible wonders and limitless beauty. Surely she could be happy there. Surely she loved him enough to forgive him.

And then how would he be any different than her husband? If he had learned anything from Pamela, it was that love can not be dictated, demanded or imprisoned. He couldn't chain her to him; he could only love her.

Was it just a week ago that he had believed he had conquered love? How naïve he had been. Mortal or immortal, love made no distinctions for rank or privilege. Love was a matter of the soul, incorporeal and not subject to the whims of man or god.

Apollo slowed and then guided Pamela to a nearby bench as the noisy group they had been walking behind came to a sudden halt. Like milling cattle they shuffled impatiently and called loudly to one another.

"It's the street; they're waiting for the light," Pamela said, sitting beside him and staring out at the dark water. She sounded almost normal, except that, like a dimmed lamp, the usual animation had faded from her face, leaving her pale and subdued. "The group's too big—it's backed up and it'll probably take two light changes for all of them to cross the street." Her sad eyes looked up at him. "After spending the week in the desert all these people make me feel kind of claustrophobic. Do we have time to sit for a minute and let them go ahead?"

"Yes," he said, putting his arm around her. She rested her head against his shoulder and snuggled into his side. "We don't have to be there the exact instant the portal reappears. We have time."

"How much time?"

"Not much. I do not want to anger Zeus any more by seeming to disregard his command to appear before him."

"What are you going to tell him?"

"The truth." He kissed her forehead. "That I found my soul mate in the modern world, and that my heart's desire is not to be parted from her."

"I hope you're granted your heart's desire as easily as I was granted mine." She lifted her face to his. As he kissed her, she breathed in his scent. His closeness soothed her. When he touched her, she could make herself believe that what he said so often was the truth—that all really would be well. Reluctantly, he ended their kiss, and her stomach tightened uncomfortably.

"It appears the crowd has moved on," Apollo said.

Pamela glanced down the suddenly empty sidewalk. "Looks like there must have been a big rush to get somewhere. It's a little weird." She felt a trickle of something lift the fine hairs on her arms and the back of her neck. Her intuition was telling her to stay there, seated on the bench beside Apollo. But before she could say anything, he was already standing up. With a thick feeling of resignation, she realized that she just didn't want him to go—that was all there was to her so-called intuition.

Distracted, the god shrugged off the strangeness of the deserted walkway. "We should go, too," Apollo said. He pulled her to her feet beside him. Keeping his arm securely around her, they walked slowly to stand alone on the curb while they waited for the light to change from red to green. It wasn't good-bye yet, he told himself. He would keep her close to him all the way through Caesars Palace and would not relinquish her until the portal was before him. Then their separation would only be temporary. Apollo murmured his next thoughts aloud to her. "My father will relent. He has been love's victim too many times not to grant our request."

"Love's victim or lust's victim?" Pamela asked.

He smiled down at her. "For my father, love and lust set the same banquet table, and Zeus enjoys the feast."

Pamela gave an unladylike, sarcastic snort. He laughed, hugging her against him. He couldn't lose her. She tilted her head up to him, and as he bent to kiss her again, the fountain sprang into life. They froze, staring at each other, and then Pamela's face blazed with happiness.

"Perfect!" she said through her laughter. "It couldn't be more perfect."

Once again, Faith Hill seemed to sing only for them.

"It is the best of omens! All will be well," Apollo said joyously. He turned and watched the dancing water.

Almost as if the music compelled him, the god walked to the railing. There was something in the air—something in which he sensed an immortal's hand. It had to be an omen sent from Zeus. Glancing over his shoulder, he grinned happily, motioning for Pamela to join him.

She smiled and nodded, but stayed where she was—just for another moment. Apollo was gazing at the sparkling waters as they geysered into the air in time to the magical song. He was so magnificent, this remarkable god who somehow was the other half of her soul. And suddenly, fiercely she believed that he would make everything right. The God of Light was her soul mate, and he would find a way to return to her.

"*. . . it's . . . ahhh . . . impossible! This kiss! This kiss!*
Unstoppable! This kiss! This kiss!"

Pamela lifted her foot to take a step forward, and a flash of movement caught at the corner of her eye. Frowning, she turned her head in time to see the car, but not in time to get out of its path as it leapt the curb and rammed into her body.

Filled with new hope, Apollo was smiling at the shooting water when he heard the first terrible screech. Insulated as he was by water and song, the sound seemed far away. Confused, he turned to see what was keeping Pamela. In wordless horror he watched as the metal beast struck her body.

"*Pamela!*" he screamed. The impact hurtled her to the busy street and directly into the oncoming traffic. Brakes squealed, and drivers veered, smashing into other cars as they tried unsuccessfully to avoid hitting her. Apollo surged forward. Dodging cars and people, he followed her bloody path to where she had finally come to rest in a crumpled heap in the center median.

Shrieking his agony, Apollo dropped to his knees beside her and pulled her broken body into his arms. His flashing, tear-filled eyes stared at the ball of light that still hovered low in the sky.

"Leave the sky!" he commanded the waning sun. "Return my powers to me!"

Pamela felt nothing, just an odd sense of wrongness. As if she had awakened in a dark room in a strange bed, she couldn't see and couldn't get her bearings. Then she heard a scream that tore through her soul. She knew it was Apollo. She tried to open her mouth and call out to him, but her body was no longer under her control. She fought against it, but her eyes closed an instant before the sun set.

Apollo knew when she died. It was one breath before the pain in his hand disappeared and immortal power filled his body. Panicked, he lay her carefully on the cement road and placed his hands on her bloody chest.

"Live!" commanded the God of Light, though he knew he was too late. Even with his immortal powers, he could not reset time. He could not undo what was already done. "No!" his tears mingled with her blood. *"No!"* he cried.

"Someone call 911!"

"Oh my god! Get an ambulance!"

"Is there a doctor here?"

Apollo heard the cries of the mortals around him. They would come and take her from him.

"No!" he screamed his rage. Standing, he threw his arms out wide. *"Be silent!"* His command shot like an arrow through the growing crowd, forming a wall of power that struck each of them deaf and dumb, turning the mortals into silent, openmouthed statues.

Then the God of Light looked down at his fallen love.

"No." He whispered the word this time. "It will not be." He made the decision quickly. He had to. If he hesitated now, it would be too late. Regardless of the consequences, it was the only way. Apollo stretched his hands out above Pamela's body. "Come to me. I command you not to depart this realm."

Beneath Apollo's outstretched hands, Pamela's body began to glow, and then a sphere of pure light lifted to hover between the god's palms.

"Apollo!"

He heard the cry behind him and, keeping the globe of light between his hands, he whirled. Like a sprite, Artemis ran through the smashed cars and silent, frozen mortals until she came close enough to see what it was her brother loomed over and what it was he held between his palms. She gasped and covered her mouth with her hands. Moving with surprising speed, Eddie rushed up beside her. As his mind tried to make sense of the scene before him, the author's face drained of all color.

"You should not have lifted the spell from him," Apollo snarled.

"I didn't know . . . I didn't think . . . Oh, my brother. What have you done?" She stared from Pamela's body to the pulsing light he gripped possessively.

"I was too late," he said brokenly. "The sun was too late. They killed her."

Artemis approached him slowly, as if he was one of her wild woodland creatures. "But what are you doing? You hold her immortal soul."

Apollo cradled the light against his body. "I will not lose her!"

"Apollo—" she began.

"No! I will not lose her!" His angry cry caused lightning to spike across the sky. "Laws of the Universe be damned. Over and over it has been said that love is the strongest force in the universe." The god's wild eyes turned to the stunned author. "You are a bard in this world. Is that not what you proclaim?"

Unable to find the words to speak, E. D. Faust could only nod.

"Then I say my love for her overrules the Laws of the Universe!"

"Apollo, you can not keep her like this. Her immortal soul will not rest in this realm. You know that," Artemis said.

"I am not going to keep her in this realm."

Artemis' eyes widened with understanding. "Hades!"

"He will know what to do. He *must* know what to do," Apollo said.

"Yes." The goddess's voice broke. "Go to your friend, my Brother. I pray that he will have an answer for you. For both of you."

His expression dazed, as if he was just noticing the extent of what his power had wrought, Apollo looked around him at the crumpled cars and frozen people.

"I will make this right," Artemis said. "Go. Pamela needs you."

"Zeus?"

"I will appear before our father. It was because of me you entered this kingdom. I began this. I should end it."

Apollo shook his head. "It was not you, Artemis. Blame the Fates if you must. Pamela and I were destined to meet."

"Then you must take her to the Underworld and petition Hades for a resolution."

"Thank you, my Sister . . ." Apollo's voice faded. Still clutching the glowing soul, the god moved with speed that was impossible for mortal eyes to behold between the cars and into Caesars Palace to the portal that waited there.

With heavy steps, Artemis approached Pamela's body.

"How could something so strong be contained in such a fragile shell?" The goddess looked down at her friend as tears washed her cheeks.

"My heart was right all along," Eddie said reverently. He approached her and then, when he was beside her, he dropped to one knee. "You truly are the Goddess Artemis."

"Yes," she said, resting one soft hand on the author's shoulder, "but I do not feel like a goddess. I feel like a woman who has just lost a very good friend." She drew a deep breath and let it out on a sob. "Look at her, Eddie. She is all broken."

For a moment Eddie hesitated. Then he reached up and patted the goddess's hand reassuringly. "She isn't here, Artemis. She's with Apollo."

"You're right. I know. It's just that . . . just that I didn't have a chance to say good-bye, or I'm sorry, or even thank you."

"Sometimes," Eddie said quietly, "you don't get to say those things. That's what it is to be a mortal. We can only try to live our lives with enough joy and passion that when our time is finished we leave behind more good memories than regrets."

"I didn't understand that before, but I do now. I think there is a part of me that from here on throughout eternity will always feel a little mortal." She smiled sadly at Pamela's body. "I think it might be the best part of me."

On impulse, Artemis bent and grasped the coin carrying her brother's image, which still hung around Pamela's neck. With a flick of her fingers it came free and pooled in her palm. "Apollo would want me to keep this for her." She closed her hand, and the coin disappeared. Then the goddess knelt beside her friend's body.

"What will you do?" Eddie asked.

"What I can," Artemis said softly.

She lifted her hands, and they began to glow with the cool white light of a full moon. "Good-bye, my friend," she murmured as she passed her luminous hands down Pamela's body—changing—rearranging—and doing what she could to make it right. When the light faded, the mortal's broken body had been replaced by the body of a beautiful young doe.

Wearily, Artemis stood. "Walk with me, Eddie. I must return and face my father."

"Of course, my Goddess."

Tucking her arm within his, he led her carefully away from the body of the fallen doe. They had almost reached the sidewalk when Artemis suddenly stopped. Scenting the air like a creature of the forest, she turned her head and narrowed her eyes. The car was battered. The front of it caved inwards and bloodied with the clear marks of where it had hit Pamela's body. Artemis stepped closer and peered within the car. The woman frozen by Apollo's spell had both hands gripping the steering wheel. Strapped securely into her seat, she was uninjured, but her eyes were wide and filled with an unspeakable terror. Artemis drew in another deep breath.

The mortal's body reeked of liquor, and not just any liquor. Artemis' keen senses recognized the sweet scent of ambrosia mixed with lust and despair and addiction. The God of the Vine's mark was there, not clearly branded, as her bond to Pamela had been. It was more hidden, though no less binding. Artemis closed her eyes against the intensity of her anger. He would pay, she promised herself. She would see to it that Bacchus paid.

When she opened her eyes, she found Eddie watching her intently.

"You know what caused this."

"I do," Artemis said.

Eddie's face hardened in anger. "Make them pay, Goddess."

"I shall, my warrior. I shall."

Resolutely, Artemis turned to face the carnage that jealousy and spite had caused. She raised her hands. Voice magnified by her immortal power, her words shimmered throughout Las Vegas as the beautiful Huntress Goddess soothed, healed, and then destroyed the last vestiges of Bacchus' malevolent spell.

"Let their spirits be free
tonight no other shall die
the doe is the miracle they see
though they know not how or why.

"Upon their immortal souls my blessings shall rain
washing their memories—easing their pain."

She dropped her hands, and pandemonium broke free around them. Shouts of "Can you believe it? It's a deer!" filled the night as people rushed into the street and the sound of an ambulance siren wailed in the distance. Through it all, Artemis simply took Eddie's arm. The two of them walked away, unseen, in a powerful bubble of immortal serenity.

"You did a kind thing, my Goddess." Eddie patted her hand as they made their way up the sidewalk that led to the main entrance of Caesars Palace.

Artemis smiled at him. "Thank you." Then she cocked her head, considering.

"Goddess?" the author asked.

"Eddie, I may not be able to return here. Olympus will find these events disturbing."

"I understand that." He hesitated and allowed his veneer of eccentric author to slip so that his heartbreak showed clearly in his eyes. "From the beginning I knew that you would not stay with me. Regardless of that, I chose to love you. I do not regret one instant of that choice.

And I shall hold your memory close to my heart as long as there is breath in my body."

"Perhaps there is a way my memory would not be all you held close to your heart," she said slowly.

The author's eyes widened in surprise.

"Eddie, have you ever heard of a kingdom called Tulsa, Oklahoma?"

CHAPTER 33

"Hades!" Apollo's voice shook the walls of the Lord of the Underworld's Great Hall.

The dark god rushed into his throne room with his wife close behind him.

"Apollo?" Hades almost didn't recognize his friend, which had nothing to do with his strange, blood-spattered clothing or the glowing sphere of light he clutched to his chest. It was the wild, crazed look in his eye that was so totally foreign to what he knew of the God of Light. "What has happened?"

"They killed her. The metal beasts. I couldn't stop them. I didn't get to her in time." Breathing heavily, he spoke in short bursts.

Hades' wife moved from beside her husband. Within Persephone's immortal body, Carolina's soul shivered as she instantly understood.

"This is Pamela," she said, gazing at the bright ball of light.

"A modern mortal's soul? You brought the soul of a modern mortal here!" Hades exclaimed.

"Of course he did," Lina's voice was hushed. "What else could he do?"

"You must make it right! You must make her Pamela again."

Lina's sharp eyes skewered the God of Light. "That's enough of that kind of talk. She is still Pamela, and you're probably scaring her." She glanced back at where her husband was standing. "My love, you must welcome her."

The Lord of the Underworld moved reluctantly. He stretched out his hand, but before he touched the light, his gaze caught Apollo's. "It is not wise to meddle with the Laws of the Universe, my friend."

"She is my soul mate," Apollo said.

The dark god shook his head sadly. "Then let us hope that the Fates are understanding." He touched his palm to the glowing ball. "You are welcome in my realm, Pamela."

The light quivered and then elongated. With a sound that was very much like a sigh, it took on form and features until Pamela was standing within the circle of Apollo's arms. Her body still carried a slight luminescence, but she had also taken on a surreal, transparent look—as if she was a half-finished watercolor of herself. With a sob, Apollo tightened his arms around her. She felt cool and too light. He was afraid if he loosened his hold on her, she would float away. She didn't move or speak.

"Pamela!" Apollo cried. "It's me. I have you. All will be well now."

A shiver passed through her almost insubstantial body. "Apollo?"

"Yes, my sweet!" He pressed his face into her hair.

She pulled back from him, looking around in confusion. She saw that she was standing in an enormous marble room with Apollo, a beautiful young woman, and a tall, dark man. Then her gaze went down to her body, and her face went blank with shock.

"Tell me this is a dream, Apollo. Tell me that pretty soon I'll wake up," Pamela's voice trembled.

"I can not," he said brokenly.

"Pamela," Lina's voice was like a warm, quiet pool. She touched the newly dead spirit lightly on her arm. "I am Carolina; you may call me Lina if you'd like. And this is my husband, Hades."

Pamela's eyes looked huge and round in her pale face.

"Hades?" she whispered. Woodenly, she lifted her translucent hand and stared at it. "I'm dead? And now I'm in . . ." Her eyes flew back to Hades, and her mouth opened, as if she wanted to scream.

"You're in Elysia," Lina told her with a gentle smile.

She took the hand Pamela still held in front of her and wrapped it in her warmth, willing the immortal powers that rested within Persephone's body to comfort her. "Specifically, you are in our palace at the edge of the Elysian Fields. The Underworld is a very beautiful place, honey. There's nothing here you need to be afraid of."

"The Underworld?" Shaking her head, Pamela looked at Apollo. "Why am I in the Greek Underworld?"

"I didn't know what else to do." Apollo's eyes pleaded with her to understand.

"No," Pamela whispered. "No, it can't be."

"You died before the sun set. I could do nothing to save you. Please forgive me. I couldn't let you go—I—I don't think I could ever let you go."

Pamela kept shaking her head and staring at him. And then she remembered. In her mind she saw the car coming towards her and knew all over again the deadly impact. With a jerky, mechanical movement, she stepped from the circle of Apollo's arms to stare wide-eyed at him.

"I don't know what we do next," he said.

"Well," Lina said matter-of-factly, "next you go with Hades and get cleaned up and into some clothes that don't have . . ." She paused and decided on different wording. "Clothes that aren't so dirty. And while you do that, I'll show Pamela around. Go on." She caught her husband's eye and raised her brows. "We'll be fine."

"I will not be long," Apollo told Pamela. She only gazed at him unresponsively as he and Hades left the room.

Lina still held Pamela's cool hand, and she gently led her toward a large silver-plated door on the far side of the room. Unresisting, the newly dead spirit followed her. Once through the door, they entered a wide hallway that was hung with jeweled chandeliers. Lina turned to the right and then again to the left. Huge glass doors opened without her touching them, and they walked out into an incredibly lovely courtyard filled with marble statues, a huge fountain, and flowers all different shades of white.

Even through the terrible knot of panic that seemed to choke rational thoughts from her mind, the designer within Pamela noticed the beauty that surrounded her.

"It's fantastic, isn't it?" Lina said. "I loved it from the first moment I set eyes on it."

Pamela looked at Lina and blinked rapidly, like a sleep-walker fighting to awaken.

"You're not really one of them, are you?"

"No," Lina shook her head, causing her chestnut-colored hair to ripple around her shapely waist. She smiled and pointed at her body. *"This* is one of them, but *this"*—she placed her hand over her heart—"is very mortal. I'm like you—a spirit that has been displaced from what they call the modern mortal world. Here, let's sit at this bench." Lina waited until Pamela had settled herself to continue. "I'm really a baker from Tulsa. It's a long story, but the end result is that Persephone and I made a deal. When it's spring and summer in Tulsa, her spirit is there in my body, and I'm here in the Underworld with Hades. Fall and winter in Oklahoma, I'm there and she frolics around Olympus or wherever in her goddess body." Lina grinned. "It's a pretty good deal, too. Oklahoma winters are nice—and the weather in Elysia"—she gestured around them—"is always perfect. And then, of course, there's Hades." Her eyes softened.

"I can't . . . I don't know if I can accept all of this." Pamela wiped a hand over her brow and then made a startled little jerk as she stared at her pale, ghostly hand. "I don't feel like me; I don't look like me."

"I know, honey, I know. It's always hard when someone dies before they're ready. And with you it's especially difficult because this isn't where you expected to end up. But I promise you that Elysia welcomes you. You'll find peace here. You don't need to be afraid. Just listen to your spirit—it knows more than you think it does."

"Peace . . ." Pamela repeated. She wasn't gasping for breath anymore and she didn't feel so afraid. Through the shock and the panic she could sense the edge of something that reminded her a little of Lina's voice. It was sweet and warm and comforting, like a late spring rain, or an afternoon nap, and it was in the air around her. A small breeze brushed against her spirit body, soothing her. It seemed to whisper her name like a mother welcoming a lost child into her arms.

"See what I mean?" Lina asked, studying her face.

Pamela drew a deep breath and looked down at her body again. This time her luminous skin didn't frighten her. Yes, it was still her—her arms and legs and the rest of her body. She lifted her hand again, studying it . . . recognizing the soul within the altered casing. The warm breeze brushed against her, caressing her with palpable acceptance and love.

"I think I'm starting to understand." Thinking, she ran her hand through her short hair, only vaguely noticing that it felt a little like passing her hand through a cool mist. She turned on the bench so that she was facing Lina. "I can believe that I can find peace here, but what about love?"

"You already know that answer, Pamela. Do you still love Apollo?"

"Of course," she said without hesitation.

Lina smiled. "That's because love is one of the few things we can actually take with us."

"But what about . . ." Pamela lifted her semitransparent hand again. "I'm not like I was before."

"No, you're not the same, but your spirit does have form and feelings. The rest is up to you and Apollo."

"Won't it be like loving a ghost for him?" Pamela said despondently.

Lina took her hand again. "I like to think of it more as loving the essence of a person."

"I'm dead." This time when she said it, her heart didn't shake, and she didn't feel like she needed to wake up from a nightmare. Random thoughts flitted through her mind— she worried about her brother and her parents and Vernelle—but her worry had a distant, otherworldly sense to it, as if she were remembering a sweet, reoccurring dream. It wasn't that she had forgotten them or stopped loving them. It was just that she already felt detached from the life she had known. She wondered if it was some kind of built-in defense mechanism of the soul, to keep her spirit from pining away for eternity for those left behind. Eternity . . . it was still incomprehensible.

"I'm dead, but I'm still me."

"Yes, honey, and you're going to be fine," Lina said. Then she looked up and smiled. "And here come our gods."

Hades and Apollo strode towards them through the flowered courtyard. The dark god had his hand on his friend's shoulder and was speaking earnestly to him as they walked. Apollo nodded in response, but when he saw Pamela, his attention turned completely to her as he hurried to where she and Lina sat. He stopped beside the bench.

"You look as bad as you did right after the snake bit you," Pamela said. "Your hand isn't still hurting you, is it?"

"No!" he said and almost laughed. "There is no injury left in my body." Apollo let his fingers lightly brush her cheek. "Are you yourself again, sweet Pamela?"

"Yes, I think I am. Somehow I'm different, but still me. Maybe more me than I have ever been," she said in a voice tinged with the wonder of it.

"And do you forgive me for stealing your soul and bringing it here?"

Pamela studied his handsome face. Lina had been right. She got to bring love with her, and a few other things— like faith and hope and forgiveness.

"All is well, Apollo. I forgive you," she said.

Silently, the God of Light fell to his knees, buried his head in her lap, and as she stroked his hair, Apollo wept.

On Mount Olympus Zeus listened to Artemis finish her story. The Huntress Goddess was spectacular in her anger, but she was also something else. She was passionate in her defense of the modern mortals. Intrigued, Zeus watched his daughter wipe tears from her beautiful face as she described the death of the mortal woman she claimed her brother loved. He could hardly believe the change in her. Artemis had never cared overly much for mortals. She wasn't cruel to them; she was simply aloof, cool, untouchable. They made sacrifices to the Huntress Goddess, petitioned for her aid, and Artemis even occasionally granted those requests as her whim struck her. But never in all the eons of her existence had Zeus known her to weep over a mortal. And she had spoken of the bard that had sheltered her and her twin with honest warmth. As if she truly cared for the mortal man. It was all fascinating.

"That poor, weak woman who was the instrument of Pamela's death was under the influence of Bacchus. I smelled his stench. It was as if she and the night had been bathed in it. The God of the Vine is culpable, and not simply for the death of an innocent. He manipulated all of the events that led to that sad night. And why?" The Huntress turned on Bacchus, who also stood in front of great Zeus where he sat on his raised throne. "For no other reason than spite and jealousy."

"For retribution!" Bacchus shrieked.

"Retribution?" Artemis cried. "How did Pamela deserve your punishment? She was kind and loyal. All she did was to love my brother and succor both of us when we were trapped in her world without our powers."

"The punishment wasn't for her. It was for you and your arrogant brother." Bacchus turned his wild, haunted eyes to Zeus. "Do you not see it? They thought they could take over my kingdom and never be touched for their trespass. They were not innocent visitors, they were usurpers!"

"Silence!" Zeus commanded as thunder growled across the sky. "It is time I pass judgment. Approach me, Bacchus."

The god walked hesitantly to the edge of Zeus' dais.

"You are my son, Bacchus, and I love you. But you are also your mother's child. She desired what she could not have. She could not be made to see reason, and so her desire cost Semele her life. Now you desire that which is not yours. Like your mother, I gave you a chance to see reason. Instead, you answered me with deceit and hatred. So you tell me, Bacchus, God of the Vine, what do you do when one of your vines ceases to bear good fruit?"

Confused, Bacchus blinked his small eyes and squinted at Zeus. "It is pruned at the end of the season, so that next season it will live again and bear good fruit."

Zeus nodded solemnly. "And that is your punishment, my son. Beginning now, at the end of every season your body will be sent to the Titans to be rent apart—pruned—by their mighty eagles. As you are born anew, take your lesson from the spent vine. Think on your wrongdoings, learn and bear new fruit."

As Bacchus shrieked in terror, Zeus raised his mighty hand, and the God of the Vine disappeared.

He turned his gaze to Artemis.

"Approach me, my Daughter."

Showing no fear, Artemis walked to the dais.

"Tell me what you learned in the Kingdom of Las Vegas," he said.

She met her father's storm gray eyes. "I have learned what it is to be mortal."

"Tell me what that means, Artemis."

"It means that I have learned that they are not weak, in-consequential beings who live and die in the blink of our eyes. They are not weak at all—it is only their mortal shells that must succumb. Within many of them are the sparks of honor and loyalty, friendship and love, and they shine so bright that if we could see them as they truly are, their light would blind even the gods. "

"And was it a valuable lesson?"

"I will carry it with me forever," she said.

"Then your lesson was learned through something more profound than any punishment I could mete out. It was learned through your own heart. Therefore, I will not add to it. The truth you carry within your heart is lesson enough. You are free to do as you will."

Artemis bowed her head, but before she could leave her father's throne room, his voice stopped her.

"One last thing, Daughter. Your brother has need of you. I grant you the power you will require to aid him. If you so choose."

Confused, Artemis bowed her head again. Of course she would aid Apollo.

"Thank you, Father."

"Do not thank me yet, Daughter. Love is often as

painful as it is sweet. Go to Apollo now." There was no mistaking the sadness in Zeus' mighty voice.

As soon as she was free of her father's presence, she closed her eyes and willed herself to the Underworld.

CHAPTER 34

"Artemis, I'm asking you to try to understand, and to try to think of a way to help me," Apollo said.

"I can't! I won't! I don't understand why you can't just leave things the way they are. Pamela seems happy. Why would she want you to change that?" Artemis plucked irritably at one of the perfect cream-colored roses that lined that part of the ornate gardens that stretched in tiers behind Hades' Palace and ended just at the edge of the Elysian Fields. As soon as she had materialized in the Underworld, she had barely had time to greet Pamela when Apollo had said he needed to speak with her and pulled her out into the gardens. She could hardly believe what he had wanted to tell her.

Apollo sighed. "I haven't talked with her about it yet. I wanted to tell you what I was thinking first, so that you could help me decide what is to be done about . . ." His voice faded as he paced restlessly back and forth along the path in front of her.

"You mean what is to be done about the insignificant fact that the God of Light is thinking of leaving Olympus. Forever."

Apollo frowned at her. "Not forever. Just for one lifetime."

"It will certainly feel like forever to an ancient world bereft of their Apollo!"

"Perhaps we could talk with Father. You said he's not angry at us anymore. Maybe I could convince him to—"

"To what! Be you. Make sure your chariot continues to usher the sun through the sky? You expect that of him?" Artemis tossed her long, golden hair back, trying to ignore the words that rang through her head: *Your brother has need of you. I grant you the power you will require to aid him. If you so choose.* Now she understood what Zeus had meant. She understood, and she hated it.

Apollo shook his head miserably and wiped a hand across his brow. "No . . . I—I don't know what to do, Sister. I just wanted one chance. It seemed the only way . . ."

Artemis' chest felt tight. "Pamela doesn't even know what you're thinking?"

"No, not yet," he admitted.

"And Hades and Lina? Have you told them what you propose?"

Apollo nodded.

"And what do they think of this plan of yours?"

"Hades thought I might be going mad. Lina understood."

"Well, I am more of Hades' mind than Lina's!"

"I thought you might be," he said wearily.

"What did you expect!"

His eyes met his hers. "I thought maybe my sister could help me find a way."

Artemis felt the slice of bittersweet pain as she made her decision. She really didn't have any choice. She loved him.

"I will guide your chariot, Brother."

"You? But how can—"

The goddess held up one slender, perfect hand, and used arrogance to stop the tears that burned hot within her eyes. "Do you doubt my powers?"

"No! I—"

"Then it's settled." She studied her well-manicured nails. "I've always thought that chariot needed an update. It's much too old-fashioned—much too"—she shuddered dramatically—"Spartan."

Apollo just stared openmouthed at her. She gave him a stern look. "Well, aren't you going to thank your sister?"

With a whoop he threw his arms around her lifted her and spun her in a circle.

Pamela's ethereal body stepped from one of the side paths. "Hey, what in the bloody buggering hell is—" Pamela gasped and covered her mouth. Then she started to laugh. "I said 'hell' and then freaked myself out." She shook her head, her wispy hair floating like sea foam around her face.

Apollo grinned and held his hand out to her. Still giggling a little, she clasped his solid, warm hand in her cool one.

"As I was saying—what is going on with you two? I could hear you yelling all the way up on the other tier."

Apollo looked at Artemis, who looked at Apollo.

"Well?" Pamela asked. "Someone tell me."

"It's your plan. You tell her," Artemis said.

"What is it?"

Apollo drew a deep breath. "I have an idea. I spoke with Hades and Lina about it, and just now I told Artemis. Between the three of them, they have made it possible."

"Mad, but possible," Artemis grumbled.

Apollo smiled fondly his sister before turning back to Pamela. "You have been here long enough to know that there are seven rivers in the Underworld."

Pamela nodded her head. "Yes."

"My idea has to do with one of them—the River Lethe."

Pamela shrugged her pale shoulders. "Okay, what's the idea?"

"You must first understand about the River Lethe," Lina said, walking up the path arm in arm with her husband.

"It is called the River of Forgetfulness," Hades said.

Apollo shook his head. "Is there no privacy in the Underworld?"

Everyone ignored him.

"The River of Forgetfulness—what does that mean?" Pamela asked.

"Its purpose is to wash a soul clean of all memories so that it can be reborn and live another lifetime," Lina explained.

Pamela met Apollo's brilliant blue eyes. "Tell me."

"If we drank of Lethe, you and I could be reborn. We would live a lifetime. We could marry, have children, and grow old together."

"But you're not mortal," Pamela said faintly. His words had brought a rush of light-headedness through her spirit. To live again? To love and have children—Apollo's children?

"Lethe will have the same effect on his spirit," Lina said. "All he needs to do is to choose to leave his immortal body, just like Persephone chooses to leave hers every six months."

"But how can he do that? How can he just stop being Apollo?"

"That's where Artemis comes in. She has agreed to make sure the Ancient World is not devoid of light while I'm absent from it."

"She has?" Pamela said, looking at the goddess.

Artemis moved her shoulders nonchalantly, and then under the pretense of smelling a milk-colored rose, she bent to the fragrant bloom and quickly turned her head away from them and wiped the wetness from her face.

Apollo took Pamela's shoulders in his hands. "We would live a mortal lifetime together. Our children would carry on after us. Think of it, Pamela!"

She felt dizzy, and she was glad Apollo was holding her so tightly. "But wait." She looked at Lina. "I thought you said that Lethe washes away memories. If we don't remember each other, how will I find him? Or he find me?"

Lina smiled and leaned into Hades, who wrapped his arm around her. "Soul mates always find one another."

"On that you have my sacred promise," Hades said.

Pamela's gaze shifted to the too-silent Artemis. "You don't want him to do this, do you?"

"I don't want to lose my brother," she said.

Apollo took one hand from Pamela's shoulder and rested it on his sister's arm. "I did not think you would lose me. I thought you would watch over me—carefully. As well as my children and my children's children."

Artemis bowed her head and put her hand over her brother's. "As I will, my Brother. On that you have my oath."

Apollo turned back to Pamela. "Then all that is left is for you to agree, sweet Pamela."

She felt as if her soul would burst with happiness. "Yes! Let's do it!"

Apollo turned to Hades and quirked one brow at his friend. "Now?"

Hades shrugged, and Lina elbowed him.

"Now is perfect," the Queen of the Underworld said.

Apollo took a step away from Pamela, who was still frowning at him in confusion. He lifted his chin regally, and Pamela thought he looked exactly like the profile that had been stamped on the old coin he had given her so long ago. She was going to tell him so, when his body suddenly quivered and then changed into solid marble as his glowing spirit stepped from it.

The God of Light's shining form turned to Hades. "Take good care of it. I will need it again someday."

"I shall, my friend."

Lina reached up and cupped his face in her hands and kissed him lightly on the lips, and then she moved back to her husband's side. "I wish you both a lifetime filled with happiness and laughter. You know the way, don't you, Apollo?"

The glowing god nodded his head.

"You're not going with us?" Pamela asked.

Lina smiled at her. "For this, you do not need the presence of the gods. This is something that souls do best without our interference."

"Then I will take my leave of you here, too," Artemis said quietly. First she went to Pamela and hugged her fiercely. "Take care of him for me," she whispered to the mortal soul her brother loved so dearly. Then she turned to Apollo and stepped into his glowing arms. Taking no heed of the tears that she now let run freely down her face, she pressed her cheek against his. "Wherever you are. Whoever you are. Know that my love and my blessing will always be with you, just as it will be with your children and your children's children."

"Thank you for understanding, my Sister. And thank you for being my light while I can not be." He kissed each of her wet cheeks.

"I love you," the Huntress Goddess said as her body faded and disappeared.

Apollo and Pamela walked silently through the tall pines that began where Hades' gardens ended. Their hands were linked, and their shoulders and hips brushed intimately against each other. Soon between the trees they began to catch the crystal reflection of moving water. The river called to them with a seductive, whispering voice. Unconsciously, they walked quicker. The trees ended, and they were standing atop a rocky bank looking down at water that glistened like liquid jewels.

"Are you afraid?" Apollo asked her.

"No," Pamela said. "You'll find me. I know you will."

"Always," he said.

Together they knelt at the edge of the water. Apollo cupped his hands and dipped them in the cold water, lifting them so Pamela could drink deeply. Then, while she watched, he dipped them again and drank. Standing, he took her into his arms and kissed her. As their spirit bodies moved together, they began to shine. Their hair and clothes suddenly whipped wildly around them, as if they were standing in the middle of a raging windstorm.

Apollo threw back his head and laughed joyously, and Pamela's shout joined his own as their souls were filled with an incredible rush of love and joy. Again, Apollo pulled his soul mate into his arms, and Pamela wrapped her glowing body around him. While they were embracing, their bodies continued to change, losing shape so that it seemed that they merged together and truly became one. Then the incandescent, blazing ball of light exploded, raining sparks into the water. From the center of the shining geyser appeared two fist-sized globes of identical light. They hovered there above the river for a moment, acclimating themselves to their new senses. Then, as if following a trail of sweet memories, they began to float downstream and toward their new beginning.

EPILOGUE

~

Kristin was so bored she thought she would die. She wished she would die. She might as well die—like there was anything else to do? It was just like her parents to force her into a stupid family vacation. Could they have let her stay home with her friends Janice and Rebecca and Ruth? Of course not, even though she had just turned thirteen. Definitely old enough to stay home alone for two tiny weeks. It totally made no sense.

So here she was, sitting on a beach while the sun was rising, all by herself. Why? Because no one else in her family got out of bed practically before noon. She was doomed to live with people who slept away the best part of the day. It was just the second day of the two-week torture her parents called vacation. She considered hurling herself into the ocean. No, she swam too well. It would take forever for her to drown.

Kristin dug her feet into the white sand and let the edge of the waves lap over her toes. She supposed she could read a book. Another book. She ran a hand through her short hair in irritation. She'd just had it cut before they left, and she couldn't get used to the feel of it—or the way it kinda stuck out sometimes, especially in front. She sighed. She probably shouldn't have cut it. She'd never get a boyfriend now. Ever. She'd die an old maid.

A shadow blocked a piece of the morning sun, and she sighed again. It was probably her little brother. Perfect.

She balled up a handful of wet sand and got ready to throw it at him when the shadow spoke.

"Hey," said a stranger's voice.

Kristin squinted and held her sandy hand up against the glare of the rising sun. And she almost passed out. It was a boy! A really hot, tall, blond boy. He looked practically sixteen. And he was smiling at her.

"Hey," she said.

"So, are you just getting up or just going to bed?" he asked.

His voice didn't even crack.

"Gettin' up," she said, trying to stop herself from staring like a retard at his eyes. They were, like, as blue as the ocean.

"Me, too," he said and flopped down next to her. "I like morning best."

"Me, too," she said.

"My family's all 'sleep still," he said.

"So's mine. They sleep forever."

"Yeah."

She couldn't believe how warm he was. He wasn't even sitting that close to her, but she could swear that waves of hotness were coming from his body. She wanted to say something to him, but she didn't want to babble. Or sound stupid.

"Hey, what's that?" he said, pointing at something that was glittering just at the edge of the surf, half covered by the sand her toes had dug up.

He leaned forward—practically touching her—and grabbed a hold of the thing, lifting it free of the sand.

"Wow!" he said.

"It's awesome," she said. She couldn't look away from the bright coin that hung from the gold chain. It shined in the growing light, and she could see that it had the head of a man stamped on it. A really cute man with curly hair.

"It's yours," he said solemnly.

"Mine? Nuh-uh."

"Yes-huh. It is. It was by your feet on your beach during your morning. It's definitely yours." He opened the little clasp and put it around her neck. It hung there like a piece of the sun. Kristin touched it. It felt warm.

"See," he said. "It fits perfectly."

He smiled at her, and Kristin thought she was going to faint. He was so unbelievably, totally cute.

"My name is Kristin," she said.

"I'm Jordan," he said.

"Hi, Jordan."

"Hi, Kristin."

They grinned at each other, and the sun exploded from the ocean and into the morning sky.

"Hey," Jordan said. "I like your hair."

"Thanks," she said and thought that maybe this summer's vacation wouldn't be such torture after all.

Neither of the teenagers noticed the tall blond woman who watched them from the shadows. *Soul mates do always find each other,* Artemis thought. *I should have never doubted you, my Brother.* The goddess wiped her eyes and smiled wistfully as she faded silently into the waiting palm trees.

Turn the page for a special preview of
P. C. Cast's next novel

Goddess of the Rose

Coming soon from Berkley Sensation!

"I've been having those dreams again."

"Dr. Ireland straightened in his chair and gave her what Mikki liked to think of as his Clinically Interested Look.

"Would you like to tell me about them?"

Mikki shifted her eyes from his. Would she like to tell him? She uncrossed then crossed her long legs, ran her hand nervously through her hair, and tried to settle back into the too plump leather chair.

"Well, they're the same as the others." She glanced at him. Noting his knowing look coupled with his raised eyebrows, she sighed and rolled her eyes. "Okay, so they have begun to change lately."

"Could you see his face this time?" Dr. Ireland asked gently.

"Almost." Mikki squinted and stared at a spot above the cozy brick fireplace. "Actually, I think I could have seen his face this time, but . . ."

"But?" the psychiatrist prompted.

"But I . . ." Mikki hesitated.

Dr. Ireland made an encouraging sound.

"But I was so preoccupied I couldn't make myself concentrate on his face," she finished in a rush.

"Preoccupied with?"

Mikki stopped staring at the hearth and met her psychiatrist's eyes. "I was preoccupied with having the most deliciously erotic dream of my life. I really didn't give a damn what his face looked like, Dr. I."

"I don't remember you describing the other dreams as being sexual in nature, Mikki," Dr. Ireland said without missing a beat.

She had to give him credit—he might be young, but he certainly wasn't easily shocked.

"That's because they weren't . . . or maybe I didn't . . . oh, I don't know, for some reason they're different now." She struggled to describe what was happening to her. "I'm telling you, Dr. I., the dreams are getting more and more real."

"As is the rest of the fantasy?"

She continued to meet his eyes. "Yes. It's like the more realistic the dreams get, the less real my life is."

"So tell me about your latest dream, Mikki."

Instead of answering him, she pulled at an errant strand of thick, strawberry-blond hair and studied him. She liked him, and not just because he was young and handsome. Okay, she should quit thinking of him as "young." He had just turned thirty, and she was only a few years his senior—this morning she just felt decades older. She narrowed her eyes and let her gaze roam down the psychiatrist's body. How much should she tell him?

Dr. Ireland was tall. Her mom would have described him in her Oklahoma twang as a long, cool drink of water. At their first meeting Mikki had thought he was kind of nerdy, but in a nice way. Her lips turned up with a hint of a smile. Actually, once she got to know him she realized that he was anything but nerdy—it was just those silly wire-rimmed glasses, that ponytail, and his gentle, studious manner that made him appear like a dork.

Upon closer inspection, an inspection Mikki had been only too happy to engage in—in fantasy form, of course, Dr. Dennis Ireland was a sensitive, successful man who topped six-foot-four and whose body was a lovely study in muscular maleness, complete with gorgeous shoulders.

He reminded her of one of those sensitive Galahad types: chivalrous, honorable, and oh-so-delectably good. Definitely a candidate for knight in shining armor.

And happily married to Lady Kim Ireland. Unfortunately. Which meant he was just more proof to support

Mikki's theory that there were no decent available men living in Tulsa over the age of thirty.

"Mikki?"

"I'm thinking of where to start."

He gave her a little half smile and settled himself into his wing-backed chair. "Take your time."

"Thanks," she said, trying to control her guilty grin, glad he was only a good psychiatrist and not a mind reader.

She took a deep breath. She really should get this dream stuff straightened out. It was becoming too weird, in a hypnotic, seductive way.

But she was stalling, and not just because she was hesitant about revealing such intimate details aloud, but also because part of her really was afraid Dr. Ireland would cure her.

She wasn't sure she wanted to be cured.

"All you have to do is talk to me," Dr. I. said gently. "We'll decide together where to go from there."

Mikki gave him a tight, appreciative smile. He really was a nice guy—even for a shrink.

"Okay, this one started the same as the others," she said, picking nervously at her fingernail polish.

"You mean in the canopy bed?"

"The *huge* canopy bed in the *enormous* bedroom," she corrected him and then nodded. "Yeah. It was the same place, only it wasn't as dark as it usually is. This time a little light was coming into the room through a whole wall of windows. I think they're called . . ." Mikki searched for the word. "Mull-something-or-other . . . panes of vertical stripes of glass. Know what I mean?"

Dr. Ireland nodded. "Mullioned windows."

"Right," she said, thinking that his geekiness did come in handy sometimes. "Well, whatever they're called I noticed them this time because they were letting in some light." Mikki let her gaze get trapped by the cheerily burning fire as she relived her dream experience. "It was such a soft pink-tinted light that I think it must have been dawn. Anyway, it woke me." She hesitated and a nervous, half laugh escaped her throat. "It even seemed odd in the dream—having my dream self wake up to experience another dream." Mikki shrugged her shoulders. "But I woke up. I was lying on my stomach and I could feel someone brushing my hair. It was wonderful. The 'whoever' was using one of those big brushes with soft, wide bristles." Mikki grinned at her psychiatrist. "I love having my hair brushed, and in my dream it made me want to stretch and purr like a happy cat."

"Sounds nice, Mikki, but not necessarily erotic," Dr. I. said, trying to keep her on track.

"I'm not at the erotic part yet. I'm just at the why-I-was-so-relaxed-and-happy part," Mikki said, giving the doctor an impatient look.

"Sorry for interrupting. Go on, Mikki."

"Okay, I was so relaxed that I could feel myself drifting. It was bizarre—like my soul had become so light that it lifted from my body. It was then that everything got freaky."

"Explain *freaky*."

"Well, there was a rush of wind. It was like the breeze had all of a sudden picked me up and carried me someplace. But not really 'me.' Just my spirit me. Then there was a settling feeling. It startled me, and I opened my eyes. I was back in my body, only now I was standing in the middle of the most incredible rose garden I have ever seen, ever even imagined." Mikki's voice lost any hint of hesitation as she fell into the description of the scene. "It was breathtaking—only I didn't want any of my breath to be taken away because I was surrounded by such amazing smells. I wanted to drink the air like wine. Roses were all around me. All my favorites: Double Delight, Chrysler Imperial, Cary Grant, Sterling Silver . . ." She sighed happily.

"How about the Mikado rose?"

Dr. Ireland's question brought her back to reality.

"No, Dr. I., I didn't see any of my namesake roses." She sat up, straightening her spine. "And I really don't think this is happening to me because my mother thought it was clever to name me after her favorite rose."

Dr. Ireland made a conciliatory gesture with his hand. "I didn't mean to imply it was, but you have to admit, Mikki"—he pronounced her nickname clearly, as if to erase the word *mikado* from the air around them—"that it is odd that roses, in some form, appear in every one of your dreams."

"Why should it be odd? You know I volunteer for the Tulsa Municipal Rose Gardens. I love it. Why shouldn't my favorite hobby figure into my dreams?"

"You're correct. Roses are an important part of your life, as they were your mother's—"

"And her mother's before her, and hers before her," Mikki interrupted.

Dr. Ireland smiled and nodded. "And it is a lovely hobby."

Mikki smiled back at him. "I'm sorry. I shouldn't be so touchy. I guess I'm running short on sleep."

Concern shadowed the psychiatrist's expression and he rustled through the file on his lap. "Is the Xanax not helping you sleep?"

"Oh, no, it's working fine," Mikki said briskly. "I guess I've just been taking too many papers home from the office and staying up too late."

Please don't ask me any more questions about that, she thought, glancing at him under her lashes. She didn't want him to know that her exhaustion had nothing to do with lack of sleep or too much work. All she wanted to do was sleep, and Xanax was the trapdoor to her dream world. And even though she never felt fully rested after she'd been to that fantasy world, she was compelled to return night after night.

"Mikki?"

"Where was I?" she floundered.

"In the beautiful rose garden."

"That's right."

Dr. Ireland glanced at his notes. "And that's where you said things 'got freaky.'"

"Yeah." Mikki let her eyes fall back to the fireplace. "For a while I just walked among the roses, touching each of them and appreciating their beauty. My guess was right, it was early morning and the air was fresh and cool; the roses were still sprinkled with dew. Everything looked like it had just been washed. The garden was circular, and the roses and their terraces formed a kind of labyrinth or maybe a maze. I wandered around and around, just enjoying myself."

Mikki's smile wavered and she paused before beginning the next part of her dream. She could feel her cheeks coloring. Her eyes shifted abruptly to meet her doctor's concerned gaze.

"You don't need to be embarrassed, Mikki."

Mikki gave him sheepish grin. "Actually, I'm more worried about shocking you than I am about being embarrassed, Dr. I."

"You won't shock me. Just tell me what you experienced."

Mikki nodded and drew a deep breath. When she resumed the retelling, her voice had taken on a husky, sexy tone that lingered sensuously between them in the little office.

"Then I felt him. I couldn't see him, but I knew he was behind me." Mikki licked her lips. Unconsciously, her hand moved to her throat. Her fingertips slowly stroked the sensitive skin at the base of her neck as she spoke. "I started walking faster, because at first I felt like I should get away from him, but soon that changed. I could hear him behind me; he was gaining on me. He wasn't being quiet or trying to hide. His noises were feral. It was as if I was being hunted by a fierce, masculine animal."

Mikki tried to force her breathing back to normal. Her body tingled. She could feel the drop of sweat that made a hot, wet path between her breasts.

"And you were afraid?"

"No," Mikki said in a whisper the psychiatrist had to lean forward and strain to hear. "That's just it. I wasn't afraid at all. It thrilled me. It excited me. I wanted him to catch me. When I ran it was only because I could tell it provoked him—and I wanted very much for him to be provoked."

"I see . . ."

"I don't think you do," Mikki said, meeting his eyes. "I was naked and laughing as I ran. It felt like the wind was my lover as it brushed over my body. I reveled in every grunt, every huff, every growl made by the beast that pursued me. And I wanted to be caught, but not until he was very, very eager to catch me."

"Did he catch you?"

Mikki's expression became introspective and her gaze moved back to the fireplace.

"Yes and no. As I said, I was running and he was chasing me. I came to a sharp corner in the labyrinth and I turned, then stumbled and fell into a pit. When I hit the bottom it should have hurt, but it didn't because my fall was cushioned." Mikki's lips curved into a seductive smile. "It was cushioned by petals. I had fallen into a pit that had been filled with a bed of rose petals. There must have been thousands of them. Their scent filled the air and caressed my body. Every inch of my naked skin felt alive against their softness. And then his hands were taking the place of the roses. They weren't soft, instead they were rough and strong and demanding. The difference in the two sensations was exquisite. He stroked my naked body, moving from my breasts down my stomach and my thighs. He caressed me exactly as I would have touched myself. It was like he had the ability to tap into my mind and he knew all of my secret desires."

Mikki paused to brush a strand of hair from her face. The psychiatrist noticed that her hand was shaking. Before he could comment, Mikki continued her story.

"It was darker in the pit than it had been in the gardens, and my vision was hazy, almost like the scent of the crushed petals had created a fog of perfume that obscured my vision. I couldn't see him, but wherever he touched me I was on fire. Before then in all of the dreams I had felt his presence, like he was an insubstantial being, a ghost or a shadow. I had known he was there, but he had never pursued me, never touched me. And I had certainly never touched him. But in the pit of roses everything changed. I could feel his hands on me, and when I reached for him I could actually touch him, too. I pulled him to me. And he . . . he felt . . ."

Mikki gulped and closed her eyes tightly in remembrance. "He felt thick and strong and incredibly big. I ran my hands up and down the width of his shoulders and his arms. It was like his muscles were living stone. And I felt something else. At first I thought he must be wearing a coat or some kind of weird costume, but the more I touched him the more I knew that he wasn't wearing anything. Anything at all, except"—Mikki swallowed around the sudden dryness in her throat—"fur. His body was covered in a thick pelt. I let my fingers sift through it, like I was stroking an enormous, muscular beast. His face was buried in my hair, right here."

Still keeping her eyes closed, Mikki's right hand moved slowly up, pulled forward a mass of her copper-colored curls, and sank her hand into them near her right ear.

"This is where his face was, so it was easy for me to hear every sound he made. When I touched him he moaned into my ear, except that it wasn't really a moan—at least not a moan a human would have made. It was a low, rumbling growl that went on and on. I know it should have scared me. I should have screamed and fought, or at the very least been petrified and frozen with fear. But I didn't want to be away from him. That horrible, wonderful beast-like sound excited me even more. I felt like I would die if I couldn't have him—all of him. Arching up to meet him, I took my hands from his chest and slid them down his huge body. He was wearing leather pants, butter-soft, skin-tight leather pants, and I could easily feel his erection through them. He was grinding it against me. I wanted to find the buckle of his pants and get them off of him. But it was too late. I was already climaxing, and all I could do was wrap my legs around him as my body exploded. The orgasm is what woke me."

P.C. Cast

Goddess of the Sea

There's a little goddess in every woman...

After her plane crashes into the sea, an Air Force Sergeant finds herself occupying the body of the mythical mermaid Undine—and falling for a sexy merman.

"[CAST HAS] A VIVID IMAGINATION
AND A WICKED SENSE OF HUMOR."
—ROMANCE READER

**Available wherever books are sold or at
www.penguin.com**

BERKLEY SENSATION
COMING IN MAY 2005

Hot Legs
by Susan Johnson
Curator Cassie Hill has sworn off men. But when a
painting is stolen, a hot-shot bounty hunter is called
in—and he's driving Cassie wild.

0-425-20355-7

Master of the Moon
by Angela Knight
A shape-shifting werewolf, Diana London is on the trail
of a killer vampiress. But her search takes an unexpected turn when erotic dreams lead her to Llyr, the king
of the faeries.

0-425-20357-3

The Moon Witch
by Linda Winstead Jones
Juliet Fyne has been kidnapped by the Emperor's
men—only to be rescued by a man whose animal
instincts tell him she's the only woman he will ever
love.

0-425-20129-5

Daring the Highlander
by Laurin Wittig
An independent young widow must help an unlikely
leader without losing her own cautious heart.

0-425-20292-5

Available wherever books are sold or at www.penguin.com

From the author of *Jane's Warlord*

Master of the Night
by Angela Knight

Enter a dazzling new world
of vampires—

American agent Erin Grayson is assigned to
seduce international businessman
Reece Champion. But she's been set up.
Reece is an agent, too—and a vampire.

"CHILLS, THRILLS...[A] SEXY TALE."
—EMMA HOLLY ON *Jane's Warlord*

0-425-19880-4

Available wherever books are sold or at
www.penguin.com

B864

FOUR BESTSELLING AUTHORS.

FOUR SPELLBINDING ORIGINAL STORIES.

ONE COLLECTION THAT'S TRULY...

Out of this World

#1 *New York Times* bestselling author
J.D. Robb

New York Times bestselling author
Laurell K. Hamilton

USA Today bestselling author
Susan Krinard

USA Today bestselling author
Maggie Shayne

0-515-13109-1

**Available wherever books are sold or at
www.penguin.com**